Jane Austen Juvenilia and Short Stories

Jane Austen

ISBN: 978-1-943862-06-1

182-21 150th Avenue
Springfield Gardens, NY, 11413
U.S.A.
http://www.palmerapublishing.com

Jane Austen Juvenilia and Short Stories/Jane Austen
978-1-943862-06-1

Printed in the United States of America

Table of Contents

Lady Suzan

I: LADY SUSAN VERNON TO MR. VERNON

Langford, Dec.

MY DEAR BROTHER,—I can no longer refuse myself the pleasure of profiting by your kind invitation when we last parted of spending some weeks with you at Churchhill, and, therefore, if quite convenient to you and Mrs. Vernon to receive me at present, I shall hope within a few days to be introduced to a sister whom I have so long desired to be acquainted with. My kind friends here are most affectionately urgent with me to prolong my stay, but their hospitable and cheerful dispositions lead them too much into society for my present situation and state of mind; and I impatiently look forward to the hour when I shall be admitted into Your delightful retirement.

I long to be made known to your dear little children, in whose hearts I shall be very eager to secure an interest I shall soon have need for all my fortitude, as I am on the point of separation from my own daughter. The long illness of her dear father prevented my paying her that attention which duty and affection equally dictated, and I have too much reason to fear that the governess to whose care I consigned her was unequal to the charge. I have therefore resolved on placing her at one of the best private schools in town, where I shall have an opportunity of leaving her myself in my way to you. I am determined, you see, not to be denied admittance at Churchhill. It would indeed give me most painful sensations to know that it were not in your power to receive me.

Your most obliged and affectionate sister,
S. VERNON.

II: LADY SUSAN VERNON TO MRS. JOHNSON

Langford.

You were mistaken, my dear Alicia, in supposing me fixed at this place for the rest of the winter: it grieves me to say how greatly you were mistaken, for I have seldom spent three months more agreeably than those which have just flown away. At present, nothing goes smoothly; the females of the family are united against me. You foretold how it would be when I first came to

Langford, and Mainwaring is so uncommonly pleasing that I was not without apprehensions for myself. I remember saying to myself, as I drove to the house, "I like this man, pray Heaven no harm come of it!" But I was determined to be discreet, to bear in mind my being only four months a widow, and to be as quiet as possible: and I have been so, my dear creature; I have admitted no one's attentions but Mainwaring's. I have avoided all general flirtation whatever; I have distinguished no creature besides, of all the numbers resorting hither, except Sir James Martin, on whom I bestowed a little notice, in order to detach him from Miss Mainwaring; but, if the world could know my motive THERE they would honour me. I have been called an unkind mother, but it was the sacred impulse of maternal affection, it was the advantage of my daughter that led me on; and if that daughter were not the greatest simpleton on earth, I might have been rewarded for my exertions as I ought.

Sir James did make proposals to me for Frederica; but Frederica, who was born to be the torment of my life, chose to set herself so violently against the match that I thought it better to lay aside the scheme for the present. I have more than once repented that I did not marry him myself; and were he but one degree less contemptibly weak I certainly should: but I must own myself rather romantic in that respect, and that riches only will not satisfy me. The event of all this is very provoking: Sir James is gone, Maria highly incensed, and Mrs. Mainwaring insupportably jealous; so jealous, in short, and so enraged against me, that, in the fury of her temper, I should not be surprized at her appealing to her guardian, if she had the liberty of addressing him: but there your husband stands my friend; and the kindest, most amiable action of his life was his throwing her off for ever on her marriage. Keep up his resentment, therefore, I charge you. We are now in a sad state; no house was ever more altered; the whole party are at war, and Mainwaring scarcely dares speak to me. It is time for me to be gone; I have therefore determined on leaving them, and shall spend, I hope, a comfortable day with you in town within this week. If I am as little in favour with Mr. Johnson as ever, you must come to me at 10 Wigmore street; but I hope this may not be the case, for as Mr. Johnson, with all his faults, is a man to whom that great word "respectable" is always given, and I am known to be so intimate with his wife, his slighting me has an awkward look.

I take London in my way to that insupportable spot, a country village; for I am really going to Churchhill. Forgive me, my dear friend, it is my last resource. Were there another place in England open to me I would prefer it. Charles Vernon is my aversion; and I am afraid of his wife. At Churchhill, however, I must remain till I have something better in view. My young lady accompanies me to town, where I shall deposit her under the care of Miss Summers, in Wigmore street, till she becomes a little more reasonable. She will made good connections there, as the girls are all of the best families. The price is immense, and much beyond what I can ever attempt to pay.

Adieu, I will send you a line as soon as I arrive in town.

Yours ever,

S. VERNON.

III: MRS. VERNON TO LADY DE COURCY

Churchhill.

My dear Mother,—I am very sorry to tell you that it will not be in our power to keep our promise of spending our Christmas with you; and we are prevented that happiness by a circumstance which is not likely to make us any amends. Lady Susan, in a letter to her brother-in-law, has declared her intention of visiting us almost immediately; and as such a visit is in all probability merely an affair of convenience, it is impossible to conjecture its length. I was by no means prepared for such an event, nor can I now account for her ladyship's conduct; Langford appeared so exactly the place for her in every respect, as well from the elegant and expensive style of living there, as from her particular attachment to Mr. Mainwaring, that I was very far from expecting so speedy a distinction, though I always imagined from her increasing friendship for us since her husband's death that we should, at some future period, be obliged to receive her. Mr. Vernon, I think, was a great deal too kind to her when he was in Staffordshire; her behaviour to him, independent of her general character, has been so inexcusably artful and ungenerous since our marriage was first in agitation that no one less amiable and mild than himself could have overlooked it all; and though, as his brother's widow, and in narrow circumstances, it was proper to render her pecuniary assistance, I cannot help thinking his pressing invitation to her to visit us at Churchhill perfectly unnecessary. Disposed, however, as he always is to think the best of everyone, her display of grief, and professions of regret, and general resolutions of prudence, were sufficient to soften his heart and make him really confide in her sincerity; but, as for myself, I am still unconvinced, and plausibly as her ladyship has now written, I cannot make up my mind till I better understand her real meaning in coming to us. You may guess, therefore, my dear madam, with what feelings I look forward to her arrival. She will have occasion for all those attractive powers for which she is celebrated to gain any share of my regard; and I shall certainly endeavour to guard myself against their influence, if not accompanied by something more substantial. She expresses a most eager desire of being acquainted with me, and makes very gracious mention of my children but I am not quite weak enough to suppose a woman who has behaved with inattention, if not with unkindness, to her own child, should be attached to any of mine. Miss Vernon is to be placed at a school in London before her mother comes to us which I am glad of, for her sake and my own. It must be to her advantage to be separated from her mother, and a girl of sixteen who has received so wretched an education, could not be a very desirable companion here.

Reginald has long wished, I know, to see the captivating Lady Susan, and we shall depend on his joining our party soon. I am glad to hear that my father continues so well; and am, with best love, &c.,

CATHERINE VERNON.

IV: MR. DE COURCY TO MRS. VERNON

Parklands.

My dear Sister,—I congratulate you and Mr. Vernon on being about to receive into your family the most accomplished coquette in England. As a very distinguished flirt I have always been taught to consider her, but it has lately fallen In my way to hear some particulars of her conduct at Langford: which prove that she does not confine herself to that sort of honest flirtation which satisfies most people, but aspires to the more delicious gratification of making a whole family miserable. By her behaviour to Mr. Mainwaring she gave jealousy and wretchedness to his wife, and by her attentions to a young man previously attached to Mr. Mainwaring's sister deprived an amiable girl of her lover.

I learnt all this from Mr. Smith, now in this neighbourhood (I have dined with him, at Hurst and Wilford), who is just come from Langford where he was a fortnight with her ladyship, and who is therefore well qualified to make the communication.

What a woman she must be! I long to see her, and shall certainly accept your kind invitation, that I may form some idea of those bewitching powers which can do so much—engaging at the same time, and in the same house, the affections of two men, who were neither of them at liberty to bestow them—and all this without the charm of youth! I am glad to find Miss Vernon does not accompany her mother to Churchhill, as she has not even manners to recommend her; and, according to Mr. Smith's account, is equally dull and proud. Where pride and stupidity unite there can be no dissimulation worthy notice, and Miss Vernon shall be consigned to unrelenting contempt; but by all that I can gather Lady Susan possesses a degree of captivating deceit which it must be pleasing to witness and detect. I shall be with you very soon, and am ever,

Your affectionate brother,
R. DE COURCY.

V: LADY SUSAN VERNON TO MRS. JOHNSON

Churchhill.

I received your note, my dear Alicia, just before I left town, and rejoice to be assured that Mr. Johnson suspected nothing of your engagement the evening before. It is undoubtedly better to deceive him entirely, and since he will be stubborn he must be tricked. I arrived here in safety, and have no reason to complain of my reception from Mr. Vernon; but I confess myself not equally satisfied with the behaviour of his lady. She is perfectly well-bred, indeed, and has the air of a woman of fashion, but her manners are not such as can persuade me of her being prepossessed in my favour. I wanted her to be delighted at seeing me. I was as amiable as possible on the occasion, but all in vain. She does not like me. To be sure when we consider that I DID take some pains to prevent my brother-in-law's marrying her, this want of cordiality is not very surprizing, and yet it shows an illiberal and vindictive spirit to resent a project which influenced me six years ago, and which never succeeded at last.

I am sometimes disposed to repent that I did not let Charles buy Vernon Castle, when we were obliged to sell it; but it was a trying circumstance, especially as the sale took place exactly at the time of his marriage; and everybody ought to respect the delicacy of those feelings which could not endure that my husband's dignity should be lessened by his younger brother's having possession of the family estate. Could matters have been so arranged as to prevent the necessity of our leaving the castle, could we have lived with Charles and kept him single, I should have been very far from persuading my husband to dispose of it elsewhere; but Charles was on the point of marrying Miss De Courcy, and the event has justified me. Here are children in abundance, and what benefit could have accrued to me from his purchasing Vernon? My having prevented it may perhaps have given his wife an unfavourable impression, but where there is a disposition to dislike, a motive will never be wanting; and as to money matters it has not withheld him from being very useful to me. I really have a regard for him, he is so easily imposed upon! The house is a good one, the furniture fashionable, and everything announces plenty and elegance. Charles is very rich I am sure; when a man has once got his name in a banking-house he rolls in money; but they do not know what to do with it, keep very little company, and never go to London but on business. We shall be as stupid as possible. I mean to win my sister-in-law's heart through the children; I know all their names already, and am going to attach myself with the greatest sensibility to one in particular, a young Frederic, whom I take on my lap and sigh over for his dear uncle's sake.

Poor Mainwaring! I need not tell you how much I miss him, how perpetually he is in my thoughts. I found a dismal letter from him on my arrival here, full of complaints of his wife and sister, and lamentations on the cruelty of his fate. I passed off the letter as his wife's, to the Vernons, and when I write to him it must be under cover to you.

Ever yours,
S. VERNON.

VI: MRS. VERNON TO MR. DE COURCY

Churchhill.

Well, my dear Reginald, I have seen this dangerous creature, and must give you some description of her, though I hope you will soon be able to form your own judgment she is really excessively pretty; however you may choose to question the allurements of a lady no longer young, I must, for my own part, declare that I have seldom seen so lovely a woman as Lady Susan. She is delicately fair, with fine grey eyes and dark eyelashes; and from her appearance one would not suppose her more than five and twenty, though she must in fact be ten years older, I was certainly not disposed to admire her, though always hearing she was beautiful; but I cannot help feeling that she possesses an uncommon union of symmetry, brilliancy, and grace. Her address to me was so gentle, frank, and even affectionate, that, if I had not known how much she has always disliked me for marrying Mr. Vernon, and that we had never met before, I should have imagined her an attached friend. One is apt, I believe, to connect assurance of manner with coquetry, and to expect that an impudent address will naturally attend an impudent mind; at least I was myself prepared for an improper degree of confidence in Lady Susan; but her countenance is absolutely sweet, and her voice and manner winningly mild. I am sorry it is so, for what is this but deceit? Unfortunately, one knows her too well. She is clever and agreeable, has all that knowledge of the world which makes conversation easy, and talks very well, with a happy command of language, which is too often used, I believe, to make black appear white. She has already almost persuaded me of her being warmly attached to her daughter, though I have been so long convinced to the contrary. She speaks of her with so much tenderness and anxiety, lamenting so bitterly the neglect of her education, which she represents however as wholly unavoidable, that I am forced to recollect how many successive springs her ladyship spent in town, while her daughter was left in Staffordshire to the care of servants, or a governess very little better, to prevent my believing what she says.

If her manners have so great an influence on my resentful heart, you may judge how much more strongly they operate on Mr. Vernon's generous temper. I wish I could be as well satisfied as he is, that it was really her choice to leave Langford for Churchhill; and if she had not stayed there for months before she discovered that her friend's manner of living did not suit her situation or feelings, I might have believed that concern for the loss of such a husband as Mr. Vernon, to whom her own behaviour was far from unexceptionable, might for a time make her wish for retirement. But I cannot forget the length of her visit to the Mainwarings, and when I reflect on the different mode of life which she led with them from that to which she must now submit, I can only suppose that the wish of establishing her reputation by following though late the path of propriety, occasioned her removal from a family where she must in reality have been particularly happy. Your friend Mr. Smith's story, however, cannot be quite correct, as she corresponds regularly with Mrs. Mainwaring. At any rate it must be exaggerated. It is scarcely possible that two men should be so grossly deceived by her at once.

Yours, &c.,
CATHERINE VERNON

VII: LADY SUSAN VERNON TO MRS. JOHNSON

Churchhill.

My dear Alicia,—You are very good in taking notice of Frederica, and I am grateful for it as a mark of your friendship; but as I cannot have any doubt of the warmth of your affection, I am far from exacting so heavy a sacrifice. She is a stupid girl, and has nothing to recommend her. I would not, therefore, on my account, have you encumber one moment of your precious time by sending for her to Edward Street, especially as every visit is so much deducted from the grand affair of education, which I really wish to have attended to while she remains at Miss Summers's. I want her to play and sing with some portion of taste and a good deal of assurance, as she has my hand and arm and a tolerable voice. I was so much indulged in my infant years that I was never obliged to attend to anything, and consequently am without the accomplishments which are now necessary to finish a pretty woman. Not that I am an advocate for the prevailing fashion of acquiring a perfect knowledge of all languages, arts, and sciences. It is throwing time away to be mistress of French, Italian, and German: music, singing, and drawing, &c., will gain a woman some applause, but will not add one lover to her list—grace and manner, after all, are of the greatest importance. I do not mean, therefore, that Frederica's acquirements should be more than superficial, and I flatter myself that she will not remain long enough at school to understand anything thoroughly. I hope to see her the wife of Sir James within a twelvemonth. You know on what I ground my hope, and it is certainly a good foundation, for school must be very humiliating to a girl of Frederica's age. And, by-the-by, you had better not invite her any more on that account, as I wish her to find her situation as unpleasant as possible. I am sure of Sir James at any time, and could make him renew his application by a line. I shall trouble you meanwhile to prevent his forming any other attachment when he comes to town. Ask him to your house occasionally, and talk to him of Frederica, that he may not forget her. Upon the whole, I commend my own conduct in this affair extremely, and regard it as a very happy instance of circumspection and tenderness. Some mothers would have insisted on their daughter's accepting so good an offer on the first overture; but I could not reconcile it to myself to force Frederica into a marriage from which her heart revolted, and instead of adopting so harsh a measure merely propose to make it her own choice, by rendering her thoroughly uncomfortable till she does accept him—but enough of this tiresome girl. You may well wonder how I contrive to pass my time here, and for the first week it was insufferably dull. Now, however, we begin to mend, our party is enlarged by Mrs. Vernon's brother, a handsome young man, who promises me some amusement. There is something about him which rather interests me, a sort of sauciness and familiarity which I shall teach him to correct. He is lively, and seems clever, and when I have inspired him with greater respect for me than his sister's kind offices have implanted, he may be an agreeable flirt. There is exquisite pleasure in subduing an insolent spirit, in making a person predetermined to dislike acknowledge one's superiority. I have disconcerted him already by my calm reserve, and it shall be my endeavour to humble the pride of these self important De Courcys still lower, to convince Mrs. Vernon that her sisterly cautions have been bestowed in vain, and to persuade Reginald that she has scandalously belied me. This project will serve at least to amuse me, and prevent my feeling so acutely this dreadful separation from you and all whom I love.

Yours ever,
S. VERNON.

VIII: MRS. VERNON TO LADY DE COURCY

Churchhill.

My dear Mother,—You must not expect Reginald back again for some time. He desires me to tell you that the present open weather induces him to accept Mr. Vernon's invitation to prolong his stay in Sussex, that they may have some hunting together. He means to send for his horses immediately, and it is impossible to say when you may see him in Kent. I will not disguise my sentiments on this change from you, my dear mother, though I think you had better not communicate them to my father, whose excessive anxiety about Reginald would subject him to an alarm which might seriously affect his health and spirits. Lady Susan has certainly contrived, in the space of a fortnight, to make my brother like her. In short, I am persuaded that his continuing here beyond the time originally fixed for his return is occasioned as much by a degree of fascination towards her, as by the wish of hunting with Mr. Vernon, and of course I cannot receive that pleasure from the length of his visit which my brother's company would otherwise give me. I am, indeed, provoked at the artifice of this unprincipled woman; what stronger proof of her dangerous abilities can be given than this perversion of Reginald's judgment, which when he entered the house was so decidedly against her! In his last letter he actually gave me some particulars of her behaviour at Langford, such as he received from a gentleman who knew her perfectly well, which, if true, must raise abhorrence against her, and which Reginald himself was entirely disposed to credit. His opinion of her, I am sure, was as low as of any woman in England; and when he first came it was evident that he considered her as one entitled neither to delicacy nor respect, and that he felt she would be delighted with the attentions of any man inclined to flirt with her. Her behaviour, I confess, has been calculated to do away with such an idea; I have not detected the smallest impropriety in it— nothing of vanity, of pretension, of levity; and she is altogether so attractive that I should not wonder at his being delighted with her, had he known nothing of her previous to this personal acquaintance; but, against reason, against conviction, to be so well pleased with her, as I am sure he is, does really astonish me. His admiration was at first very strong, but no more than was natural, and I did not wonder at his being much struck by the gentleness and delicacy of her manners; but when he has mentioned her of late it has been in terms of more extraordinary praise; and yesterday he actually said that he could not be surprised at any effect produced on the heart of man by such loveliness and such abilities; and when I lamented, in reply, the badness of her disposition, he observed that whatever might have been her errors they were to be imputed to her neglected education and early marriage, and that she was altogether a wonderful woman. This tendency to excuse her conduct or to forget it, in the warmth of admiration, vexes me; and if I did not know that Reginald is too much at home at Churchhill to need an invitation for lengthening his visit, I should regret Mr. Vernon's giving him any. Lady Susan's intentions are of course those of absolute coquetry, or a desire of universal admiration; I cannot for a moment imagine that she has anything more serious in view; but it mortifies me to see a young man of Reginald's sense duped by her at all.

I am, &c.,
CATHERINE VERNON.

IX: MRS. JOHNSON TO LADY S. VERNON

Edward Street.

My dearest Friend,—I congratulate you on Mr. De Courcy's arrival, and I advise you by all means to marry him; his father's estate is, we know, considerable, and I believe certainly entailed. Sir Reginald is very infirm, and not likely to stand in your way long. I hear the young man well spoken of; and though no one can really deserve you, my dearest Susan, Mr. De Courcy may be worth having. Mainwaring will storm of course, but you easily pacify him; besides, the most scrupulous point of honour could not require you to wait for HIS emancipation. I have seen Sir James; he came to town for a few days last week, and called several times in Edward Street. I talked to him about you and your daughter, and he is so far from having forgotten you, that I am sure he would marry either of you with pleasure. I gave him hopes of Frederica's relenting, and told him a great deal of her improvements. I scolded him for making love to Maria Mainwaring; he protested that he had been only in joke, and we both laughed heartily at her disappointment; and, in short, were very agreeable. He is as silly as ever.

Yours faithfully,
ALICIA.

X: LADY SUSAN VERNON TO MRS. JOHNSON

Churchhill.

I am much obliged to you, my dear Friend, for your advice respecting Mr. De Courcy, which I know was given with the full conviction of its expediency, though I am not quite determined on following it. I cannot easily resolve on anything so serious as marriage; especially as I am not at present in want of money, and might perhaps, till the old gentleman's death, be very little benefited by the match. It is true that I am vain enough to believe it within my reach. I have made him sensible of my power, and can now enjoy the pleasure of triumphing over a mind prepared to dislike me, and prejudiced against all my past actions. His sister, too, is, I hope, convinced how little the ungenerous representations of anyone to the disadvantage of another will avail when opposed by the immediate influence of intellect and manner. I see plainly that she is uneasy at my progress in the good opinion of her brother, and conclude that nothing will be wanting on her part to counteract me; but having once made him doubt the justice of her opinion of me, I think I may defy, her. It has been delightful to me to watch his advances towards intimacy, especially to observe his altered manner in consequence of my repressing by the cool dignity of my deportment his insolent approach to direct familiarity. My conduct has been equally guarded from the first, and I never behaved less like a coquette in the whole course of my life, though perhaps my desire of dominion was never more decided. I have subdued him entirely by sentiment and serious conversation, and made him, I may venture to say, at least half in love with me, without the semblance of the most commonplace flirtation. Mrs. Vernon's consciousness of deserving every sort of revenge that it can be in my power to inflict for her ill-offices could alone enable her to perceive that I am actuated by any design in behaviour so gentle and unpretending. Let her think and act as she chooses, however. I have never yet found that the advice of a sister could prevent a young man's being in love if he chose. We are advancing now to some kind of confidence, and in short are likely to be engaged in a sort of platonic friendship. On my side you may be sure of its never being more, for if I were not attached to another person as much as I can be to anyone, I should make a point of not bestowing my affection on a man who had dared to think so meanly of me. Reginald has a good figure and is not unworthy the praise you have heard given him, but is still greatly inferior to our friend at Langford. He is less polished, less insinuating than Mainwaring, and is comparatively deficient in the power of saying those delightful things which put one in good humour with oneself and all the world. He is quite agreeable enough, however, to afford me amusement, and to make many of those hours pass very pleasantly which would otherwise be spent in endeavouring to overcome my sister-in-law's reserve, and listening to the insipid talk of her husband. Your account of Sir James is most satisfactory, and I mean to give Miss Frederica a hint of my intentions very soon.

Yours, &c.,
S. VERNON.

XI: MRS. VERNON TO LADY DE COURCY

Churchhill

I really grow quite uneasy, my dearest mother, about Reginald, from witnessing the very rapid increase of Lady Susan's influence. They are now on terms of the most particular friendship, frequently engaged in long conversations together; and she has contrived by the most artful coquetry to subdue his judgment to her own purposes. It is impossible to see the intimacy between them so very soon established without some alarm, though I can hardly suppose that Lady Susan's plans extend to marriage. I wish you could get Reginald home again on any plausible pretence; he is not at all disposed to leave us, and I have given him as many hints of my father's precarious state of health as common decency will allow me to do in my own house. Her power over him must now be boundless, as she has entirely effaced all his former ill-opinion, and persuaded him not merely to forget but to justify her conduct. Mr. Smith's account of her proceedings at Langford, where he accused her of having made Mr. Mainwaring and a young man engaged to Miss Mainwaring distractedly in love with her, which Reginald firmly believed when he came here, is now, he is persuaded, only a scandalous invention. He has told me so with a warmth of manner which spoke his regret at having believed the contrary himself. How sincerely do I grieve that she ever entered this house! I always looked forward to her coming with uneasiness; but very far was it from originating in anxiety for Reginald. I expected a most disagreeable companion for myself, but could not imagine that my brother would be in the smallest danger of being captivated by a woman with whose principles he was so well acquainted, and whose character he so heartily despised. If you can get him away it will be a good thing.

Yours, &c.,
CATHERINE VERNON.

XII: SIR REGINALD DE COURCY TO HIS SON

Parklands.

I know that young men in general do not admit of any enquiry even from their nearest relations into affairs of the heart, but I hope, my dear Reginald, that you will be superior to such as allow nothing for a father's anxiety, and think themselves privileged to refuse him their confidence and slight his advice. You must be sensible that as an only son, and the representative of an ancient family, your conduct in life is most interesting to your connections; and in the very important concern of marriage especially, there is everything at stake—your own happiness, that of your parents, and the credit of your name. I do not suppose that you would deliberately form an absolute engagement of that nature without acquainting your mother and myself, or at least, without being convinced that we should approve of your choice; but I cannot help fearing that you may be drawn in, by the lady who has lately attached you, to a marriage which the whole of your family, far and near, must highly reprobate. Lady Susan's age is itself a material objection, but her want of character is one so much more serious, that the difference of even twelve years becomes in comparison of small amount. Were you not blinded by a sort of fascination, it would be ridiculous in me to repeat the instances of great misconduct on her side so very generally known.

Her neglect of her husband, her encouragement of other men, her extravagance and dissipation, were so gross and notorious that no one could be ignorant of them at the time, nor can now have forgotten them. To our family she has always been represented in softened colours by the benevolence of Mr. Charles Vernon, and yet, in spite of his generous endeavours to excuse her, we know that she did, from the most selfish motives, take all possible pains to prevent his marriage with Catherine.

My years and increasing infirmities make me very desirous of seeing you settled in the world. To the fortune of a wife, the goodness of my own will make me indifferent, but her family and character must be equally unexceptionable. When your choice is fixed so that no objection can be made to it, then I can promise you a ready and cheerful consent; but it is my duty to oppose a match which deep art only could render possible, and must in the end make wretched. It is possible her behaviour may arise only from vanity, or the wish of gaining the admiration of a man whom she must imagine to be particularly prejudiced against her; but it is more likely that she should aim at something further. She is poor, and may naturally seek an alliance which must be advantageous to herself; you know your own rights, and that it is out of my power to prevent your inheriting the family estate. My ability of distressing you during my life would be a species of revenge to which I could hardly stoop under any circumstances.

I honestly tell you my sentiments and intentions: I do not wish to work on your fears, but on your sense and affection. It would destroy every comfort of my life to know that you were married to Lady Susan Vernon; it would be the death of that honest pride with which I have hitherto considered my son; I should blush to see him, to hear of him, to think of him. I may perhaps do no good but that of relieving my own mind by this letter, but I felt it my duty to tell you that your partiality for Lady Susan is no secret to your friends, and to warn you against her. I should be glad to hear your reasons for disbelieving Mr. Smith's intelligence; you had no doubt of its authenticity a month ago. If you can give me your assurance of having no design beyond enjoying the conversation of a clever woman for a short period, and of yielding admiration only to her beauty and abilities, without being blinded by them to her faults, you will restore me to happiness; but, if you cannot do this, explain to me, at least, what has occasioned so great an alteration in your opinion of her.

I am, &c., &c,
REGINALD DE COURCY

XIII: LADY DE COURCY TO MRS. VERNON

Parklands.

My dear Catherine,—Unluckily I was confined to my room when your last letter came, by a cold which affected my eyes so much as to prevent my reading it myself, so I could not refuse Your father when he offered to read it to me, by which means he became acquainted, to my great vexation, with all your fears about your brother. I had intended to write to Reginald myself as soon as my eyes would let me, to point out, as well as I could, the danger of an intimate acquaintance, with so artful a woman as Lady Susan, to a young man of his age, and high expectations. I meant, moreover, to have reminded him of our being quite alone now, and very much in need of him to keep up our spirits these long winter evenings. Whether it would have done any good can never be settled now, but I am excessively vexed that Sir Reginald should know anything of a matter which we foresaw would make him so uneasy. He caught all your fears the moment he had read your letter, and I am sure he has not had the business out of his head since. He wrote by the same post to Reginald a long letter full of it all, and particularly asking an explanation of what he may have heard from Lady Susan to contradict the late shocking reports. His answer came this morning, which I shall enclose to you, as I think you will like to see it. I wish it was more satisfactory; but it seems written with such a determination to think well of Lady Susan, that his assurances as to marriage, &c., do not set my heart at ease. I say all I can, however, to satisfy your father, and he is certainly less uneasy since Reginald's letter. How provoking it is, my dear Catherine, that this unwelcome guest of yours should not only prevent our meeting this Christmas, but be the occasion of so much vexation and trouble! Kiss the dear children for me.

Your affectionate mother,
C. DE COURCY.

XIV: MR. DE COURCY TO SIR REGINALD

Churchhill.

My dear Sir,—I have this moment received your letter, which has given me more astonishment than I ever felt before. I am to thank my sister, I suppose, for having represented me in such a light as to injure me in your opinion, and give you all this alarm. I know not why she should choose to make herself and her family uneasy by apprehending an event which no one but herself, I can affirm, would ever have thought possible. To impute such a design to Lady Susan would be taking from her every claim to that excellent understanding which her bitterest enemies have never denied her; and equally low must sink my pretensions to common sense if I am suspected of matrimonial views in my behaviour to her. Our difference of age must be an insuperable objection, and I entreat you, my dear father, to quiet your mind, and no longer harbour a suspicion which cannot be more injurious to your own peace than to our understandings. I can have no other view in remaining with Lady Susan, than to enjoy for a short time (as you have yourself expressed it) the conversation of a woman of high intellectual powers. If Mrs. Vernon would allow something to my affection for herself and her husband in the length of my visit, she would do more justice to us all; but my sister is unhappily prejudiced beyond the hope of conviction against Lady Susan. From an attachment to her husband, which in itself does honour to both, she cannot forgive the endeavours at preventing their union, which have been attributed to selfishness in Lady Susan; but in this case, as well as in many others, the world has most grossly injured that lady, by supposing the worst where the motives of her conduct have been doubtful. Lady Susan had heard something so materially to the disadvantage of my sister as to persuade her that the happiness of Mr. Vernon, to whom she was always much attached, would be wholly destroyed by the marriage. And this circumstance, while it explains the true motives of Lady Susan's conduct, and removes all the blame which has been so lavished on her, may also convince us how little the general report of anyone ought to be credited; since no character, however upright, can escape the malevolence of slander. If my sister, in the security of retirement, with as little opportunity as inclination to do evil, could not avoid censure, we must not rashly condemn those who, living in the world and surrounded with temptations, should be accused of errors which they are known to have the power of committing.

I blame myself severely for having so easily believed the slanderous tales invented by Charles Smith to the prejudice of Lady Susan, as I am now convinced how greatly they have traduced her. As to Mrs. Mainwaring's jealousy it was totally his own invention, and his account of her attaching Miss Mainwaring's lover was scarcely better founded. Sir James Martin had been drawn in by that young lady to pay her some attention; and as he is a man of fortune, it was easy to see HER views extended to marriage. It is well known that Miss M. is absolutely on the catch for a husband, and no one therefore can pity her for losing, by the superior attractions of another woman, the chance of being able to make a worthy man completely wretched. Lady Susan was far from intending such a conquest, and on finding how warmly Miss Mainwaring resented her lover's defection, determined, in spite of Mr. and Mrs. Mainwaring's most urgent entreaties, to leave the family. I have reason to imagine she did receive serious proposals from Sir James, but her removing to Langford immediately on the discovery of his attachment, must acquit her on that article with any mind of common candour. You will, I am sure, my dear Sir, feel the truth of this, and will hereby learn to do justice to the character of a very injured woman. I know that Lady Susan in coming to Churchhill was governed only by the most honourable and amiable intentions; her prudence and economy are exemplary, her regard for Mr. Vernon equal even to HIS deserts; and her wish of obtaining my sister's good opinion merits a better return than it has received. As a mother she is unexceptionable; her solid affection for her child is shown by placing her in hands where her education will be properly attended to; but because she has not the blind and weak partiality of most mothers, she is accused of wanting maternal tenderness. Every person of sense, however, will know how to value and commend her well-directed affection, and will join me in wishing that Frederica Vernon may prove more worthy than she has yet done of her mother's tender care. I have now, my dear father, written my real sentiments of Lady Susan; you will know from this letter how highly I admire her abilities, and esteem her character; but if you are not equally convinced by my full and solemn assurance that your fears have been most idly created, you will deeply mortify and distress me.

I am, &c., &c.,
R. DE COURCY.

XV: MRS. VERNON TO LADY DE COURCY

Churchhill

My dear Mother,—I return you Reginald's letter, and rejoice with all my heart that my father is made easy by it: tell him so, with my congratulations; but, between ourselves, I must own it has only convinced ME of my brother's having no PRESENT intention of marrying Lady Susan, not that he is in no danger of doing so three months hence. He gives a very plausible account of her behaviour at Langford; I wish it may be true, but his intelligence must come from herself, and I am less disposed to believe it than to lament the degree of intimacy subsisting, between them implied by the discussion of such a subject. I am sorry to have incurred his displeasure, but can expect nothing better while he is so very eager in Lady Susan's justification. He is very severe against me indeed, and yet I hope I have not been hasty in my judgment of her. Poor woman! though I have reasons enough for my dislike, I cannot help pitying her at present, as she is in real distress, and with too much cause. She had this morning a letter from the lady with whom she has placed her daughter, to request that Miss Vernon might be immediately removed, as she had been detected in an attempt to run away. Why, or whither she intended to go, does not appear; but, as her situation seems to have been unexceptionable, it is a sad thing, and of course highly distressing to Lady Susan. Frederica must be as much as sixteen, and ought to know better; but from what her mother insinuates, I am afraid she is a perverse girl. She has been sadly neglected, however, and her mother ought to remember it. Mr. Vernon set off for London as soon as she had determined what should be done. He is, if possible, to prevail on Miss Summers to let Frederica continue with her; and if he cannot succeed, to bring her to Churchhill for the present, till some other situation can be found for her. Her ladyship is comforting herself meanwhile by strolling along the shrubbery with Reginald, calling forth all his tender feelings, I suppose, on this distressing occasion. She has been talking a great deal about it to me. She talks vastly well; I am afraid of being ungenerous, or I should say, TOO well to feel so very deeply; but I will not look for her faults; she may be Reginald's wife! Heaven forbid it! but why should I be quicker-sighted than anyone else? Mr. Vernon declares that he never saw deeper distress than hers, on the receipt of the letter; and is his judgment inferior to mine? She was very unwilling that Frederica should be allowed to come to Churchhill, and justly enough, as it seems a sort of reward to behaviour deserving very differently; but it was impossible to take her anywhere else, and she is not to remain here long. "It will be absolutely necessary," said she, "as you, my dear sister, must be sensible, to treat my daughter with some severity while she is here; a most painful necessity, but I will ENDEAVOUR to submit to it. I am afraid I have often been too indulgent, but my poor Frederica's temper could never bear opposition well: you must support and encourage me; you must urge the necessity of reproof if you see me too lenient." All this sounds very reasonable. Reginald is so incensed against the poor silly girl. Surely it is not to Lady Susan's credit that he should be so bitter against her daughter; his idea of her must be drawn from the mother's description. Well, whatever may be his fate, we have the comfort of knowing that we have done our utmost to save him. We must commit the event to a higher power.

Yours ever, &c.,
CATHERINE VERNON.

XVI: LADY SUSAN TO MRS. JOHNSON

Churchhill.

Never, my dearest Alicia, was I so provoked in my life as by a letter this morning from Miss Summers. That horrid girl of mine has been trying to run away. I had not a notion of her being such a little devil before, she seemed to have all the Vernon milkiness; but on receiving the letter in which I declared my intention about Sir James, she actually attempted to elope; at least, I cannot otherwise account for her doing it. She meant, I suppose, to go to the Clarkes in Staffordshire, for she has no other acquaintances. But she shall be punished, she shall have him. I have sent Charles to town to make matters up if he can, for I do not by any means want her here. If Miss Summers will not keep her, you must find me out another school, unless we can get her married immediately. Miss S. writes word that she could not get the young lady to assign any cause for her extraordinary conduct, which confirms me in my own previous explanation of it, Frederica is too shy, I think, and too much in awe of me to tell tales, but if the mildness of her uncle should get anything out of her, I am not afraid. I trust I shall be able to make my story as good as hers. If I am vain of anything, it is of my eloquence. Consideration and esteem as surely follow command of language as admiration waits on beauty, and here I have opportunity enough for the exercise of my talent, as the chief of my time is spent in conversation.

Reginald is never easy unless we are by ourselves, and when the weather is tolerable, we pace the shrubbery for hours together. I like him on the whole very well; he is clever and has a good deal to say, but he is sometimes impertinent and troublesome. There is a sort of ridiculous delicacy about him which requires the fullest explanation of whatever he may have heard to my disadvantage, and is never satisfied till he thinks he has ascertained the beginning and end of everything. This is one sort of love, but I confess it does not particularly recommend itself to me. I infinitely prefer the tender and liberal spirit of Mainwaring, which, impressed with the deepest conviction of my merit, is satisfied that whatever I do must be right; and look with a degree of contempt on the inquisitive and doubtful fancies of that heart which seems always debating on the reasonableness of its emotions. Mainwaring is indeed, beyond all compare, superior to Reginald—superior in everything but the power of being with me! Poor fellow! he is much distracted by jealousy, which I am not sorry for, as I know no better support of love. He has been teazing me to allow of his coming into this country, and lodging somewhere near INCOG.; but I forbade everything of the kind. Those women are inexcusable who forget what is due to themselves, and the opinion of the world.

Yours ever,

S. VERNON.

XVII: MRS. VERNON TO LADY DE COURCY

Churchhill.

My dear Mother,—Mr. Vernon returned on Thursday night, bringing his niece with him. Lady Susan had received a line from him by that day's post, informing her that Miss Summers had absolutely refused to allow of Miss Vernon's continuance in her academy; we were therefore prepared for her arrival, and expected them impatiently the whole evening. They came while we were at tea, and I never saw any creature look so frightened as Frederica when she entered the room. Lady Susan, who had been shedding tears before, and showing great agitation at the idea of the meeting, received her with perfect self-command, and without betraying the least tenderness of spirit. She hardly spoke to her, and on Frederica's bursting into tears as soon as we were seated, took her out of the room, and did not return for some time. When she did, her eyes looked very red and she was as much agitated as before. We saw no more of her daughter. Poor Reginald was beyond measure concerned to see his fair friend in such distress, and watched her with so much tender solicitude, that I, who occasionally caught her observing his countenance with exultation, was quite out of patience. This pathetic representation lasted the whole evening, and so ostentatious and artful a display has entirely convinced me that she did in fact feel nothing. I am more angry with her than ever since I have seen her daughter; the poor girl looks so unhappy that my heart aches for her. Lady Susan is surely too severe, for Frederica does not seem to have the sort of temper to make severity necessary. She looks perfectly timid, dejected, and penitent. She is very pretty, though not so handsome as her mother, nor at all like her. Her complexion is delicate, but neither so fair nor so blooming as Lady Susan's, and she has quite the Vernon cast of countenance, the oval face and mild dark eyes, and there is peculiar sweetness in her look when she speaks either to her uncle or me, for as we behave kindly to her we have of course engaged her gratitude.

Her mother has insinuated that her temper is intractable, but I never saw a face less indicative of any evil disposition than hers; and from what I can see of the behaviour of each to the other, the invariable severity of Lady Susan and the silent dejection of Frederica, I am led to believe as heretofore that the former has no real love for her daughter, and has never done her justice or treated her affectionately. I have not been able to have any conversation with my niece; she is shy, and I think I can see that some pains are taken to prevent her being much with me. Nothing satisfactory transpires as to her reason for running away. Her kind-hearted uncle, you may be sure, was too fearful of distressing her to ask many questions as they travelled. I wish it had been possible for me to fetch her instead of him. I think I should have discovered the truth in the course of a thirty-mile journey. The small pianoforte has been removed within these few days, at Lady Susan's request, into her dressing-room, and Frederica spends great part of the day there, practising as it is called; but I seldom hear any noise when I pass that way; what she does with herself there I do not know. There are plenty of books, but it is not every girl who has been running wild the first fifteen years of her life, that can or will read. Poor creature! the prospect from her window is not very instructive, for that room overlooks the lawn, you know, with the shrubbery on one side, where she may see her mother walking for an hour together in earnest conversation with Reginald. A girl of Frederica's age must be childish indeed, if such things do not strike her. Is it not inexcusable to give such an example to a daughter? Yet Reginald still thinks Lady Susan the best of mothers, and still condemns Frederica as a worthless girl! He is convinced that her attempt to run away proceeded from no, justifiable cause, and had no provocation. I am sure I cannot say that it HAD, but while Miss Summers declares that Miss Vernon showed no signs of obstinacy or perverseness during her whole stay in Wigmore Street, till she was detected in this scheme, I cannot so readily credit what Lady Susan has made him, and wants to make me believe, that it was merely an impatience of restraint and a desire of escaping from the tuition of masters which brought on the plan of an elopement. O Reginald, how is your judgment enslaved! He scarcely dares even allow her to be handsome, and when I speak of her beauty, replies only that her eyes have no brilliancy! Sometimes he is sure she is deficient in understanding, and at others that her temper only is in fault. In short, when a person is always to deceive, it is impossible to be consistent. Lady Susan finds it necessary that Frederica should be to blame, and probably has sometimes judged it expedient to excuse her of ill-nature and sometimes to lament her want of sense. Reginald is only repeating after her ladyship.

I remain, &c., &c.,
CATHERINE VERNON.

XVIII: FROM THE SAME TO THE SAME

Churchhill.

My dear Mother,—I am very glad to find that my description of Frederica Vernon has interested you, for I do believe her truly deserving of your regard; and when I have communicated a notion which has recently struck me, your kind impressions in her favour will, I am sure, be heightened. I cannot help fancying that she is growing partial to my brother. I so very often see her eyes fixed on his face with a remarkable expression of pensive admiration. He is certainly very handsome; and yet more, there is an openness in his manner that must be highly prepossessing, and I am sure she feels it so. Thoughtful and pensive in general, her countenance always brightens into a smile when Reginald says anything amusing; and, let the subject be ever so serious that he may be conversing on, I am much mistaken if a syllable of his uttering escapes her. I want to make him sensible of all this, for we know the power of gratitude on such a heart as his; and could Frederica's artless affection detach him from her mother, we might bless the day which brought her to Churchhill. I think, my dear mother, you would not disapprove of her as a daughter. She is extremely young, to be sure, has had a wretched education, and a dreadful example of levity in her mother; but yet I can pronounce her disposition to be excellent, and her natural abilities very good. Though totally without accomplishments, she is by no means so ignorant as one might expect to find her, being fond of books and spending the chief of her time in reading. Her mother leaves her more to herself than she did, and I have her with me as much as possible, and have taken great pains to overcome her timidity. We are very good friends, and though she never opens her lips before her mother, she talks enough when alone with me to make it clear that, if properly treated by Lady Susan, she would always appear to much greater advantage. There cannot be a more gentle, affectionate heart; or more obliging manners, when acting without restraint; and her little cousins are all very fond of her.

> Your affectionate daughter,
> C. VERNON

XIX: LADY SUSAN TO MRS. JOHNSON

Churchhill.

You will be eager, I know, to hear something further of Frederica, and perhaps may think me negligent for not writing before. She arrived with her uncle last Thursday fortnight, when, of course, I lost no time in demanding the cause of her behaviour; and soon found myself to have been perfectly right in attributing it to my own letter. The prospect of it frightened her so thoroughly, that, with a mixture of true girlish perverseness and folly, she resolved on getting out of the house and proceeding directly by the stage to her friends, the Clarkes; and had really got as far as the length of two streets in her journey when she was fortunately missed, pursued, and overtaken. Such was the first distinguished exploit of Miss Frederica Vernon; and, if we consider that it was achieved at the tender age of sixteen, we shall have room for the most flattering prognostics of her future renown. I am excessively provoked, however, at the parade of propriety which prevented Miss Summers from keeping the girl; and it seems so extraordinary a piece of nicety, considering my daughter's family connections, that I can only suppose the lady to be governed by the fear of never getting her money. Be that as it may, however, Frederica is returned on my hands; and, having nothing else to employ her, is busy in pursuing the plan of romance begun at Langford. She is actually falling in love with Reginald De Courcy! To disobey her mother by refusing an unexceptionable offer is not enough; her affections must also be given without her mother's approbation. I never saw a girl of her age bid fairer to be the sport of mankind. Her feelings are tolerably acute, and she is so charmingly artless in their display as to afford the most reasonable hope of her being ridiculous, and despised by every man who sees her.

Artlessness will never do in love matters; and that girl is born a simpleton who has it either by nature or affectation. I am not yet certain that Reginald sees what she is about, nor is it of much consequence. She is now an object of indifference to him, and she would be one of contempt were he to understand her emotions. Her beauty is much admired by the Vernons, but it has no effect on him. She is in high favour with her aunt altogether, because she is so little like myself, of course. She is exactly the companion for Mrs. Vernon, who dearly loves to be firm, and to have all the sense and all the wit of the conversation to herself: Frederica will never eclipse her. When she first came I was at some pains to prevent her seeing much of her aunt; but I have relaxed, as I believe I may depend on her observing the rules I have laid down for their discourse. But do not imagine that with all this lenity I have for a moment given up my plan of her marriage. No; I am unalterably fixed on this point, though I have not yet quite decided on the manner of bringing it about. I should not chuse to have the business brought on here, and canvassed by the wise heads of Mr. and Mrs. Vernon; and I cannot just now afford to go to town. Miss Frederica must therefore wait a little.

Yours ever,
S. VERNON.

XX: MRS. VERNON TO LADY DE COURCY

Churchhill

We have a very unexpected guest with us at present, my dear Mother: he arrived yesterday. I heard a carriage at the door, as I was sitting with my children while they dined; and supposing I should be wanted, left the nursery soon afterwards, and was half-way downstairs, when Frederica, as pale as ashes, came running up, and rushed by me into her own room. I instantly followed, and asked her what was the matter. "Oh!" said she, "he is come— Sir James is come, and what shall I do?" This was no explanation; I begged her to tell me what she meant. At that moment we were interrupted by a knock at the door: it was Reginald, who came, by Lady Susan's direction, to call Frederica down. "It is Mr. De Courcy!" said she, colouring violently. "Mamma has sent for me; I must go." We all three went down together; and I saw my brother examining the terrified face of Frederica with surprize. In the breakfast-room we found Lady Susan, and a young man of gentlemanlike appearance, whom she introduced by the name of Sir James Martin—the very person, as you may remember, whom it was said she had been at pains to detach from Miss Mainwaring; but the conquest, it seems, was not designed for herself, or she has since transferred it to her daughter; for Sir James is now desperately in love with Frederica, and with full encouragement from mamma. The poor girl, however, I am sure, dislikes him; and though his person and address are very well, he appears, both to Mr. Vernon and me, a very weak young man. Frederica looked so shy, so confused, when we entered the room, that I felt for her exceedingly. Lady Susan behaved with great attention to her visitor; and yet I thought I could perceive that she had no particular pleasure in seeing him. Sir James talked a great deal, and made many civil excuses to me for the liberty he had taken in coming to Churchhill—mixing more frequent laughter with his discourse than the subject required—said many things over and over again, and told Lady Susan three times that he had seen Mrs. Johnson a few evenings before. He now and then addressed Frederica, but more frequently her mother. The poor girl sat all this time without opening her lips—her eyes cast down, and her colour varying every instant; while Reginald observed all that passed in perfect silence. At length Lady Susan, weary, I believe, of her situation, proposed walking; and we left the two gentlemen together, to put on our pelisses. As we went upstairs Lady Susan begged permission to attend me for a few moments in my dressing-room, as she was anxious to speak with me in private. I led her thither accordingly, and as soon as the door was closed, she said: "I was never more surprized in my life than by Sir James's arrival, and the suddenness of it requires some apology to you, my dear sister; though to ME, as a mother, it is highly flattering. He is so extremely attached to my daughter that he could not exist longer without seeing her. Sir James is a young man of an amiable disposition and excellent character; a little too much of the rattle, perhaps, but a year or two will rectify THAT: and he is in other respects so very eligible a match for Frederica, that I have always observed his attachment with the greatest pleasure; and am persuaded that you and my brother will give the alliance your hearty approbation. I have never before mentioned the likelihood of its taking place to anyone, because I thought that whilst Frederica continued at school it had better not be known to exist; but now, as I am convinced that Frederica is too old ever to submit to school confinement, and have, therefore, begun to consider her union with Sir James as not very distant, I had intended within a few days to acquaint yourself and Mr. Vernon with the whole business. I am sure, my dear sister, you will excuse my remaining silent so long, and agree with me that such circumstances, while they continue from any cause in suspense, cannot be too cautiously concealed. When you have the happiness of bestowing your sweet little Catherine, some years hence, on a man who in connection and character is alike unexceptionable, you will know what I feel now; though, thank Heaven, you cannot have all my reasons for rejoicing in such an event. Catherine will be amply provided for, and not, like my Frederica, indebted to a fortunate establishment for the comforts of life." She concluded by demanding my congratulations. I gave them somewhat awkwardly, I believe; for, in fact, the sudden disclosure of so important a matter took from me the power of speaking with any clearness, She thanked me, however, most affectionately, for my kind concern in the welfare of herself and daughter; and then said: "I am not apt to deal in professions, my dear Mrs. Vernon, and I never had the convenient talent of affecting sensations foreign to my heart; and therefore I trust you will believe me when I declare, that much as I had heard in your praise before I knew you, I had no idea that I should ever love you as I now do; and I must further say that your friendship towards me is more particularly gratifying because I have reason to believe that some attempts were made to prejudice you against me. I only wish that they, whoever they are, to whom I am indebted for such kind intentions, could see the terms on which we now are together, and understand the real affection we feel for each other; but I will not detain you any longer. God bless you, for your goodness to me and my girl, and continue to you all your present happiness." What can one say of such a woman, my dear mother? Such earnestness such solemnity of expression! and yet I cannot help suspecting the truth of everything she says. As for Reginald, I believe he does not know what to make of the matter. When Sir James came, he appeared all astonishment and perplexity; the folly of the young man and the confusion of Frederica entirely engrossed him; and though a little private discourse with Lady Susan has since had its effect, he is still hurt, I am sure, at her allowing of such a man's attentions to her daughter. Sir James invited himself with great composure to remain here a few days—hoped we would not think it odd, was aware of its being very impertinent, but he took the liberty of a relation; and concluded by wishing, with a laugh, that he might be really one very soon. Even Lady Susan seemed a little disconcerted by this forwardness; in her heart I am persuaded she sincerely wished him gone. But something must be done for this poor girl, if her feelings are such as both I and her uncle believe them to be. She must not be sacrificed to policy or ambition, and she must not be left to suffer from the dread of it. The girl whose heart can distinguish Reginald De Courcy, deserves, however he may slight her, a better fate than to be Sir James Martin's wife. As soon as I can get her alone, I will discover the real truth; but she seems to wish to avoid me. I hope this does not proceed from anything wrong, and that I shall not find out I have thought too well of her. Her behaviour to Sir James certainly speaks the greatest consciousness and embarrassment, but I see nothing in it more like encouragement. Adieu, my dear mother.

Yours, &c.,

C. VERNON.

XXI: MISS VERNON TO MR DE COURCY

Sir,—I hope you will excuse this liberty; I am forced upon it by the greatest distress, or I should be ashamed to trouble you. I am very miserable about Sir James Martin, and have no other way in the world of helping myself but by writing to you, for I am forbidden even speaking to my uncle and aunt on the subject; and this being the case, I am afraid my applying to you will appear no better than equivocation, and as if I attended to the letter and not the spirit of mamma's commands. But if you do not take my part and persuade her to break it off, I shall be half distracted, for I cannot bear him. No human being but YOU could have any chance of prevailing with her. If you will, therefore, have the unspeakably great kindness of taking my part with her, and persuading her to send Sir James away, I shall be more obliged to you than it is possible for me to express. I always disliked him from the first: it is not a sudden fancy, I assure you, sir; I always thought him silly and impertinent and disagreeable, and now he is grown worse than ever. I would rather work for my bread than marry him. I do not know how to apologize enough for this letter; I know it is taking so great a liberty. I am aware how dreadfully angry it will make mamma, but I remember the risk.

I am, Sir, your most humble servant,

F. S. V.

XXII: LADY SUSAN TO MRS. JOHNSON

Churchhill.

This is insufferable! My dearest friend, I was never so enraged before, and must relieve myself by writing to you, who I know will enter into all my feelings. Who should come on Tuesday but Sir James Martin! Guess my astonishment, and vexation—for, as you well know, I never wished him to be seen at Churchhill. What a pity that you should not have known his intentions! Not content with coming, he actually invited himself to remain here a few days. I could have poisoned him! I made the best of it, however, and told my story with great success to Mrs. Vernon, who, whatever might be her real sentiments, said nothing in opposition to mine. I made a point also of Frederica's behaving civilly to Sir James, and gave her to understand that I was absolutely determined on her marrying him. She said something of her misery, but that was all. I have for some time been more particularly resolved on the match from seeing the rapid increase of her affection for Reginald, and from not feeling secure that a knowledge of such affection might not in the end awaken a return. Contemptible as a regard founded only on compassion must make them both in my eyes, I felt by no means assured that such might not be the consequence. It is true that Reginald had not in any degree grown cool towards me; but yet he has lately mentioned Frederica spontaneously and unnecessarily, and once said something in praise of her person. HE was all astonishment at the appearance of my visitor, and at first observed Sir James with an attention which I was pleased to see not unmixed with jealousy; but unluckily it was impossible for me really to torment him, as Sir James, though extremely gallant to me, very soon made the whole party understand that his heart was devoted to my daughter. I had no great difficulty in convincing De Courcy, when we were alone, that I was perfectly justified, all things considered, in desiring the match; and the whole business seemed most comfortably arranged. They could none of them help perceiving that Sir James was no Solomon; but I had positively forbidden Frederica complaining to Charles Vernon or his wife, and they had therefore no pretence for interference; though my impertinent sister, I believe, wanted only opportunity for doing so. Everything, however, was going on calmly and quietly; and, though I counted the hours of Sir James's stay, my mind was entirely satisfied with the posture of affairs. Guess, then, what I must feel at the sudden disturbance of all my schemes; and that, too, from a quarter where I had least reason to expect it. Reginald came this morning into my dressing-room with a very unusual solemnity of countenance, and after some preface informed me in so many words that he wished to reason with me on the impropriety and unkindness of allowing Sir James Martin to address my daughter contrary to her inclinations. I was all amazement. When I found that he was not to be laughed out of his design, I calmly begged an explanation, and desired to know by what he was impelled, and by whom commissioned, to reprimand me. He then told me, mixing in his speech a few insolent compliments and ill-timed expressions of tenderness, to which I listened with perfect indifference, that my daughter had acquainted him with some circumstances concerning herself, Sir James, and me which had given him great uneasiness. In short, I found that she had in the first place actually written to him to request his interference, and that, on receiving her letter, he had conversed with her on the subject of it, in order to understand the particulars, and to assure himself of her real wishes. I have not a doubt but that the girl took this opportunity of making downright love to him. I am convinced of it by the manner in which he spoke of her. Much good may such love do him! I shall ever despise the man who can be gratified by the passion which he never wished to inspire, nor solicited the avowal of. I shall always detest them both. He can have no true regard for me, or he would not have listened to her; and SHE, with her little rebellious heart and indelicate feelings, to throw herself into the protection of a young man with whom she has scarcely ever exchanged two words before! I am equally confounded at HER impudence and HIS credulity. How dared he believe what she told him in my disfavour! Ought he not to have felt assured that I must have unanswerable motives for all that I had done? Where was his reliance on my sense and goodness then? Where the resentment which true love would have dictated against the person defaming me—that person, too, a chit, a child, without talent or education, whom he had been always taught to despise? I was calm for some time; but the greatest degree of forbearance may be overcome, and I hope I was afterwards sufficiently keen. He endeavoured, long endeavoured, to soften my resentment; but that woman is a fool indeed who, while insulted by accusation, can be worked on by compliments. At length he left me, as deeply provoked as myself; and he showed his anger more. I was quite cool, but he gave way to the most violent indignation; I may therefore expect it will the sooner subside, and perhaps his may be vanished for ever, while mine will be found still fresh and implacable. He is now shut up in his apartment, whither I heard him go on leaving mine. How unpleasant, one would think, must be his reflections! but some people's feelings are incomprehensible. I have not yet tranquillised myself enough to see Frederica. SHE shall not soon forget the occurrences of this day; she shall find that she has poured forth her tender tale of love in vain, and exposed herself for ever to the contempt of the whole world, and the severest resentment of her injured mother.

Your affectionate
S. VERNON.

XXIII: MRS. VERNON TO LADY DE COURCY

Churchhill.

Let me congratulate you, my dearest Mother! The affair which has given us so much anxiety is drawing to a happy conclusion. Our prospect is most delightful, and since matters have now taken so favourable a turn, I am quite sorry that I ever imparted my apprehensions to you; for the pleasure of learning that the danger is over is perhaps dearly purchased by all that you have previously suffered. I am so much agitated by delight that I can scarcely hold a pen; but am determined to send you a few short lines by James, that you may have some explanation of what must so greatly astonish you, as that Reginald should be returning to Parklands. I was sitting about half an hour ago with Sir James in the breakfast parlour, when my brother called me out of the room. I instantly saw that something was the matter; his complexion was raised, and he spoke with great emotion; you know his eager manner, my dear mother, when his mind is interested. "Catherine," said he, "I am going home to-day; I am sorry to leave you, but I must go: it is a great while since I have seen my father and mother. I am going to send James forward with my hunters immediately; if you have any letter, therefore, he can take it. I shall not be at home myself till Wednesday or Thursday, as I shall go through London, where I have business; but before I leave you," he continued, speaking in a lower tone, and with still greater energy, "I must warn you of one thing—do not let Frederica Vernon be made unhappy by that Martin. He wants to marry her; her mother promotes the match, but she cannot endure the idea of it. Be assured that I speak from the fullest conviction of the truth of what I say; I Know that Frederica is made wretched by Sir James's continuing here. She is a sweet girl, and deserves a better fate. Send him away immediately; he is only a fool: but what her mother can mean, Heaven only knows! Good bye," he added, shaking my hand with earnestness; "I do not know when you will see me again; but remember what I tell you of Frederica;

you MUST make it your business to see justice done her. She is an amiable girl, and has a very superior mind to what we have given her credit for." He then left me, and ran upstairs. I would not try to stop him, for I know what his feelings must be. The nature of mine, as I listened to him, I need not attempt to describe; for a minute or two I remained in the same spot, overpowered by wonder of a most agreeable sort indeed; yet it required some consideration to be tranquilly happy. In about ten minutes after my return to the parlour Lady Susan entered the room. I concluded, of course, that she and Reginald had been quarrelling; and looked with anxious curiosity for a confirmation of my belief in her face. Mistress of deceit, however, she appeared perfectly unconcerned, and after chatting on indifferent subjects for a short time, said to me, "I find from Wilson that we are going to lose Mr. De Courcy—is it true that he leaves Churchhill this morning?" I replied that it was. "He told us nothing of all this last night," said she, laughing, "or even this morning at breakfast; but perhaps he did not know it himself. Young men are often hasty in their resolutions, and not more sudden in forming than unsteady in keeping them. I should not be surprised if he were to change his mind at last, and not go." She soon afterwards left the room. I trust, however, my dear mother, that we have no reason to fear an alteration of his present plan; things have gone too far. They must have quarrelled, and about Frederica, too. Her calmness astonishes me. What delight will be yours in seeing him again; in seeing him still worthy your esteem, still capable of forming your happiness! When I next write I shall be able to tell you that Sir James is gone, Lady Susan vanquished, and Frederica at peace. We have much to do, but it shall be done. I am all impatience to hear how this astonishing change was effected. I finish as I began, with the warmest congratulations.

Yours ever, &c.,
CATH. VERNON.

XXIV: FROM THE SAME TO THE SAME

Churchhill.

Little did I imagine, my dear Mother, when I sent off my last letter, that the delightful perturbation of spirits I was then in would undergo so speedy, so melancholy a reverse. I never can sufficiently regret that I wrote to you at all. Yet who could have foreseen what has happened? My dear mother, every hope which made me so happy only two hours ago has vanished. The quarrel between Lady Susan and Reginald is made up, and we are all as we were before. One point only is gained. Sir James Martin is dismissed. What are we now to look forward to? I am indeed disappointed; Reginald was all but gone, his horse was ordered and all but brought to the door; who would not have felt safe? For half an hour I was in momentary expectation of his departure. After I had sent off my letter to you, I went to Mr. Vernon, and sat with him in his room talking over the whole matter, and then determined to look for Frederica, whom I had not seen since breakfast. I met her on the stairs, and saw that she was crying. "My dear aunt," said she, "he is going—Mr. De Courcy is going, and it is all my fault. I am afraid you will be very angry with me, but indeed I had no idea it would end so." "My love," I replied, "do not think it necessary to apologize to me on that account. I shall feel myself under an obligation to anyone who is the means of sending my brother home, because," recollecting myself, "I know my father wants very much to see him. But what is it you have done to occasion all this?" She blushed deeply as she answered: "I was so unhappy about Sir James that I could not help—I have done something very wrong, I know; but you have not an idea of the misery I have been in: and mamma had ordered me never to speak to you or my uncle about it, and—" "You therefore spoke to my brother to engage his interference," said I, to save her the explanation. "No, but I wrote to him—I did indeed, I got up this morning before it was light, and was two hours about it; and when my letter was done I thought I never should have courage to give it. After breakfast however, as I was going to my room, I met him in the passage, and then, as I knew that everything must depend on that moment, I forced myself to give it. He was so good as to take it immediately. I dared not look at him, and ran away directly. I was in such a fright I could hardly breathe. My dear aunt, you do not know how miserable I have been." "Frederica" said I, "you ought to have told me all your distresses. You would have found in me a friend always ready to assist you. Do you think that your uncle or I should not have espoused your cause as warmly as my brother?" "Indeed, I did not doubt your kindness," said she, colouring again, "but I thought Mr. De Courcy could do anything with my mother; but I was mistaken: they have had a dreadful quarrel about it, and he is going away. Mamma will never forgive me, and I shall be worse off than ever." "No, you shall not," I replied; "in such a point as this your mother's prohibition ought not to have prevented your speaking to me on the subject. She has no right to make you unhappy, and she shall NOT do it. Your applying, however, to Reginald can be productive only of good to all parties. I believe it is best as it is. Depend upon it that you shall not be made unhappy any longer." At that moment how great was my astonishment at seeing Reginald come out of Lady Susan's dressing-room. My heart misgave me instantly. His confusion at seeing me was very evident. Frederica immediately disappeared. "Are you going?" I said; "you will find Mr. Vernon in his own room." "No, Catherine," he replied, "I am not going. Will you let me speak to you a moment?" We went into my room. "I find," he continued, his confusion increasing as he spoke, "that I have been acting with my usual foolish impetuosity. I have entirely misunderstood Lady Susan, and was on the point of leaving the house under a false impression of her conduct. There has been some very great mistake; we have been all mistaken, I fancy. Frederica does not know her mother. Lady Susan means nothing but her good, but she will not make a friend of her. Lady Susan does not always know, therefore, what will make her daughter happy. Besides, I could have no right to interfere. Miss Vernon was mistaken in applying to me. In short, Catherine, everything has gone wrong, but it is now all happily settled. Lady Susan, I believe, wishes to speak to you about it, if you are at leisure." "Certainly," I replied, deeply sighing at the recital of so lame a story. I made no comments, however, for words would have been vain.

Reginald was glad to get away, and I went to Lady Susan, curious, indeed, to hear her account of it. "Did I not tell you," said she with a smile, "that your brother would not leave us after all?" "You did, indeed," replied I very gravely; "but I flattered myself you would be mistaken." "I should not have hazarded such an opinion," returned she, "if it had not at that moment occurred to me that his resolution of going might be occasioned by a conversation in which we had been this morning engaged, and which had ended very much to his dissatisfaction, from our not rightly understanding each other's meaning. This idea struck me at the moment, and I instantly determined that an accidental dispute, in which I might probably be as much to blame as himself, should not deprive you of your brother. If you remember, I left the room almost immediately. I was resolved to lose no time in clearing up those mistakes as far as I could. The case was this—Frederica had set herself violently against marrying Sir James." "And can your ladyship wonder that she should?" cried I with some warmth; "Frederica has an excellent understanding, and Sir James has none." "I am at least very far from regretting it, my dear sister," said she; "on the contrary, I am grateful for so favourable a sign of my daughter's sense. Sir James is certainly below par (his boyish manners make him appear worse); and had Frederica possessed the penetration and the abilities which I could have wished in my daughter, or had I even known her to possess as much as she does, I should not have been anxious for the match." "It is odd that you should alone be ignorant of your daughter's sense!" "Frederica never does justice to herself; her manners are shy and childish, and besides she is afraid of me. During her poor father's life she was a spoilt child; the severity which it has since been necessary for me to show has alienated her affection; neither has she any of that brilliancy of intellect, that genius or vigour of mind which will force itself forward." "Say rather that she has been unfortunate in her education!" "Heaven knows, my dearest Mrs. Vernon, how fully I am aware of that; but I would wish to forget every circumstance that might throw blame on the memory of one whose name is sacred with me." Here she pretended to cry; I was out of patience with her. "But what," said I, "was your ladyship going to tell me about your disagreement with my brother?" "It originated in an action of my daughter's, which equally marks her want of judgment and the unfortunate dread of me I have been mentioning—she wrote to Mr. De Courcy." "I know she did; you had forbidden her speaking to Mr. Vernon or to me on the cause of her distress; what could she do, therefore, but apply to my brother?" "Good God!" she exclaimed, "what an opinion you must have of me! Can you possibly suppose that I was aware of her unhappiness! that it was my object to make my own child miserable, and that I had forbidden her speaking to you on the subject from a fear of your interrupting the diabolical scheme? Do you think me destitute of every honest, every natural feeling? Am I capable of consigning HER to everlasting: misery whose welfare it is my first earthly duty to promote? The idea is horrible!" "What, then, was your intention when you insisted on her silence?" "Of what use, my dear sister, could be any application to you, however the affair might stand? Why should I subject you to entreaties which I refused to attend to myself? Neither for your sake nor for hers, nor for my own, could such a thing be desirable. When my own resolution was taken I could nor wish for the interference, however friendly, of another person. I was mistaken, it is true, but I believed myself right." "But what was this mistake to which your ladyship so often alludes! from whence arose so astonishing a misconception of your daughter's feelings! Did you not know that she disliked Sir James?" "I knew that he was not absolutely the man she would have chosen, but I was persuaded that her objections to him did not arise from any perception of his deficiency. You must not question me, however, my dear sister, too minutely on this point," continued she, taking me affectionately by the hand; "I honestly own that there is something to conceal. Frederica makes me very unhappy! Her applying to Mr. De Courcy hurt me particularly." "What is it you mean to infer," said I, "by this appearance of mystery? If you think your daughter at all attached to Reginald, her objecting to Sir James could not less deserve to be attended to than if the cause of her objecting had been a consciousness of his folly; and why should your ladyship, at any rate, quarrel with my brother for an interference which, you must know, it is not in his nature to refuse when urged in such a manner?"

"His disposition, you know, is warm, and he came to expostulate with me; his compassion all alive for this ill-used girl, this heroine in distress! We misunderstood each other: he believed me more to blame than I really was; I considered his interference less excusable than I now find it. I have a real regard for him, and was beyond expression mortified to find it, as I thought, so ill bestowed We were both warm, and of course both to blame. His resolution of leaving Churchhill is consistent with his general eagerness. When I understood his intention, however, and at the same time began to think that we had been perhaps equally mistaken in each other's meaning, I resolved to have an explanation before it was too late. For any member of your family I must always feel a degree of affection, and I own it would have sensibly hurt me if my acquaintance with Mr. De Courcy had ended so gloomily. I have now only to say further, that as I am convinced of Frederica's having a reasonable dislike to Sir James, I shall instantly inform him that he must give up all hope of her. I reproach myself for having even, though innocently, made her unhappy on that score. She shall have all the retribution in my power to make; if she value her own happiness as much as I do, if she judge wisely, and command herself as she ought, she may now be easy. Excuse me, my dearest sister, for thus trespassing on your time, but I owe it to my own character; and after this explanation I trust I am in no danger of sinking in your opinion." I could have said, "Not much, indeed!" but I left her almost in silence. It was the greatest stretch of forbearance I could practise. I could not have stopped myself had I begun. Her assurance! her deceit! but I will not allow myself to dwell on them; they will strike you sufficiently. My heart sickens within me. As soon as I was tolerably composed I returned to the parlour. Sir James's carriage was at the door, and he, merry as usual, soon afterwards took his leave. How easily does her ladyship encourage or dismiss a lover! In spite of this release, Frederica still looks unhappy: still fearful, perhaps, of her mother's anger; and though dreading my brother's departure, jealous, it may be, of his staying. I see how closely she observes him and Lady Susan, poor girl! I have now no hope for her. There is not a chance of her affection being returned. He thinks very differently of her from what he used to do; he does her some justice, but his reconciliation with her mother precludes every dearer hope. Prepare, my dear mother, for the worst! The probability of their marrying is surely heightened! He is more securely hers than ever. When that wretched event takes place, Frederica must belong wholly to us. I am thankful that my last letter will precede this by so little, as every moment that you can be saved from feeling a joy which leads only to disappointment is of consequence.

Yours ever, &c.,
CATHERINE VERNON.

XXV: LADY SUSAN TO MRS. JOHNSON

Churchhill.

I call on you, dear Alicia, for congratulations: I am my own self, gay and triumphant! When I wrote to you the other day I was, in truth, in high irritation, and with ample cause. Nay, I know not whether I ought to be quite tranquil now, for I have had more trouble in restoring peace than I ever intended to submit to—a spirit, too, resulting from a fancied sense of superior integrity, which is peculiarly insolent! I shall not easily forgive him, I assure you. He was actually on the point of leaving Churchhill! I had scarcely concluded my last, when Wilson brought me word of it. I found, therefore, that something must be done; for I did not choose to leave my character at the mercy of a man whose passions are so violent and so revengeful. It would have been trifling with my reputation to allow of his departing with such an impression in my disfavour; in this light, condescension was necessary. I sent Wilson to say that I desired to speak with him before he went; he came immediately. The angry emotions which had marked every feature when we last parted were partially subdued. He seemed astonished at the summons, and looked as if half wishing and half fearing to be softened by what I might say. If my countenance expressed what I aimed at, it was composed and dignified; and yet, with a degree of pensiveness which might convince him that I was not quite happy. "I beg your pardon, sir, for the liberty I have taken in sending for you," said I; "but as I have just learnt your intention of leaving this place to-day, I feel it my duty to entreat that you will not on my account shorten your visit here even an hour. I am perfectly aware that after what has passed between us it would ill suit the feelings of either to remain longer in the same house: so very great, so total a change from the intimacy of friendship must render any future intercourse the severest punishment; and your resolution of quitting Churchhill is undoubtedly in unison with our situation, and with those lively feelings which I know you to possess. But, at the same time, it is not for me to suffer such a sacrifice as it must be to leave relations to whom you are so much attached, and are so dear. My remaining here cannot give that pleasure to Mr. and Mrs. Vernon which your society must; and my visit has already perhaps been too long. My removal, therefore, which must, at any rate, take place soon, may, with perfect convenience, be hastened; and I make it my particular request that I may not in any way be instrumental in separating a family so affectionately attached to each other. Where I go is of no consequence to anyone; of very little to myself; but you are of importance to all your connections." Here I concluded, and I hope you will be satisfied with my speech. Its effect on Reginald justifies some portion of vanity, for it was no less favourable than instantaneous. Oh, how delightful it was to watch the variations of his countenance while I spoke! to see the struggle between returning tenderness and the remains of displeasure. There is something agreeable in feelings so easily worked on; not that I envy him their possession, nor would, for the world, have such myself; but they are very convenient when one wishes to influence the passions of another. And yet this Reginald, whom a very few words from me softened at once into the utmost submission, and rendered more tractable, more attached, more devoted than ever, would have left me in the first angry swelling of his proud heart without deigning to seek an explanation. Humbled as he now is, I cannot forgive him such an instance of pride, and am doubtful whether I ought not to punish him by dismissing him at once after this reconciliation, or by marrying and teazing him for ever. But these measures are each too violent to be adopted without some deliberation; at present my thoughts are fluctuating between various schemes. I have many things to compass: I must punish Frederica, and pretty severely too, for her application to Reginald; I must punish him for receiving it so favourably, and for the rest of his conduct. I must torment my sister-in-law for the insolent triumph of her look and manner since Sir James has been dismissed; for, in reconciling Reginald to me, I was not able to save that ill-fated young man; and I must make myself amends for the humiliation to which I have stooped within these few days. To effect all this I have various plans. I have also an idea of being soon in town; and whatever may be my determination as to the rest, I shall probably put THAT project in execution; for London will be always the fairest field of action, however my views may be directed; and at any rate I shall there be rewarded by your society, and a little dissipation, for a ten weeks' penance at Churchhill. I believe I owe it to my character to complete the match between my daughter and Sir James after having so long intended it. Let me know your opinion on this point. Flexibility of mind, a disposition easily biassed by others, is an attribute which you know I am not very desirous of obtaining; nor has Frederica any claim to the indulgence of her notions at the expense of her mother's inclinations. Her idle love for Reginald, too! It is surely my duty to discourage such romantic nonsense. All things considered, therefore, it seems incumbent on me to take her to town and marry her immediately to Sir James. When my own will is effected contrary to his, I shall have some credit in being on good terms with Reginald, which at present, in fact, I have not; for though he is still in my power, I have given up the very article by which our quarrel was produced, and at best the honour of victory is doubtful. Send me your opinion on all these matters, my dear Alicia, and let me know whether you can get lodgings to suit me within a short distance of you.

Your most attached
S. VERNON.

XXVI: MRS. JOHNSON TO LADY SUSAN

Edward Street.

I am gratified by your reference, and this is my advice: that you come to town yourself, without loss of time, but that you leave Frederica behind. It would surely be much more to the purpose to get yourself well established by marrying Mr. De Courcy, than to irritate him and the rest of his family by making her marry Sir James. You should think more of yourself and less of your daughter. She is not of a disposition to do you credit in the world, and seems precisely in her proper place at Churchhill, with the Vernons. But you are fitted for society, and it is shameful to have you exiled from it. Leave Frederica, therefore, to punish herself for the plague she has given you, by indulging that romantic tender-heartedness which will always ensure her misery enough, and come to London as soon as you can. I have another reason for urging this: Mainwaring came to town last week, and has contrived, in spite of Mr. Johnson, to make opportunities of seeing me. He is absolutely miserable about you, and jealous to such a degree of De Courcy that it would be highly unadvisable for them to meet at present. And yet, if you do not allow him to see you here, I cannot answer for his not committing some great imprudence—such as going to Churchhill, for instance, which would be dreadful! Besides, if you take my advice, and resolve to marry De Courcy, it will be indispensably necessary to you to get Mainwaring out of the way; and you only can have influence enough to send him back to his wife. I have still another motive for your coming: Mr. Johnson leaves London next Tuesday; he is going for his health to Bath, where, if the waters are favourable to his constitution and my wishes, he will be laid up with the gout many weeks. During his absence we shall be able to chuse our own society, and to have true enjoyment. I would ask you to Edward Street, but that once he forced from me a kind of promise never to invite you to my house; nothing but my being in the utmost distress for money should have extorted it from me. I can get you, however, a nice drawing-room apartment in Upper Seymour Street, and we may be always together there or here; for I consider my promise to Mr. Johnson as comprehending only (at least in his absence) your not sleeping in the house. Poor Mainwaring gives me such histories of his wife's jealousy. Silly woman to expect constancy from so charming a man! but she always was silly—intolerably so in marrying him at all, she the heiress of a large fortune and he without a shilling: one title, I know, she might have had, besides baronets. Her folly in forming the connection was so great that, though Mr. Johnson was her guardian, and I do not in general share HIS feelings, I never can forgive her.

Adieu. Yours ever,
ALICIA.

XXVII: MRS. VERNON TO LADY DE COURCY

Churchhill.

This letter, my dear Mother, will be brought you by Reginald. His long visit is about to be concluded at last, but I fear the separation takes place too late to do us any good. She is going to London to see her particular friend, Mrs. Johnson. It was at first her intention that Frederica should accompany her, for the benefit of masters, but we overruled her there. Frederica was wretched in the idea of going, and I could not bear to have her at the mercy of her mother; not all the masters in London could compensate for the ruin of her comfort. I should have feared, too, for her health, and for everything but her principles—there I believe she is not to be injured by her mother, or her mother's friends; but with those friends she must have mixed (a very bad set, I doubt not), or have been left in total solitude, and I can hardly tell which would have been worse for her. If she is with her mother, moreover, she must, alas! in all probability be with Reginald, and that would be the greatest evil of all. Here we shall in time be in peace, and our regular employments, our books and conversations, with exercise, the children, and every domestic pleasure in my power to procure her, will, I trust, gradually overcome this youthful attachment. I should not have a doubt of it were she slighted for any other woman in the world than her own mother. How long Lady Susan will be in town, or whether she returns here again, I know not. I could not be cordial in my invitation, but if she chuses to come no want of cordiality on my part will keep her away. I could not help asking Reginald if he intended being in London this winter, as soon as I found her ladyship's steps would be bent thither; and though he professed himself quite undetermined, there was something in his look and voice as he spoke which contradicted his words. I have done with lamentation; I look upon the event as so far decided that I resign myself to it in despair. If he leaves you soon for London everything will be concluded.

Your affectionate, &c.,
C. VERNON.

XXVIII: MRS. JOHNSON TO LADY SUSAN

Edward Street.

My dearest Friend,—I write in the greatest distress; the most unfortunate event has just taken place. Mr. Johnson has hit on the most effectual manner of plaguing us all. He had heard, I imagine, by some means or other, that you were soon to be in London, and immediately contrived to have such an attack of the gout as must at least delay his journey to Bath, if not wholly prevent it. I am persuaded the gout is brought on or kept off at pleasure; it was the same when I wanted to join the Hamiltons to the Lakes; and three years ago, when I had a fancy for Bath, nothing could induce him to have a gouty symptom.

I am pleased to find that my letter had so much effect on you, and that De Courcy is certainly your own. Let me hear from you as soon as you arrive, and in particular tell me what you mean to do with Mainwaring. It is impossible to say when I shall be able to come to you; my confinement must be great. It is such an abominable trick to be ill here instead of at Bath that I can scarcely command myself at all. At Bath his old aunts would have nursed him, but here it all falls upon me; and he bears pain with such patience that I have not the common excuse for losing my temper.

Yours ever,
ALICIA.

XXIX: LADY SUSAN VERNON TO MRS. JOHNSON

Upper Seymour Street.

My dear Alicia,—There needed not this last fit of the gout to make me detest Mr. Johnson, but now the extent of my aversion is not to be estimated. To have you confined as nurse in his apartment! My dear Alicia, of what a mistake were you guilty in marrying a man of his age! just old enough to be formal, ungovernable, and to have the gout; too old to be agreeable, too young to die. I arrived last night about five, had scarcely swallowed my dinner when Mainwaring made his appearance. I will not dissemble what real pleasure his sight afforded me, nor how strongly I felt the contrast between his person and manners and those of Reginald, to the infinite disadvantage of the latter. For an hour or two I was even staggered in my resolution of marrying him, and though this was too idle and nonsensical an idea to remain long on my mind, I do not feel very eager for the conclusion of my marriage, nor look forward with much impatience to the time when Reginald, according to our agreement, is to be in town. I shall probably put off his arrival under some pretence or other. He must not come till Mainwaring is gone. I am still doubtful at times as to marrying; if the old man would die I might not hesitate, but a state of dependance on the caprice of Sir Reginald will not suit the freedom of my spirit; and if I resolve to wait for that event, I shall have excuse enough at present in having been scarcely ten months a widow. I have not given Mainwaring any hint of my intention, or allowed him to consider my acquaintance with Reginald as more than the commonest flirtation, and he is tolerably appeased. Adieu, till we meet; I am enchanted with my lodgings.

Yours ever,
S. VERNON.

XXX: LADY SUSAN VERNON TO MR. DE COURCY

Upper Seymour Street.

I have received your letter, and though I do not attempt to conceal that I am gratified by your impatience for the hour of meeting, I yet feel myself under the necessity of delaying that hour beyond the time originally fixed. Do not think me unkind for such an exercise of my power, nor accuse me of instability without first hearing my reasons. In the course of my journey from Churchhill I had ample leisure for reflection on the present state of our affairs, and every review has served to convince me that they require a delicacy and cautiousness of conduct to which we have hitherto been too little attentive. We have been hurried on by our feelings to a degree of precipitation which ill accords with the claims of our friends or the opinion of the world. We have been unguarded in forming this hasty engagement, but we must not complete the imprudence by ratifying it while there is so much reason to fear the connection would be opposed by those friends on whom you depend. It is not for us to blame any expectations on your father's side of your marrying to advantage; where possessions are so extensive as those of your family, the wish of increasing them, if not strictly reasonable, is too common to excite surprize or resentment. He has a right to require; a woman of fortune in his daughter-in-law, and I am sometimes quarrelling with myself for suffering you to form a connection so imprudent; but the influence of reason is often acknowledged too late by those who feel like me. I have now been but a few months a widow, and, however little indebted to my husband's memory for any happiness derived from him during a union of some years, I cannot forget that the indelicacy of so early a second marriage must subject me to the censure of the world, and incur, what would be still more insupportable, the displeasure of Mr. Vernon. I might perhaps harden myself in time against the injustice of general reproach, but the loss of HIS valued esteem I am, as you well know, ill-fitted to endure; and when to this may be added the consciousness of having injured you with your family, how am I to support myself? With feelings so poignant as mine, the conviction of having divided the son from his parents would make me, even with you, the most miserable of beings. It will surely, therefore, be advisable to delay our union—to delay it till appearances are more promising—till affairs have taken a more favourable turn. To assist us In such a resolution I feel that absence will be necessary. We must not meet. Cruel as this sentence may appear, the necessity of pronouncing it, which can alone reconcile it to myself, will be evident to you when you have considered our situation in the light in which I have found myself imperiously obliged to place it. You may be—you must be—well assured that nothing but the strongest conviction of duty could induce me to wound my own feelings by urging a lengthened separation, and of insensibility to yours you will hardly suspect me. Again, therefore, I say that we ought not, we must not, yet meet. By a removal for some months from each other we shall tranquillise the sisterly fears of Mrs. Vernon, who, accustomed herself to the enjoyment of riches, considers fortune as necessary everywhere, and whose sensibilities are not of a nature to comprehend ours. Let me hear from you soon—very soon. Tell me that you submit to my arguments, and do not reproach me for using such. I cannot bear reproaches:

my spirits are not so high as to need being repressed. I must endeavour to seek amusement, and fortunately many of my friends are in town; amongst them the Mainwarings; you know how sincerely I regard both husband and wife.

I am, very faithfully yours,
S. VERNON

XXXI: LADY SUSAN TO MRS. JOHNSON

Upper Seymour Street.

My dear Friend,—That tormenting creature, Reginald, is here. My letter, which was intended to keep him longer in the country, has hastened him to town. Much as I wish him away, however, I cannot help being pleased with such a proof of attachment. He is devoted to me, heart and soul. He will carry this note himself, which is to serve as an introduction to you, with whom he longs to be acquainted. Allow him to spend the evening with you, that I may be in no danger of his returning here. I have told him that I am not quite well, and must be alone; and should he call again there might be confusion, for it is impossible to be sure of servants. Keep him, therefore, I entreat you, in Edward Street. You will not find him a heavy companion, and I allow you to flirt with him as much as you like. At the same time, do not forget my real interest; say all that you can to convince him that I shall be quite wretched if he remains here; you know my reasons—propriety, and so forth. I would urge them more myself, but that I am impatient to be rid of him, as Mainwaring comes within half an hour. Adieu!

S VERNON

XXXII: MRS. JOHNSON TO LADY SUSAN

Edward Street.

My dear Creature,—I am in agonies, and know not what to do. Mr. De Courcy arrived just when he should not. Mrs. Mainwaring had that instant entered the house, and forced herself into her guardian's presence, though I did not know a syllable of it till afterwards, for I was out when both she and Reginald came, or I should have sent him away at all events; but she was shut up with Mr. Johnson, while he waited in the drawing-room for me. She arrived yesterday in pursuit of her husband, but perhaps you know this already from himself. She came to this house to entreat my husband's interference, and before I could be aware of it, everything that you could wish to be concealed was known to him, and unluckily she had wormed out of Mainwaring's servant that he had visited you every day since your being in town, and had just watched him to your door herself! What could I do! Facts are such horrid things! All is by this time known to De Courcy, who is now alone with Mr. Johnson. Do not accuse me; indeed, it was impossible to prevent it. Mr. Johnson has for some time suspected De Courcy of intending to marry you, and would speak with him alone as soon as he knew him to be in the house. That detestable Mrs. Mainwaring, who, for your comfort, has fretted herself thinner and uglier than ever, is still here, and they have been all closeted together. What can be done? At any rate, I hope he will plague his wife more than ever. With anxious wishes,

Yours faithfully,
ALICIA.

XXXIII: LADY SUSAN TO MRS. JOHNSON

Upper Seymour Street.

This eclaircissement is rather provoking. How unlucky that you should have been from home! I thought myself sure of you at seven! I am undismayed however. Do not torment yourself with fears on my account; depend on it, I can make my story good with Reginald. Mainwaring is just gone; he brought me the news of his wife's arrival. Silly woman, what does she expect by such manoeuvres? Yet I wish she had stayed quietly at Langford. Reginald will be a little enraged at first, but by to-morrow's dinner, everything will be well again.

Adieu!

S. V.

XXXIV: MR. DE COURCY TO LADY SUSAN

—Hotel

I write only to bid you farewell, the spell is removed; I see you as you are. Since we parted yesterday, I have received from indisputable authority such a history of you as must bring the most mortifying conviction of the imposition I have been under, and the absolute necessity of an immediate and eternal separation from you. You cannot doubt to what I allude. Langford! Langford! that word will be sufficient. I received my information in Mr. Johnson's house, from Mrs. Mainwaring herself. You know how I have loved you; you can intimately judge of my present feelings, but I am not so weak as to find indulgence in describing them to a woman who will glory in having excited their anguish, but whose affection they have never been able to gain.

R. DE COURCY.

XXXV: LADY SUSAN TO MR. DE COURCY

Upper Seymour Street.

I will not attempt to describe my astonishment in reading the note this moment received from you. I am bewildered in my endeavours to form some rational conjecture of what Mrs. Mainwaring can have told you to occasion so extraordinary a change in your sentiments. Have I not explained everything to you with respect to myself which could bear a doubtful meaning, and which the ill-nature of the world had interpreted to my discredit? What can you now have heard to stagger your esteem for me? Have I ever had a concealment from you? Reginald, you agitate me beyond expression, I cannot suppose that the old story of Mrs. Mainwaring's jealousy can be revived again, or at least be LISTENED to again. Come to me immediately, and explain what is at present absolutely incomprehensible. Believe me the single word of Langford is not of such potent intelligence as to supersede the necessity of more. If we ARE to part, it will at least be handsome to take your personal leave—but I have little heart to jest; in truth, I am serious enough; for to be sunk, though but for an hour, in your esteem Is a humiliation to which I know not how to submit. I shall count every minute till your arrival.

S. V.

XXXVI: MR. DE COURCY TO LADY SUSAN

——Hotel.

Why would you write to me? Why do you require particulars? But, since it must be so, I am obliged to declare that all the accounts of your misconduct during the life, and since the death of Mr. Vernon, which had reached me, in common with the world in general, and gained my entire belief before I saw you, but which you, by the exertion of your perverted abilities, had made me resolved to disallow, have been unanswerably proved to me; nay more, I am assured that a connection, of which I had never before entertained a thought, has for some time existed, and still continues to exist, between you and the man whose family you robbed of its peace in return for the hospitality with which you were received into it; that you have corresponded with him ever since your leaving Langford; not with his wife, but with him, and that he now visits you every day. Can you, dare you deny it? and all this at the time when I was an encouraged, an accepted lover! From what have I not escaped! I have only to be grateful. Far from me be all complaint, every sigh of regret. My own folly had endangered me, my preservation I owe to the kindness, the integrity of another; but the unfortunate Mrs. Mainwaring, whose agonies while she related the past seemed to threaten her reason, how is SHE to be consoled! After such a discovery as this, you will scarcely affect further wonder at my meaning in bidding you adieu. My understanding is at length restored, and teaches no less to abhor the artifices which had subdued me than to despise myself for the weakness on which their strength was founded.

R. DE COURCY.

XXXVII: LADY SUSAN TO MR. DE COURCY

Upper Seymour Street.

I am satisfied, and will trouble you no more when these few lines are dismissed. The engagement which you were eager to form a fortnight ago is no longer compatible with your views, and I rejoice to find that the prudent advice of your parents has not been given in vain. Your restoration to peace will, I doubt not, speedily follow this act of filial obedience, and I flatter myself with the hope of surviving my share in this disappointment.

S. V.

XXXVIII: MRS. JOHNSON TO LADY SUSAN VERNON

Edward Street

I am grieved, though I cannot be astonished at your rupture with Mr. De Courcy; he has just informed Mr. Johnson of it by letter. He leaves London, he says, to-day. Be assured that I partake in all your feelings, and do not be angry if I say that our intercourse, even by letter, must soon be given up. It makes me miserable; but Mr. Johnson vows that if I persist in the connection, he will settle in the country for the rest of his life, and you know it is impossible to submit to such an extremity while any other alternative remains. You have heard of course that the Mainwarings are to part, and I am afraid Mrs. M. will come home to us again; but she is still so fond of her husband, and frets so much about him, that perhaps she may not live long. Miss Mainwaring is just come to town to be with her aunt, and they say that she declares she will have Sir James Martin before she leaves London again. If I were you, I would certainly get him myself. I had almost forgot to give you my opinion of Mr. De Courcy; I am really delighted with him; he is full as handsome, I think, as Mainwaring, and with such an open, good-humoured countenance, that one cannot help loving him at first sight. Mr. Johnson and he are the greatest friends in the world. Adieu, my dearest Susan, I wish matters did not go so perversely. That unlucky visit to Langford! but I dare say you did all for the best, and there is no defying destiny.

Your sincerely attached
ALICIA.

XXXIX: LADY SUSAN TO MRS. JOHNSON

Upper Seymour Street.

My dear Alicia,—I yield to the necessity which parts us. Under circumstances you could not act otherwise. Our friendship cannot be impaired by it, and in happier times, when your situation is as independent as mine, it will unite us again in the same intimacy as ever. For this I shall impatiently wait, and meanwhile can safely assure you that I never was more at ease, or better satisfied with myself and everything about me than at the present hour. Your husband I abhor, Reginald I despise, and I am secure of never seeing either again. Have I not reason to rejoice? Mainwaring is more devoted to me than ever; and were we at liberty, I doubt if I could resist even matrimony offered by HIM. This event, if his wife live with you, it may be in your power to hasten. The violence of her feelings, which must wear her out, may be easily kept in irritation. I rely on your friendship for this. I am now satisfied that I never could have brought myself to marry Reginald, and am equally determined that Frederica never shall. To-morrow, I shall fetch her from Churchhill, and let Maria Mainwaring tremble for the consequence. Frederica shall be Sir James's wife before she quits my house, and she may whimper, and the Vernons may storm, I regard them not. I am tired of submitting my will to the caprices of others; of resigning my own judgment in deference to those to whom I owe no duty, and for whom I feel no respect. I have given up too much, have been too easily worked on, but Frederica shall now feel the difference. Adieu, dearest of friends; may the next gouty attack be more favourable! and may you always regard me as unalterably yours,

S. VERNON

XL: LADY DE COURCY TO MRS. VERNON

My dear Catherine,—I have charming news for you, and if I had not sent off my letter this morning you might have been spared the vexation of knowing of Reginald's being gone to London, for he is returned. Reginald is returned, not to ask our consent to his marrying Lady Susan, but to tell us they are parted for ever. He has been only an hour in the house, and I have not been able to learn particulars, for he is so very low that I have not the heart to ask questions, but I hope we shall soon know all. This is the most joyful hour he has ever given us since the day of his birth. Nothing is wanting but to have you here, and it is our particular wish and entreaty that you would come to us as soon as you can. You have owed us a visit many long weeks; I hope nothing will make it inconvenient to Mr. Vernon; and pray bring all my grand-children; and your dear niece is included, of course; I long to see her. It has been a sad, heavy winter hitherto, without Reginald, and seeing nobody from Churchhill. I never found the season so dreary before; but this happy meeting will make us young again. Frederica runs much in my thoughts, and when Reginald has recovered his usual good spirits (as I trust he soon will) we will try to rob him of his heart once more, and I am full of hopes of seeing their hands joined at no great distance.

Your affectionate mother,
C. DE COURCY

XLI: MRS. VERNON TO LADY DE COURCY

Churchhill.

My dear Mother,—Your letter has surprized me beyond measure! Can it be true that they are really separated—and for ever? I should be overjoyed if I dared depend on it, but after all that I have seen how can one be secure And Reginald really with you! My surprize is the greater because on Wednesday, the very day of his coming to Parklands, we had a most unexpected and unwelcome visit from Lady Susan, looking all cheerfulness and good-humour, and seeming more as if she were to marry him when she got to London than as if parted from him for ever. She stayed nearly two hours, was as affectionate and agreeable as ever, and not a syllable, not a hint was dropped, of any disagreement or coolness between them. I asked her whether she had seen my brother since his arrival in town; not, as you may suppose, with any doubt of the fact, but merely to see how she looked. She immediately answered, without any embarrassment, that he had been kind enough to call on her on Monday; but she believed he had already returned home, which I was very far from crediting. Your kind invitation is accepted by us with pleasure, and on Thursday next we and our little ones will be with you. Pray heaven, Reginald may not be in town again by that time! I wish we could bring dear Frederica too, but I am sorry to say that her mother's errand hither was to fetch her away; and, miserable as it made the poor girl, it was impossible to detain her. I was thoroughly unwilling to let her go, and so was her uncle; and all that could be urged we did urge; but Lady Susan declared that as she was now about to fix herself in London for several months, she could not be easy if her daughter were not with her for masters, &c. Her manner, to be sure, was very kind and proper, and Mr. Vernon believes that Frederica will now be treated with affection. I wish I could think so too. The poor girl's heart was almost broke at taking leave of us. I charged her to write to me very often, and to remember that if she were in any distress we should be always her friends. I took care to see her alone, that I might say all this, and I hope made her a little more comfortable; but I shall not be easy till I can go to town and judge of her situation myself. I wish there were a better prospect than now appears of the match which the conclusion of your letter declares your expectations of. At present, it is not very likely,

Yours ever, &c.,
C. VERNON

Conclusion

This correspondence, by a meeting between some of the parties, and a separation between the others, could not, to the great detriment of the Post Office revenue, be continued any longer. Very little assistance to the State could be derived from the epistolary intercourse of Mrs. Vernon and her niece; for the former soon perceived, by the style of Frederica's letters, that they were written under her mother's inspection! and therefore, deferring all particular enquiry till she could make it personally in London, ceased writing minutely or often. Having learnt enough, in the meanwhile, from her open-hearted brother, of what had passed between him and Lady Susan to sink the latter lower than ever in her opinion, she was proportionably more anxious to get Frederica removed from such a mother, and placed under her own care; and, though with little hope of success, was resolved to leave nothing unattempted that might offer a chance of obtaining her sister-in-law's consent to it. Her anxiety on the subject made her press for an early visit to London; and Mr. Vernon, who, as it must already have appeared, lived only to do whatever he was desired, soon found some accommodating business to call him thither. With a heart full of the matter, Mrs. Vernon waited on Lady Susan shortly after her arrival in town, and was met with such an easy and cheerful affection, as made her almost turn from her with horror. No remembrance of Reginald, no consciousness of guilt, gave one look of embarrassment; she was in excellent spirits, and seemed eager to show at once by ever possible attention to her brother and sister her sense of their kindness, and her pleasure in their society. Frederica was no more altered than Lady Susan; the same restrained manners, the same timid look in the presence of her mother as heretofore, assured her aunt of her situation being uncomfortable, and confirmed her in the plan of altering it. No unkindness, however, on the part of Lady Susan appeared. Persecution on the subject of Sir James was entirely at an end; his name merely mentioned to say that he was not in London; and indeed, in all her conversation, she was solicitous only for the welfare and improvement of her daughter, acknowledging, in terms of grateful delight, that Frederica was now growing every day more and more what a parent could desire. Mrs. Vernon, surprized and incredulous, knew not what to suspect, and, without any change in her own views, only feared greater difficulty in accomplishing them. The first hope of anything better was derived from Lady Susan's asking her whether she thought Frederica looked quite as well as she had done at Churchhill, as she must confess herself to have sometimes an anxious doubt of London's perfectly agreeing with her. Mrs. Vernon, encouraging the doubt, directly proposed her niece's returning with them into the country. Lady Susan was unable to express her sense of such kindness, yet knew not, from a variety of reasons, how to part with her daughter; and as, though her own plans were not yet wholly fixed, she trusted it would ere long be in her power to take Frederica into the country herself, concluded by declining entirely to profit by such unexampled attention. Mrs. Vernon persevered, however, in the offer of it, and though Lady Susan continued to resist, her resistance in the course of a few days seemed somewhat less formidable. The lucky alarm of an influenza decided what might not have been decided quite so soon. Lady Susan's maternal fears were then too much awakened for her to think of anything but Frederica's removal from the risk of infection; above all disorders in the world she most dreaded the influenza for her daughter's constitution!

Frederica returned to Churchhill with her uncle and aunt; and three weeks afterwards, Lady Susan announced her being married to Sir James Martin. Mrs. Vernon was then convinced of what she had only suspected before, that she might have spared herself all the trouble of urging a removal which Lady Susan had doubtless resolved on from the first. Frederica's visit was nominally for six weeks, but her mother, though inviting her to return in one or two affectionate letters, was very ready to oblige the whole party by consenting to a prolongation of her stay, and in the course of two months ceased to write of her absence, and in the course of two or more to write to her at all. Frederica was therefore fixed in the family of her uncle and aunt till such time as Reginald De Courcy could be talked, flattered, and finessed into an affection for her which, allowing leisure for the conquest of his attachment to her mother, for his abjuring all future attachments, and detesting the sex, might be reasonably looked for in the course of a twelvemonth. Three months might have done it in general, but Reginald's feelings were no less lasting than lively. Whether Lady Susan was or was not happy in her second choice, I do not see how it can ever be ascertained; for who would take her assurance of it on either side of the question? The world must judge from probabilities; she had nothing against her but her husband, and her conscience. Sir James may seem to have drawn a harder lot than mere folly merited; I leave him, therefore, to all the pity that anybody can give him. For myself, I confess that I can pity only Miss Mainwaring; who, coming to town, and putting herself to an expense in clothes which impoverished her for two years, on purpose to secure him, was defrauded of her due by a woman ten years older than herself.

The Watsons

Chapter I

The first winter assembly in the town of D. in Surrey was to be held on Tuesday, October 13th and it was generally expected to be a very good one. A long list of county families was confidently run over as sure of attending, and sanguine hopes were entertained that the Osbornes themselves would be there. The Edwards' invitation to the Watsons followed, of course. The Edwards were people of fortune, who lived in the town and kept their coach. The Watsons inhabited a village about three miles distant, were poor, and had no close carriage; and ever since there had been balls in the place, the former were accustomed to invite the latter to dress, dine, and sleep at their house on every monthly return throughout the winter. On the present occasion, as only two of Mr. Watson's children were at home, and one was always necessary as companion to himself, for he was sickly and had lost his wife, one only could profit by the kindness of their friends. Miss Emma Watson, who was very recently returned to her family from the care of an aunt who had brought her up, was to make her first public appearance in the neighbourhood, and her eldest sister, whose delight in a ball was not lessened by a ten years' enjoyment, had some merit in cheerfully undertaking to drive her and all her finery in the old chair to D. on the important morning.

As they splashed along the dirty lane, Miss Watson thus instructed and cautioned her inexperienced sister: --

"I dare say it will be a very good ball, and among so many officers you will hardly want partners. You will find Mrs. Edwards' maid very willing to help you, and I would advise you to ask Mary Edwards' opinion if you are at all at a loss, for she has a very good taste. If Mr. Edwards does not lose his money at cards, you will stay as late as you can wish for; if he does, he will hurry you home perhaps -- but you are sure of some comfortable soup. I hope you will be in good looks. I should not be surprised if you were to be thought one of the prettiest girls in the room; there is a great deal in novelty. Perhaps Tom Musgrave may take notice of you; but I would advise you by all means not to give him any encouragement. He generally pays attention to every new girl; but he is a great flirt, and never means anything serious."

"I think I have heard you speak of him before," said Emma; "who is he?"

"A young man of very good fortune, quite independent, and remarkably agreeable, -- a universal favourite wherever he goes. Most of the girls hereabout are in love with him, or have been. I believe I am the only one among them that have escaped with a whole heart; and yet I was the first he paid attention to when he came into this country six years ago; and very great attention did he pay me. Some people say that he has never seemed to like any girl so well since, though he is always behaving in a particular way to one or another."

"And how came your heart to be the only cold one?" said Emma, smiling.

"There was a reason for that," replied Miss Watson, changing colour, -- "I have not been very well used among them, Emma. I hope you will have better luck."

"Dear sister, I beg your pardon if I have unthinkingly given you pain."

"When first we knew Tom Musgrave," continued Miss Watson, without seeming to hear her, "I was very much attached to a young man of the name of Purvis, a particular friend of Robert's, who used to be with us a great deal. Everybody thought it would have been a match."

A sigh accompanied these words, which Emma respected in silence; but her sister after a short pause went on.

"You will naturally ask why it did not take place, and why he is married to another woman, while I am still single. But you must ask her, not me, -- you must ask Penelope. Yes, Emma, Penelope was at the bottom of it all. She thinks everything fair for a husband. I trusted her; she set him against me, with a view of gaining him herself, and it ended in his discontinuing his visits, and soon after marrying somebody else. Penelope makes light of her conduct, but I think such treachery very bad. It has been the ruin of my happiness. I shall never love any man as I loved Purvis. I do not think Tom Musgrave should be named with him in the same day."

"You quite shock me by what you say of Penelope," said Emma. "Could a sister do such a thing? Rivalry, treachery between sisters! I shall be afraid of being acquainted with her. But I hope it was not so; appearances were against her."

"You do not know Penelope. There is nothing she would not do to get married. She would as good as tell you so herself. Do not trust her with any secrets of your own, take warning by me, do not trust her; she has her good qualities, but she has no faith, no honour, no scruples, if she can promote her own advantage. I wish with all my heart she was well married. I declare I had rather have her well married than myself."

"Than yourself! yes, I can suppose so. A heart wounded like yours can have little inclination for matrimony."

"Not much indeed -- but you know we must marry. I could do very well single for my own part; a little company, and a pleasant ball now and then, would be enough for me, if one could be young forever; but my father cannot provide for us, and it is very bad to grow old and be poor and laughed at. I have lost Purvis, it is true; but very few people marry their first loves. I should not refuse a man because he was not Purvis. Not that I can ever quite forgive Penelope."

Emma shook her head in acquiescence.

"Penelope, however, has had her troubles," continued Miss Watson. "She was sadly disappointed in Tom Musgrave, who afterwards transferred his attentions from me to her, and whom she was very fond of; but he never means anything serious, and when he had trifled with her long enough, he began to slight her for Margaret, and poor Penelope was very wretched. And since then she has been trying to make some match at Chichester, -- she won't tell us with whom; but I believe it is a rich old Dr. Harding, uncle to the friend she goes to see; and she has taken a vast deal of trouble about him, and given up a great deal of time to no purpose as yet. When she went away the other day, she said it should be the last time. I suppose you did not know what her particular business was at Chichester, nor guess at the object which could take her away from Stanton just as you were coming home after so many years' absence."

"No indeed, I had not the smallest suspicion of it. I considered her engagement to Mrs. Shaw just at that time as very unfortunate for me. I had hoped to find all my sisters at home, to be able to make an immediate friend of each."

"I suspect the Doctor to have had an attack of the asthma, and that she was hurried away on that account. The Shaws are quite on her side, -- at least, I believe so; but she tells me nothing. She professes to keep her own counsel; she says, and truly enough, that `Too many cooks spoil the broth.'"

"I am sorry for her anxieties," said Emma; "but I do not like her plans or her opinions. I shall be afraid of her. She must have too masculine and bold a temper. To be so bent on marriage, to pursue a man merely for the sake of situation, is a sort of thing that shocks me; I cannot understand it. Poverty is a great evil; but to a woman of education and feeling it ought not, it cannot be the greatest. I would rather be teacher at a school (and I can think of nothing worse) than marry a man I did not like."

"I would rather do anything than be teacher at a school," said her sister. "I have been at school, Emma, and know what a life they lead; you never have. I should not like marrying a disagreeable man any more than yourself; but I do not think there are many very disagreeable men; I think I could like any good-humoured man with a comfortable income. I suppose my aunt brought you up to be rather refined."

"Indeed I do not know. My conduct must tell you how I have been brought up. I am no judge of it myself. I cannot compare my aunt's method with any other person's, because I know no other."

"But I can see in a great many things that you are very refined. I have observed it ever since you came home, and I am afraid it will not be for your happiness. Penelope will laugh at you very much."

"That will not be for my happiness, I an sure. If my opinions are wrong, I must correct them; if they are above my situation, I must endeavour to conceal them; but I doubt whether ridicule -- Has Penelope much wit?"

"Yes; she has great spirits, and never cares what she says."

"Margaret is more gentle, I imagine?"

"Yes; especially in company. She is all gentleness and mildness when anybody is by; but she is a little fretful and perverse among ourselves. Poor creature! She is possessed with the notion of Tom Musgrave's being more seriously in love with her than he ever was with anybody else, and is always expecting him to come to the point. This is the second time within this twelvemonth that she has gone to spend a month with Robert and Jane on purpose to egg him on by her absence; but I am sure she is mistaken, and that he will no more follow her to Croydon now than he did last March. He will never marry unless he can marry somebody very great, -- Miss Osborne, perhaps, or something in that style."

"Your account of this Tom Musgrave, Elizabeth, gives me very little inclination for his acquaintance."

"You are afraid of him; I do not wonder at you."

"No, indeed; I dislike and despise him."

"Dislike and despise Tom Musgrave! No, that you never can. I defy you not to be delighted with him if he takes notice of you. I hope he will dance with you; and I dare say he will, unless the Osbornes come with a large party, and then he will not speak to anybody else."

"He seems to have most engaging manners!" said Emma. "Well, we shall see how irresistible Mr. Tom Musgrave and I find each other. I suppose I shall know him as soon as I enter the ball-room; he must carry some of his charm in his face."

"You will not find him in the ball-room, I can tell you; you will go early, that Mrs. Edwards may get a good place by the fire, and he never comes till late; if the Osbornes are coming, he will wait in the passage and come in with them. I should like to look in upon you, Emma. If it was but a good day with my father, I would wrap myself up, and James should drive me over as soon as I had made tea for him; and I should be with you by the time the dancing began."

"What! Would you come late at night in this chair?"

"To be sure I would. There, I said you were very refined, and that's an instance of it."

Emma for a moment made no answer. At last she said, --

"I wish, Elizabeth, you had not made a point of my going to this ball; I wish you were going instead of me. Your pleasure would be greater than mine. I am a stranger here, and know nobody but the Edwardses; my enjoyment, therefore, must be very doubtful. Yours, among all your acquaintance, would be certain. It is not too late to change. Very little apology could be requisite to the Edwardses, who must be more glad of your company than of mine, and I should most readily return to my father; and should not be at all afraid to drive this quiet old creature home. Your clothes I would undertake to find means of sending to you."

"My dearest Emma," cried Elizabeth, warmly, "do you think I would do such a thing? Not for the universe! But I shall never forget your good-nature in proposing it. You must have a sweet temper indeed! I never met with anything like it! And would you really give up the ball that I might be able to go to it? Believe me, Emma, I am not so selfish as that comes to. No; though I am nine years older than you are, I would not be the means of keeping you from being seen. You are very pretty, and it would be very hard that you should not have as fair a chance as we have all had to make your fortune. No, Emma, whoever stays at home this winter, it sha'n't be you. I am sure I should never have forgiven the person who kept me from a ball at nineteen."

Emma expressed her gratitude, and for a few minutes they jogged on in silence. Elizabeth first spoke: --

"You will take notice who Mary Edwards dances with?"

"I will remember her partners, if I can; but you know they will be all strangers to me."

"Only observe whether she dances with Captain Hunter more than once, -- I have my fears in that quarter. Not that her father or mother like officers; but if she does, you know, it is all over with poor Sam. And I have promised to write him word who she dances with."

"Is Sam attached to Miss Edwards?"

"Did not you know that?"

"How should I know it? How should I know in Shropshire what is passing of that nature in Surrey? It is not likely that circumstances of such delicacy should have made any part of the scanty communication which passed between you and me for the last fourteen years."

"I wonder I never mentioned it when I wrote. Since you have been at home, I have been so busy with my poor father and our great wash that I have had no leisure to tell you anything; but, indeed, I concluded you knew it all. He has been very much in love with her these two years, and it is a great disappointment to him that he cannot always get away to our balls; but Mr. Curtis won't often spare him, and just now it is a sickly time at Guildford."

"Do you suppose Miss Edwards inclined to like him?"

"I am afraid not: you know she is an only child, and will have at least ten thousand pounds."

"But still she may like our brother."

"Oh, no! The Edwards look much higher. Her father and mother would never consent to it. Sam is only a surgeon, you know. Sometimes I think she does like him. But Mary Edwards is rather prim and reserved; I do not always know what she would be at."

"Unless Sam feels on sure grounds with the lady herself, it seems a pity to me that he should be encouraged to think of her at all."

"A young man must think of somebody," said Elizabeth, "and why should not he be as lucky as Robert, who has got a good wife and six thousand pounds?"

"We must not all expect to be individually lucky," replied Emma. "The luck of one member of a family is luck to all."

"Mine is all to come, I am sure," said Elizabeth, giving another sigh to the remembrance of Purvis. "I have been unlucky enough; and I cannot say much for you, as my aunt married again so foolishly. Well, you will have a good ball, I daresay. The next turning will bring us to the turnpike: you may see the church-tower over the hedge, and the White Hart is close by it. I shall long to know what you think of Tom Musgrave."

Such were the last audible sounds of Miss Watson's voice, before they passed through the turnpike-gate, and entered on the pitching of the town, the jumbling and noise of which made farther conversation most thoroughly undesirable. The old mare trotted heavily on, wanting no direction of the reins to take the right turning, and making only one blunder, in proposing to stop at the milliner's before she drew up towards Mr. Edwards' door. Mr. Edwards lived in the best house in the street, and the best in the place, if Mr. Tomlinson, the banker, might be indulged in calling his newly erected house at the end of the town, with a shrubbery and sweep, in the country.

Mr. Edwards' house was higher than most of its neighbours, with four windows on each side the door, the windows guarded by posts and chains, and the door approached by a flight of stone steps.

"Here we are," said Elizabeth, as the carriage ceased moving, "safely arrived, and by the market clock we have been only five-and-thirty minutes coming; which I think is doing pretty well, though it would be nothing for Penelope. Is not it a nice town? The Edwards have a noble house, you see, and they live quite in style. The door will be opened by a man in livery, with a powdered head, I can tell you."

Emma had seen the Edwardses only one morning at Stanton; they were therefore all but strangers to her; and though her spirits were by no means insensible to the expected joys of the evening, she felt a little uncomfortable in the thought of all that was to precede them. Her conversation with Elizabeth, too, giving her some very unpleasant feelings with respect to her own family, had made her more open to disagreeable impressions from any other cause, and increased her sense of the awkwardness of rushing into intimacy on so slight an acquaintance.

There was nothing in the manner of Mrs. or Miss Edwards to give immediate change to these ideas. The mother, though a very friendly woman, had a reserved air, and a great deal of formal civility; and the daughter, a genteel-looking girl of twenty-two, with her hair in papers, seemed very naturally to have caught something of the style of her mother, who had brought her up. Emma was soon left to know what they could be, by Elizabeth's being obliged to hurry away; and some very languid remarks on the probable brilliancy of the ball were all that broke, at intervals, a silence of half an hour, before they were joined by the master of the house. Mr. Edwards had a much easier and more communicative air than the ladies of the family; he was fresh from the street, and he came ready to tell whatever might interest. After a cordial reception of Emma, he turned to his daughter with, --

"Well, Mary, I bring you good news: the Osbornes will certainly be at the ball tonight. Horses for two carriages are ordered from the White Hart to be at Osborne Castle by nine."

"I am glad of it," observed Mrs. Edwards, "because their coming gives a credit to our assembly. The Osbornes being known to have been at the first ball, will dispose a great many people to attend the second. It is more than they deserve; for in fact, they add nothing to the pleasure of the evening: they come so late and go so early; but great people have always their charm."

Mr. Edwards proceeded to relate every other little article of news which his morning's lounge had supplied him with, and they chatted with greater briskness, till Mrs. Edwards' moment for dressing arrived, and the young ladies were carefully recommended to lose no time. Emma was shown to a very comfortable apartment, and as soon as Mrs. Edwards' civilities could leave her to herself, the happy occupation, the first bliss of a ball, began. The girls, dressing in some measure together, grew unavoidably better acquainted. Emma found in Miss Edwards the show of good sense, a modest unpretending mind, and a great wish of obliging; and when they returned to the parlour where Mrs. Edwards was sitting, respectably attired in one of the two satin gowns which went through the winter, and a new cap from the milliner's, they entered it with much easier feelings and more natural smiles than they had taken away. Their dress was now to be examined: Mrs. Edwards acknowledged herself too old-fashioned to approve of every modern extravagance, however sanctioned; and though complacently viewing her daughter's good looks, would give but a qualified admiration; and Mr. Edwards, not less satisfied with Mary, paid some compliments of good-humoured gallantry to Emma at her expense. The discussion led to more intimate remarks, and Miss Edwards gently asked Emma if she were not often reckoned very like her youngest brother. Emma thought she could perceive a faint blush accompany the question, and there seemed something still more suspicious in the manner in which Mr. Edwards took up the subject.

"You are paying Miss Emma no great compliment, I think, Mary," said he, hastily. "Mr. Sam Watson is a very good sort of young man, and I dare say a very clever surgeon; but his complexion has been rather too much exposed to all weathers to make a likeness to him very flattering."

Mary apologised, in some confusion, --

"She had not thought a strong likeness at all incompatible with very different degrees of beauty. There might be resemblance in countenance, and the complexion and even the features be very unlike."

"I know nothing of my brother's beauty," said Emma, "for I have not seen him since he was seven years old; but my father reckons us alike."

"Mr. Watson!" cried Mr. Edwards; "well, you astonish me. There is not the least likeness in the world; your brother's eyes are grey, yours are brown; he has a long face and a wide mouth. My dear, do you perceive the least resemblance?"

"Not the least. Miss Emma Watson puts me very much in mind of her eldest sister, and sometimes I see a look of Miss Penelope, and once or twice there has been a glance of Mr. Robert, but I cannot perceive any likeness to Mr. Samuel."

"I see the likeness between her and Miss Watson," replied Mr. Edwards, "very strongly, but I am not sensible of the others. I do not much think she is like any of the family but Miss Watson; but I am very sure there is no resemblance between her and Sam."

This matter was settled, and they went to dinner.

"Your father, Miss Emma, is one of my oldest friends," said Mr. Edwards, as he helped her to wine, when they were drawn round the fire to enjoy their dessert. "We must drink to his better health. It is a great concern to me, I assure you, that he should be such an invalid. I know nobody who likes a game of cards, in a social way, better than he does, and very few people that play a fairer rubber. It is a thousand pities that he should be so deprived of the pleasure. For now we have a quiet little Whist Club, that meets three times a week at the White Hart; and if he could but have his health, how much he would enjoy it!"

"I dare say he would, sir; and I wish, with all my heart, he were equal to it."

"Your club would be better fitted for an invalid," said Mrs. Edwards, "if you did not keep it up so late."

This was an old grievance.

"So late, my dear! What are you talking of?" cried the husband, with sturdy pleasantry. "We are always at home before midnight. They would laugh at Osborne Castle to hear you call that late; they are but just rising from dinner at midnight."

"That is nothing to the purpose," retorted the lady, calmly. "The Osbornes are to be no rule for us. You had better meet every night, and break up two hours sooner."

So far the subject was very often carried; but Mr. and Mrs. Edwards were so wise as never to pass that point; and Mr. Edwards now turned to something else. He had lived long enough in the idleness of a town to become a little of a gossip, and having some anxiety to know more of the circumstances of his young guest than had yet reached him, he began with, --

"I think, Miss Emma, I remember your aunt very well, about thirty years ago; I am pretty sure I danced with her in the old rooms at Bath, the year before I married. She was a very fine woman then; but like other people, I suppose, she is grown somewhat older since that time. I hope she is likely to be happy in her second choice."

"I hope so; I believe so, sir," said Emma, in some agitation.

"Mr. Turner had not been dead a great while, I think?"

"About two years, sir."

"I forget what her name is now."

"O'Brien."

"Irish! ah, I remember; and she is gone to settle in Ireland. I do wonder that you should not wish to go with her into that country, Miss Emma; but it must be a great deprivation to her, poor lady!, after bringing you up like a child of her own."

"I was not so ungrateful, sir," said Emma, warmly, "as to wish to be anywhere but with her. It did not suit them, it did not suit Captain O'Brien that I should be of the party."

"Captain!" repeated Mrs. Edwards. "The gentleman is in the army then?"

"Yes, ma'am."

"Aye, there is nothing like your officers for captivating the ladies, young or old. There is no resisting a cockade, my dear."

"I hope there is," said Mrs. Edwards, gravely, with a quick glance at her daughter; and Emma had just recovered from her own perturbation in time to see a blush on Miss Edwards' cheek, and in remembering what Elizabeth had said of Captain Hunter, to wonder and waver between his influence and her brother's.

"Elderly ladies should be careful how they make a second choice," observed Mr. Edwards.

"Carefulness -- discretion should not be confined to elderly ladies or to a second choice," added his wife. "They are quite as necessary to young ladies in their first."

"Rather more so, my dear," replied he; "because young ladies are likely to feel the effects of it longer. When an old lady plays the fool, it is not in the course of nature that she should suffer from it many years."

Emma drew her hand across her eyes; and Mrs. Edwards, on perceiving it, changed the subject to one of less anxiety to all.

With nothing to do but to expect the hour of setting off, the afternoon was long to the two young ladies; and though Miss Edwards was rather discomposed at the very early hour which her mother always fixed for going, that early hour itself was watched for with some eagerness.

The entrance of the tea-things at seven o'clock was some relief; and luckily Mr. and Mrs. Edwards always drank a dish extraordinary and ate an additional muffin when they were going to sit up late, which lengthened the ceremony almost to the wished-for moment.

Chapter II

At a little before eight, the Tomlinsons' carriage was heard to go by -- which was the constant signal for Mrs. Edwards to order hers to the door; and in a very few minutes the party were transported from the quiet and warmth of a snug parlour to the bustle, noise, and draughts of air of the broad entrance passage of an inn. Mrs. Edwards, carefully guarding her own dress, while she attended with yet greater solicitude to the proper security of her young charges' shoulders and throats, led the way up the wide staircase, while no sound of a ball but the first scrape of one violin blessed the ears of her followers; and Miss Edwards, on hazarding the anxious inquiry of whether there were many people come yet, was told by the waiter, as she knew she should, that "Mr. Tomlinson's family were in the room."

In passing along a short gallery to the assembly-room, brilliant in lights before them, they were accosted by a young man in a morning-dress and boots, who was standing in the doorway of a bed-chamber, apparently on purpose to see them go by.

"Ah! Mrs. Edwards, how do you do? How do you do, Miss Edwards?" he cried, with an easy air. "You are determined to be in good time, I see, as usual. The candles are but this moment lit."

"I like to get a good seat by the fire, you know, Mr. Musgrave," replied Mrs. Edwards.

"I am this moment going to dress," said he. "I am waiting for my stupid fellow. We shall have a famous ball. The Osbornes are certainly coming; you may depend upon that, for I was with Lord Osborne this morning."

The party passed on. Mrs. Edwards' satin gown swept along the clean floor of the ball-room to the fireplace at the upper end, where one party only were formally seated, while three or four officers were lounging together, passing in and out from the adjoining card-room. A very stiff meeting between these near neighbours ensued; and as soon as they were all duly placed again, Emma, in the low whisper which became the solemn scene, said to Miss Edwards, --

"The gentleman we passed in the passage was Mr. Musgrave, then; he is reckoned remarkably agreeable, I understand?"

Miss Edwards answered hesitatingly, "Yes; he is very much liked by many people; but we are not very intimate."

"He is rich, is not he?"

"He has about eight or nine hundred pounds a year, I believe. He came into possession of it when he was very young, and my father and mother think it has given him rather an unsettled turn. He is no favourite with them."

The cold and empty appearance of the room and the demure air of the small cluster of females at one end of it, began soon to give way. The inspiriting sound of other carriages was heard, and continual accessions of portly chaperons and strings of smartly-dressed girls were received, with now and then a fresh gentleman straggler, who, if not enough in love to station himself near any fair creature, seemed glad to escape into the card-room.

Among the increasing number of military men, one now made his way to Miss Edwards with an air of empressement which decidedly said to her companion, "I am Captain Hunter"; and Emma, who could not but watch her at such a moment, saw her looking rather distressed, but by no means displeased, and heard an engagement formed for the two first dances, which made her think her brother Sam's a hopeless case.

Emma in the meanwhile was not unobserved or unadmired herself. A new face, and a very pretty one, could not be slighted. Her name was whispered from one party to another; and no sooner had the signal been given by the orchestra's striking up a favourite air, which seemed to call the young to their duty and people the centre of the room, than she found herself engaged to dance with a brother officer, introduced by Captain Hunter.

Emma Watson was not more than of the middle height, well made and plump, with an air of healthy vigour. Her skin was very brown, but clear, smooth, and glowing, which, with a lively eye, a sweet smile, and an open countenance, gave beauty to attract, and expression to make that beauty improve on acquaintance. Having no reason to be dissatisfied with her partner, the evening began very pleasantly to her, and her feelings perfectly coincided with the reiterated observation of others, that it was an excellent ball. The two first dances were not quite over when the returning sound of carriages after a long interruption called general notice, and "The Osbornes are coming! The Osbornes are coming!" was repeated round the room. After some minutes of extraordinary bustle without and watchful curiosity within, the important party, preceded by the attentive master of the inn to open a door which was never shut, made their appearance. They consisted of Lady Osborne; her son, Lord Osborne; her daughter, Miss Osborne; Miss Carr, her daughter's friend; Mr. Howard, formerly tutor to Lord Osborne, now clergyman of the parish in which the castle stood; Mrs. Blake, a widow sister who lived with him; her son, a fine boy of ten years old; and Mr. Tom Musgrave, who probably, imprisoned within his own room, had been listening in bitter impatience to the sound of the music for the last half-hour. In their progress up the room, they paused almost immediately behind Emma to receive the compliments of some acquaintance; and she heard Lady Osborne observe that they had made a point of coming early for the gratification of Mrs. Blake's little boy, who was uncommonly fond of dancing. Emma looked at them all as they passed, but chiefly and with most interest on Tom Musgrave, who was certainly a genteel, good-looking young man. Of the females, Lady Osborne had by much the finest person; though nearly fifty, she was very handsome, and had all the dignity of rank.

Lord Osborne was a very fine young man; but there was an air of coldness, of carelessness, even of awkwardness about him, which seemed to speak him out of his element in a ball-room. He came, in fact, only because it was judged expedient for him to please the borough; he was not fond of women's company, and he never danced. Mr. Howard was an agreeable-looking man, a little more than thirty.

At the conclusion of the two dances, Emma found herself, she knew not how, seated amongst the Osborne set; and she was immediately struck with the fine countenance and animated gestures of the little boy, as he was standing before his mother, wondering when they should begin.

"You will not be surprised at Charles' impatience," said Mrs. Blake, a lively, pleasant-looking little woman of five or six and thirty, to a lady who was standing near her, "when you know what a partner he is to have. Miss Osborne has been so very kind as to promise to dance the two first dances with him."

"Oh, yes! we have been engaged this week," cried the boy, "and we are to dance down every couple."

On the other side of Emma, Miss Osborne, Miss Carr, and a party of young men were standing engaged in very lively consultation; and soon afterwards she saw the smartest officer of the set walking off to the orchestra to order the dance, while Miss Osborne, passing before her to her little expecting partner, hastily said: "Charles, I beg your pardon for not keeping my engagement, but I am going to dance these two dances with Colonel Beresford. I know you will excuse me, and I will certainly dance with you after tea"; and without staying for an answer, she turned again to Miss Carr, and in another minute was led by Colonel Beresford to begin the set. If the poor little boy's face had in its happiness been interesting to Emma, it was infinitely more so under this sudden reverse; he stood the picture of disappointment, with crimsoned cheeks, quivering lips, and eyes bent on the floor. His mother, stifling her own mortification, tried to soothe his with the prospect of Miss Osborne's second promise; but though he contrived to utter, with an effort of boyish bravery, "Oh, I do not mind it!" it was very evident, by the unceasing agitation of his features, that he minded it as much as ever.

Emma did not think or reflect; she felt and acted. "I shall be very happy to dance with you, sir, if you like it," said she, holding out her hand with the most unaffected good-humour. The boy, in one moment restored to all his first delight, looked joyfully at his mother; and stepping forwards with an honest and simple "Thank you, ma'am," was instantly ready to attend his new acquaintance. The thankfulness of Mrs. Blake was more diffuse; with a look most expressive of unexpected pleasure and lively gratitude, she turned to her neighbour with repeated and fervent acknowledgments of so great and condescending a kindness to her boy. Emma, with perfect truth, could assure her that she could not be giving greater pleasure than she felt herself; and Charles being provided with his gloves and charged to keep them on, they joined the set which was now rapidly forming, with nearly equal complacency. It was a partnership which could not be noticed without surprise. It gained her a broad stare from Miss Osborne and Miss Carr as they passed her in the dance. "Upon my word, Charles, you are in luck," said the former, as she turned him; "you have got a better partner than me"; to which the happy Charles answered "Yes."

Tom Musgrave, who was dancing with Miss Carr, gave her many

inquisitive glances; and after a time Lord Osborne himself came, and under pretence of talking to Charles, stood to look at his partner. Though rather distressed by such observation, Emma could not repent what she had done, so happy had it made both the boy and his mother; the latter of whom was continually making opportunities of addressing her with the warmest civility. Her little partner, she found, though bent chiefly on dancing, was not unwilling to speak, when her questions or remarks gave him anything to say; and she learnt, by a sort of inevitable inquiry, that he had two brothers and a sister, that they and their mamma all lived with his uncle at Wickstead, that his uncle taught him Latin, that he was very fond of riding, and had a horse of his own given him by Lord Osborne; and that he had been out once already with Lord Osborne's hounds.

At the end of these dances, Emma found they were to drink tea; Miss Edwards gave her a caution to be at hand, in a manner which convinced her of Mrs. Edwards' holding it very important to have them both close to her when she moved into the tea-room; and Emma was accordingly on the alert to gain her proper station. It was always the pleasure of the company to have a little bustle and crowd when they adjourned for refreshment. The tea-room was a small room within the card-room; and in passing through the latter, where the passage was straitened by tables, Mrs. Edwards and her party were for a few moments hemmed in. It happened close by Lady Osborne's casino table; Mr. Howard, who belonged to it, spoke to his nephew; and Emma, on perceiving herself the object of attention both to Lady Osborne and him, had just turned away her eyes in time to avoid seeming to hear her young companion delightedly whisper aloud, "Oh, uncle! do look at my partner; she is so pretty!" As they were immediately in motion again, however, Charles was hurried off without being able to receive his uncle's suffrage. On entering the tea-room, in which two long tables were prepared, Lord Osborne was to be seen quite alone at the end of one, as if retreating as far as he could from the ball, to enjoy his own thoughts and gape without restraint. Charles instantly pointed him out to Emma. "There's Lord Osborne; let you and I go and sit by him."

"No, no," said Emma, laughing; "you must sit with my friends."

Charles was now free enough to hazard a few questions in his turn. "What o'clock was it?"

"Eleven."

"Eleven! and I am not at all sleepy. Mamma said I should be asleep before ten. Do you think Miss Osborne will keep her word with me, when tea is over?"

"Oh, yes! I suppose so"; though she felt that she had no better reason to give than that Miss Osborne had not kept it before.

"When shall you come to Osborne Castle?"

"Never, probably. I am not acquainted with the family."

"But you may come to Wickstead and see mamma, and she can take you to the castle. There is a monstrous curious stuffed fox there, and a badger; anybody would think they were alive. It is a pity you should not see them."

On rising from tea, there was again a scramble for the pleasure of being first out of the room, which happened to be increased by one or two of the card-parties having just broken up, and the players being disposed to move exactly the different way. Among these was Mr. Howard, his sister leaning on his arm; and no sooner were they within reach of Emma, than Mrs Blake, calling her notice by a friendly touch, said, "Your goodness to Charles, my dear Miss Watson, brings all his family upon you. Give me leave to introduce my brother, Mr. Howard." Emma curtsied, the gentleman bowed, made a hasty request for the honour of her hand in the two next dances, to which as hasty an affirmative was given, and they were immediately impelled in opposite directions. Emma was very well pleased with the circumstance; there was a quietly cheerful, gentlemanlike air in Mr. Howard which suited her; and in a few minutes afterwards the value of her engagement increased, when, as she was sitting in the card-room, somewhat screened by a door, she heard Lord Osborne, who was lounging on a vacant table near her, call Tom Musgrave towards him and say, "Why do not you dance with that beautiful Emma Watson? I want you to dance with her, and I will come and stand by you."

"I was determining on it this very moment, my lord; I'll be introduced and dance with her directly."

"Aye, do; and if you find she does not want much talking to, you may introduce me by and by."

"Very well, my lord; if she is like her sisters, she will only want to be listened to. I will go this moment. I shall find her in the tea-room. That stiff old Mrs. Edwards has never done tea."

Away he went, Lord Osborne after him; and Emma lost no time in hurrying from her corner exactly the other way, forgetting in her haste that she left Mrs. Edwards behind.

"We had quite lost you," said Mrs. Edwards, who followed her with Mary in less than five minutes. "If you prefer this room to the other, there is no reason why you should not be here; but we had better all be together."

Emma was saved the trouble of apologizing, by their being joined at the moment by Tom Musgrave, who requesting Mrs. Edwards aloud to do him the honour of presenting him to Miss Emma Watson, left that good lady without any choice in the business, but that of testifying by the coldness of her manner that she did it unwillingly. The honour of dancing with her was solicited without loss of time; and Emma, however she might like to be thought a beautiful girl by lord or commoner, was so little disposed to favour Tom Musgrave himself that she had considerable satisfaction in avowing her previous engagement. He was evidently surprised and discomposed. The style of her last partner had probably led him to believe her not overpowered with applications.

"My little friend Charles Blake," he cried, "must not expect to engross you the whole evening. We can never suffer this. It is against the rules of the assembly, and I am sure it will never be patronised by our good friend here, Mrs. Edwards; she is by much too nice a judge of decorum to give her license to such a dangerous particularity --"

"I am not going to dance with Master Blake, sir!"

The gentleman, a little disconcerted, could only hope he might be fortunate another time, and seeming unwilling to leave her, though his friend Lord Osborne was waiting in the doorway for the result, as Emma with some amusement perceived, he began to make civil inquiries after her family.

"How comes it that we have not the pleasure of seeing your sisters here this evening? Our assemblies have been used to be so well treated by them that we do not know how to take this neglect."

"My eldest sister is the only one at home, and she could not leave my father."

"Miss Watson the only one at home! You astonish me! It seems but the day before yesterday that I saw them all three in this town. But I am afraid I have been a very sad neighbour of late. I hear dreadful complaints of my negligence wherever I go, and I confess it is a shameful length of time since I was at Stanton. But I shall now endeavour to make myself amends for the past."

Emma's calm courtesy in reply must have struck him as very unlike the encouraging warmth he had been used to receive from her sisters, and gave him probably the novel sensation of doubting his own influence, and of wishing for more attention than she bestowed. The dancing now recommenced; Miss Carr being impatient to call, everybody was required to stand up; and Tom Musgrave's curiosity was appeased on seeing Mr. Howard come forward and claim Emma's hand.

"That will do as well for me," was Lord Osborne's remark, when his friend carried him the news, and he was continually at Howard's elbow during the two dances.

The frequency of his appearance there was the only unpleasant part of the engagement, the only objection she could make to Mr. Howard. In himself, she thought him as agreeable as he looked; though chatting on the commonest topics, he had a sensible, unaffected way of expressing himself, which made them all worth hearing, and she only regretted that he had not been able to make his pupil's manners as unexceptionable as his own. The two dances seemed very short, and she had her partner's authority for considering them so. At their conclusion the Osbornes and their train were all on the move.

"We are off at last," said his lordship to Tom. "How much longer do you stay in this heavenly place -- till sunrise?"

"No, faith! my lord; I have had quite enough of it. I assure you, I shall not show myself here again when I have had the honour of attending Lady

Osborne to her carriage. I shall retreat in as much secrecy as possible to the most remote corner of the house, where I shall order a barrel of oysters, and be famously snug."

"Let me see you soon at the castle, and bring me word how she looks by daylight."

Emma and Mrs. Blake parted as old acquaintance, and Charles shook her by the hand, and wished her "good-bye" at least a dozen times. From Miss Osborne and Miss Carr she received something like a jerking curtsey as they passed her; even Lady Osborne gave her a look of complacency, and his lordship actually came back, after the others were out of the room, to "beg her pardon," and look in the window-seat behind her for the gloves which were visibly compressed in his hand. As Tom Musgrave was seen no more, we may suppose his plan to have succeeded, and imagine him mortifying with his barrel of oysters in dreary solitude, or gladly assisting the landlady in her bar to make fresh negus for the happy dancers above. Emma could not help missing the party by whom she had been, though in some respects unpleasantly, distinguished; and the two dances which followed and concluded the ball were rather flat in comparison with the others. Mr. Edwards having played with good luck, they were some of the last in the room.

"Here we are back again, I declare," said Emma, sorrowfully, as she walked into the dining-room, where the table was prepared, and the neat upper maid was lighting the candles. "My dear Miss Edwards, how soon it is at an end! I wish it could all come over again."

A great deal of kind pleasure was expressed in her having enjoyed the evening so much; and Mr. Edwards was as warm as herself in the praise of the fullness, brilliancy, and spirit of the meeting, though as he had been fixed the whole time at the same table in the same room, with only one change of chairs, it might have seemed a matter scarcely perceived; but he had won four rubbers out of five, and everything went well. His daughter felt the advantage of this gratified state of mind, in the course of the remarks and retrospections which now ensued over the welcome soup.

"How came you not to dance with either of the Mr. Tomlinsons, Mary?" said her mother.

"I was always engaged when they asked me."

"I thought you were to have stood up with Mr. James the two last dances; Mrs. Tomlinson told me he was gone to ask you, and I had heard you say two minutes before that you were not engaged."

"Yes, but there was a mistake; I had misunderstood. I did not know I was engaged. I thought it had been for the two dances after, if we stayed so long; but Captain Hunter assured me it was for those very two."

"So you ended with Captain Hunter, Mary, did you?" said her father. "And whom did you begin with?"

"Captain Hunter," was repeated in a very humble tone.

"Hum! That is being constant, however. But who else did you dance with?"

"Mr. Norton and Mr. Styles."

"And who are they?"

"Mr. Norton is a cousin of Captain Hunter's."

"And who is Mr. Styles?"

"One of his particular friends."

"All in the same regiment," added Mrs. Edwards. "Mary was surrounded by red-coats all the evening. I should have been better pleased to see her dancing with some of our old neighbours, I confess."

"Yes, yes; we must not neglect our old neighbours. But if these soldiers are quicker than other people in a ball-room, what are young ladies to do?"

"I think there is no occasion for their engaging themselves so many dances beforehand, Mr. Edwards."

"No, perhaps not; but I remember, my dear, when you and I did the same."

Mrs. Edwards said no more, and Mary breathed again. A good deal of good-humoured pleasantry followed; and Emma went to bed in charming spirits, her head full of Osbornes, Blakes, and Howards.

The next morning brought a great many visitors. It was the way of the place always to call on Mrs. Edwards the morning after a ball, and this neighbourly inclination was increased in the present instance by a general spirit of curiosity on Emma's account, as everybody wanted to look again at the girl who had been admired the night before by Lord Osborne. Many were the eyes, and various the degrees of approbation with which she was examined. Some saw no fault, and some no beauty. With some her brown skin was the annihilation of every grace, and others could never be persuaded that she was half so handsome as Elizabeth Watson had been ten years ago. The morning passed quickly away in discussing the merits of the ball with all this succession of company; and Emma was at once astonished by finding it two o'clock, and considering that she had heard nothing of her father's chair. After this discovery, she had walked twice to the window to examine the street, and was on the point of asking leave to ring the bell and make inquiries, when the light sound of a carriage driving up to the door set her heart at ease. She stepped again to the window, but instead of the convenient though very un-smart family equipage, perceived a neat curricle. Mr. Musgrave was shortly afterwards announced, and Mrs. Edwards put on her very stiffest look at the sound. Not at all dismayed, however, by her chilling air, he paid his compliments to each of the ladies with no unbecoming ease, and continuing to address Emma, presented her a note, which "he had the honour of bringing from her sister, but to which he must observe a verbal postscript from himself would be requisite."

The note, which Emma was beginning to read rather before Mrs. Edwards had entreated her to use no ceremony, contained a few lines from Elizabeth importing that their father, in consequence of being unusually well, had taken the sudden resolution of attending the visitation that day, and that as his road lay quite wide from D., it was impossible for her to come home till the following morning, unless the Edwardses would send her, which was hardly to be expected, or she could meet with any chance conveyance, or did not mind walking so far. She had scarcely run her eye through the whole, before she found herself obliged to listen to Tom Musgrave's farther account.

"I received that note from the fair hands of Miss Watson only ten minutes ago," said he; "I met her in the village of Stanton, whither my good stars prompted me to turn my horses' heads. She was at that moment in quest of a person to employ on the errand, and I was fortunate enough to convince her that she could not find a more willing or speedy messenger than myself. Remember, I say nothing of my disinterestedness. My reward is to be the indulgence of conveying you to Stanton in my curricle. Though they are not written down, I bring your sister's orders for the same."

Emma felt distressed; she did not like the proposal -- she did not wish to be on terms of intimacy with the proposer; and yet, fearful of encroaching on the Edwardses, as well as wishing to go home herself, she was at a loss how entirely to decline what he offered. Mrs. Edwards continued silent, either not understanding the case, or waiting to see how the young lady's inclination lay. Emma thanked him, but professed herself very unwilling to give him so much trouble. "The trouble was of course honour, pleasure, delight, -- what had he or his horses to do?" Still she hesitated, -- "She believed she must beg leave to decline his assistance; she was rather afraid of the sort of carriage. The distance was not beyond a walk." Mrs. Edwards was silent no longer. She inquired into the particulars, and then said, "We shall be extremely happy, Miss Emma, if you can give us the pleasure of your company till tomorrow; but if you cannot conveniently do so, our carriage is quite at your service, and Mary will be pleased with the opportunity of seeing your sister."

This was precisely what Emma had longed for, and she accepted the offer most thankfully, acknowledging that as Elizabeth was entirely alone, it was her wish to return home to dinner. The plan was warmly opposed by their visitor, --

"I cannot suffer it, indeed. I must not be deprived of the happiness of escorting you. I assure you there is not a possibility of fear with my horses. You might guide them yourself. Your sisters all know how quiet they are; they have none of them the smallest scruple in trusting themselves with me, even on a race-course. Believe me," added he, lowering his voice, "you are quite safe, -- the danger is only mine."

Emma was not more disposed to oblige him for all this.

"And as to Mrs. Edwards' carriage being used the day after a ball, it is a thing quite out of rule, I assure you -- never heard of before. The old coachman will look as black as his horses -- won't he Miss Edwards?"

No notice was taken. The ladies were silently firm, and the gentleman found himself obliged to submit.

"What a famous ball we had last night!" he cried, after a short pause. "How long did you keep it up after the Osbornes and I went away?"

"We had two dances more."

"It is making it too much of a fatigue, I think, to stay so late. I suppose your set was not a very full one."

"Yes; quite as full as ever, except the Osbornes. There seemed no vacancy anywhere; and everybody danced with uncommon spirit to the very last."

Emma said this, though against her conscience.

"Indeed! perhaps I might have looked in upon you again, if I had been aware of as much, for I am rather fond of dancing than not. Miss Osborne is a charming girl, is not she?"

"I do not think her handsome," replied Emma, to whom all this was chiefly addressed.

"Perhaps she is not critically handsome, but her manners are delightful. And Fanny Carr is a most interesting little creature. You can imagine nothing more naive or piquante; and what do you think of Lord Osborne, Miss Watson?"

"He would be handsome even though he were not a lord, and perhaps, better bred; more desirous of pleasing and showing himself pleased in a right place."

"Upon my word, you are severe upon my friend! I assure you Lord Osborne is a very good fellow."

"I do not dispute his virtues, but I do not like his careless air."

"If it were not a breach of confidence," replied Tom, with an important look, "perhaps I might be able to win a more favourable opinion of poor Osborne."

Emma gave him no encouragement, and he was obliged to keep his friend's secret. He was also obliged to put an end to his visit, for Mrs. Edwards having ordered her carriage, there was no time to be lost on Emma's side in preparing for it. Miss Edwards accompanied her home; but as it was dinner-hour at Stanton, stayed with them only a few minutes.

Chapter III

"Now, my dear Emma," said Miss Watson, as soon as they were alone, "you must talk to me all the rest of the day without stopping, or I shall not be satisfied; but, first of all, Nanny shall bring in the dinner. Poor thing! You will not dine as you did yesterday, for we have nothing but some fried beef. How nice Mary Edwards looks in her new pelisse! And now tell me how you like them all, and what I am to say to Sam. I have begun my letter, Jack Stokes is to call for it tomorrow, for his uncle is going within a mile of Guildford the next day."

Nanny brought in the dinner.

"We will wait upon ourselves," continued Elizabeth, "and then we shall lose no time. And so, you would not come home with Tom Musgrave?"

"No, you had said so much against him that I could not wish either for the obligation or the intimacy which the use of his carriage must have created. I should not even have liked the appearance of it."

"You did very right; though I wonder at your forbearance, and I do not think I could have done it myself. He seemed so eager to fetch you that I could not say no, though it rather went against me to be throwing you together, so well as I knew his tricks; but I did long to see you, and it was a clever way of getting you home. Besides, it won't do to be too nice. Nobody could have thought of the Edwardses' letting you have their coach, after the horses being out so late. But what am I to say to Sam?"

"If you are guided by me, you will not encourage him to think of Miss Edwards. The father is decidedly against him, the mother shows him no favour, and I doubt his having any interest with Mary. She danced twice with Captain Hunter, and I think shows him in general as much encouragement as is consistent with her disposition and the circumstances she is placed in. She once mentioned Sam, and certainly with a little confusion; but that was perhaps merely owing to the consciousness of his liking her, which may very probably have come to her knowledge."

"Oh, dear! yes. She has heard enough of that from us all. Poor Sam! he is out of luck as well as other people. For the life of me, Emma, I cannot help feeling for those that are crossed in love. Well, now begin, and give me an account of everything as it happened."

Emma obeyed her, and Elizabeth listened with very little interruption till she heard of Mr. Howard as a partner.

"Dance with Mr. Howard! Good heavens! you don't say so! Why, he is quite one of the great and grand ones. Did you not find him very high?"

"His manners are of a kind to give me much more ease and confidence than Tom Musgrave's."

"Well, go on. I should have been frightened out of my wits to have had anything to do with the Osbornes' set."

Emma concluded her narration.

"And so you really did not dance with Tom Musgrave at all; but you must have liked him, -- you must have been struck with him altogether."

"I do not like him, Elizabeth. I allow his person and air to be good, and that his manners to a certain point -- his address rather -- is pleasing, but I see nothing else to admire in him. On the contrary, he seems very vain, very conceited, absurdly anxious for distinction, and absolutely contemptible in some of the measures he takes for becoming so. There is a ridiculousness about him that entertains me, but his company gives me no other agreeable emotion."

"My dearest Emma! You are like nobody else in the world. It is well Margaret is not by. You do not offend me, though I hardly know how to believe you; but Margaret would never forgive such words."

"I wish Margaret could have heard him profess his ignorance of her being out of the country; he declared it seemed only two days since he had seen her."

"Aye, that is just like him; and yet this is the man she will fancy so desperately in love with her. He is no favourite of mine, as you well know, Emma; but you must think him agreeable. Can you lay your hand on your heart, and say you do not?"

"Indeed, I can, both hands, and spread to their widest extent."

"I should like to know the man you do think agreeable."

"His name is Howard."

"Howard! Dear me; I cannot think of him but as playing cards with Lady Osborne, and looking proud. I must own, however, that it is a relief to me to find you can speak as you do of Tom Musgrave. My heart did misgive me that you would like him too well. You talked so stoutly beforehand, that I was sadly afraid your brag would be punished. I only hope it will last, and that he will not come on to pay you much attention. It is a hard thing for a woman to stand against the flattering ways of a man, when he is bent upon pleasing her."

As their quietly sociable little meal concluded, Miss Watson could not help observing how comfortably it had passed.

"It is so delightful to me," said she, "to have things going on in peace and good-humour. Nobody can tell how much I hate quarrelling. Now, though we have had nothing but fried beef, how good it has all seemed! I wish everybody were as easily satisfied as you; but poor Margaret is very snappish, and Penelope owns she had rather have quarrelling going on than nothing at all."

Mr. Watson returned in the evening not the worse for the exertion of the day, and, consequently pleased with what he had done, and glad to talk of it over his own fireside. Emma had not foreseen any interest to herself in the occurrences of a visitation; but when she heard Mr. Howard spoken of as the preacher, and as having given them an excellent sermon, she could not help listening with a quicker ear.

"I do not know when I have heard a discourse more to my mind," continued Mr. Watson, "or one better delivered. He reads extremely well, with great propriety, and in a very impressive manner, and at the same time without any theatrical grimace or violence. I own I do not like much action in the pulpit; I do not like the studied air and artificial inflexions of voice which your very popular and most admired preachers generally have. A simple delivery is much better calculated to inspire devotion, and shows a much better taste. Mr. Howard read like a scholar and a gentleman."

"And what had you for dinner, sir?" said his eldest daughter.

He related the dishes, and told what he had ate himself.

"Upon the whole," he added, "I have had a very comfortable day. My old friends were quite surprised to see me amongst them, and I must say that everybody paid me great attention, and seemed to feel for me as an invalid. They would make me sit near the fire; and as the partridges were pretty high, Dr. Richards would have them sent away to the other end of the table, `that they might not offend Mr. Watson,' which I thought very kind of him. But what pleased me as much as anything was Mr. Howard's attention. There is a pretty steep flight of steps up to the room we dine in, which do not quite agree with my gouty foot; and Mr. Howard walked by me from the bottom to the top, and would make me take his arm. It struck me as very becoming in so young a man; but I am sure I had no claim to expect it, for I never saw him before in my life. By the by, he inquired after one of my daughters; but I do not know which. I suppose you know among yourselves."

Chapter IV

On the third day after the ball, as Nanny, at five minutes before three, was beginning to bustle into the parlour with the tray and the knife-case, she was suddenly called to the front door by the sound of as smart a rap as the end of a riding-whip could give; and though charged by Miss Watson to let nobody in, returned in half a minute with a look of awkward dismay to hold the parlour door open for Lord Osborne and Tom Musgrave. The surprise of the young ladies may be imagined. No visitors would have been welcome at such a moment, but such visitors as these -- such a one as Lord Osborne at least, a nobleman and a stranger -- was really distressing.

He looked a little embarrassed himself, as, on being introduced by his easy, voluble friend, he muttered something of doing himself the honour of waiting upon Mr. Watson. Though Emma could not but take the compliment of the visit to herself, she was very far from enjoying it. She felt all the inconsistency of such an acquaintance with the very humble style in which they were obliged to live; and having in her aunt's family been used to many of the elegancies of life, was fully sensible of all that must be open to the ridicule of richer people in her present home. Of the pain of such feelings, Elizabeth knew very little. Her simple mind, or juster reason, saved her from such mortification; and though shrinking under a general sense of inferiority, she felt no particular shame. Mr. Watson, as the gentlemen had already heard from Nanny, was not well enough to be down-stairs. With much concern they took their seats; Lord Osborne near Emma, and the convenient Mr. Musgrave, in high spirits at his own importance, on the other side of the fireplace, with Elizabeth. He was at no loss for words; but when Lord Osborne had hoped that Emma had not caught cold at the ball, he had nothing more to say for some time, and could only gratify his eye by occasional glances at his fair neighbour. Emma was not inclined to give herself much trouble for his entertainment; and after hard labour of mind, he produced the remark of its being a very fine day, and followed it up with the question of, "Have you been walking this morning?"

"No, my lord; we thought it too dirty."

"You should wear half-boots." After another pause: "Nothing sets off a neat ankle more than a half-boot; nankeen galoshed with black looks very well. Do not you like half-boots?"

"Yes; but unless they are so stout as to injure their beauty, they are not fit for country walking."

"Ladies should ride in dirty weather. Do you ride?"

"No, my lord."

"I wonder every lady does not; a woman never looks better than on horseback."

"But every woman may not have the inclination, or the means."

"If they knew how much it became them, they would all have the inclination; and I fancy, Miss Watson, when once they had the inclination, the means would soon follow."

"Your lordship thinks we always have our own way. That is a point on which ladies and gentlemen have long disagreed; but without pretending to decide it, I may say that there are some circumstances which even women cannot control. Female economy will do a great deal my lord: but it cannot turn a small income into a large one."

Lord Osborne was silenced. Her manner had been neither sententious nor sarcastic; but there was a something in its mild seriousness, as well as in the words themselves, which made his lordship think; and when he addressed her again, it was with a degree of considerate propriety totally unlike the half-awkward, half-fearless style of his former remarks. It was a new thing with him to wish to please a woman; it was the first time that he had ever felt what was due to a woman in Emma's situation; but as he wanted neither in sense nor a good disposition, he did not feel it without effect.

"You have not been long in this country, I understand," said he, in the tone of a gentleman. "I hope you are pleased with it."

He was rewarded by a gracious answer, and a more liberal full view of her face than she had yet bestowed. Unused to exert himself, and happy in contemplating her, he then sat in silence for some minutes longer, while Tom Musgrave was chattering to Elizabeth; till they were interrupted by Nanny's approach, who, half-opening the door and putting in her head, said, --

"Please, ma'am, master wants to know why he ben't to have his dinner?"

The gentlemen, who had hitherto disregarded every symptom, however positive, of the nearness of that meal, now jumped up with apologies, while Elizabeth called briskly after Nanny "to tell Betty to take up the fowls."

"I am sorry it happens so," she added, turning good-humouredly towards

Musgrave, "but you know what early hours we keep."

Tom had nothing to say for himself; he knew it very well, and such honest simplicity, such shameless truth, rather bewildered him. Lord Osborne's parting compliments took some time, his inclination for speech seeming to increase with the shortness of the term for indulgence. He recommended exercise in defiance of dirt; spoke again in praise of half-boots; begged that his sister might be allowed to send Emma the name of her shoemaker; and concluded with saying, "My hounds will be hunting this country next week. I believe they will throw off at Stanton Wood on Wednesday at nine o'clock. I mention this in hopes of your being drawn out to see what's going on. If the morning's tolerable, pray do us the honour of giving us your good wishes in person."

The sisters looked on each other with astonishment when their visitors had withdrawn.

"Here's an unaccountable honour!" cried Elizabeth, at last. "Who would have thought of Lord Osborne's coming to Stanton? He is very handsome; but Tom Musgrave looks all to nothing the smartest and most fashionable man of the two. I am glad he did not say anything to me; I would not have had to talk to such a great man for the world. Tom was very agreeable, was not he? But did you hear him ask where Miss Penelope and Miss Margaret were, when he first came in? It put me out of patience. I am glad Nanny had not laid the cloth, however -- it would have looked so awkward; just the tray did not signify." To say that Emma was not flattered by Lord Osborne's visit would be to assert a very unlikely thing, and describe a very odd young lady; but the gratification was by no means unalloyed: his coming was a sort of notice which might please her vanity, but did not suit her pride; and she would rather have known that he wished the visit without presuming to make it, than have seen him at Stanton.

Among other unsatisfactory feelings, it once occurred to her to wonder why Mr. Howard had not taken the same privilege of coming, and accompanied his lordship; but she was willing to suppose that he had either known nothing about it, or had declined any share in a measure which carried quite as much impertinence in its form as good-breeding. Mr. Watson was very far from being delighted when he heard what had passed; a little peevish under immediate pain, and ill-disposed to be pleased, he only replied, --

"Phoo! phoo! what occasion could there be for Lord Osborne's coming? I have lived here fourteen years without being noticed by any of the family. It is some foolery of that idle fellow, Tom Musgrave. I cannot return the visit. I would not if I could." And when Tom Musgrave was met with again, he was commissioned with a message of excuse to Osborne Castle, on the too-sufficient plea of Mr. Watson's infirm state of health.

Chapter V

A week or ten days rolled quietly away after this visit before any new bustle arose to interrupt even for half a day the tranquil and affectionate intercourse of the two sisters, whose mutual regard was increasing with the intimate knowledge of each other which such intercourse produced. The first circumstance to break in on this security was the receipt of a letter from Croydon to announce the speedy return of Margaret, and a visit of two or three days from Mr. and Mrs. Robert Watson, who undertook to bring her home, and wished to see their sister Emma.

It was an expectation to fill the thoughts of the sisters at Stanton, and to busy the hours of one of them at least; for as Jane had been a woman of fortune, the preparations for her entertainment were considerable; and as Elizabeth had at all times more goodwill than method in her guidance of the house, she could make no change without a bustle. An absence of fourteen years had made all her brothers and sisters strangers to Emma, but in her expectation of Margaret there was more than the awkwardness of such an alienation; she had heard things which made her dread her return; and the day which brought the party to Stanton seemed to her the probable conclusion of almost all that had been comfortable in the house.

Robert Watson was an attorney at Croydon, in a good way of business; very well satisfied with himself for the same, and for having married the only daughter of the attorney to whom he had been clerk, with a fortune of six thousand pounds. Mrs. Robert was not less pleased with herself for having had that six thousand pounds, and for being now in possession of a very smart house in Croydon, where she gave genteel parties and wore fine clothes. In her person there was nothing remarkable; her manners were pert and conceited. Margaret was not without beauty; she had a slight pretty figure, and rather wanted countenance than good features; but the sharp and anxious expression of her face made her beauty in general little felt. On meeting her long-absent sister, as on every occasion of show, her manner was all affection and her voice all gentleness; continual smiles and a very slow articulation being her constant resource when determined on pleasing.

She was now so "delighted to see dear, dear Emma," that she could hardly speak a word in a minute.

"I am sure we shall be great friends," she observed with much sentiment, as they were sitting together. Emma scarcely knew how to answer such a proposition, and the manner in which it was spoken she could not attempt to equal. Mrs. Robert Watson eyed her with much familiar curiosity and triumphant compassion: the loss of the aunt's fortune was uppermost in her mind at the moment of meeting; and she could not but feel how much better it was to be the daughter of a gentleman of property in Croydon than the niece of an old woman who threw herself away on an Irish captain. Robert was carelessly kind, as became a prosperous man and a brother; more intent on settling with the post-boy, inveighing against the exorbitant advance in posting, and pondering over a doubtful half-crown, than on welcoming a sister who was no longer likely to have any property for him to get the direction of.

"Your road through the village is infamous, Elizabeth," said he; "worse than ever it was. By Heaven! I would indict it if I lived near you. Who is surveyor now?"

There was a little niece at Croydon to be fondly inquired after by the kind-hearted Elizabeth, who regretted very much her not being of the party.

"You are very good," replied her mother, "and I assure you it went very hard with Augusta to have us come away without her. I was forced to say we were only going to church, and promise to come back for her directly. But you know it would not do to bring her without her maid, and I am as particular as ever in having her properly attended to."

"Sweet little darling!" cried Margaret. "It quite broke my heart to leave her."

"Then why was you in such a hurry to run away from her?" cried Mrs. Robert. "You are a sad, shabby girl. I have been quarrelling with you all the way we came, have not I? Such a visit as this, I never heard of! You know how glad we are to have any of you with us, if it be for months together; and I am sorry" (with a witty smile) "we have not been able to make Croydon agreeable this autumn."

"My dearest Jane, do not overpower me with your raillery. You know what inducements I had to bring me home. Spare me, I entreat you. I am no match for your arch sallies."

"Well, I only beg you will not set your neighbours against the place. Perhaps Emma may be tempted to go back with us and stay till Christmas, if you don't put in your word."

Emma was greatly obliged. "I assure you we have very good society at Croydon. I do not much attend the balls, they are rather too mixed; but our parties are very select and good. I had seven tables last week in my drawing-room. Are you fond of the country? How do you like Stanton?"

"Very much," replied Emma, who thought a comprehensive answer most to the purpose. She saw that her sister-in-law despised her immediately. Mrs. Robert Watson was indeed wondering what sort of a home Emma could possibly have been used to in Shropshire, and setting it down as certain that the aunt could never have had six thousand pounds.

"How charming Emma is," whispered Margaret to Mrs. Robert, in her most languishing tone. Emma was quite distressed by such behaviour; and she did not like it better when she heard Margaret five minutes afterwards say to Elizabeth in a sharp, quick accent, totally unlike the first, "Have you heard from Pen since she went to Chichester? I had a letter the other day. I don't find she is likely to make anything of it. I fancy she'll come back `Miss

Penelope,' as she went."

Such, she feared, would be Margaret's common voice when the novelty of her own appearance were over; the tone of artificial sensibility was not recommended by the idea. The ladies were invited upstairs to prepare for dinner.

"I hope you will find things tolerably comfortable, Jane," said Elizabeth, as she opened the door of the spare bedchamber.

"My good creature," replied Jane, "use no ceremony with me, I entreat you. I am one of those who always take things as they find them. I hope I can put up with a small apartment for two or three nights without making a piece of work. I always wish to be treated quite en famille when I come to see you. And now I do hope you have not been getting a great dinner for us. Remember, we never eat suppers."

"I suppose," said Margaret, rather quickly to Emma, "you and I are to be together; Elizabeth always takes care to have a room to herself."

"No. Elizabeth gives me half hers."

"Oh!" in a softened voice, and rather mortified to find that she was not ill-used, "I am sorry I am not to have the pleasure of your company, especially as it makes me nervous to be much alone."

Emma was the first of the females in the parlour again; on entering it she found her brother alone.

"So, Emma," said he, "you are quite a stranger at home. It must seem odd enough for you to be here. A pretty piece of work your Aunt Turner has made of it! By Heaven! a woman should never be trusted with money. I always said she ought to have settled something on you, as soon as her husband died."

"But that would have been trusting me with money," replied Emma; "and I am a woman too."

"It might have been secured to your future use, without your having any power over it now. What a blow it must have been upon you! To find yourself, instead of heiress of 8,000 or 9,000 l., sent back a weight upon your family, without a sixpence. I hope the old woman will smart for it."

"Do not speak disrespectfully of her; she was very good to me, and if she has made an imprudent choice, she will suffer more from it herself than I can possibly do."

"I do not mean to distress you, but you know everybody must think her an old fool. I thought Turner had been reckoned an extraordinarily sensible, clever man. How the devil came he to make such a will?"

"My uncle's sense is not at all impeached in my opinion by his attachment to my aunt. She had been an excellent wife to him. The most liberal and enlightened minds are always the most confiding. The event has been unfortunate; but my uncle's memory is, if possible, endeared to me by such a proof of tender respect for my aunt."

"That's odd sort of talking. He might have provided decently for his widow, without leaving everything that he had to dispose of, or any part of it, at her mercy."

"My aunt may have erred," said Emma, warmly; "she has erred, but my uncle's conduct was faultless. I was her own niece, and he left to herself the power and the pleasure of providing for me."

"But unluckily she has left the pleasure of providing for you to your father, and without the power. That's the long and short of the business. After keeping you at a distance from your family for such a length of time as must do away all natural affection among us, and breeding you up (I suppose) in a superior style, you are returned upon their hands without a sixpence."

"You know," replied Emma, struggling with her tears, "my uncle's melancholy state of health. He was a greater invalid than my father. He could not leave home."

"I do not mean to make you cry," said Robert, rather softened, -- and after a short silence, by way of changing the subject, he added: "I am just come from my father's room; he seems very indifferent. It will be a sad break up when he dies. Pity you can none of you get married! You must come to Croydon as well as the rest, and see what you can do there. I believe if Margaret had had a thousand or fifteen hundred pounds, there was a young man who would have thought of her."

Emma was glad when they were joined by the others; it was better to look at her sister-in-law's finery than listen to Robert, who had equally irritated and grieved her. Mrs. Robert, exactly as smart as she had been at her own party, came in with apologies for her dress.

"I would not make you wait," said she; "so I put on the first thing I met with. I am afraid I am a sad figure. My dear Mr. W.," (to her husband) "you have not put any fresh powder in your hair."

"No, I do not intend it. I think there is powder enough in my hair for my wife and sisters."

"Indeed, you ought to make some alteration in your dress before dinner when you are out visiting, though you do not at home."

"Nonsense."

"It is very odd you should not like to do what other gentlemen do. Mr. Marshall and Mr. Hemmings change their dress every day of their lives before dinner. And what was the use of my putting up your last new coat, if you are never to wear it?"

"Do be satisfied with being fine yourself, and leave your husband alone."

To put an end to this altercation and soften the evident vexation of her sister-in-law, Emma (though in no spirits to make such nonsense easy), began to admire her gown. It produced immediate complacency.

"Do you like it?" said she. "I am very happy. It has been excessively admired; but sometimes I think the pattern too large. I shall wear one tomorrow that I think you will prefer to this. Have you seen the one I gave Margaret?"

Dinner came, and except when Mrs. Robert looked at her husband's head, she continued gay and flippant, chiding Elizabeth for the profusion on the table, and absolutely protesting against the entrance of the roast turkey, which formed the only exception to "You see your dinner." "I do beg and entreat that no turkey may be seen today. I am really frightened out of my wits with the number of dishes we have already. Let us have no turkey, I beseech you."

"My dear," replied Elizabeth, "the turkey is roasted, and it may just as well come in as stay in the kitchen. Besides, if it is cut, I am in hopes my father may be tempted to eat a bit, for it is rather a favourite dish."

"You may have it in, my dear; but I assure you I sha'n't touch it."

Mr. Watson had not been well enough to join the party at dinner, but was prevailed on to come down and drink tea with them.

"I wish we may be able to have a game of cards tonight," said Elizabeth to Mrs. Robert, after seeing her father comfortably seated in his arm-chair.

"Not on my account, my dear, I beg. You know I am no card-player. I think a snug chat infinitely better. I always say cards are very well sometimes to break a formal circle, but one never wants them among friends."

"I was thinking of its being something to amuse my father," said Elizabeth, "if it was not disagreeable to you. He says his head won't bear whist, but perhaps if we make a round game he may be tempted to sit down with us."

"By all means, my dear creature. I am quite at your service; only do not oblige me to choose the game, that's all. Speculation is the only round game at Croydon now, but I can play anything. When there is only one or two of you at home, you must be quite at a loss to amuse him. Why do you not get him to play at cribbage? Margaret and I have played at cribbage most nights that we have not been engaged."

A sound like a distant carriage was at this moment caught; everybody listened; it became more decided; it certainly drew nearer. It was an unusual sound for Stanton at any time of the day, for the village was on no very public road, and contained no gentleman's family but the rector's. The wheels rapidly approached; in two minutes the general expectation was answered; they stopped beyond a doubt at the garden-gate of the parsonage. "Who could it be? It was certainly a postchaise. Penelope was the only creature to be thought of; she might perhaps have met with some unexpected opportunity of returning." A pause of suspense ensued. Steps were distinguished along the paved foot-way, which led under the windows of the house to the front door, and then within the passage. They were the steps of a man. It could not be Penelope. It must be Samuel. The door opened, and displayed Tom Musgrave in the wrap of a traveller. He had been in London, and was now on his way home, and he had come half-a-mile out of his road merely to call for ten minutes at Stanton. He loved to take people by surprise with sudden visits at extraordinary seasons, and, in the present instance, had had the additional motive of being able to tell the Miss Watsons, whom he depended on finding sitting quietly employed after tea, that he was going home to an eight-o'clock dinner.

As it happened, however, he did not give more surprise than he received, when, instead of being shown into the usual little sitting-room, the door of the best parlour (a foot larger each way than the other) was thrown open, and he beheld a circle of smart people whom he could not immediately recognize arranged, with all the honours of visiting, round the fire, and Miss Watson seated at the best Pembroke table, with the best tea-things before her. He stood a few seconds in silent amazement. "Musgrave!" ejaculated Margaret, in a tender voice. He recollected himself, and came forward, delighted to find such a circle of friends, and blessing his good fortune for the unlooked-for indulgence. He shook hands with Robert, bowed and smiled to the ladies, and did everything very prettily; but as to any particularity of address or emotion towards Margaret, Emma, who closely observed him, perceived nothing that did not justify Elizabeth's opinion, though Margaret's modest smiles imported that she meant to take the visit to herself. He was persuaded without much difficulty to throw off his great-coat and drink tea with them. For "whether he dined at eight or nine," as he observed, "was a matter of very little consequence"; and without seeming to seek, he did not turn away from the chair close by Margaret, which she was assiduous in providing him. She had thus secured him from her sisters, but it was not immediately in her power to preserve him from her brother's claims; for as he came avowedly from London, and had left it only four hours ago, the last current report as to public news, and the general opinion of the day, must be understood before Robert could let his attention be yielded to the less national and important demands of the women. At last, however, he was at liberty to hear Margaret's soft address, as she spoke her fears of his having had a most terrible cold, dark, dreadful journey.

"Indeed, you should not have set out so late."

"I could not be earlier," he replied. "I was detained chatting at the Bedford by a friend. All hours are alike to me. How long have you been in the country, Miss Margaret?"

"We only came this morning; my kind brother and sister brought me home this very morning. 'Tis singular, is not it?"

"You were gone a great while, were not you? A fortnight, I suppose?"

"You may call a fortnight a great while, Mr. Musgrave," said Mrs. Robert, sharply; "but we think a month very little. I assure you we bring her home at the end of a month much against our will."

"A month! Have you really been gone a month? 'Tis amazing how time flies."

"You may imagine," said Margaret, in a sort of whisper, "what are my sensations in finding myself once more at Stanton; you know what a sad visitor I make. And I was so excessively impatient to see Emma; I dreaded the meeting, and at the same time longed for it. Do you not comprehend the sort of feeling?"

"Not at all," cried he, aloud: "I could never dread a meeting with Miss Emma Watson -- or any of her sisters."

It was lucky that he added that finish.

"Were you speaking to me?" said Emma, who had caught her own name.

"Not absolutely," he answered; "but I was thinking of you, as many at a greater distance are probably doing at this moment. Fine open weather, Miss Emma, charming season for hunting."

"Emma is delightful, is not she?" whispered Margaret; "I have found her more than answer my warmest hopes. Did you ever see anything more perfectly beautiful? I think even you must be a convert to a brown complexion."

He hesitated. Margaret was fair herself, and he did not particularly want to compliment her; but Miss Osborne and Miss Carr were likewise fair, and his devotion to them carried the day.

"Your sister's complexion," said he, at last, "is as fine as a dark complexion can be; but I still profess my preference of a white skin. You have seen Miss Osborne? She is my model for a truly feminine complexion, and she is very fair."

"Is she fairer than me?"

Tom made no reply. "Upon my honour, ladies," said he, giving a glance over his own person, "I am highly indebted to your condescension for admitting me in such dishabille into your drawing-room. I really did not consider how unfit I was to be here, or I hope I should have kept my distance. Lady Osborne would tell me that I were growing as careless as her son, if she saw me in this condition."

The ladies were not wanting in civil returns, and Robert Watson, stealing a view of his own head in an opposite glass, said with equal civility, --

"You cannot be more in dishabille than myself. We got here so late that I had not time even to put a little fresh powder in my hair."

Emma could not help entering into what she supposed her sister-in-law's feelings at the moment.

When the tea-things were removed, Tom began to talk of his carriage; but the old card-table being set out, and the fish and counters, with a tolerably clean pack, brought forward from the buffet by Miss Watson, the general voice was so urgent with him to join their party that he agreed to allow himself another quarter of an hour. Even Emma was pleased that he would stay, for she was beginning to feel that a family party might be the worst of all parties; and the others were delighted.

"What's your game?" cried he, as they stood round the table.

"Speculation, I believe," said Elizabeth. "My sister recommends it, and I fancy we all like it. I know you do, Tom."

"It is the only round game played at Croydon now," said Mrs. Robert; "we never think of any other. I am glad it is a favourite with you."

"Oh, me!" said Tom. "Whatever you decide on will be a favourite with me. I have had some pleasant hours at speculation in my time, but I have not been in the way of it now for a long while. Vingt-un is the game at Osborne Castle. I have played nothing but vingt-un of late. You would be astonished to hear the noise we make there -- the fine old lofty drawing-room rings again. Lady Osborne sometimes declares she cannot hear herself speak. Lord Osborne enjoys it famously, and he makes the best dealer without exception that I ever beheld, -- such quickness and spirit, he lets nobody dream over their cards. I wish you could see him overdraw himself on both his own cards. It is worth anything in the world!"

"Dear me!" cried Margaret, "why should not we play at vingt-un? I think it is a much better game than speculation. I cannot say I am very fond of speculation."

Mrs. Robert offered not another word in support of the game. She was quite vanquished, and the fashions of Osborne Castle carried it over the fashions of Croydon.

"Do you see much of the parsonage family at the castle, Mr. Musgrave?" said Emma, as they were taking their seats.

"Oh, yes; they are almost always there. Mrs. Blake is a nice little good-humoured woman; she and I are sworn friends; and Howard's a very gentlemanlike, good sort of fellow! You are not forgotten, I assure you, by any of the party. I fancy you must have a little cheek-glowing now and then, Miss Emma. Were not you rather warm last Saturday about nine or ten o'clock in the evening? I will tell you how it was, -- I see you are dying to know. Says Howard to Lord Osborne --"

At this interesting moment he was called on by the others to regulate the game, and determine some disputable point; and his attention was so totally engaged in the business, and afterwards by the course of the game, as never to revert to what he had been saying before; and Emma, though suffering a good deal from curiosity, dared not remind him.

He proved a very useful addition to their table. Without him, it would have been a party of such very near relations as could have felt little interest, and perhaps maintained little complaisance; but his presence gave variety and secured good manners. He was, in fact, excellently qualified to shine at a round game, and few situations made him appear to greater advantage. He played with spirit, and had a great deal to say; and, though no wit himself, could sometimes make use of the wit of an absent friend, and had a lively way of retailing a common-place or saying a mere nothing, that had great effect at a card-table. The ways and good jokes of Osborne Castle were now added to his ordinary means of entertainment. He repeated the smart sayings of one lady, detailed the oversights of another, and indulged them even with a copy of Lord Osborne's style of overdrawing himself on both cards.

The clock struck nine while he was thus agreeably occupied; and when Nanny came in with her master's basin of gruel, he had the pleasure of observing to Mr. Watson that he should leave him at supper while he went home to dinner himself. The carriage was ordered to the door, and no entreaties for his staying longer could now avail; for he well knew that if he stayed he must sit down to supper in less than ten minutes, which to a man whose heart had been long fixed on calling his next meal a dinner, was quite insupportable. On finding him determined to go, Margaret began to wink and nod at Elizabeth to ask him to dinner for the following day, and Elizabeth at last not able to resist hints which her own hospitable, social temper more than half seconded, gave the invitation: "Would he give Robert the meeting, they should be very happy?"

"With the greatest pleasure" was his first reply. In a moment afterwards, "That is, if I can possibly get here in time; but I shoot with Lord Osborne, and therefore must not engage. You will not think of me unless you see me." And so he departed, delighted with the uncertainty in which he had left it.

Chapter VI

Margaret, in the joy of her heart under circumstances which she chose to consider as peculiarly propitious, would willingly have made a confidante of Emma when they were alone for a short time the next morning, and had proceeded so far as to say, "The young man who was here last night, my dear Emma, and returns today, is more interesting to me than perhaps you may be aware --"; but Emma, pretending to understand nothing extraordinary in the words, made some very inapplicable reply, and jumping up, ran away from a subject which was odious to her feelings. As Margaret would not allow a doubt to be repeated of Musgrave's coming to dinner, preparations were made for his entertainment much exceeding what had been deemed necessary the day before; and taking the office of superintendence entirely from her sister, she was half the morning in the kitchen herself, directing and scolding.

After a great deal of indifferent cooking and anxious suspense, however, they were obliged to sit down without their guest. Tom Musgrave never came; and Margaret was at no pains to conceal her vexation under the disappointment, or repress the peevishness of her temper. The peace of the party for the remainder of that day and the whole of the next, which comprised the length of Robert's and Jane's visit, was continually invaded by her fretful displeasure and querulous attacks. Elizabeth was the usual object of both. Margaret had just respect enough for her brother's and sister's opinion to behave properly by them, but Elizabeth and the maids could never do anything right; and Emma, whom she seemed no longer to think about, found the continuance of the gentle voice beyond her calculation short. Eager to be as little among them as possible, Emma was delighted with the alternative of sitting above with her father, and warmly entreated to be his constant companion each evening; and as Elizabeth loved company of any kind too well not to prefer being below at all risks; as she had rather talk of Croydon with Jane, with every interruption of Margaret's perverseness, than sit with only her father, who frequently could not endure talking at all, -- the affair was so settled, as soon as she could be persuaded to believe it no sacrifice on her sister's part. To Emma, the change was most acceptable and delightful. Her father, if ill, required little more than gentleness and silence, and being a man of sense and education, was, if able to converse, a welcome companion. In his chamber Emma was at peace from the dreadful mortifications of unequal society and family discord; from the immediate endurance of hard-hearted prosperity, low-minded conceit, and wrong-headed folly, engrafted on an untoward disposition. She still suffered from them in the contemplation of their existence, in memory and in prospect; but for the moment, she ceased to be tortured by their effects. She was at leisure; she could read and think, though her situation was hardly such as to make reflection very soothing. The evils arising from the loss of her uncle were neither trifling nor likely to lessen; and when thought had been freely indulged, in contrasting the past and the present, the employment of mind and dissipation of unpleasant ideas which only reading could produce made her thankfully turn to a book.

The change in her home, society, and style of life, in consequence of the death of one friend and the imprudence of another, had indeed been striking. From being the first object of hope and solicitude to an uncle who had formed her mind with the care of a parent, and of tenderness to an aunt whose amiable temper had delighted to give her every indulgence; from being the life and spirit of a house where all had been comfort and elegance, and the expected heiress of an easy independence, she was become of importance to no one, -- a burden on those whose affections she could not expect, an addition in a house already overstocked, surrounded by inferior minds, with little chance of domestic comfort, and as little hope of future support. It was well for her that she was naturally cheerful, for the change had been such as might have plunged weak spirits in despondence.

She was very much pressed by Robert and Jane to return with them to Croydon, and had some difficulty in getting a refusal accepted, as they thought too highly of their own kindness and situation to suppose the offer could appear in a less advantageous light to anybody else. Elizabeth gave them her interest, though evidently against her own, in privately urging Emma to go.

"You do not know what you refuse, Emma," said she, "nor what you have to bear at home. I would advise you by all means to accept the invitation; there is always something lively going on at Croydon. You will be in company almost every day, and Robert and Jane will be very kind to you. As for me, I shall be no worse off without you than I have been used to be; but poor Margaret's disagreeable ways are new to you, and they would vex you more than you think for, if you stay at home."

Emma was of course uninfluenced, except to greater esteem for Elizabeth, by such representations, and the visitors departed without her.

A Note from Austen Leigh's Memoir on Jane Austen

According to Austen-Leigh's Memoir:

"When the author's sister, Cassandra, showed the manuscript of this work to some of her nieces, she also told them something of the intended story; for with this dear sister -- though, I believe, with no one else -- Jane seems to have talked freely of any work that she might have in hand. Mr. Watson was soon to die; and Emma to become dependent for a home on her narrow-minded sister-in-law and brother. She was to decline an offer of marriage from Lord Osborne, and much of the interest of the tale was to arise from Lady Osborne's love for Mr. Howard, and his counter affection for Emma, whom he was finally to marry."

Sandition

Chapter 1

A gentleman and a lady travelling from Tunbridge towards that part of the Sussex coast which lies between Hastings and Eastbourne, being induced by business to quit the high road and attempt a very rough lane, were overturned in toiling up its long a scent, half rock, half sand.

The accident happened just beyond the only gentleman's house near the lane a house which their driver, on being first required to take that direction, had conceived to be necessarily their object and had with most unwilling looks been constrained to pass by.

He had grumbled and shaken his shoulders and pitied and cut his horses so sharply that he might have been open to the suspicion of overturning them on purpose (especially as the carriage was not his master's own) if the road had not indisputably become worse than before, as soon as the premises of the said house were left behind expressing with a most portentous countenance that, beyond it, no wheels but cart wheels could safely proceed.

The severity of the fall was broken by their slow pace and the narrowness of the lane; and the gentleman having scrambled out and helped out his companion, they neither of them at first felt more than shaken and bruised. But the gentleman had, in the course of the extrication, sprained his foot; and soon becoming sensible of it, was obliged in a few moments to cut short both his remonstrances to the driver and his congratulations to his wife and himself and sit down on the bank, unable to stand.

"There is something wrong here," said he, putting his hand to his anle. "But never mind, my dear," looking up at her with a smile, "it could not have happened, you know, in a better place Good out of evil. The very thing perhaps to be wished for. We shall soon get relief. There, I fancy, lies my cure," pointing to the neat-looking end of a cottage, which was seen romantically situated among wood on a high eminence at some little distance "Does not that promise to Be the very place?"

His wife fervently hoped it was; but stood, terrified and anxious, neither able to do or suggest anything, and receiving her first real comfort from the sight of several persons now coming to their assistance.

The accident had been discerned from a hayfield adjoining the house they had passed. And the persons who approached were a well-looking, hale, gentlemanlike man of middle age, the proprietor of the place, who happened to be among his haymakers at the time, and three or four of the ablest of them summoned to attend their master to say nothing of all the rest of the field, men, women and children, not very far off.

Mr. Heywood, such was the name of the said proprietor, advanced with a very civil salutation, much concern for the accident, some surprise at anybody's attempting that road in a carriage, and ready offers of assistance.

His courtesies were received with good breeding and gratitude, and while one or two of the men lent their help to the driver in getting the carriage upright again, the traveller said, "You are extremely obliging, sir, and I take you at your word The injury to my leg is, I dare say, very trifling. But it is always best in these cases, you know, to have a surgeon's opinion without loss of time; and as the road does not seem in a favourable state for my getting up to his house myself, I will thank you to send off one of these good people for the surgeon."

"The surgeon!" exclaimed Mr. Heywood. "I am afraid you will find no surgeon at hand here, but I dare say we shall do very well without him."

"Nay sir, if he is not in the way, his partner will do just as well or rather better. I would rather see his partner. Indeed I would prefer the attendance of his partner. One of these good people can be with him in three minutes, I am sure. I need not ask whether I see the house," looking towards the cottage, "for excepting your own, we have passed none in this place which can be the abode of a gentleman."

Mr. Heywood looked very much astonished.

"What, sir! Are you expecting to find a surgeon in that cottage? We have neither surgeon nor partner in the parish, I assure you."

"Excuse me, sir," replied the other. "I am sorry to have the appearance of contradicting you, but from the extent of the parish or some other cause you may not be aware of the fact stay can I be mistaken in the place? Am I not in Willingden? Is not this Willingden?"

"Yes, sir, this is certainly Willingden."

"Then, sir, I can bring proof of your having a surgeon in the parish, whether you may know it or not. Here, sir," taking out his pocket book, "if you will do me the favor of casting your eye over these advertisements which I cut out myself from the Morning Post and the Kentish Gazette only yesterday morning in London, I think you will be convinced that I am not speaking at random.

You will find in it an advertisement of the dissolution of a partnership in the medical line in your own parish exttensive business undeniable character respectable references wishing to form a separate establishment. You will find it at full length, sir,' offering the two little oblong extracts.

"Sir, if you were to show me all the newspapers that are printed in one week throughout the kingdom, you would not persuade me of there being a surgeon in Willingden," said Mr. Heywood with a good-humoured smile. "Having lived here ever since I was born, man and boy fifty-seven years, I think I must have known of such a person. At least I may venture to say that he has not much business. To be sure, if gentlemen were to be often attempting this lane in post-chaises, it might not be a bad speculation for a surgeon to get a house at the top of the hill. But as to that cottage, I can assure you, sir, that it is in fact, in spite of its spruce air at this distance, as indifferent a double tenement as any in the parish, and that my shepherd lives at one end and three old women at the other."

He took the pieces of paper as he spoke, and, having looked them over, added, "I believe I can explain it, sir. Your mistake is in the place.

There are two Willingdens in this country. And your advertisements must refer to the other, which is Great Willingden or Willingden Abbots, and lies seven miles off on the other side of Battle. Quite down in the weald. And we, sir," he added, speaking rather proudly, "are not in the weald."

"Not down in the weald, I am sure," replied the traveller pleasantly. "It took us half an hour to climb your hill. Well, I dare say it is as you say and I have made an abominably stupid blunder.

All done in a moment. The advertisements did not catch my eye till the last half hour of our being in town everything in the hurry and confusion which always attend a short stay there. One is never able to complete anything in the way of business, you know, till the carriage is at the door. So satisfying myself with a brief inquiry, and finding we were actually to pass within a mile or two of a Willingden, I sought no farther.... My dear" (to his wife) "I am very sorry to have brought you into this scrape.

But do not be alarmed about my leg. It gives me no pain while I am quiet. And as soon as these good people have succeeded in setting the carriage to rights and turning the horses round, the best thing we can do will be to measure back our steps into the turnpike road and proceed to Hailsham, and so home without attempting anything farther. Two hours take us home from Hailsham.

And once at home, we have our remedy at hand, you know. A little of our own bracing sea air will soon set me on my feet again. Depend upon it, my dear, it is exactly a case for the sea.

Saline air and immersion will be the very thing. My sensations tell me so already."

In a most friendly manner Mr. Heywood here interposed, entreating them not to think of proceeding till the ankle had been examined and some refreshment taken, and very cordially pressing them to make use of his house for both purposes.

"We are always well stocked," said he, "with all the common remedies for sprains and bruises. And I will answer for the pleasure it will give my wife and daughters to be of service to you in every way in their power."

A twinge or two, in trying to move his foot, disposed the traveller to think rather more than he had done at first of the benefit of immediate assistance; and consulting his wife in the few words of "Well, my dear, I believe it will be better for us,' he turned again to Mr. Heywood.

'Before we accept your hospitaliey sir, and in order to do away with any unfavourable impression which the sort of wild-goose chase you find me in may have given rise to allow me to tell you who we are. My name is Parker, Mr. Parker of Sanditon; this lady, my wife, Mrs. Parker. We are on our road home from London. My name perhaps though I am by no means the first of my family holding landed property in the parish of Sanditon may be unknown at this distance from the coast. But Sanditon itself everybody has heard of Sanditon. The favourite for a young and rising bathing-place certainly the favourite spot of all that are to be found along the coast of Sussex; the most favoured by nature, and promising to be the most chosen by man."

"Yes, I have heard of Sanditon," replied Mr. Heywood. "Every five years, one hears of some new place or other starting up by the sea and growing the fashion. How they can half of them be filled is the wonder! Where people can be found with money and time to go to them! Bad things for a country sure to raise the price of provisions and make the poor good for nothing as I dare say you find, sir."

"Not at all, sir, not at all," cried Mr. Parker eagerly. "Quite the contrary, I assure you. A common idea, but a mistaken one.

It may apply to your large, overgrown places like Brighton or Worthing or Eastbourne but not to a small village like Sanditon, precluded by its size from experiencing any of the evils of civilization; while the growth of the place, the buildings, the nursery grounds, the demand for everything and the sure resort of the very best company those regular, steady, private families of thorough gentility and character who are a blessing everywhere excite the industry of the poor and diffuse comfort and improvement among them of every sort. No sir, I assure you, Sanditon is not a place " "I do not mean to take exception to any place in particular,"

answered Mr. Heywood. "I only think our coast is too full of them altogether. But had we not better try to get you " Our coast too full!" repeated Mr. Parker. "On that point perhaps we may not totally disagree. At least there are enough. Our coast is abundant enough. It demands no more. Everybody's taste and everybody's finances may be suited. And those good people who are trying to add to the number are, in my opinion, excessively absurd and must soon find themselves the dupes of their own fallacious calculations. Such a place as Sanditon, sir, I may say was wanted, was called for. Nature had marked it out, had spoken in most intelligible characters. The finest, purest sea breeze on the coast acknowledged to be so excellent bathing fine hard sand deep water ten yards from the shore no mud no weeds no slimy rocks. Never was there a place more palpably designed by nature for the resort of the invalid the very spot which thousands seemed in need of! The most desirable distance from London! One complete, measured mile nearer than Eastbourne. Only conceive, sir, the advantage of saving a whole mile in a long journey. But Brinshore, sir, which I dare say you have in your eye the attempts of two or three speculating people about Brinshore this last year to raise that paltry hamlet lying as it does between a stagnant marsh, a bleak moor and the constant effluvia of a ridge of putrefying seaweed can end in nothing but their own disappointment.

What in the name of common sense is to recommend Brinshore? A most insalubrious air roads proverbially detestable water brackish beyond example, impossible to get a good dish of tea within three miles of the place. And as for the soil it is so cold and ungrateful that it can hardly be made to yield a cabbage. Depend upon it, sir, that this is a most faithful Brinshore not in the smallest degree exaggerated and if you have heard it differently spoken of " "Sir, I never heard it spoken of in my life before," said Mr.

Heywood. "I did not know there was such a place in the world."

"You did not! There, my dear," turning with exultation to his wife, "you see how it is. So much for the celebrity of Brinshore! This gentleman did not know there was such a place in the world.

Why, in truth, sir, I fancy we may apply to Brinshore that line of the poet Cowper in his the religious cottager, as opposed to Voltaire She, never heard of half a mile from home."

"With all my heart, sir apply any verses you like to it. But I want to see something applied to your leg. And I am sure by your lady's countenance that she is quite of my opinion and thinks it a pity to lose any more time. And here come my girls to speak for themselves and their mother." Two or three genteel-looking young women, followed by as many maid servants, were now seen issuing from the house. "I began to wonder the bustle should not have reached them. A thing of this kind soon makes a stir in a lonely place like ours, Now, sir, let us see how you can be best conveyed into the house."

The young ladies approached and said everything that was proper to recommend their father's offers, and in an unaffected manner calculated to make the strangers easy. As Mrs. parker was etceedingly anxious for relief and her husband by this time not much less disposed for it a very few civil scruples were enough; especially as the carriage, being now set up, was discovered to have received such injury on the fallen side as to be unfit for present use. Mr. Parker was therefore carried into the house and his carriage wheeled off to a vacant barn.

Chapter 2

The acquaintance, thus oddly begun, was neither short nor unimportant. For a whole fortnight the travellers were fixed at Willingden, Mr. Parker's sprain proving too serious for him to move sooner. He had fallen into very good hands. The Heywoods were a thoroughly respectable family and every possible attention was paid, in the kindest and most unpretending manner, to both husband and wife. He was waited on and nursed, and she cheered and comforted with unremitting kindness; and as every office of hospitality and friendliness was received as it ought, as there was not more good will on one side than gratitude on the other, nor any deficiency of generally pleasant manners in either, they grew to like each other in the course of that fortnight exceedingly well.

Mr. parker's character and history were soon unfolded. All that he understood of himself, he readily told, for he was very openhearted; and where he might be himself in the dark, his conversation was still giving information to such of the Heywoods as could observe. By such he was perceived to be an enthusiast on the subject of Sanditon, a complete enthusiast. Sanditon, the success of Sanditon as a small, fashionable bathing place, was the object for which he seemed to live.

A very few years ago, it had been a quiet village of no pretensions; but some natural advantages in its position and some accidental circumstances having stiggested to himself and the other principal landholder the probability of its becoming a profitable speculation, they had engaged in it, and planned and built, and praised and puffed, and raised it to something of young renown; and Mr. Parker could now think of very little besides.

The facts which, in more direct communication, he laid before them were that he was about five and thirty, had been married very happily married seven years, and had four sweet children at home; that he was of a respectable family and easy, though not large, fortune; no profession succeeding as eldest son to the property which two or three generations had been holding and accumulating before him; that he had two brothers and two sisters, all single and all independent the eldest of the two former indeed, by collateral inheritance, quite as well provided for as himself.

His object in quitting the high road to hunt for an advertising surgeon was also plainly stated. It had not proceeded from any intention of spraining his ankle or doing himself any other injury for the good of such surgeon, nor (as Mr. Heywood had been apt to suppose) from any design of entering into partnership with him; it was merely in consequence of a wish to establish some medical man at Sanditon, which the nature of the advertisement induced him to expect to accomplish in Willingden. He was convinced that the advantage of a medical man at hand would very materially promote the rise and prosperity of the place, would in fact tend to bring a prodigious influx; nothing else was wanting. He had strong reason to believe that one family had been deterred last year from trying Sanditon on that account and probably very many more and his own sisters, who were sad invalids and whom he was very anxious to get to Sanditon this summer, could hardly be expected to hazard themselves in a place where they could not have immediate medical advice.

Upon the whole, Mr. parker was evidently an amiable family man, fond of wife, children, brothers and sisters, and generally kind-hearted; liberal, gentlemanlike, easy to please; of a sanguine turn of mind, with more imagination than judgement. And Mrs.

Parker was as evidently a gentle, amiable, sweet-tempered woman, the properest wife in the world for a man of strong understanding but not of a capacity to supply the cooler reflection which her own husband sometimes needed; and so entirely waiting to be guided on every occasion that whether he was risking his fortune or spraining his ankle, she remained equally useless.

Sanditon was a second wife and four children to him, hardly less dear, and certainly more engrossing. He could talk of it forever. It had indeed the highest claims; not only those of birthplace, property and home; it was his mine, his lottery, his speculation and his hobby horse; his occupation, his hope and his futurity.

He was extremely desirous of drawing his good friends at Willingden thither; and his endeavours in the cause were as grateful and disinterested as they were warm. He wanted to secre the promise of a visit, to get as many of the family as his own house would contain to follow him to Sanditon as soon as possible; and, healthy as they all undeniably were, foresaw that every one of them would be benefited by the sea.

He held it indeed as certain that no person could be really well, no person (however upheld for the present by fortuitous aids of exercise and spirits in a semblance of health) could be really in a state of secure and permanent health without spending at least six weeks by the sea every year. The sea air and sea bathing together were nearly infallible, one or the other of them being a match for every disorder of the stomach, the lungs or the blood.

They were anti-spasmodic, anti-pulmonary, anti-septic, anti-billious and anti-rheumatic. Nobody could catch cold by the sea; nobody wanted appetite by the sea; nobody wanted spirits; nobody wanted strength. Sea air was healing, softening, relaxing fortifying and bracing seemingly just as was wanted sometimes one, sometimes the other. If the sea breeze failed, the sea-bath was the certain corrective; and where bathing disagreed, the sea air alone was evidently designed by nature for the cure.

His eloquence, however, could not prevail. Mr. and Mrs.

Heywood never left home. Marrying early and having a very numerous family, their movements had, long been limited to one small circle; and they were older in habits than in age. Excepting two journeys to London in the year to receive his dividends, Mr.

Heywood went no farther than his feet or his well-tried old horse could carry him; and Mrs. Heywood's adventurings were only now and then to visit her neighbours in the old coach which had been new when they married and fresh-lined on their eldest son's coming of age ten years ago.

They had a very pretty property; enough, had their family been of reasonable limits, to have allowed them a very gentlemanlike share of luxuries and change; enough for them to have indulged in a new carriage and better roads, an occasional month at Tunbridge Wells, and symptoms of the gout and a winter at Bath, But the maintenance, education and fitting out of fourteen children demanded a very quiet, settled, careful course of life, and obliged them to be stationary and healthy at Willingden. What prudence had at first enjoined was now rendered pleasant by habit. They never left home and they had gratification in saying so.

But very far from wishing their children to do the same, they were glad to promote their getting out into the world as much as possible. They stayed at home that their children might get out; and, while making that home extremely comfortable, welcomed every change from it which could give useful connections or respectable acquaintance to sons or daughters.

When Mr. and Mrs. Parker, therefore, ceased from soliciting a family visit and bounded their views to carrying back one daughter with them, no difficulties were started. It was general pleasure and consent.

Their invitation was to Miss Charlotte Heywood, a very pleasing young woman of two and twenty, the eldest of the daughters at home and the one who, under her mother's directions, had been particularly useful and obliging to them; who had attended them most and knew them best.

Charlotte was to go: with excellent health, to bathe and be better if she could; to receive every possible pleasure which Sanditon could made to supply by the gratitude of those she went with; and to buy new parasols, new gloves and new brooches for her sisters and herself at the library, which Mr. Parker was anxiously wishing to support.

All that Mr. Heywood himself could be persuaded to promise was that he would send everyone to Sanditon who asked his advice, and that nothing should ever induce him (as far as the future could be answered for) to spend even five shilling at Brinstore.

Chapter 3

Every neighbourhood should have a great lady. The great lady of Sanditon was Lady Denham; and in their journey from Willingden to the coast, Mr. Parker gave Charlotte a more detailed account of her than had been called for before. She had been necessarily often mentioned at Willingden for being his colleague in speculation, Sanditon itself could not be talked of long without the introduction of Lady Denham. That she was a very rich old lady, who had buried two husbands, who knew the value of money, and was very much looked up to and had a poor cousin living with her, were facts already known; but some further particulars of her history and her character served to lighten the tediousness of a long hill, or a heavy bit of road, and to give the visiting young lady a suitable knowledge of the person with whom she might now expect to be daily associating.

Lady Denham had been a rich Miss Brereton, born to wealth but not to education. Her first husband had been a Mr. Hollis, a man of considerable property in the country, of which a large share of the parish of Sanditon, with manor and mansion house, made a part. He had been an elderly man when she married him, her own age about thirty. Her motives for such a match could be little understood at the distance of forty years, but she had so well nursed and pleased Mr. Hollis that at his death he left her everything all his estates, and all at her disposal.

After a widowhood of some years, she had been induced to marry again. The late Sir Harry Denham, of Denham Park in the neighbourhood of Sanditon, had succeeded in removing her and her large income to his own domains, but he could not succeed in the views of permanently enriching his family which were attributed to him. She had been too wary to put anything out of her own power and when, on Sir Harry's decease, she returned again to her own house at Sanditon, she was said to have made this boast to a friend: "that though she had got nothing but her title from the family, still she had given nothing for it. For the title, it was to be supposed, she had married; and Mr. Parker acknowledged there being just such a degree of value for it apparent now as to give her conduct that natural explanation.

"There is at times," said he, "a little self-importance but it is not offensive and there are moments, there are points, when her love of money is carried greatly too far. But she is a good-natured woman, a very good-natured woman a very obliging, friendly neighbour; a cheerful, independent, valuable character and her faults may be entirely imputed to her want of education. She has good natural sense, but quite uncultivated. She has a fine active mind as well as a fine healthy frame for a woman of seventy, and enters into the improvement of Sanditon with a spirit truly admirable. Though now and then, a littleness will appear. She cannot look forward quite as I would have her and takes alarm at a trifling present expense without considering what returns it will make her in a year or two. That is, we think differently. We now and then see things differently, Miss Heywood. Those who tell their own story, you know, must be listened to with caution.

When you see us in contact, you will judge for yourself."

Lady Denham was indeed a great lady beyond the common wants of society, for she had many thousands a year to bequeath, and three distinct sets of people to be courted by: her own relations, who might very reasonably wish for her original thirty thousand pounds among them; the legal heirs of Mr. Hollis, who must hope to be more indebted to her sense of justice than he had allowed them to be to his; and those members of the Denham family whom her second husband had hoped to make a good bargain for.

By all of these, or by branches of them, she had no doubt been long, and still continued to be, well attacked; and of these three divisions, Mr. parker did not hesitate to say that Mr. Hollis's kindred were the least in favour and Sir Harry Denham's the most. The former, he believed, had done themselves irremediable harm by expressions of very unwise and unjustifiable resentment at the time of Mr. Hollis's death; the latter had the advantage of being the remnant of a connection which she certainly valued, of having been known to her frosn their childhood and of being always at hand to preserve their interest by reasonable attention.

Sir Edward, the present baronet, nephew to Sir Harry, resided constantly at Denham Park; and Mr. Parker had little doubt that he and his sister, Miss Denham, who lived with him, would be principally remembered in her will. He sincerely hoped it. Miss Denham had a very small provision; and her brother was a poor man for his rank in society.

"He is a warm friend to Sanditon," said Mr. Parker, "and his hand would be as liberal as his heart, had he the power. He would be a noble coadjutor! As it is, he does what he can and is running up a tasteful little cottage orne on a strip of waste ground Lady Denham has granted him, which I have no doubt we shall have many a candidate for before the end even of this season."

Till within the last twelvemonth, Mr. Parker had considered Sir Edward as standing without a rival, as having the fairest chance of succeeding to the greater part of all that she had to give; but there were now another person's claims to be taken into account those of the young female relation whom Lady Denham had been induced to receive into her family. After having always protested against any such addition, and long and often enjoyed the repeated defeats she had given to every attempt of her relations to introduce this young lady or that young lady as a companion at Sanditon House, she had brought back with her from London last Michaelmas a Miss Brereton, who bid fair by her merits to vie in favour with Sir Edward and to secure for herself and her family that share of the accumulated property which they had certainly the best right to inherit.

Mr. parker spoke warmly of Clara Brereton, and the interest of his story increased very much with the introduction of such a character. Charlotte listened with more than amusement now; it was solicitude and enjoyment, as she heard her described to be lovely, amiable, gentle, unassuming, conducting herself uniformly with great good sense, and evidently gaining by her innate worth on the affections of her patroness. Beauty, sweetness, poverty and dependence do not want the imagination of a man to operate upon; with due exceptions, woman feels for woman very promptly and compassionately. He gave the particulars which had led to Clara's admission at Sanditon as no bad exemplification of that mixture of character that union of littleness with kindness and good sense, even liberality which he saw in Lady Denham.

After having avoided London for many years, principally on account of these very cousins who were continually writing, inviting and tormenting her, and whom she was determined to keep at a distance, she had been obliged to go there last Michaelmas with the certainty of being detained at least a fortnight.

She had gone to a hotel, living by her own account as prudently as possible to defy the reputed expensiveness of such a home, and at the end of three days calling for her bill that she might judge of her state. Its amount was such as determined her on staying not another hour in the house, and she was preparing in all the anger and perturbation of her belief in very gross imposition and her ignorance of where to go for better usage to leave the hotel at all hazards, when the cousins, the politic and lucky cousins, who seemed always to have a spy on her, introduced themselves at this important moment; and learning her situation, persuaded her to accept such a home for the rest of her stay as their humbler house in a very inferior part of London could offer.

She went, was delighted with her welcome and the hospitality and attention she received from everybody; found her good cousins the Breretons beyond her expectation worthy people; and finally was impelled by a personal knowledge of their narrow income and pecuniary difficulties to invite one of the girls of the family to pass the winter with her.

The invitation was to one, for six months, with the probability of another being then to take her place; but in selecting the one, Lady Denham had shown the good part of her character For, passing by the actual daughters of the house, she had chosen Clara, a niece, more helpless and more pitiable of course than any a dependent on poverty an additional burden on an encumbered circle; and one who had been so low in every worldly view as, with all her natural endowments and powers, to have been preparing for a situation little better than a nursery maid.

Clara had returned with her and by her good sense and merit had now, to all appearance, secured a very strong hold in Lady Denham's regard. The six months had long been over and not a syllable was breathed of any change or exchange. She was a general favourite. The influence of her steady conduct and mild, gentle temper was felt by everybody. The prejudices which had met her at first, in some quarters, were all dissipated. She was felt to be worthy of trust, to be the very companion who would guide and soften Lady Denham, who would enlarge her mind and open her hand. She was as thoroughly amiable as she was lovely; and since having had the advantage of their Sanditon breezes, that loveliness was complete.

Chapter 4

"And whose very snug-looking place is this?" said Charlotte as, in a sheltered dip within two miles of the sea, they passed close by a moderate-sized house, well fenced and planted, and rich in the garden, orchard and meadows which are the best embellishments of such a dwelling. "It seems to have as many comforts about it as Willingden."

"Ah," said Mr. parker. "This is my old house, the house of my forefathers, the house where I and all my brothers and sisters were born and bred, and where my own three eldest children were born; where Mrs. Parker and I lived till within the last two years, till our new house was finished. I am glad you are pleased with it. It is an honest old place; and Hillier keeps it in very good order. I have given it up, you know, to the man who occupies the chief of my land. He gets a better house by it, and I, a rather better situation! One other hill brings us to Sanditon modern Sanditon a beautiful spot. Our ancestors, you know, always built in a hole, Here were we, pent down in this little contracted nook, without air or view, only one mile and three quarters from the noblest expanse of ocean between the South Foreland and Land's End, and without the smallest advantage from it. You will not think I have made a bad exchange when we reach Trafalgar House which by the bye, I almost wish I had not named Trafalgar for Waterloo is more the thing now. However, Waterloo is in reserve; and if we have encouragement enough this year for a little crescent to be ventured on (as I trust we shall) then we shall be able to call it Waterloo Cresent and the name joined to the form of the building, which always takes, will give us the command of lodgers. In a good season we should have more applications than we could attend to."

"It was always a very comfortable house," said Mrs. Parker, looking at it through the back window with something like the fondness of regret. "And such a nice garden such an excellent garden."

"Yes, my love, but that we may be said to carry with us. It supplies us, as before, with all the fruit and vegetables we want.

And we have, in fact, all the comfort of an excellent kitchen garden without the constant eyesore of its formalities or the yearly nuisance of its decaying vegetation. Who can endure a cabbage bed in October?"

"Oh dear, yes. We are quite as well off for gardenstuff as ever we were; for if it is forgot to be brought at any time, we can always buy what we want at Sanditon House. The gardener there is glad enough to supply us. But it was a nice place for the children to run about in. So shady in summer!"

"My dear, we shall have shade enough on the hill, and more than enough in the course of a very few years. The growth of my plantations is a general astonishment. In the meanwhile we have the canvas awning which gives us the most complete comfort within doors. And you can get a parasol at Whitby's for little Mary at any time, or a large bonnet at Jebb's. And as for the boys, I must say I would rather them run about in the sunshine than not. I am sure we agree, my dear, in wishing our boys to be as hardy as possible."

"Yes indeed, I am sure we do. And I will get Mary a little parasol, which will make her as proud as can be. How grave she will walk about with it and fancy herself quite a little woman.

Oh, I have not the smallest doubt of our being a great deal better off where we are now. If we any of us want to bathe, we have not a quarter of a mile to go. But you know," still looking back, "one loves to look at an old friend at a place where one has been happy The Milliers did not seem to feel the storms last winter at all. I remember seeing Mrs. Millier after one of those dreadful nights, when we had been literally rocked in our bed, and she did not seem at all aware of the wind being anything more than common."

"Yes, yes, that's likely enough. We have all the grandeur of the storm with less real danger because the wind, meeting with nothing to oppose or confine it around our house, simply rages and passes on; while down in this gutter, nothing is known of the state of the air below the tops of the trees; and the inhabitants may be taken totally unawares by one of those dreadful currents, which do more mischief in a valley when they do arise than an open country ever experiences in the heaviest gale. But, my dear love, as to gardenstuff, you were saying that any accidental omission is supplied in a moment by Lady Denham's gardener.

But it occurs to me that we ought to go elsewhere upon such occasions, and that old Stringer and his son have a higher claim.

I encouraged him to set up, you know, and am afraid he does not do very well. That is, there has not been time enough yet.

He will do very well beyond a doubt. But at first it is uphill work, and therefore we must give him what help we can. When any vegetables or fruit happen to be wanted and it will not be amiss to have them often wanted, to have something or other forgotten most days; just to have a nominal supply, you know, that poor old Andrew may not lose his daily job but in fact to buy the chief of our consumption from the Stringers."

"Very well, my love, that can be easily done. And cook will be satisfied, which will be a great comfort, for she is always complaining of old Andrew now and says he never brings her what she wants. There now the old house is quite left behind. What is it your brother Sidney says about its being a hospital?"

"Oh, my dear Mary, merely a joke of his. He pretends to advise me to make a hospital of it. He pretends to laugh at my improvements. Sidney says anything, you know. He has always said what he chose, of and to us all. Most families have such a member among them, I believe, Miss Heywood. There is someone in most families privileged by superior abilities or spirits to say anything. In ours, it is Sidney, who is a very clever young man and with great powers of pleasing. He lives too much in the world to be settled; that is his only fault. He is here and there and everywhere. I wish we may get him to Sanditon. I should like to have you acquainted with him. And it would be a fine thing for the place! Such a young man as Sidney, with his neat equipage and fashionable air. You and I, Mary, know what effect it might have. Many a respectable family, many a careful mother, many a pretty daughter might it secure us to the prejudice of Eastbourne and Hastings."

They were now approaching the church and neat village of old Sanditon, which stood at the foot of the hill they were afterwards to ascend a hill whose side was covered with the woods and enclosures of Sanditon House and whose height ended in an open down where the new buildings might soon be looked for. A branch only of the valley, winding more obliquely towards the sea, gave a passage to an inconsiderable stream, and formed at its mouth a third habitable division in a small cluster of fishermen's houses. The original village contained little more than cottages; but the spirit of the day had been caught, as Mr. Parker observed with delight to Charlotte, and two Dr three of the best of them were smartened up with a white curtain and "Lodgings to let" and farther on, in the little green court of an old farm house, two females in elegant white were actually to be seen with their books and camp stools; and in turning the corner of the baker's shop, the sound of a harp might be heard through the upper casement, Such sights and sounds were highly blissful to Mr. Parker.

Not that he had any personal concern in the success of the village itself; for considering it as too remote from the beach, he had done nothing there; but it was a most valuable proof of the increasing fashion of the place altogether. If the village could attract, the hill might be nearly full. He anticipated an amazing season. At the same time last year (late in July) there had not been a single lodger in the village! Nor did he remember any during the whole summer, excepting one family of children who came from London for sea air after the whooping cough, and whose mother would not let them be nearer the shore for fear of their tumbling in.

'Civilization, civilization indeed!" cried Mr. Parker, delighted.

"Look, my dear Mary, look at William Heeley's windows. Blue shoes, and nankin boots! Who would have expected such a sight at a shoemaker"s in old Sanditon! This is new within the month. There was no blue shoe when we passed this way a month ago. Glorious indeed! Well, I think I have done something in my day. Now, for our hill, our health-breathing hill."

In ascending, they passed the lodge gates of Sanditon House and saw the top of the house itself among its groves. It was the last building of former days in that line of the parish. A little higher up, the modern began; and in crossing the down, a prospect House, a Bellevue Cottage and a Denham Place were to be looked at by Charlotte with the calmness of amused curiosity, and by Mr. parker with the eager eye which hoped to see scarcely any empty houses. More bills at the windows than he had calculated on, and a smaller show of company on the hill fewer carriages, fewer walkers. He had fancied it just the time of day for them to be all returning from their airings to dinner; but the sands and the Terrace always attracted some, and the tide must be flowing about half-tide now. He longed to be on the sands, the cliffs, at his own house, and everywhere out of his house at once. His spirits rose with the very sight of the sea and he could almost feel his ankle getting stronger already.

Trafalgar House, on the most elevated spot on the down, was a light, elegant building, standing in a small lawn with a very young plantation round it, about a hundred yards from the brow of a steep but not very lofty cliff, and the nearest to it of every building, excepting one short row of smart-looking houses called the Terrace, with a broad walk in front, aspiring to be the Mall of the place. In this row were the best milliner's shop and the library a little detached from it, the hotel and billiard room. Here began the descent to the beach and to the bathing machines. And this was therefore the favourite spot for beautey and fashion.

At Trafalgar House, rising at a little distance behind the Terrace, the travellers were safely set down; and all was happiness and joy between Papa and Mama and their children; while Charlotte, having received possession of her apartment, found amusement enough in standing at her ample Venetian window and looking over the miscellaneous foreground of unfinished buildings, waving linen and tops of houses, to the sea, dancing and sparkling in sunshine and freshness.

Chapter 5

When they met before dinner, Mr. Parker was looking over letters.

"Not a line from Sidney!" said he. "He is an idle fellow. I sent him an account of my accident from Willingden and thought he would have vouchsafed me an answer. But perhaps it implies that he is coming himself. I trust it may. But here is a letter from one of my sisters. They never fail me. Women are the only correspondents to be depended on. Now, Mary," smiling at his wife, "before I open it, what shall we guess as to the state of health of those it comes from or rather what would Sidney say if he were here? Sidney is a saucy fellow, Miss Heywood.

And you must know, he will have it there is a good deal of imagination in my two sisters' complaints. But it really is not so or very little. They have wretched health, as you have heard us say frequently, and are subject to a variety of very serious disorders. Indeed, I do not believe they know what a day's health is. And at the same time, they are such excellent useful women and have so much energy of character that where any good is to be done, they force themselves on exertions which, to those who do not thoroughly know them, have an extraordinary appearance.

But there is really no affectation about them, you know. They have only weaker constitutions and stronger minds than are often met with, either separate or together. And our youngest brother, who lives with them and who is not much above twenty, I am sorry to say is almost as great an invalid as themselves. He is so delicate that he can engage in no profession. Sidney laughs at him. But it really is no joke, though Sidney often makes me laugh at them all in spite of myself. Now, if he were here, I know he would be offering odds that either Susan, Diana or Arthur would appear by this letter to have been at the point of death within the last month."

Having run his eye over the letter, he shook his head and began, "No chance of seeing them at Sanditon I am sorry to say. A very indifferent account of them indeed. Seriously, a very indifferent account. Mary, you will be quite sorry to hear how ill they have been and are. Miss Heywood, if you will give me leave, I will read Diana's letter aloud. I like to have my friends acquainted with each other and I am afraid this is the only sort of acquaintance I shall have the means of accomplishing between you. And I can have no scruple on Diana's account; for her letters show her exactly as she is, the most active, friendly, warm-hearted being in existence, and therefore must give a good impression."

He read: My dear Tom, we were all much grieved at Wour accident, and if you had not described yourself asfallen into such very good hands, I should have been with you at all hazards the day after the receipt of your letter, though it found me suffering under a more severe attack than usual of my old grievance, spasmodic bile, and hardly able to crawlfrom my bed to the sofa. But how were you treated? Send me more Particulars in your next. If indeed a simple sprain, as you denominate it, nothing would have been so judicious as friction, friction by the hand alone, supposing it could be applied instantly.

Two years ago I happened to be calling on Mrs. Sheldon when her coachman sprained hisfoot as he was cleaning the carriage and could hardly limp into the house, but by the immediate use offriction alone steadily perservered in (and I rubbed his ankle with my own handfor six hours without intermission) he was wellin three days.

Many thanks, my dear Tom, for the kindness with respect to us, which had so large a share in bringing onyour accident.

But pray never run into perilagain in looking for an apothecary on our account, for hadyou the most experienced man in his line settled at Sanditon, it would be no recommendation to us. We have entirely done with the whole medical tribe.

We have consulted physician after physician in vain, till we are quite convinced that they can do nothing for us and that we must trust to our own knowledge of our own wretched constitutions for any relief. But if you think it advisable for the interest of the place to get a medical man there, I will undertake the commission with pleasure, and have no doubt of succeeding. I could soon put the necessary irons in the fire. As for getting to Sanditon myself, it is quite an impossibility.

I grieve to say that I dare not attempt it but my feelings tell me too plainly that, in my present state, the sea air would probably be the death of me. And neither of my dear companions will leave me or I would promote their going down to you for a fortnight. But in truth, I doubt whether Susan"s nerves would be equal to the effort. She has been suffering much from the headache, and six leeches a day for ten days together relieved her so little that we thought it right to change our measures, and being convinced on examination that mach of the evillay in her gum, I persuaded her to attack the disorder there. She has accordingly had three teeth drawn, and is decidedly better, but her nerves are a good deal deranged. She can only speak in a whisper andfainted away twice this morning on poor Arthur's trying to suppress a cough. He, I am happy to say, is tolerably well though more languid than I like and I fear for his liver. I have heard nothing of Sidney since your being together in town, but conclude his scheme to the Isle of Wight has not taken place or we should have seen him in his way.

Most sincerely do we wish you a good season at Sanditon, and though we cannot contribute to your beau monde in person, we are doing our utmost to sendyou company worth having and think we may safely reckon on securing you two large families. One a rich West Indianfrom Surrey, the other a most respectable Girls Boarding School, or Academy, from Camberwell. I will not tell you how many people I have employed in the business wheel within wheel. But success more than repays. Yours most affectionately etcetera. "Well," said Mr. parker, as he finished. "Though I dare sa Sidney might find something extremely entertaining in this letter and make us laugh for half an hour together, I declare I , by myself can see nothing in it but what is either very pitiable or very creditable.

With all their sufferings, you perceive how much they ar occupied in promoting the good of others! So anxious for Sanditon! Two large families one for Prospect House prob ably, the other for Number two Denham place or the end house of the Terrace, with extra beds at the hotel. I told you my sister were excellent women, Miss Heywood."

"And I am sure they must be very extraordinary ones," sai Charlotte. "I am astonished at the cheerful style of the letter, considering the state in which both sisters appear to be. Thre teeth drawn at once frightful! Your sister Diana seems almost as ill as possible, but those three teeth of your sister Susan s ar more distressing than all the rest."

"Oh, they are so used to the operation to every operation and have such fortitude!"

"Your sisters know what they are about, I dare say, but their measures seem to touch on extremes. I feel that in any illness I should be so anxious for professional advice, so very little venturesome for myself or anybody I loved! But then, we have been so healthy a family that I can be no judge of what the habit of self-doctoring may do."

"Why to own the truth," said Mrs. Parker, "I do think the Miss Parkers carry it too far sometimes. And so do you, my love, you know. You often think they would be better if they would leave themselves more alone and especially Arthur. I know you think it agreat pity they should give him such a turn for being ill."

"Well, well, my dear Mary, I grant you, it is unfortunate for poor Arthur that at his time of life he should be encouraged to give way to indisposition. It is bad that he should be fancying himself too sickly for any profession and sit down at one and twenty, on the interest of his own little fortune, without any idea of attempting to improve it or of engaging in any occupation that may be of use to himself or others. But let us talk of pleasanter things."

These two large families are just what we wanted. But here is something at hand pleasanter stillMorgan with his "Dinner on table."

Chapter 6

The party were very soon moving after dinner. Mr. Parker could not be satisfied without an early visit to the library and the library subscription book; and Charlotte was glad to see as much and as quickly as possible where all was new.

They were out in the very quietest part of a watering-place day, when the important business of dinner or of sitting after dinner was going on in almost every inhabited lodging. Here and there might be seen a solitary elderly man, who was forced to move early and walk for health; but in general, it was a thorough pause of company.

It was emptiness and tranquillity on the Terrace, the cliffs and the sands. The shops were deserted. The straw hats and pendant lace seemed left to their fate both within the house and without, and Mrs. Whitby at the library was sitting in her inner room, reading one of her own novels for want of employment.

The list of subscribers was but commonplace. The Lady Denham, Miss Brereton, Mr. and Mrs. Parker, Sir Edward Denham and Miss Denham, whose names might be said to lead off the season, were followed by nothing better than: Mrs. Mathews, Miss Mathews, Miss E. Mathews, Miss H. Mathews; Dr. and Mrs.

Brown; Mr. Richard pratt; Lieutenant Smith R.N.; Captain Little Limehouse; Mrs. Jane Fisher, Miss Fisher, Miss Scroggs; Reverend Mr. Hanking; Mr. Beard Solicitor, Grays Inn; Mrs.

Davis and Miss Merryweather.

Mr. parker could not but feel that the list was not only without distinction but less numerous than he had hoped. It was but July, however, and August and September were the months. And besides, the promised large families from Surrey and Camberwell were an ever-ready consolation.

Mrs. Whitby came forward without delay from her literary recess, delighted to see Mr. Parker, whose manners recommended him to everybody, and they were fully occupied in their various civilities and communications; while Charlotte, having added her name to the list as the first offering to the success of the season, was busy in some immediate purchases for the further good of everybody as soon as Miss Whitby could be hurried down from her toilette, with all her glossy curls and smart trinkets, to wait on her.

The library, of course, afforded everything: all the useless things in the world that could not be done without; and among so many pretty temptations, and with so much good will for Mr.

parker to encourage expenditure, Charlotte began to feel that she must check herself or rather she reflected that at two and twenty there could be no excuse for her doing otherwise and that it would not do for her to be spending all her money the very first evening. She took up a book; it happened to be a volume of Camilla. She had not Camilla's youth, and had no intention of having her distress; so she turned from the drawers of rings and brooches, repressed further solicitation and paid for what she had bought.

For her particular gratification, they were then to take a turn on the cliff; but as they quitted the library they were met by two ladies whose arrival made an alteration necessary: Lady Denham and Miss Brereton. They had been to Trafalgar House and been directed thence to the library; and though Lady Denham was a great deal too active to regard the walk of a mile as anything requiring rest, and talked of going home again directly, the parkers knew that to be pressed into their house and obliged to take her tea with them would suit her best; and therefore the stroll on the cliff gave way to an immediate return home.

"No, no," said her Ladyship. "I will not have you hurry your tea on my account. I know you like your tea late. My early hours are not to put my neighbours to inconvenience. No, no, Miss Clara and I will get back to our own tea. We came out with no other thought. We wanted just to see you and make sure of your being really come but we get back to our own tea. " She went on however towards Trafalgar House and took possession of the drawing room very quietly without seeming to hear a word of Mrs. parker's orders to the servant, as they entered, to bring tea directly. Charlotte was fully consoled for the loss of her walk by finding herself in company with those whom the conversation of the morning had given her a great curiosity to see. She obsetved them well.

Lady Denham was of middle height, stout, upright and alert in her motions, with a shrewd eye and self-satisfied air but not an unagreeable countenance; and though her manner was rather downright and abrupt, as of a person who valued herself on being free-spoken, there was a good humour and cordiality about her a civility and readiness to be acquainted with Charlotte herself and a heartiness of welcome towards her old friends which was inspiring the good will she seemed to feel.

And as for Miss Brereton, her appearance so completely justified Mr. parker's praise that Charlotte thought she had never beheld a more lovely or more interesting young woman. Elegantly tall, regularly handsome, with great delicacy of complexion and soft blue eyes, a sweetly modest and yet naturally graceful address, Charlotte could see in her only the most perfect representation of whatever heroine might be most beautiful and bewitching in all the numerous volumes they had left behind on Mrs. Whitby's shelves. perhaps it might be partly owing to her having just issued from a circulating library but she could not separate the idea of a complete heroine from Clara Brereton. Her situation with Lady Denham so very much in favour of it! She seemed placed with her on purpose to be ill-used. Such poverty and dependence joined to such beauty and merit seemed to leave no choice in the business.

These feelings were not the result of any spirit of romance in Charlotte herself. No, she was a very sober-minded young lady, sufficiently well-read in novels to supply her imagination with amusement, but not at all unreasonably influenced by them; and while she pleased herself the first five minutes with fancying the persecution which ought to be the lot of the interesting Clara, especially in the form of the most barbarous conduct on Lady Denham's side, she found no reluctance to admit from subsequent observation that they appeared to be on very comfortable terms.

She could see nothing worse in Lady Denham than the sort of old-fashioned formality of always calling her Miss Clara; nor anything objectionable in the degree of observance and attention which Clara paid. On one side it seemed protecting kindness, on the other grateful and affectionate respect.

The conversation turned entirely upon Sanditon, its present number of visitants and the chances of a good season.

It was evident that Lady Denham had more anxiety, more fears of loss, than her coadjutor. She wanted to have the place fill faster and seemed to have many harassing apprehensions of the lodgings being in some instances underlet. Miss Diana parker's two large families were not forgotten.

"Very good, very good," said her Ladyship. "A West Indy family and a school. That sounds well. That will bring money."

"No people spend more freely, I believe, than West Indians," observed Mr. parker.

"Aye, so I have heard; and because they have full purses fancy themselves equal, maybe, to your old country families. But then, they who scatter their money so freely never think of whether they may not be doing mischief by raising the price of things. And I have heard that's very much the case with your West-injines.

And if they come among us to raise the price of our necessaries of life, we shall not much thank them, Mr. Parker."

"My dear Madam, they can only raise the price of consumable articles by such an extraordinary demand for them and such a diffusion of money among us as must do us more good than harm.

Our butchers and bakers and traders in general cannot get rich without bringing prosperity to us. If they do not gain, our rents must be insecure; and in proportion to their profit must be ours eventually in the increased value of our houses."

"Oh! well. But I should not like to have butcher's meat raised, though. And I shall keep it down as long as I can. Aye, that young lady smiles, I see. I dare say she thinks me an odd sort of creature; but she will come to care about such matters herself in time. Yes, yes, my dear, depend upon it, you will be thinking of the price of butcher's meat in time, though you may not happen to have quite such a servants' hall to feed as I have. And I do believe those are best off that have fewest servants. I am not a woman of parade as all the world knows, and if it was not for what I owe to poor Mr. Hollis's memory, I should never keep up Sanditon House as I do. (t is not for my own pleasure. Well, Mr. Parker, and the other is a boarding school, a French boarding school, is it? No harm in that. They'll stay their six weeks.

And out of such a number, who knows but some may be consumptive and want asses' milk; and I have two milch asses at this present time. But perhaps the little Misses may hurt the furniture.

I hope they will have a good sharp governess to look after them."

Poor Mr. parker got no more credit from Lady Denham than he had from his sisters for the object which had taken him to Willingden.

"Lord! my dear sir," she cried. "How could you think of such a thing? I am very sorry you met with your accident, but upon my word, you deserved it. Going after a doctor! Why, what should we do with a doctor here? It would be only encouraging our servants and the poor to fancy themselves ill if there was a doctor at hand. Oh! pray, let us have none of the tribe at Sanditon. We go on very well as we are. There is the sea and the downs and my milch asses. And I have told Mrs. Whitby that if anybody inquires for a chamber-horse, they may be supplied at a fair rate poor Mr. Hollis's chamber-horse, as good as new and what can people want for more? Here have I lived seventy good years in the world and never took physic above twice and never saw the face of a doctor in all my life on my own account. And I verily believe if my poor dear Sir Harry had never seen one neither, he would have been alive now. Ten fees, one after another, did the man take who sent him out of the world. I beseech you Mr. Parker, no doctors here." The tea things were brought in. "Oh, my dear Mrs. parker, you should not indeed why would you do so? I was just upon the point of wishing you good evening. But since you are so very neighbourly, I believe Miss Clara and I must stay."

Chapter 7

The popularity of the Parkers brought them some visitors the very next morning; amongst them, Sir Edward Denham and his sister who having been at Sanditon House, drove on to pay their compliments; and the duty of letter writing being accomplished, Charlotte was settled with Mrs. parker in the drawing room in time to see them all.

The Denhams were the only ones to excite particular attention.

Charlotte was glad to complete her knowledge of the family by an introduction to them; and found them, the better half at least (for while single, the gentleman may sometimes be thought the better half of the pair) not unworthy of notice.

Miss Denham was a fine young woman, but cold and reserved, giving the idea of one who felt her consequence with pride and her poverty with discontent, and who was immediately gnawed by the want of a handsomer equipage than the simple gig in which they travelled, and which their groom was leading about still in her sight.

Sir Edward was much her superior in air and manner certainly handsome, but yet more to be remarked for his very good address and wish of paying attention and giving pleasure. He came into the room remarkably well, talked much and very much to Charlotte, by whom he chanced to be placed and she soon perceived that he had a fine countenance, a most pleasing gentleness of voice and a great deal of conversation. She liked him. Sober-minded as she was, she thought him agreeable and did not quarrel with the suspicion of his finding her equally so, which would arise from his evidently disregarding his sister's motion to go, and persisting in his station and his discourse.

I make no apologies for my heroine's vanity. If there are young ladies in the world at her time of life more dull of fancy and more careless of pleasing, I know them not and never wish to know them.

At last, from the low French windows of the drawing room which commanded the road and all the paths across the down, Charlotte and Sir Edward as they sat could not but observe Lady Denham and Miss Brereton walking by; and there was instantly a slight change in Sir Edward's countenance with an anxious glance after them as they proceeded followed by an early proposal to his sister, not merely for moving, but for walking on together to the Terrace, which altogether gave a hasty turn to Charlotte's fancy, cured her of her half-hour's fever, and placed her in a more capable state of judging, when Sir Edward was gone, of how agreeable he had actually been. "perhaps there was a good deal in his air and address; and his title did him no harm."

She was very soon in his company again. The first object of the Parkers, when their house was cleared of morning visitors, was to get out themselves. The Terrace was the attraction to all.

Everybody who walked must begin with the Terrace; and there, seated on one of the two green benches by the gravel walk, they found the united Denham party; but though united in the gross, very distinctly divided again: the two superior ladies being at one end of the bench, and Sir Edward and Miss Brereton at the other.

Charlotte s first glance told her that Sir Edward's air was that of a lover. There could be no doubt of his devotion to Clara. How Clara received it was less obvious, but she was inclined to think not very favourably; for though sitting thus apart with him (which probably she might not have been able to preveno her air was calm and grave.

That the young lady at the other end of the bench was doing penance was indubitable. The difference in Miss Denham's countenance, the change from Miss Denham sitting in cold grandeur in Mrs. parker's drawing room, to be kept from silence by the efforts of others, to Miss Denham at Lady Denham's elbow, listening and talking with smiling attention or solicitous eagerness, was very striking and very amusing or very melancholy, just as satire or morality might prevail. Miss Denham's character was pretty well decided with Charlotte.

Sir Edward's required longer observation. He surprised her by quitting Clara immediately on their all joining and agreeing to walk, and by addressing his attentions entirely to herself.

Stationing himself close by her, he seemed to mean to detach her as much as possible from the rest of the party and to give her the whole of his conversation. He began, in a tone of great taste and feeling, to talk of the sea and the sea shore; and ran with energy through all the usual phrases employed in praise of their sublimity and descriptive of the undescribable emotions they excite in the mind of sensibility. The terrific grandeur of the ocean in a storm, its glass surface in a calm, its gulls and its samphire and the deep fathoms of its abysses, its quick vicissitudes, its direful deceptions, its mariners tempting it in sunshine and overwhelmed by the sudden tempest all were eagerly and fluently touched; rather commonplace perhaps, but doing very well from the lips of a handsome Sir Edward, and she could not but think him a man of feeling, till he began to stagger her by the number of his quotations and the bewilderment of some of his sentences.

"Do you remember," said he, "Scott's beautiful lines on the sea? Oh! what a description they convey! They are never out of my thoughts when I walk here. That man who can read them unmoved must have the nerves of an assassin! Heaven defend me from meeting such a man unarmed."

"What description do you mean?" said Charlotte. "I remember none at this moment, of the sea, in either of Scott s poems.

"Do you not indeed? Nor can I exactly recall the beginning at this moment. But you cannot have forgotten his description of woman—

Oh. Woman in our hours of ease Delicious! Delicious! Had he written nothing more, he would have been immortal. And then again, that unequalled, unrivalled address to parental affection

Some feelings are to mortals given

With less of earth in them than heaven etcetera.

But while we are on the subject of poetry, what think you, Miss Heywood, of Burns's lines to his Mary? Oh! there is pathos to madden one! If ever there was a man who felt, it was Burns.

Montgomery has all the fire of poetry, Wordsworth has the true soul of it, Campbell in his pleasures of hope has touched the extreme of our sensations

Like angels' visits, few and far between.

Can you conceive anything more subduing, more melting, more fraught with the deep sublime than that line? But Burns I confess my sense of his pre-eminence, Miss Heywood. If Scott has a fault, it is the want of passion. Tender, elegant, descriptive but tame. The man who cannot do justice to the attributes of woman is my contempt. Sometimes indeed a flash of feeling seems to irradiate him, as in the lines we were speaking of

Oh. Woman in our hours of ease

But Burns is always on fire. His soul was the altar in which lovely woman sat enshrined, his spirit truly breathed the immortal incense which is her due."

"I have read several of Burns's poems with great delight," said Charlotte as soon as she had time to speak. "But I am not poetic enough to separate a man's poetry entirely from his character; and poor Burns's known irregularities greatly interrupt my enjoyment of his lines. I have difficulty in depending on the truth of his feelings as a lover. I have not faith in the sincerity of the affections of a man of his description. He felt and he wrote and he forgot."

"Oh! no, no," exclaimed Sir Edward in an ecstasy. "He was all ardour and truth! His genius and his susceptibilities might lead him into some aberrations but who is perfect? It were hyper-criticism, it were pseudo-philosophy to expect from the soul of high-toned genius the grovellings of a common mind. The coruscations of talent, elicited by impassioned feeling in the breast of man, are perhaps incompatible with some of the prosaic decencies of life; nor can you, loveliest Miss Heywood," speaking with an air of deep sentiment, "nor can any woman be a fair judge of what a man may be propelled to say, write or do by the sovereign impulses of illimitable ardour."

This was very fine but if Charlotte understood it at all, not very moral; and being moreover by no means pleased with his extraordinary style of compliment, she gravely answered, "I really know nothing of the matter. This is a charming day.

The wind, I fancy, must be southerly."

"Happy, happy wind, to engage Miss Heywood's thoughts!"

She began to think him downright silly. His choosing to walk with her, she had learnt to understand. It was done to pique Miss Brereton. She had read it, in an anxious glance or two on his side; but why he should talk so much nonsense, unless he could do no better, was unintelligible. He seemed very sentimental, very full of some feeling or other, and very much addicted to all the newest-fashioned hard words, had not a very clear brain, she presumed, and talked a good deal by rote. The future might explain him further.

But when there was a proposition for going into the library, she felt that she had had quite enough of Sir Edward for one morning and very gladly accepted Lady Denham's invitation of remaining on the Terrace with her. The others all left them, Sir Edward with looks of very gallant despair in tearing himself away, and they united their agreeableness; that is, Lady Denham, like a true great lady, talked and talked only of her own concerns, and Charlotte listened, amused in considering the contrast between her two companions. Certainly there was no strain of doubtful sentiment nor any phrase of difficult interpretation in Lady Denham's discourse. Taking hold of Charlotte's arm with the ease of one who felt that any notice from her was an honour, and communicative from the influence of the same conscious importance or a natural love of talking, she immediately said in a tone of great satisfaction and with a look of arch sagacity, "Miss Esther wants me to invite her and her brother to spend a week with me at Sanditon House, as I did last summer. But I shan't. She has been trying to get round me every way with her praise of this and her praise of that; but I saw what she was about.

I saw through it all. I am not very easily taken in, my dear."

Charlotte could think of nothing more harmless to be said than the simple enquiry of "Sir Edward and Miss Denham?"

"Yes, my dear. My young folks, as I call them sometimes, for I take them very much by the hand. I had them with me last summer, about this time, for a week; from Monday to Monday; and very delighted and thankful they were. For they are very good young people, my dear. I would not have you think that I only notice them for poor dear Sir Harry's sake. No, no; they are very deserving themselves or, trust me, they would not be so much in my company. I am not the woman to help anybody blindfold.

I always take care to know what I am about and who I have to deal with before I stir a finger. I do not think I was ever over-reached in my life. And that is a good deal for a woman to say that has been married twice. Poor dear Sir Harry, between ourselves, thought at first to have got more. But, with a bit of a sigh, he is gone, and we must not find fault with the dead.

Nobody could live happier together than us and he was a very honourable man, quite the gentleman of ancient family. And when he died, I gave Sir Edward his gold watch."

She said this with a look at her companion which implied its right to produce a great impression; and seeing no rapturous astonishment in Charlotte s countenance, added quickly, "He did not bequeath it to his nephew, my dear. It was no bequest. It was not in the will. He only told me, and that but once, that he should wish his nephew to have his watch; but it need not have been binding if I had not chose it."

"Very kind indeed! Very handsome!" said Charlotte, absolutely forced to affect admiration.

"Yes, my dear, and it is not the only kind thing I have done by him. I have been a very liberal friend to Sir Edward. And poor young man, he needs it bad enough. For though I am only the dowager, my dear, and he is the heir, things do not stand between us in the way they commonly do between those two parties. Not a shilling do I receive from the Denham estate. Sir Edward has no payments to make me. He don't stand uppermost, believe me. It is I that help him. "Indeed! He is a very fine young man, particularly elegant in his address." This was said chiefly for the sake of saying something, but Charlotte directly saw that it was laying her open to suspicion by Lady Denham's giving a shrewd glance at her and replying, "Yes, yes, he is very well to look at. And it is to be hoped that some lady of large fortune will think so, for Sir Edward must marry for money. He and I often talk that matter over. A handsome young fellow like him will go smirking and smiling about and paying girls compliments, but he knows he must marry for money. And Sir Edward is a very steady young man in the main and has got very good notions.

"Sir Edward Denham," said Charlotte, "with such personal advantages may be almost stire of getting a woman of fortune, if he chooses it."

This glorious sentiment seemed quite to remove suspicion.

"Aye my dear, that's very sensibly said," cried Lady Denham.

"And if we could but get a young heiress to Sanditon! But heiresses are monstrous scarce! I do not think we have had an heiress here or even a co since Sanditon has been a public place. Families come after families but, as far as I can learn, it is not one in a hundred of them that have any real property, landed or funded. An income perhaps, but no property. Clergymen maybe, or lawyers from town, or half-pay officers, or widows with only a jointure. And what good can such people do anybody? Except just as they take our empty houses and, between ourselves, I think they are great fools for not staying at home. Now if we could get a young heiress to be sent here for her health and if she was ordered to drink asses' milk I could supply her and, as soon as she got well, have her fall in love with Sir Edward!"

"That would be very fortunate indeed."

"And Miss Esther must marry somebody of fortune too. She must get a rich husband. Ah, young ladies that have no money are very much to be pitied! But," after a short pause, "if Miss Esther thinks to talk me into inviting them to come and stay at Sanditon Mouse, she will find herself mistaken. Matters are altered with me since last summer, you know. I have Miss Clara with me now which makes a great difference."

She spoke this so seriously that Charlotte instantly saw in it the evidence of real penetration and prepared for some fuller remarks; but it was followed only by, "I have no fancy for having my house as full as an hotel. I should not choose to have my two housemaids' time taken up all the morning in dusting out bed rooms. They have Miss Clara's room to put to rights as well as my own every day. If they had hard places, they would want higher wages."

For objections of this nature, Charlotte was not prepared. She found it so impossible even to affect sympathy that she could say nothing. Lady Denham soon added, with great glee, "And besides all this, my dear, am I to be filling my house to the prejudice of Sanditon? If people want to be by the sea, why don't they take lodgings? Here are a great many empty houses three on this very Terrace. No fewer than three lodging papers staring me in the face at this very moment, Numbers three, four and eight. Eight, the corner house, may be too large for them, but either of the two others are nice little snug houses, very fit for a young gentleman and his sister. And so, my dear, the next time Miss Esther begins talking about the dampness of Denham park and the good bathing always does her, I shall advise them to come and take one of these lodgings for a fortnight. Don t you think that will be very fair? Charity begins at home, you know."

Charlotte's feelings were divided between amusement and indignation, but indignation had the larger and the increasing share. She kept her countenance and she kept a civil silence.

She could not carry her forbearance farther, but without attempting to listen longer, and only conscious that Lady Denham was still talking on in the same way, allowed her thoughts to form themselves into such a meditation as this: "She is thoroughly mean. I had not expected anything so bad. Mr. parker spoke too mildly of her. His judgement is evidently not to be trusted. His own good nature misleads him. He is too kind-hearted to see clearly. I must judge for myself. And their very connection prejudices him. He has persuaded her to engage in the same speculation, and because their object in that line is the same, he fancies she feels like him in others. But she is very, very mean. I can see no good in her. Poor Miss Brereton! And she makes everybody mean about her. This poor Sir Edward and his sister how far nature meant them to be respectable I cannot tell but they are obliged to be mean in their servility to her.

And I am mean, too, in giving her my attention with the appearance of coinciding with her. Thus it is, when rich people are sordid."

Chapter 8

The two ladies continued walking together till rejoined by the others, who, as they issued from the library, were followed by a young Whitby running off with five volumes under his arm to Sir Edward's gig; and Sir Edward, approaching Charlotte, said, "You may perceive what has been our occupation. My sister wanted my counsel in the selection of some books. We have many leisure hours and read a great deal. I am no indiscriminate novel reader. The mere trash of the common circulating library I hold in the highest contempt. You will never hear me advocating those puerile emanations which detail nothing but discordant principles incapable of amalgamation, or those vapid tissues of ordinary occurrences from which no useful deductions can be drawn. In vain may we put them into a literary alembic; we distil nothing which can add to science. You understand me, I am sure?"

"I am not quite certain that I do. But if you will describe the sort of novels which you do approve, I dare say it will give me a clearer idea."

Most willingly, fair questioner. The novels which I approve are such as display human nature with grandeur; such as show her in the sublimities of intense feeling; such as exhibit the progress of strong passion from the first germ of incipient susceptibility to the utmost energies of reason half-dethroned; where we see the strong spark of woman's captivations elicit such fire in the soul of man as leads him though at the risk of some aberration from the strict line of primitive obligations to hazard all, dare all, achieve all ttj obtain her. Such are the works which I peruse with delight and, I hope I may say, with amelioration. They hold forth the most splendid portraitures of high conceptions, unbounded views, illimitable ardour, indomitable decision.

And even when the event is mainly anti-prosperous to the high-toned machinations of the prime character the potent, pervading hero of the story it leaves us full of generous emotions for him; our hearts are paralysed.

It would be pseudo-philosophy to assert that we do not feel more enwrapped by the brilliancy of his career than by the tranquil and morbid virtues of any opposing character. Our approbation of the latter is but eleemosynary. These are the novels which enlarge the primitive capabilities of the heart; and it cannot impugn the sense or be any dereliction of the character of the most anti-puerile man, to be conversant with them.

"If I understand you aright," said Charlotte, "our taste in novels is not at all the same."

And here they were obliged to part, Miss Denham being much too tired of them all to stay any longer.

The truth was that Sir Edward, whom circumstances had confined very much to one spot, had read more sentimental novels than agreed with him. His fancy had been early caught by all the impassioned and most exceptionable parts of Richardson's.

And such authors as had since appeared to tread in Richardson's steps (so far as man's determined pursuit of woman in defiance of every opposition of feeling and convenience was concerned) had since occupied the greater part of his literary hours, and formed his character.

With a perversity of judgement which must be attributed to his not having by nature a very strong head, the graces, the spirit, the sagacity and the perserverance of the villain of the story out-weighed all his absurdities and all his atrocities with Sir Edward.

With him such conduct was genius, fire and feeling. It interested and inflamed him. And he was always more anxious for its success, and mourned over its discomfitures with more tenderness, than could ever have been contemplated by the authors. Though he owed many of his ideas to this sort of reading, it would be unjust to say that he read nothing else or that his language was not formed on a more general knowledge of modern literature.

He read all the essays, letters, tours and criticisms of the day; and with the same ill-luck which made him derive only false principles from lessons of morality, and incentives to vice from the history of its overthrow, he gathered only hard words and involved st'ntences from the style of our most approved writers.

Sir Edward's great object in life was to be seductive. With such personal advantages as he knew himself to possess, and such talents as he did also give himself credit for, he regarded it as his duty. He felt that he was formed to be a dangerous man, quite in the line of the Lovelaces. The very name of Sir Edward, he thought, carried some degree of fascination with it.

To be generally gallant and assiduous about the fair, to make fine speeches to every pretty girl, was but the inferior part of the character he had to play. Miss Heywood, or any other young woman with any pretensions to beauty, he was entitled (according to his own views of society) to approach with high compliment and rhapsody on the slightest acquaintance.

But it was Clara alone on whom he had serious designs; it was Clara whom he meant to seduce her seduction was quite determined on. Her situation in every way called for it. She was his rival in Lady Denham's favour; she was young, lovely and dependent. He had very early seen the necessity of the case, and had now been long trying with cautious assiduity to make an impression on her heart and to undermine her principles. Clara saw through him and had not the least intention of being seduced; but she bore with him patiently enough to confirm the sort of attachment which her personal charms had raised. A greater degree of discouragement indeed would not have affected Sir Edward. He was armed against the highest pitch of disdain or aversion. If she could not be won by affection, he must carry her off. He knew his business.

Already had he had many musings on the subject. If he were constrained so to act, he must naturally wish to strike out something new, to exceed those who had gone before him; and he felt a strong curiosity to ascertain whether the neighbourhood of Timbuctu might not afford some solitary house adapted for Clara's reception.

But the expense, alas! of measures in that masterly style was ill-suited to his purse; and prudence obliged him to prefer the quietest sort of ruin and disgrace for the object of his affections to the more renowned.

Chapter 9

One day, soon after Charlotte's arrival at Sanditon she had the pleasure of seeing, just as she ascended from the sands to the Terrace, a gentleman's carriage with post horses standing at the door of the hotel, as very lately arrived and by the quantity of luggage being taken off bringing, it might be hoped, some respectable family determined on a long residence.

Delighted to have such good news for Mr. and Mrs. parker, who had both gone home some time before, she proceeded to Trafalgar House with as much alacrity as could remain after having contended for the last two hours with a very fine wind blowing directly on shore. But she had not reached the little lawn when she saw a lady walking nimbly behind her at no great distance; and convinced that it could be no acquaintance of her own, she resolved to hurry on and get into the house if possible before her.

But the stranger's pace did not allow this to be accomplished.

Charlotte was on the steps and had rung but the door was not open when the other crossed the lawn; and when the servant appeared, they were just equally ready for entering the house.

The ease of the lady, her "How do you do, Morgan?" and Morgan's looks on seeing her were a moment's astonishment; but another moment brought Mr. parker into the hall to welcome the sister he had seen from the drawing room; and Charlotte was soon introduced to Miss Diana parker.

There was a great deal of surprise but still more pleasure in seeing her. Nothing could be kinder than her reception from both husband and wife. How did she come? And with whom? And they were so glad to find her equal to the journey! And that she was to belong to them was taken as a matter of course.

Miss Diana parker was about four and thirty, of middling height and slender; delicate looking rather than sickly; with an agreeable face and a very animated eye; her manners resembling her brother's in their ease and frankness, though with more decision and less mildness in her tone.

She began an account of herself without delay. Thanking them for their invitation but "that was quite out of the question for they were all three come and meant to get into lodgings and make some stay."

"All three come! What! Susan and Arthur! Susan able to come too! This is better and better."

"Yes, we are actually all come. Cite unavoidable. Nothing else to be done. You shall hear all about it. But my dear Mary, send for the children I long to see them."

"And how has Susan borne the journey? And how is Arthur? And why do we not see him here with you?"

"Susan has borne it wonderfully. She had not a wink of sleep either the night before we set out or last night at Chichester, and as this is not so common with her as with me, I have had a thousand fears for her. But she has kept up wonderfully no hysterics of consequence till we came within sight of poor old Sanditon and the attack was not very violent nearly over by the time we reached your hotel so that we got her out of the carriage extremely well with only Mr. Woodcock's assistance.

And when I left her she was directing the disposal of the luggage and helping old Sam uncord the trunks. She desired her best love with a thousand regrets at being so poor a creature that she could not come with me. And as for poor Arthur, he would not have been unwilling himself, but there is so much wind that I did not think he could safely venture for I am sure there is lumbago hanging about him; and so I helped him on with his great coat and sent him off to the Terrace to take us lodgings. Miss Heywood must have seen our carriage standing at the hotel. I knew Miss Heywood the moment I saw her before me on the down. My dear Tom, I am so glad to see you walk so well. Let me feel your ankle. That's right; all right and clean. The play of your sinews a very little affected, barely perceptible. Well, now for the explanation of my being here. I told you in my letter of the two considerable families I was hoping to secure for you, the West Indians and the seminary."

Here Mr. parker drew his chair still nearer to his sister and took her hand again most affectionately as he answered, "Yes, yes, how active and how kind you have been!"

"The West Indians," she continued, "whom I look upon as the most desirable of the two, as the best of the good, prove to be a Mrs. Griffiths and her family. I know them only through others.

You must have heard me mention Miss Capper, the particular friend of my very particular friend Fanny Noyce. Now, Miss Capper is extremely intimate with a Mrs. Darling, who is on terms of constant correspondence with Mrs. Griffiths herself. Only a short chain, you see, between us, and not a link wanting. Mrs.

Griffiths meant to go to the sea for her young people s benefit, had fixed on the coast of Sussex but was undecided as to the where, wanted something private, and wrote to ask the opinion of her friend Mrs. Darling. Miss Capper happened to be staying with Mrs. Darling when Mrs. Griffiths' letter arrived and was consulted on the question. She wrote the same day to Fanny Noyce and mentioned it to her; and Fanny, all alive for us, instantly took up her pen and forwarded the circumstance to me except as to names, which have but lately transpired. There was but one thing for me to do. I answered Fanny's letter by the same post and pressed for the recommendation of Sanditon. Fanny had feared your having no house large enough to receive such a family. But I seem to be spinning out my story to an endless length. You see how it was all managed. I had the pleasure of hearing soon afterwards by the same simple link of connection that Sanditon had been recommended by Mrs. Darling, and that the West Indians were very much disposed to go thither. This was the state of the case when I wrote to you. But two days ago yes, the day before yesterday I heard again from Fanny Noyce, saying that she had heard from Miss Capper, who by a letter from Mrs. Darling understood that Mrs. Griffiths had expressed herself in a letter to Mrs. Darling more doubtingly on the subject of Sanditon. Am I clear? I would be anything rather than not clear."

"Oh, perfectly, perfectly. Well?"

"The reason of this hesitation was her having no connections in the place, and no means of ascertaining that she should have good accommodations on arriving there; and she was particularly careful and scrupulous on all those matters more on account of a certain Miss Lambe, a young lady probably a niece under her care than on her own account or her daughters". Miss Lambe has an immense fortune richer than all the rest and very delicate health. One sees clearly enough by all this the sort of woman Mrs. Griffiths must be: as helpless and indolent as wealth and a hot climate are apt to make us. But we are not born to equal energy. What was to be done? I had a few moments' indecision, whether to offer to write to you or to Mrs. Whitby to secure them a house; but neither pleased me. I hate to employ others when I am equal to act myself; and my conscience told me that this was an occasion which called for me. Here was a family of helpless invalids whom I might essentially serve. I sounded Susan. The same thought had occurred to her. Arthur made no difficulties. Our plan was arranged immediately, we were off yesterday morning at six, left Chichester at the same hour today and here we are."

"Excellent! Excellent!" cried Mr. parker. "Diana, you are unequalled in serving your friends and doing good to all the world. I know nobody like you. Mary, my love, is not she a wonderful creature? Well, and now, what house do you design to engage for them? What is the size of their family?"

"I do not at all know," replied his sister, "have not the least idea, never heard any particulars; but I am very sure that the largest house at Sanditon cannot be too large. They are more likely to want a second. I shall take only one, however, and that but for a week certain. Miss Heywood, I astonish you. You hardly know what to make of me. I see by your looks that you are not used to such quick measures."

The words "unaccountable officiousness!" "activity run mad!"

had just passed through Charlotte's mind, but a civil answer was easy.

"I dare say I do look surprised," said she, "because these are very great exertions, and I know what invalids both you and your sister are.

"Invalids indeed. I trust there are not three people in England who have so sad a right to that appellation! But my dear Miss Heywood, we are sent into this world to be as extensively useful as possible, and where some degree of strength of mind is given, it is not a feeble body which will excuse us or incline us to excuse ourselves. The world is pretty much divided between the weak of mind and the strong; between those who can act and those who cannot; and it is the bounden duty of the capable to let no opportunity of being useful escape them. My sister's complaints and mine are happily not often of a nature to threaten existence immediately. And as long as we can exert ourselves to be of use to others, I am convinced that the body is the better for the refreshment the mind receives in doing its duty. While I have been travelling with this object in view, I have been perfectly well."

The entrance of the children ended this little panegyric on her own disposition; and after having noticed and caressed them all, she prepared to go.

"Cannot you dine with us? Is not it possible to prevail on you to dine with us?" was then the cry. And that being absolutely negatived, it was, "And when shall we see you again? And how can we be of use to you?" And Mr. Parker warmly offered his assistance in taking the house for Mrs. Griffiths.

"I will come to you the moment I have dined," said he, "and we will go about together."

But this was immediately declined.

"No, my dear Tom, upon no account in the world shall you stir a step on any business of mine. Your ankle wants rest. I see by the position of your foot that you have used it too much already.

No, I shall go about my house-taking directly. Our dinner is not ordered till six; and by that time I hope to have completed it. It is now only half past four. As to seeing me again today, I cannot answer for it. The others will be at the hotel all the evening and delighted to see you at any time; but as soon as I get back I shall hear what Arthur has done about our own lodgings, and probably the moment dinner is over shall be out again on business relative to them, for we hope to get into some lodgings or other and be settled after breakfast tomorrow. I have not much confidence in poor Arthur's skill for lodging-taking, but he seemed to like the commission."

"I think you are doing too much," said Mr. Parker. "You will knock yourself up. You should not move again after dinner."

"No, indeed you should not, cried his wife, "for dinner is such a mere name with you all that it can do you no good. I know what your appetites are."

"My appetite is very much mended, I assure you, lately. I have been taking some bitters of my own decocting, which have done wonders. Susan never eats, I grant you; and just at present I shall want nothing. I never eat for about a week after a journey.

But as for Arthur, he is only too much disposed for food. We are often obliged to check him."

"But you have not told me anything of the other family coming to Sanditon," said Mr. Parker as he walked with her to the door of the house. "The Camberwell Seminary. Have we a good chance of them?; "Oh, certain. Quite certain. I had forgotten them for the moment. But I had a letter three days ago from my friend Mrs.

Charles Dupuis which assured me of Camberwell. Camberwell will be here to a certainty, and very soon. That good woman I do not know her name not being so wealthy and independent as Mrs. Griffiths, can travel and choose for herself. I will tell you how I got at her. Mrs. Charles Dupuis lives almost next door to a lady, who has a relation lately settled at Clapham, who actually attends the seminary and gives lessons on eloquence and belles lettres to some of the girls. I got this man a hare from one of Sidney's friends; and he recommended Sanditon. Without my appearing however Mrs. Charles Dupuis managed it all."

Chapter 10

It was not a week since Miss Diana parker had been told by her feelings that the sea air would probably, in her present state, be the death of her; and now she was at Sanditon, intending to make some stay and without appearing to have the slightest recollection of having written or felt any such thing.

It was impossible for Charlotte not to suspect a good deal of fancy in such an extraordinary state of health. Disorders and recoveries so very much out of the common way seemed more like the amusement of eager minds in want of employment than of actual afflictions and relief. The parkers were no doubt a family of imagination and quick feelings, and while the eldest brother found vent for his superfluity of sensation as a projector, the sisters were perhaps driven to dissipate theirs in the invention of odd complaints. The whole of their mental vivacity was evidently not so employed; part was laid out in a zeal for being useful. It would seem that they must either be very busy for the good of others or else extremely ill themselves.

Some natural delicacy of constitution, in fact, with an unfortunate turn for medicine, especially quack medicine, had given them an early tendency at various times to various disorders; the rest of their sufferings was from fancy, the love of distinction and the love of the wonderful. They had charitable hearts and many amiable feelings; but a spirit of restless activity and the glory of doing more than anybody else had their share in every exertion of benevolence; and there was vanity in all they did, as well as in all they endured.

Mr. and Mrs. Parker spent a great part of the evening at the hotel; but Charlotte had only two or three views of Miss Diana posting over the down after a house for this lady whom she had never seen and who had never employed her. She was not made acquainted with the others till the following day when, being removed into lodgings and all the party continuing quite well, their brother and sister and herself were entreated to drink tea with them.

They were in one of the Terrace houses; and she found them arranged for the evening in a small neat drawing room with a beautiful view of the sea if they had chosen it; but though it had been a very fair English summer day, not only was there no open window, but the sofa and the table and the establishment in general was all at the other end of the room by a brisk fire.

Miss Parker, whom, remembering the three teeth drawn in one day, Charlotte approached with a peculiar degree of respectful compassion, was not very unlike her sister in person or manner, though more thin and worn by illness and medicine, more relaxed in air and more subdued in voice. She talked, however, the whole evening as incessantly as Diana; and excepting that she sat with salts in her hand, took drops two or three times from one out of several phials already at home on the mantelpiece and made a great many odd faces and contortions, Charlotte could perceive no symptoms of illness which she, in the boldness of her own good health, would not have undertaken to cure by putting out the fire, opening the window and disposing of the drops and the salts by means of one or the other.

She had had considerable curiosity to see Mr. Arthur Parker; and having fancied him a very puny, delicate-looking young man, materially the smallest of a not very robust family, was astonished to find him quite as tall as his brother and a great deal stouter, broad made and lusty, and with no other look of an invalid than a sodden complexion.

Diana was evidently the chief of the family principal mover and actor. She had been on her feet the whole morning, on Mrs.

Griffiths' business or their own, and was still the most alert of the three.

Susan had only superintended their final removal from the hotel, bringing two heavy boxes herself, and Arthur had found the air so cold that he had merely walked from one house to the other as nimbly as he could, and boasted much of sitting by the fire till he had cooked up a very good one.

Diana, whose exercise had been too domestic to admit of calculation but who, by her own account, had not once sat down during the space of seven hours, confessed herself a little tired. She had been too successful, however, for much fatigue; for not only had she by walking and talking down a thousand difficulties at last secured a proper house at eight guineas per week for Mrs.

Griffiths; she had also opened so many treaties with cooks, housemaids, washerwomen and bathing women that Mrs.

Griffiths would have little more to do on her arrival than to wave her hand and collect them around her for choice. Her concluding effort in the cause had been a few polite lines of information to Mrs. Griffiths herself, time not allowing for the circuitous train of intelligence which had been hitherto kept up; and she was now regaling in the delight of opening the first trenches of an acquaintance with such a powerful discharge of unexpected obligation.

Mr. and Mrs. Parker and Charlotte had seen two post chaises crossing the down to the hotel as they were setting off, a joyful sight and full of speculation. The Miss parkers and Arthur had also seen something; they could distinguish from their window that there was an arrival at the hotel, but not its amount. Their visitors answered for two hack chaises. Could it be the Camberwell Seminary? No, no. Had there been a third carriage, perhaps it might; but it was very generally agreed that two hack chaises could never contain a seminary. Mr. parker was confident of another new family.

When they were all finally seated, after some removals to look at the sea and the hotel, Charlotte's place was by Arthur, who was sitting next to the fire with a degree of enjoyment which gave a good deal of merit to his civility in wishing her to take his chair.

There was nothing dubious in her manner of declining it and he sat down again with much satisfaction. She drew back her chair to have all the advantage of his person as a screen and was very thankful for every inch of back and shoulders beyond her preconceived idea. Arthur was heavy in eye as well as figure but by no means indisposed to talk; and while the other four were chiefly engaged together, he evidently felt it no penance to have a fine young woman next to him, requiring in common politeness some attention; as his brother, who felt the decided want of some motive for action, some powerful object of animation for him, observed with considerable pleasure. Such was the influence of youth and bloom that he began even to make a sort of apology for having a fire.

"We should not have had one at home," said he, "but the sea air is always damp. I am not afraid of anything so much as damp."

"I am so fortunate," said Charlotte, "as never to know whether the air is damp or dry. It has always some property that is wholesome and invigorating to me."

"I like the air too, as well as anybody can," replied Arthur. "I am very fond of standing at an open window when there is no wind. But, unluckily, a damp air does not like me. It gives me the rheumatism. You are not rheumatic, I suppose?"

"Not at all."

"That's a great blessing. But perhaps you are nervous?"

"No, I believe not. I have no idea that I am.' "I am very nervous. To say the truth, nerves are the worst part of my complaints in my opinion. My sisters think me bilious, but I doubt it."

"You are quite in the right to doubt it as long as you possibly can, I am sure."

"If I were bilious," he continued, "you know, wine would disagree with me, but it always does me good. The more wine I drink in moderation the better I am. I am always best of an evening. If you had seen me today before dinner, you would have thought me a very poor creature.

Charlotte could believe it. She kept her countenance, however, and said, "As far as I can understand what nervous complaints are, I have a great idea of the efficacy of air and exercise for them daily, regular exercise and I should recommend rather more of it to you than I suspect you are in the habit of taking."

"Oh, I am very fond of exercise myself," he replied, "and I mean to walk a great deal while I am here, if the weather is temperate."

I shall be out every morning before breakfast and take several turns upon the Terrace, and you will often see me at Trafalgar House."

"But you do not call a walk to Trafalgar House much exercise?"

Not as to mere distance, but the hill is so steep! Walking up that hill, in the middle of the day, would throw me into such a perspiration! You would see me all in a bath by the time I got there! I am very subject to perspiration, and there cannot be a surer sign of nervousness."

They were now advancing so deep in physics that Charlotte viewed the entrance of the servant with the tea things as a very fortunate interruption. It produced a great and immediate change. The young man's attentions were instantly lost. He took his own cocoa from the tray, which seemed provided with almost as many teapots as there were persons in company Miss parker drinking one sort of herb tea and Miss Diana another and turning completely to the fire, sat coddling and cooking it to his own satisfaction and toasting some slices of bread, brought up ready-prepared in the toast rack; and till it was all done, she heard nothing of his voice but the murmuring of a few broken sentences of self-approbation and success. When his toils were over, however, he moved back his chair into as gallant a line as ever, and proved that he had not been working only for himself by his earnest invitation to her to take both cocoa and toast.

She was already helped to tea which surprised him, so totally self-engrossed had he been.

"I thought I should have been in time," said he, "but cocoa rakes a great deal of boiling."

"I am much obliged to you," replied Charlotte. "But I prefer tea."

"Then I will help myself," said he. "A large dish of rather weak cocoa every evening agrees with me better than anything."

It struck her, however, as he poured out this rather weak cocoa, that it came forth in a very fine, dark-coloured stream; and at the same moment, his sisters both crying out, "Oh, Arthur, you get your cocoa stronger and stronger every evening," with Arthur's somewhat conscious reply of "Tis rather stronger than it should be tonight," convinced her that Arthur was by no means so fond of being starved as they could desire or as he felt proper himself.

He was certainly very happy to turn the conversation on dry toast and hear no more of his sisters.

"I hope you will eat some of this toast," said he. "I reckon myself a very good toaster. I never burn my toasts, I never put them too near the fire at first. And yet, you see, there is not a corner but what is well browned. I hope you like dry toast.

"With a reasonable quantity of butter spread over it, very much," said Charlotte, "but not otherwise.

"No more do I," said he, exceedingly pleased. "We think quite alike there. So far from dry toast being wholesome, I think it a very bad thing for the stomach. Without a little butter to soften it, it hurts the coats of the stomach. I am sure it does. I will have the pleasure of spreading some for you directly, and afterwards I will spread some for myself. Very bad indeed for the coats of the stomach but there is no convincing some people.

It irritates and acts like a nutmeg grater."

He could not get command of the butter, however, without a struggle; his sisters accusing him of eating a great deal too much and declaring he was not to be trusted, and he maintaining that he only ate enough to secure the coats of his stomach, and besides, he only wanted it now for Miss Heywood. Such a plea must prevail. He got the butter and spread away for her with an accuracy of judgement which at least delighted himself. But when her toast was done and he took his own in hand, Charlotte could hardly contain herself as she saw him watching his sisters while he scrupulously scraped off almost as much butter as he put on, and then seizing an odd moment for adding a great dab just before it went into his mouth.

Certainly, Mr. Arthur Parker's enjoyments in invalidism were very different from his sisters' by no means so spiritualised.

A good deal of earthy dross hung about him. Charlotte could not but suspect him of adopting that line of life principally for the indulgence of an indolent temper, and to be determined on having no disorders but such as called for warm rooms and good nourishment. In one particular, however, she soon found that he had caught something from them. "What!" said he. "Do you venture upon two dishes of strong green tea in one evening? What nerves you must have! How I envy you. Now, if I were to swallow only one such dish, what do you think its effect would be upon me?"

"Keep you awake perhaps all night," replied Charlotte, meaning to overthrow his attempts at surprise by the grandeur of her own conceptions.

"Oh, if that were all!" he exclaimed. "No. It acts on me like poison and would entirely take away the use of my right side before I had swallowed it five minutes. It sounds almost incredible, but it has happened to me so often that I cannot doubt it. The use of my right side is entirely taken away for several hours ! " "It sounds rather odd to be sure," answered Charlotte coolly, "but I dare say it would be proved to be the simplest thing in the world by those who have studied right sides and green tea scientifically and thoroughly understand all the possibilities of their action on each other."

Soon after tea, a letter was brought to Miss Diana Parker from the hotel.

"From Mrs. Charles Dupuis," said she, "some private hand,"

and having read a few lines, exclaimed aloud, "Well, this is very extraordinary! Very extraordinary indeed! That both should have the same name. Two Mrs. Griffiths! This is a letter of recommendation and introduction to me of the lady from Camberwell and her name happens to be Griffiths too."

A few more lines, however, and the colour rushed into her cheeks and with much perturbation, she added, "The oddest thing that ever was! A Miss Lambe too! A young West Indian of large fortune. But it cannot be the same. Impossible that it should be the same."

She read the letter aloud for comfort. It was merely to introduce the bearer, Mrs. Griffiths from Camberwell, and the three young ladies under her care to Miss Diana Parker's notice. Mrs.

Griffiths, being a stranger at Sanditon, was anxious for a respectable introduction; and Mrs. Charles Dupuis, therefore, at the instance of the intermediate friend, provided her with this letter, knowing that she could not do her dear Diana a greater kindness than by giving her the means of being useful. "Mrs. Griffiths' chief solicitude would be for the accommodation and comfort of one of the young ladies under her care, a Miss Lambe, a young West Indian of large fortune in delicate health."

It was very strange! Very remarkable! Very extraordinary! But they were all agreed in determining it to be impossible that there should not be two families; such a totally distinct set of people as were concerned in the reports of each made that matter quite certain. There must be two families. Impossible to be otherwise.

"Impossible" and "Impossible" were repeated over and over again with great fervour. An accidental resemblance of names and circumstances, however striking at first, involved nothing really incredible; and so it was settled.

Miss Diana herself derived an immediate advantage to counter balance her perplexity. She must put her shawl over her shoulders and be running about again. Tired as she was, she must instantly repair to the hotel to investigate the truth and offer her services.

Chapter 11

It would not do. Not all that the whole Parker race could say among themselves could produce a happier catastrophe than that the family from Surrey and the family from Camberwell were one and the same. The rich West Indians and the young ladies' seminary had all entered Sanditon in those two hack chaises. The Mrs. Griffiths who, in her friend Mrs. Darling's hands, had wavered as to coming and been unequal to the journey, was the very same Mrs. Griffiths whose plans were at the same period (under another representation) perfectly decided, and who was without fears or difficulties.

All that had the appearance of incongruity in the reports of the two might very fairly be placed to the account of the vanity, the ignorance or the blunders of the many engaged in the cause by the vigilance and caution of Miss Diana parker. Her intimate friends must be officious like herself; and the subject had supplied letters and extracts and messages enough to make everything appear what it was not.

Miss Diana probably felt a little awkward on being first obliged to admit her mistake. A long journey from Hampshire taken for nothing, a brother disappointed, an expensive house on her hands for a week must have been some of her immediate reflections; and much worse than all the rest must have been the sensation of being less clear-sighted and infallible than she had believed herself. No part of it, however, seemed to trouble her for long. There were so many to share in the shame and the blame that probably, when she had divided out their proper portions to Mrs. Darling, Miss Capper, Fanny Noyce, Mrs, Charles Dupuis and Mrs. Charles Dupuis's neighbour, there might be a mere trifle of reproach remaining for herself. At any rate, she was seen all the following morning walking about after lodgings with Mrs. Griffiths as alert as ever.

Mrs. Griffiths was a very well-behaved, genteel kind of woman, who supported herself by receiving such great girls and young ladies as wanted either masters for finishing their education or a home for beginning their displays. She had several more under her care than the three who were now come to Sanditon, but the others all happened to be absent. Of these three, and indeed of all, Miss Lambe was beyond comparison the most important and precious, as she paid in proportion to her fortune. She was about seventeen, half mulatto, chilly and tender, had a maid of her own, was to have the best room in the lodgings, and was always of the first consequence in every plan of Mrs. Griffiths.

The other girls, two Miss Beauforts, were just such young ladies as may be met with in at least one family out of three throughout the kingdom. They had tolerable complejtions, showy figures, an upright decided carriage and an assured look; they were very accomplished and very ignorant, their time being divided between such pursuits as might attract admiration, and those labours and expedients of dexterous ingenuity by which they could dress in a style much beyond what they ought to have afforded; they were some of the first in every change of fashion. And the object of all was to captivate some man of much better fortune than their own.

Mrs. Griffiths had preferred a small, retired place like Sanditon on Miss Lambe's account; and the Miss Beauforts, though naturally preferring anything to smallness and retirement, having in the course of the spring been involved in the inevitable expense of six new dresses each for a three-days visit, were constrained to be satisfied with Sanditon also till their circumstances were retrieved.

There, with the hire of a harp for one and the purchase of some drawing paper for the other and all the finery they could already command, they meant to be very economical, very elegant and very secluded; with the hope, on Miss Beaufort's side, of praise and celebrity from all who walked within the sound of her instrument, and on Miss Letitia's, of curiosity and rapture in all who came near her while she sketched; and to both, the consolation of meaning to be the most stylish girls in the place.

The particular introduction of Mrs. Griffiths to Miss Diana Parker secured them immediately an acquaintance with the Trafalgar House family and with the Denhams; and the Miss Beauforts were soon satisfied with "the circle in which they moved in Sanditon," to use a proper phrase, for everybody must now "move in a circle" to the prevalence of which rotatory motion is perhaps to be attributed the giddiness and false steps of many.

Lady Denham had other motives for calling on Mrs. Griffiths besides attention to the Parkers. In Miss Lambe, here was the very young lady, sickly and rich, whom she had been asking for; and she made the acquaintance for Sir Edward's sake and the sake of her milch asses.

How it might answer with regard to the baronet remained to be proved but, as to the animals, she soon found that all her calculations of profit would be vain. Mrs. Griffiths would not allow Miss Lambe to have the smallest sympton of a decline or any complaint which asses' milk could possibly relieve. Miss Lambe was "under the constant care of an experienced physician,"
and his prescriptions must be their rule. And except in favour of some tonic pills, which a cousin of her own had a property in, Mrs. Griffiths never deviated from the strict medicinal page.

The corner house of the Terrace was the one in which Miss Diana parker had the pleasure of settling her new friends; and considering that it commanded in front the favourite lounge of all the visitors at Sanditon, and on one side whatever might be going on at the hotel, there could not have been a more favourable spot for the seclusion of the Miss Beauforts. And accordingly, long before they had suited themselves with an instrument or with drawing paper, they had, by the frequenC of their appearance at the low windows upstairs in order to close the blinds, or open the blinds, to arrange a flower pot on the balcony, or look at nothing through a telescope, attracted many an eye upwards and made many a gazer gaze again.

A little novelty has a great effect in so small a place. The Miss Beauforts, who would have been nothing at Brighton, could not move here without notice. And even Mr. Arthur Parker, though little disposed for supernumerary exertion, always quitted the Terrace in his way to his brother's by this corner house for the sake of a glimpse of the Miss Beauforts though it was half a quarter of a mile round about and added two steps to the ascent of the hill.

Chapter 12

Charlotte had been ten days at Sanditon without seeing Sanditon House, every attempt at calling on Lady Denham having been defeated by meeting with her beforehand. But now it was to be more resolutely undertaken, at a more early hour, that nothing might be neglected of attention to Lady Denham or amusement to Charlotte.

"And if you should find a favourable opening, my love," said Mr. Parker, who did not mean to go with them, "I think you had better mention the poor Mullins's situation and sound her Ladyship as to a subscription for them. I am not fond of charitable subscriptions in a place of this kind it is a sort of tax upon all that come. Yet as their distress is very great and I almost promised the poor woman yesterday to get something done for her, I believe we must set a subscription on foot, and, therefore, the sooner the better; and Lady Denham's name at the head of the list will be a very necessary beginning. You will not dislike speaking to her about it, Mary?"

'-I will do whatever you wish me," replied his wife, "but you would do it so much better yourself. I shall not know what to say."

"My dear Mary," he cried. "It is impossible you can be really at a loss. Nothing can be more simple. You have only to state the present afflicted situation of the family, their earnest application to me, and my being willing to promote a little subscription for their relief, provided it meet with her approbation."

'-The easiest thing in the world," cried Miss Diana Parker, who happened to be calling on them at the moment. All said and done in less time than you have been talking of it now. And while you are on the subject of subscriptions, Mary, I will thank you to mention a very melancholy case to Lady Denham which has been represented to me in the most affecting terms. There is a poor woman in Worcestershire, whom some friends of mine are exceedingly interested about, and I have undertaken to collect whatever I can for her. If you would mention the circumstance to Lady Denham! Lady Denham can give, if she is properly attacked. And I look upon her to be the sort of person who, when once she is prevailed on to undraw her purse, would as readily give ten guineas as five. And therefore, if you find her in a giving mood, you might as well speak in favour of another charity which I and a few more have very much at heart the establishment of a Charitable Repository at Burton on Trent.

And then there is the family of the poor man who was hung last assizes at York, though we really have raised the sum we wanted for putting them all out, yet if you can get a guinea from her on their behalf, it may as well be done."

"My dear Diana!" exclaimed Mrs. parker, "I could no more mention these things to Lady Denham than I could fly."

"Where's the difficulty? I wish I could go with you myself.

But in five minutes I must be at Mrs. Griffiths to encourage Miss Lambe in taking her first dip. She is so frightened, poor thing, that I promised to come and keep up her spirits and go in the machine with her if she wished it. And as soon as that is over, I must hurry home, for Susan is to have leeches at one o clock which will be a three hours' business. Therefore I really have not a moment to spare. Besides that, between ourselves, I ought to be in bed myself at this present time for I am hardly able to stand; and when the leeches have done, I dare say we shall both go to our rooms for the rest of the day."

"-I am sorry to hear it, indeed. But if this is the case I hope Arthur will come to us."

"-If Arthur takes my advice, he will go to bed too, for if he stays up by himself he will certainly eat and drink more than he ought.

But you see, Mary, how impossible it is for me to go with you to Lady Denham's."

Upon second thoughts, Mary," said her husband. "I will not trouble you to speak about the Mullinses. I will take an opportunity of seeing Lady Denham myself. I know how little it suits you to be pressing matters upon a mind at all unwilling."

His application thus withdrawn, his sister could say no more in support of hers, which was his object, as he felt all their impropriety and all the certainty of their ill effect upon his own better claim. Mrs. Parker was delighted at this release and set off very happy with her friend and her little girl on this walk to Sanditon House.

It was a close, misty morning and, when they reached the brow of the hill, they could not for some time make out what sort of carriage it was which they saw coming up. It appeared at different moments to be everything from a gig to a phaeton, from one horse to four; and just as they were concluding in favour of a tandem, little Mary's young eyes distinguished the coachman and she eagerly called out, "It is Uncle Sidney, Mama, it is indeed."

And so it proved. Mr. Sidney parker, driving his servant in a very neat carriage, was soon opposite to them, and they all sropped for a few minutes. The manners of the Parkers were always pleasant among themselves; and it was a very friendly meeting between Sidney and his sister-in-law, who was most kindly taking it for granted that he was on his way to Trafalgar House.

This he declined, however. He was "just come from Eastbourne proposing to spend two or three days, as it might happen, at Sanditon" but the hotel must be his quarters. He was expecting to be joined there by a friend or two.

The rest was common enquiries and remarks, with kind notice of little Mary, and a very well-bred bow and proper address to Miss Heywood on her being named to him. And they parted to meet again within a few hours. Sidney parker was about seven or eight and twenty, very good-looking, with a decided air of ease and fashion and a lively countenance.

This adventure afforded agreeable discussion for some time.

Mrs. Parker entered into all her husband's joy on the occasion and exulted in the credit which Sidney's arrival would give to the place.

The road to Sanditon House was a broad, handsome, planted approach between fields, leading at the end of a quarter of a mile through second gates into grounds which, though not extensive, had all the beauty and respectability which an abundance of very fine timber could give. These entrance gates were so much in a corner of the grounds or paddock, so near to one of its boundaries, that an outside fence was at first almost pressing on the road, till an angle here and a curve there threw them to a better distance.

The fence was a proper park paling in excellent condition, with clusters of fine elms or rows of old thorns following its line almost everywhere. Almost must be stipulated, for there were vacant spaces, and through one of these, Charlotte, as soon as they entered the enclosure, caught a glimpse over the pales of something white and womanish in the field on the other side. It was something which immediately brought Miss Brereton into her head; and stepping to the pales, she saw indeedand very decidedly, in spite of the mist Miss Brereton seated not far before her at the foot of the bank which sloped down from the outside of the paling and which a narrow path seemed to skirt along Miss Brereton seated, apparently very composedly, and Sir Edward Denham by her side.

They were sitting so near each other and appeared so closely engaged in gentle conversation that Charlotte instantly felt she had nothing to do but to step back again and say not a word. privacy was certainly their object. lt could not but strike her rather unfavourably with regard to Clara; but hers was a situation which must not be judged with severity. She was glad to perceive that nothing had been discerned by Mrs. parker. If Charlotte had not been considerably the taller of the two, Miss Brereton's white ribbons might not have fallen within the ken of her more observant eyes.

Among other points of moralising reflection which the sight of this tete-a-tete produced, Charlotte could not but think of the extreme difficulty which secret lovers must have in finding a proper spot for their stolen interviews. Here perhaps they had thought themselves so perfectly secure from observation the whole field open before them; a steep bank and pales never crossed by the foot of man at their back, and a great thickness of air to aid them as well! Yet here she had seen them. They were really ill-used.

The house was large and handsome. Two servants appeared to admit them and everything had a suitable air of property and order, Lady Denham valued herself upon her liberal establishment and had great enjoyment in the order and importance of her style of living. They were shown into the usual sitting room, well proportioned and well furnished, though it was furniture rather originally good and extremely well kept than new or showy. And as Lady Denham was not there, Charlotte had leisure to look about her and to be told by Mrs. Parker that the whole-length portrait of a stately gentleman which, placed over the mantelpiece, caught the eye immediately, was the picture of Sir Henry Denham; and that one among many miniatures in another part of the room, little conspicuous, represented Mr. Hollis. poor Mr. Hollis! lt was impossible not to feel him hardly used: to be obliged to stand back in his own house and see the best place by the fire constantly occupied by Sir H. D.

Plan of A Novel

Scene to be in the Country, Heroine the Daughter of a Clergyman, one who after having lived much in the World had retired from it and settled in a Curacy, with a very small fortune of his own. -- He, the most excellent Man that can be imagined, perfect in Character, Temper, and Manners -- without the smallest drawback or peculiarity to prevent his being the most delightful companion to his Daughter from one year's end to the other. -- Heroine a faultless Character herself, -- perfectly good, with much tenderness and sentiment, and not the least Wit -- very highly accomplished, understanding modern Languages and (generally speaking) everything that the most accomplished young Women learn, but particularly excelling in Music -- her favorite pursuit -- and playing equally well on the PianoForte and Harp -- and singing in the first stile. Her Person quite beautiful -- dark eyes and plump cheeks. -- Book to open with the description of Father and Daughter -- who are to converse in long speeches, elegant Language -- and a tone of high serious sentiment. -- The Father to be induced, at his Daughter's earnest request, to relate to her the past events of his Life. This Narrative will reach through the greatest part of the first volume -- as besides all the circumstances of his attachment to her Mother and their Marriage, it will comprehend his going to sea as Chaplain to a distinguished naval character about the Court, his going afterwards to Court himself, which introduced him to a great variety of Characters and involved him in many interesting situations, concluding with his opinions on the Benefits to result from Tithes being done away, and his having buried his own Mother (Heroine's lamented Grandmother) in consequence of the High Priest of the Parish in which she died refusing to pay her Remains the respect due to them. The Father to be of a very literary turn, an Enthusiast in Literature, nobody's Enemy but his own -- at the same time most zealous in discharge of his Pastoral Duties, the model of an exemplary Parish Priest. -- The heroine's friendship to be sought after by a young woman in the same Neighborhood, of Talents and Shrewdness, with light eyes and a fair skin, but having a considerable degree of Wit, Heroine shall shrink from the acquaintance.

From this outset, the Story will proceed, and contain a striking variety of adventures. Heroine and her Father never above a fortnight together in one place, he being driven from his Curacy by the vile arts of some totally unprincipled and heart-less young Man, desperately in love with the Heroine, and pursuing her with unrelenting passion. -- No sooner settled in one Country of Europe than they are necessitated to quit it and retire to another -- always making new acquaintance, and always obliged to leave them. -- This will of course exhibit a wide variety of Characters -- but there will be no mixture; the scene will be forever shifting from one Set of People to another -- but All the Good will be unexceptionable in every respect -- and there will be no foibles or weaknesses but with the Wicked, who will be completely depraved and infamous, hardly a resemblance of humanity left in them. -- Early in her career, in the progress of her first removals, Heroine must meet with the Hero -- all perfection of course -- and only prevented from paying his addresses to her by some excess of refinement. -- Wherever she goes, somebody falls in love with her, and she receives repeated offers of Marriage -- which she refers wholly to her Father, exceedingly angry that he should not be first applied to. -- Often carried away by the anti-hero, but rescued either by her Father or by the Hero -- often reduced to support herself and her Father by her Talents and work for her Bread; continually cheated and defrauded of her hire, worn down to a Skeleton, and now and then starved to death. -- At last, hunted out of civilized Society, denied the poor Shelter of the humblest Cottage, they are compelled to retreat into Kamschatka where the poor Father, quite worn down, finding his end approaching, throws himself on the Ground, and after 4 or 5 hours of tender advice and parental Admonition to his miserable Child, expires in a fine burst of Literary Enthusiasm, intermingled with Invectives against holders of Tithes. -- Heroine inconsolable for some time -- but afterwards crawls back towards her former Country -- having at least 20 narrow escapes from falling into the hands of the Anti-hero -- and at last in the very nick of time, turning a corner to avoid him, runs into the arms of the Hero himself, who having just shaken off the scruples which fettered him before, was at the very moment setting off in pursuit of her. -- The Tenderest and completest éclaircissement takes place, and they are happily united. -- Throughout the whole work, Heroine to be in the most elegant Society and living in high style. The name of the work not to be Emma, but of the same sort as *Sense and Sensibility* and *Pride and Prejudice*.

Sir Charles Grandison

Dramatis Personae

Men

> Sir Charles Grandison
> Sir Hargrave Pollexfen
> Lord L.
> Lord G.
> Mr Reeves
> Mr Selby
> Mr Beacham

Women

> Milliner
> Sally
> Mrs Selby
> Miss Selby
> Miss Ane Selby
> Bridget
> Jenny
> Harriot Byron
> Miss Jervois
> Lady L.
> Miss Grandison
> Mrs Reeves
> Mrs Awberry
> Miss Awberry
> Miss Sally

Act The First

Scene the First
Mr. Reeve's House. Enter Mrs. Reeves & the Milliner at different doors.

MRS. R.:
So, you have brought the dresses, have you?

MIL.:

I have brought the young Lady's dress, & Mistress says you may depend upon having yours this Evening.

MRS. R.:

Well, tell her to be sure & bring it. But let us see the dress that is come.

She takes the Bandbox out of the Milliner's hands.

MIL.:

Have you other commands Madam?

MRS. R.:

No, you may go. Miss Byron & I will come to morrow & pay you.

Exit Milliner.

MRS. R.:

Come, I will see whether she has made it right. Oh! but here is Miss Byron coming. I think it is but fair to let her see it first.

Enter Miss Byron with a work bag in her harm.

MRS. R.:

Here my dear, here is your dress come. I hope it will fit, for if it does not she will hardly have time to alter it.

MISS B.:

We will take it up stairs if you please & look at it, for Mr. Reeves is coming, & we shall have some of his Raillery.

Exeunt in an hurry.

Enter Mr. Reeves.

MR. R.:

So, for once in a way I have got the coast clear of Dresses & Band boxes; & I hope my wife & Miss Byron will continue to keep their Milliner in their own rooms, or any where so as they are not in my way. Why, if I had not had a little spirit the other day I should have had them in my own study.

Enter Sally.

SALLY.:

Do you know where Miss Byron is Sir? -

MR. R.:

She is up in her own room I beleive. -

Sally curtseys & goes off. -

MR. R.:

Sally, Sally. -

Re-enter Sally.

SALLY.:

Sir -

MR. R.:

Tell Thomas to bring out the Bay horse.

SALLY.:

Yes Sir.

Exit Sally.

MR. R.
Well, I must go & get on my boots - & by that time the horse will be out. -

Scene 2d
Mr. Reeves' house.
Mr. Reeves entering in a great hurry at one door, & running out at the other, calls behind the Scenes. -

MR. R.:
John, run all over London & see if you can find the Chairman or Chair that took Miss Byron. You know what number it was. - Thomas, run for Dr. Smith directly.
He comes in again in great agitation.

Enter Bridget.

BRID.:
Mistress is rather better Sir, & begs you will send for Dr. Smith.
MR. R.:
I have, I have.

Exit Bridget, exit Mr. Reeves at different doors. - calls behind the Scenes -

MR. R.:
William, run to Mr. Greville's Lodgings & if he is at home - Stop William, Come in here: -

(He comes in again, takes out his writing box & writes a note in great haste.)

MR. R.:
Here William is a note. Carry it to Mr. Greville's -

Exit William.
Enter Thomas

THOS.:
Dr. Smith, Sir.
MR. R.:
Shew him up stairs to your Mistress.

Enter John.

JOHN.:
I cannot find either the Chair or the Chairman Sir and Wilson is not come within Sir.

MR. R.:
Well, she must be carried out into the country I think. - You go to Paddington & tell Thomas to go to Hampstead, & see if you can find her, & I will go to Clapham.

Exit Mr. Reeves.

Act The Second

Scene 1st
Paddington -. The curtain draws up & discovers Miss Byron, Mrs. Awberry.

MRS. A.:
But my dear young Lady, think what a large fortune Sir Hargrave has got, & he intends you nothing but marriage -

MISS. B.:
Oh! Mrs. Awberry, do you think I can marry a man whom I always disliked & now I hate? Is this not your House? Cannot you favour my Escape? -

MRS. A.:
My dear Madam that is impossible without detection. You know Sir Hargrave is here & there & everywhere.

MISS. B.:
My dear Mrs. Awberry you shall have all the money in this purse if you will release me. -

Sir Hargrave burst into the room.

SIR H.:
Mrs. Awberry I see you are not to be trusted with her, you are so tender-hearted. And you Madam! -

He snatches the purse out of her hand & flings it on the ground. He goes to the door & calls

SIR H.:

Mr - We are ready. -

Enter a Clergyman & his Clerk.

SIR H.:
Miss Awberry you will be the Bridemaid if you please. -

He takes hold of Miss Byron's hand.

SIR H.:
Now Madam, all your purses will not save you. -

The Clergyman takes a book out of his pocket. Miss Byron screams & faints away. Miss Sally Awberry runs in.

MISS A.:
Sally, Sally, bring a glass of water directly.

Mrs. Awberry takes out her Salts & applies them to Miss Byron's nose.

SIR H.:
I wish Women were not quite so delicate, with all their faints and fits! -

Miss Byron revives. Miss Sally returns with a glass of water & offers it to Miss Byron who drinks some.

MRS A.:
What a long time you have been Child! If she faints again I shall send your Sister. -
SALLY. (aside):
I am glad of it. -
SIR H.:
Come Sir, we will try again. -

Takes hold of Miss Byron's hand, Miss Awberry goes behind her.

CLERGN: reads.
Dearly beloved -

She dashes the book out of his hand. -

CLERGN: picking it up again -
Oh! my poor book!
SIR H.:

Begin again Sir, if you please. You shall be well paid for your trouble.

CLERGN: reading again.

Dearly Beloved -

Miss Byron snatches the book out of his hand & flings it into the fire, exclaiming

MISS. B.:

Burn, quick, quick. -

The clergn runs to the fire & cries out

CLERGN:

Oh! Sir Hargrave you must buy me another. -

SIR H.:

I will Sir, & twenty more if you will do the business. - Is the book burnt? -

MRS. A.:

Yes, Sir - & we cannot lend you one in its place, for we have lost the key of the closet where we keep our Prayerbooks.

SIR H.:

Well Sir, I beleive we must put it off for the present. And if we are not married in this house we shall be in mine in the Forest.

CLERGN:

Then I may go Sir I suppose. Remember the Prayer book. -

SIR H.:

Yes Sir.

Exit Clergyman & his Clerk.

SIR H.:

I shall be very much obliged to you Mrs. A. if you & the young Ladies will go out of the room for an instant. I will see if I cannot reason with this perverse girl. -

MRS. A.:

Here Deb & Sal, come out.

Exeunt Mrs e Miss A's.

MISS. B.:

Oh! do not leave me alone with him, let me go out too.

She runs to the door. Sir H. follows her. She gets half way through the door, & he in shutting it squeezes her. She screams & faints. He carries her away in his arms to a Chair, & rings the bell violently.

Enter Mrs. A. & her daughters

SIR H.:
Bring some water directly.

Both the daughters go out. Miss Byron revives, & exclaims

MISS. B.:
So, I hope you have killed me at last.

Re-enter Miss Awberry with the water. Sir Hargrave takes the glass & gives it to Miss B.

MISS. B.:
No I thank you. I do not want anything that can give me life.
SIR H.
Well Miss Awberry you had better get out the Cloak. It is four o'clock & she may as well die in my house as in yours.
MRS. A.:
Shall I order the Chariot Sir? -
SIR H.:
If you please Ma'am.

Miss A. takes a long Cloak out of a Closet and attempts to put it round Miss B. - Miss B. struggles.

SIR H.:
I will put on Miss Awberry if she will not let you.

He puts it on.

SIR H.:
Will you help me lead her down stairs Miss Awberry?
MISS A.:
Yes Sir.

They both take hold of Miss B. - Enter Sally Awberry.

SALLY.:
Can I be of any service Sir? -
SIR H.:
You may hold the Candle.

Sally takes the Candle. Exeunt. –

Act The Third

Scene 1
Colnebrook -

Enter Miss Grandison & Miss Byron.

MISS. B.:
And where is this brother of yours to whom I am so much andebted.

MISS G.:
Safe in St. James Square I hope. - But why my dear will you continue to think yourself so much endebted to him, when he only did his duty?

MISS. B.:
But what must he have thought of me in such a dress? - Oh! these odious Masquerades!

MISS G.:
La! my dear, what does it signify what he thinks? He will understand it all in time. Come if your stomach pains you, you had better go to bed again.

MISS. B.:
No, it does not pain me at all. But how kind it was in my cousin Reeves to come and see me.

MISS G.:
Yes he is a very nice Man. I like him very much. He disputes charmingly, - I thought he would have got the better of me. - Well but my dear Harriet, you have had a letter today. How does my Grandmama Shirley do, & my Uncle & Aunt Selby and my Cousins Lucy & Nancy?

MISS. B.:
They are all very well I thank you, & my Grandmama thinks herself under the greatest obligation to Sir Charles for being both her & his Harriet's Deliverer, for it he had not rescued me, she would have died of a broken hearth. -

MISS G.:
Well really I am very glad he saved you for both your sakes. My brother is a charming Man. I always catch him doing some good action. We all wish him to be married but he has no time for Love. - At least he appears to have none. For he is constantly going about from one place to another. But what for, we cannot tell. And we have such a high respect for him that we never interfere in his affairs. - I will return in a minute. I am going to fetch my work bag.

Exit Miss G. -

MISS. B.:

What an odd Brother is this! If he is so fond of them, why should he wish them not to know his affairs? -

Re-enter Miss G.

MISS G.:

What is the matter Harriet? What makes you so dull Child? - I shall take care not to leave you by yourself again in an hurry, if on my return I am to find these gloomy fits have taken hold of you. Come, I will play you your favourite tune Laure & Lenze.

MISS. B.:

I was thinking of Sir Hargrave Pollexfen. But be so good as to play my tune.

MISS G.:

I will directly.

She goes to the Harpsichord & plays - After she has done playing she comes to Miss B. & says

MISS G.:

Come, it is time for you to go to bed. It is 4 o'clock & you have been up ever since 12.

Exeunt.

Scene 2
Curtain draws up & discovers Miss G. reading in the Library.

MISS G.:

Well I think this book would suit Harriet. But here is Sir Charles come home I beleive. I will go & see. Oh! here he is. -

Enter Sir Charles. She goes to him. He takes hold of her hand.

SIR C.:

No more colds I hope my dear Charlotte - but above all, how does our lovely Charge do?

MISS G.:

Oh! Much better. She got up at 12, & I have but just sent her to bed.

SIR C.:

When do you expect Lord & Lady L.? -

MISS G.:

This Evening, about six or seven o'clock.

SIR C.:

Indeed! I am very glad of it.

Enter Jenny.

JEN.:
Miss Byron would be glad to speak with you Ma'am.
MISS G.:
Very well, I will come to her.
SIR C.:
How is your Cold Jenny?
JEN.:
Quite well I thank you Sir.

Curtsies & exit.

MISS G.:
You will excuse me for a minute Sir Charles. I must obey my summons.

Exit.

SIR C.:
Certainly. Well I must go & speak to Frederic.

Exit. -

Scene 3
Curtain draws up & discovers Lord & Lady L. & Sir Charles & Miss G. at Tea.
-

SIR C.:
So my Lord, you have heard of our new Sister?
LORD L.:
Yes Sir Charles, and Miss G. by her description of her, has made me long to see her. -
MISS G.:
Frederic. - Take this to Sir Charles. - (holding some Tea.)
SIR C.:
I hope you will not be disappointed when you see her. - I might say We, for I have hardly seen her yet.
MISS G.:
I hope you do not think of me a flatterer Sir Charles.
SIR C.:
Certainly not my dear Charlotte.
LADY L.:
I assure you Charlotte can flatter sometimes.
MISS G.:

Oh! For shame Caroline. I thought you knew better then to tell tales. Lord L. will you have any more tea?

LORD L.:

No I thank you Charlotte.

LADY L.:

But Charlotte how do we come by our new Sister? I have not heard that yet.

MISS G.:

Well, we will go & take a walk in the Garden & talk about it. Frederic you may take away. Come Caroline make haste, or the fit will be off. - Gentlemen, will you accompany us? -

SIR C.:

Lord L. will you?

LORD L:

Certainly.

SIR C:

Yes, we will go Charlotte. -

MISS G.:

Come, make haste the fit is almost off.

Exeunt.

Act The Fourth

Scene 1

Colnebrook. Curtain draws up & discovers Sir C. & Miss G., Lord L. & MISS. B.:

MISS G.:

What an impudent fellow Lord G., is to make you wait so Sir Charles. - Oh! he is a poor creature.

SIR C.:

Have patience my dear Charlotte. Something most likely has detained him.

MISS G.:

Indeed Sir Charles, you are too forgiving. If he were to serve to me so, he would not get into favour for some time. - What say you Harriot? -

MISS. B.:

Indeed Miss G. you are too severe. - Besides, as Sir Charles says, something may detain him; & it is a different thing making a Lady wait on a Gentleman. But here ought to be an end of your severity, for the object of it I believe is come. I hear him in the Hall.

Enter Lord G.

LORD G.:

I am afraid I have been making you wait Gentlemen.

MISS G.:

Well, you need not be afraid any longer, for you certainly have.

SIR C.:

Fye Charlotte! - I do not think that was civillest thing in the world to say.

LORD G.:

I hope I have not offended you Madam.

MISS G.:

Yes you have, for making my dear brother wait.

SIR C.:

I will not be bribed into liking your wit Charlotte. - But where is Caroline all this while? -

MISS G.:

She is gone out in her Chariot with Emily - but I wonder Sir Charles you did not enquire after your favourite Sister before.

LORD L.:

I am sure Miss G. you cannot reproach your brother with partiality. Bur Sir Charles is it not time for us to go out riding? - If it is not, I am sure Miss G. might have spared her severity on Lord G.

SIR C.:

I assure you Lord L. that I had not forgot it, but I think it is too late to go out now. It is 3 o'clock. Now Charlotte hold your tongue. I am sure some raillery is coming out.

He rings the bell.

MISS G.:

I will not hold my tongue Sir Charles.

SIR C.:

Then Charlotte if you speak, do not let us have any severity.

MISS G.:

Very well, I will be good. Harriot, what is the matter, Child? You look languid. I will ring the bell for some Broth for you.

SIR C.:

Spare yourself that trouble my dear Charlotte, I have just rung it.

Enter Frederic

SIR C.:

Bring some sandwiches & a bason of broth Frederic.

Exit Frederic.

MISS G.:
Harriot, should you like your broth up in your own room better? -
MISS. B.:
If you please.
MISS G.:
Well, we will take it up with us.

Enter Frederic with the Sandwiches & the Broth. He sets it down upon the Table. Exit Fred. - Miss G. takes the broth.

MISS G.:
Come Harriot. -

Exit Miss B. & Miss G.
Sir C. hands the Sandwiches.

SIR C.:
How long Caroline has been gone! I hope no more Sir Hargrave Pollexfens have run away with her & Emily. -

Enter Lady L. Miss G. & Miss J. Lord L. goes to meet her, takes her hand & leads her to a Sopha.

MISS G.:
Lord! What a Loving Couple they are.
SIR C.:
Charlotte, hold your tongue.
LORD L.:
And where have you been to my dear Caroline?
LADY L.:
Only shopping. But Charlotte where is Miss B.?
MISS G.:
Very safe in her own room. I always send her away when she gapes.
LADY L.:
Poor Creature! I hope she does not gape too often. But seriously Charlotte, is she worse or better? -
MISS G.:
Law! Lady L. you are so afraid I shall not take care of her. - Why, she is just as she is always is - languid at 3 o'clock. I beleive it is because Lord G. always comes about at that time; & she is so sorry to see her poor Charlotte

plagued so! -

MISS JERVOIS.:

Dear Miss G. who plagues you? I am sure Lord G. does not.

MISS G.:

Emily you do not know anything of the matter. You must hold your tongue till it is your turn to be called upon. -

MISS J.:

Well Miss G. I think it is you who teaze him, but he will certainly get the better of you at last. He did once you know. And I do not know what you mean by its being my turn to be called upon.

MISS G.:

Why, when it is your turn to be married. But you had better not get on Lord G.'s side; you will be worsted certainly. But come is not it time to dress? (looks at her watch) Dear me! It is but four.

LORD L.:

You need not say "But" Charlotte, for you know we are to dine at 1/2 after 4, to day.

MISS G.:

Indeed my Lord, my Lady did not tell me so. Well, I will pardon her this time. Come then Let us go, if it is time.

Exeunt Ladies.

LORD L.:

What an odd girl is Charlotte. But you must not despair Lord G. I beleive she likes you tho' she wont own it. I hope Miss Byron when she is recovered will have a little influence over her.

SIR C.:

Indeed I hope so too. Miss Byron is a charming young woman. I think from what I have seen of her, her mind is a complete as her person. She is the happy medium between Gravity & over liveliness. She is lively or grave as the occasion requires.

LORD G.:

Indeed she is a delightful young woman, & only Miss G. can equal her. I do not mean any offence to Lady L.

LORD L.:

Indeed my Lord I do not take it as such. Caroline is grave, Charlotte is lively, I am fond of gravity, you most likely are fond of Loveliness.

Enter a Footman

FOOTMAN.:

Dinner is on Table my Lord. -

LORD L.:

Very well.

Exit Footman
Enter Lady L. Miss G. Miss B & Miss J.

LORD L.:
Dinner is upon Table my dear Caroline.
LADY L.:
Indeed. Come Harriet & all of you. -

Exeunt.

Act The Fifth

Scene 1
Library at Colnebrook. Sir Charles & Mr. Selby.

MR. S.:
But my dear Sir Charles my neice is but 18. I never will allow her to marry till she is 22. I shall take her back into Northamptonshire if you have done nothing but put such notions into the girl's head. I had no notion of my Harriet's coming to this. And besides Sir C. I never will allow her to marry you till Lady Clementina della Porretta is married. -

SIR C.:
Mr. Selby that has been my objection for some time to making my proposal to Miss B. But yesterday I received some Letters from Italy in which they have great hopes of Lady Clementina's being soon persuaded to marry. She wishes me in the same letter to set her the example by marrying an English woman. I admire Miss Byron very much, but I will never marry her against your consent. And if you had not told me she was 18, I should have thought her quite as much as 22. I do not mean by her looks but by her prudence.

MR. S.:
Upon my word you are a fine fellow, you have done away all my objections, & if you can get Harriot's consent you have mine. I hope she will not be nice, for if she do not get a husband now, she never may for she has refused all the young Gentry of our Neighbourhood. And as to her fortune I will tell you plainly she has no more than 14,000£.

SIR C.:
As the her fortune it is no object to me. Miss Byron herself is a Jewel of inestimable value. Her understanding more than makes up for want of fortune. And now if we can bring Lord G. & my Sister Charlotte together we

shall have a double wedding. But I am afraid Charlotte is too lively for matrimony.

MR. S.:

Oh! Yes, your sister is a fine girl, only she is too nice about an husband. Adsheart! I hope you wo'nt have such a plague with my Harriot, as I had with my Dame Selby. Well, but it is three o'clock. I will go & break it to her. Sir Charles, you may come & stay at the door till you are admitted, you know.

Exeunt. -

Scene 2
Drawing room. Lady L. Miss G. Miss B. & Miss J.

MISS G.:

There is something monstrous frightful to be sure my dear Harriot in marrying a man that one likes.

LADY L.:

My dear Charlotte, you overpower Harriot with your Raillery. - I dare say you will feel the same fright when you marry Lord G. -

MISS G.:

I will tell you Lady L. - To tell you a secret I am not likely to marry Lord G. - for I want to be married at home, & my brother will not consent to it.

MISS J.:

Oh! fye! Miss Grandison, I wonder how you could think of it.

MISS. B.:

Indeed Charlotte, I am of Emily's opinion. Are not you Lady L.?

LADY L.:

Certainly. And I know my brother will let as few people be by at the Ceremony as possible.

MISS G.:

I see you are all joined in concert against me; but before I give up, I will take the liberty to chuse how many people I like to be by. -

LADY L.:

I am sure Harriot will not object to that. Shall you Harriot? -

MISS. B.:

Oh! not at all. Indeed I wish myself to have but few people by. Lord Bless me! I do beleive here are my Aunt & Cousins come.

MISS G.:

I suppose Mrs. Reeves has brought her Marmouset with her.

Enter Mr. & Mrs. Reeves, Mrs. Selby, Lucy & Nancy. -

MISS BYRON: *rising & meeting Mrs. Selby.*

Oh! how do you do, my dear Aunt? - How does my Grandmama do ? -

MRS. S.:

She is pretty well my Love, & she would have come, but she thought the Journey too long for her to undertake.

MISS. B.:

Lucy e Nancy are you quite rid of your colds? And Mrs. Reeves! - I did not expect this favour. - Let me introduce you all to my friends. -

She introduces them.

MISS G.:

Mrs. Reeves, have you not brought your Baby? -

MRS. R.:

No she would not take that liberty. I wanted her to do it, because I knew you would excuse it. Miss Byron, where are the Bridegrooms? -

LADY L.:

I will go & call them, & my Lord. -

Exit Lady L.

MISS. B.:

Lucy, were the roads very good? -

LUCY.:

Indeed they were very good.

MR. R.:

Yes, our ponies went on fast enough.

MISS G.:

Did you ride Sir?

MR. R.:

No Ma'am, we came in our phaeton, & the Selbys in their Coach. -

Enter Lady L. - with the 4 Gentlemen. She introduces them.

MR. S.:

Mrs. Selby, here is the Bridegroom of your Harriot. Adsheart! we shall have a double marriage, as sure as two - & two - make four. And here is the other Bridegroom.

(pointing to Lord G.)

MISS G.:

Yes, this is my Man sure enough. I wish, I had a better one to shew you. But he is better than he was.

SIR C.:

Fye! Charlotte, I am sure you have nothing to complain of in Lord G. And if you will make a good wife, I will answer for it he will a Husband. - And I hope you will be as happy, as I promise myself Miss Byron & I shall be. - And I hope she will have no reason to lament having chosen me for Husband. -

The Curtain Falls.

Juvenilia — Volume the First

Frederic & Elfrida

To Miss Lloyd

MY DEAR MARTHA

As a small testimony of the gratitude I feel for your late generosity to me in finishing my muslin Cloak, I beg leave to offer you this little production of your sincere Freind

THE AUTHOR

Chapter 1

THE Uncle of Elfrida was the Father of Frederic; in other words, they were first cousins by the Father's side.

Being both born in one day & both brought up at one school, it was not wonderfull that they should look on each other with something more than bare politeness. They loved with mutual sincerity, but were both determined not to transgress the rules of Propriety by owning their attachment, either to the object beloved, or to any one else.

They were exceedingly handsome and so much alike, that it was not every one who knew them apart. Nay, even their most intimate freinds had nothing to distinguish them by, but the shape of the face, the colour of the Eye, the length of the Nose, & the difference of the complexion.

Elfrida had an intimate freind to whom, being on a visit to an Aunt, she wrote the following Letter.

TO MISS DRUMMOND

DEAR CHARLOTTE

I should be obliged to you, if you would buy me, during your stay with Mrs. Williamson, a new & fashionable Bonnet, to suit the complexion of your

E. FALKNOR

Charlotte, whose character was a willingness to oblige every one, when she returned into the Country, brought her Freind the wished-for Bonnet, & so ended this little adventure, much to the satisfaction of all parties.

On her return to Crankhumdunberry (of which sweet village her father was Rector), Charlotte was received with the greatest Joy by Frederic &

Elfrida, who, after pressing her alternately to their Bosoms, proposed to her to take a walk in a Grove of Poplars which led from the Parsonage to a verdant Lawn enamelled with a variety of variegated flowers & watered by a purling Stream, brought from the Valley of Tempé by a passage under ground.

In this Grove they had scarcely remained above 9 hours, when they were suddenly agreeably surprized by hearing a most delightfull voice warble the following stanza.

SONG

That Damon was in love with me
   I once thought & beleiv'd
But now that he is not I see,
   I fear I was deceiv'd.

No sooner were the lines finished than they beheld by a turning in the Grove 2 elegant young women leaning on each other's arm, who immediately on perceiving them, took a different path & disappeared from their sight.

Chapter 2

As Elfrida & her companions had seen enough of them to know that they were neither the 2 Miss Greens, nor Mrs. Jackson and her Daughter, they could not help expressing their surprise at their appearance; till at length recollecting, that a new family had lately taken a House not far from the Grove, they hastened home, determined to lose no no time in forming an acquaintance with 2 such amiable & worthy Girls, of which family they rightly imagined them to be a part.

Agreable to such a determination, they went that very evening to pay their respects to Mrs. Fitzroy & her two Daughters. On being shewn into an elegant dressing room, ornamented with festoons of artificial flowers, they were struck with the engaging Exterior & beautifull outside of Jezalinda, the eldest of the young Ladies; but e'er they had been many minutes seated, the Wit & Charms which shone resplendent in the conversation of the amiable Rebecca enchanted them so much, that they all with one accord jumped up and exclaimed:

"Lovely & too charming Fair one, notwithstanding your forbidding Squint, your greasy tresses & your swelling Back, which are more frightfull than imagination can paint or pen describe, I cannot refrain from expressing my raptures, at the engaging Qualities of your Mind, which so amply atone for the Horror with which your first appearance must ever inspire the unwary visitor."

"Your sentiments so nobly expressed on the different excellencies of Indian & English Muslins, & the judicious preference you give the former, have excited in me an admiration of which I can alone give an adequate idea, by assuring you it is nearly equal to what I feel for myself."

Then making a profound Curtesy to the amiable & abashed Rebecca, they left the room & hurried home.

From this period, the intimacy between the Families of Fitzroy, Drummond, and Falknor daily increased, till at length it grew to such a pitch, that they did not scruple to kick one another out of the window on the slightest provocation.

During this happy state of Harmony, the eldest Miss Fitzroy ran off with the Coachman & the amiable Rebecca was asked in marriage by Captain Roger of Buckinghamshire.

Mrs. Fitzroy did not approve of the match on account of the tender years of the young couple, Rebecca being but 36 & Captain Roger little more than 63. To remedy this objection, it was agreed that they should wait a little while till they were a good deal older.

Chapter 3

IN the mean time, the parents of Frederic proposed to those of Elfrida an union between them, which being accepted with pleasure, the wedding cloathes were bought & nothing remained to be settled but the naming of the Day.

As to the lovely Charlotte, being importuned with eagerness to pay another visit to her Aunt, she determined to accept the invitation & in consequence of it walked to Mrs. Fitzroy's to take leave of the amiable Rebecca, whom she found surrounded by Patches, Powder, Pomatum, & Paint, with which she was vainly endeavouring to remedy the natural plainness of her face.

"I am come, my amiable Rebecca, to take my leave of you for the fortnight I am destined to spend with my aunt. Beleive me, this separation is painfull to me, but it is as necessary as the labour which now engages you."

"Why to tell you the truth, my Love," replied Rebecca, "I have lately taken it into my head to think (perhaps with little reason) that my complexion is by no means equal to the rest of my face & have therefore taken, as you see, to white & red paint which I would scorn to use on any other occasion, as I hate art."

Charlotte, who perfectly understood the meaning of her freind's speech, was too good-temper'd & obliging to refuse her what she knew she wished, --

a compliment; & they parted the best freinds in the world.

With a heavy heart & streaming Eyes did she ascend the lovely vehicle which bore her from her freinds & home; but greived as she was, she little thought in what a strange & different manner she should return to it.

On her entrance into the city of London, which was the place of Mrs. Williamson's abode, the postilion, whose stupidity was amazing, declared & declared even without the least shame or Compunction, that having never been informed, he was totally ignorant of what part of the Town he was to drive to.

Charlotte, whose nature we have before intimated was an earnest desire to oblige every one, with the greatest Condescension & Good humour informed him that he was to drive to Portland Place, which he accordingly did & Charlotte soon found herself in the arms of a fond Aunt.

Scarcely were they seated as usual, in the most affectionate manner in one chair, than the Door suddenly opened & an aged gentleman with a sallow face & old pink Coat, partly by intention & partly thro' weakness was at the feet of the lovely Charlotte, declaring his attachment to her & beseeching her pity in the most moving manner.

Not being able to resolve to make any one miserable, she consented to become his wife; where upon the Gentleman left the room & all was quiet.

Their quiet however continued but a short time, for on a second opening of the door a young & Handsome Gentleman with a new blue coat entered & intreated from the lovely Charlotte, permission to pay to her his addresses.

There was a something in the appearance of the second Stranger, that influenced Charlotte in his favour, to the full as much as the appearance of the first: she could not account for it, but so it was.

Having therefore, agreable to that & the natural turn of her mind to make every one happy, promised to become his Wife the next morning, he took his leave & the two Ladies sat down to Supper on a young Leveret, a brace of Partridges, a leash of Pheasants & a Dozen of Pigeons.

Chapter 4

IT was not till the next morning that Charlotte recollected the double engagement she had entered into; but when she did, the reflection of her past folly operated so strongly on her mind, that she resolved to be guilty of a greater, & to that end threw herself into a deep stream which ran thro her Aunt's pleasure Grounds in Portland Place.

She floated to Crankhumdunberry where she was picked up & buried; the following epitaph, composed by Frederic, Elfrida, & Rebecca, was placed on her tomb.

EPITAPH

Here lies our friend who having promis-ed
That unto two she would be marri-ed
Threw her sweet Body & her lovely face
Into the Stream that runs thro' Portland Place.

These sweet lines, as pathetic as beautifull, were never read by any one who passed that way, without a shower of tears, which if they should fail of exciting in you, Reader, your mind must be unworthy to peruse them.

Having performed the last sad office to their departed freind, Frederic & Elfrida together with Captain Roger & Rebecca returned to Mrs. Fitzroy's, at whose feet they threw themselves with one accord & addressed her in the following Manner.

"Madam"

"When the sweet Captain Roger first addressed the amiable Rebecca, you alone objected to their union on account of the tender years of the Parties. That plea can be no more, seven days being now expired, together with the lovely Charlotte, since the Captain first spoke to you on the subject."

"Consent then Madam to their union & as a reward, this smelling Bottle which I enclose in my right hand, shall be yours & yours forever; I never will claim it again. But if you refuse to join their hands in 3 days time, this dagger which I enclose in my left shall be steeped in your heart's blood."

"Speak then, Madam, & decide their fate & yours."

Such gentle & sweet persuasion could not fail of having the desired effect. The answer they received, was this.

"My dear young freinds"

"The arguments you have used are too just & too eloquent to be withstood; Rebecca, in 3 days time, you shall be united to the Captain."

This speech, than which nothing could be more satisfactory, was received with Joy by all; & peace being once more restored on all sides, Captain Roger intreated Rebecca to favour them with a Song, in compliance with which request, having first assured them that she had a terrible cold, she sung as follows.

SONG

When Corydon went to the fair
  He bought a red ribbon for Bess,
With which she encircled her hair
  & made herself look very fess.

Chapter 5

AT the end of 3 days Captain Roger and Rebecca were united, and immediately after the Ceremony set off in the Stage Waggon for the Captain's seat in Buckinghamshire.

The parents of Elfrida, alltho' they earnestly wished to see her married to Frederic before they died, yet knowing the delicate frame of her mind could ill bear the least exertion & rightly judging that naming her wedding day would be too great a one, forebore to press her on the subject.

Weeks & Fortnights flew away without gaining the least ground; the Cloathes grew out of fashion & at length Capt. Roger & his Lady arrived, to pay a visit to their Mother & introduce to her their beautifull Daughter of eighteen.

Elfrida, who had found her former acquaintance were growing too old & too ugly to be any longer agreable, was rejoiced to hear of the arrival of so pretty a girl as Eleanor, with whom she determined to form the strictest freindship.

But the Happiness she had expected from an acquaintance with Eleanor, she soon found was not to be received, for she had not only the mortification of finding herself treated by her as little less than an old woman, but had actually the horror of perceiving a growing passion in the Bosom of Frederic for the Daughter of the amiable Rebecca.

The instant she had the first idea of such an attachment, she flew to Frederic & in a manner truly heroick, spluttered out to him her intention of being married the next Day.

To one in his predicament who possessed less personal Courage than Frederic was master of, such a speech would have been Death; but he, not being the least terrified, boldly replied:

"Damme, Elfrida, you may be married tomorrow, but I won't."

This answer distressed her too much for her delicate Constitution. She accordingly fainted & was in such a hurry to have a succession of fainting fits, that she had scarcely patience enough to recover from one before she fell into another.

Tho' in any threatening Danger to his Life or Liberty, Frederic was as bold as brass, yet in other respects his heart was as soft as cotton & immediately on hearing of the dangerous way Elfrida was in, he flew to her & finding her better than he had been taught to expect, was united to her Forever. –

Jack and Alice

Is respectfully inscribed to Francis William Austen Esq. Midshipman on board his Majesty's Ship the Perseverance by his obedient humble Servant

The Author

Chapter 1

MR. JOHNSON was once upon a time about 53; in a twelve-month afterwards he was 54, which so much delighted him that he was determined to celebrate his next Birthday by giving a Masquerade to his Children & Freinds. Accordingly on the Day he attained his 55th year, tickets were dispatched to all his Neighbours to that purpose. His acquaintance indeed in that part of the World were not very numerous, as they consisted only of Lady Williams, Mr. & Mrs. Jones, Charles Adams & the 3 Miss Simpsons, who composed the neighbourhood of Pammydiddle & formed the Masquerade.

Before I proceed to give an account of the Evening, it will be proper to describe to my reader the persons and Characters of the party introduced to his acquaintance.

Mr. & Mrs. Jones were both rather tall & very passionate, but were in other respects good tempered, wellbehaved People. Charles Adams was an amiable, accomplished, & bewitching young Man; of so dazzling a Beauty that none but Eagles could look him in the Face.

Miss Simpson was pleasing in her person, in her Manners, & in her Disposition; an unbounded ambition was her only fault. Her second sister Sukey was Envious, Spitefull, & Malicious. Her person was short, fat & disagreable. Cecilia (the youngest) was perfectly handsome, but too affected to be pleasing.

In Lady Williams every virtue met. She was a widow with a handsome Jointure & the remains of a very handsome face. Tho' Benevolent & Candid, she was Generous & sincere; Tho' Pious & Good, she was Religious & amiable, & Tho Elegant & Agreable, she was Polished & Entertaining.

The Johnsons were a family of Love, & though a little addicted to the Bottle & the Dice, had many good Qualities.

Such was the party assembled in the elegant Drawing Room of Johnson Court, amongst which the pleasing figure of a Sultana was the most remarkable of the female Masks. Of the Males, a Mask representing the Sun was the most universally admired. The Beams that darted from his Eyes were like those of that glorious Luminary, tho' infinitely superior. So strong were they that no one dared venture within half a mile of them; he had therefore the best part of the Room to himself, its size not amounting to more than 3 quarters of a mile in length & half a one in breadth. The Gentleman at last finding the feirceness of his beams to be very inconvenient to the concourse, by obliging them to croud together in one corner of the room, half shut his eyes, by which means the Company discovered him to be Charles Adams in his plain green Coat, without any mask at all.

When their astonishment was a little subsided, their attention was attracted by 2 Dominos who advanced in a horrible Passion; they were both very tall, but seemed in other respects to have many good qualities. "These" said the witty Charles, "these are Mr. & Mrs. Jones." and so indeed they were.

No one could imagine who was the Sultana! Till at length, on her addressing a beautifull Flora who was reclining in a studied attitude on a couch, with "Oh Cecilia, I wish I was really what I pretend to be", she was discovered by the never failing genius of Charles Adams to be the elegant but ambitious Caroline Simpson, & the person to whom she addressed herself, he rightly imagined to be her lovely but affected sister Cecilia.

The Company now advanced to a Gaming Table where sat 3 Dominos (each with a bottle in their hand) deeply engaged; but a female in the character of Virtue fled with hasty footsteps from the shocking scene, whilst a little fat woman, representing Envy, sat alternately on the foreheads of the 3 Gamesters. Charles Adams was still as bright as ever; he soon discovered the party at play to be the 3 Johnsons, Envy to be Sukey Simpson & Virtue to be Lady Williams.

The Masks were then all removed & the Company retired to another room, to partake of an elegant & well managed Entertainment, after which, the Bottle being pretty briskly pushed about by the 3 Johnsons, the whole party (not excepting even Virtue) were carried home, Dead Drunk.

Chapter 2

FOR three months did the Masquerade afford ample subject for conversation to the inhabitants of Pammydiddle; but no character at it was so fully expatiated on as Charles Adams. The singularity of his appearance, the beams which darted from his eyes, the brightness of his Wit, & the whole tout ensemble of his person had subdued the hearts of so many of the young Ladies, that of the six present at the Masquerade but five had returned uncaptivated. Alice Johnson was the unhappy sixth whose heart had not been able to withstand the power of his Charms. But as it may appear strange to my Readers, that so much worth & Excellence as he possessed should have conquered only hers, it will be necessary to inform them that the Miss Simpsons were defended from his Power by Ambition, Envy, & Self-admiration.

Every wish of Caroline was centered in a titled Husband; whilst in Sukey such superior excellence could only raise her Envy not her Love, & Cecilia was too tenderly attached to herself to be pleased with any one besides. As for Lady Williams and Mrs. Jones, the former of them was too sensible to fall in love with one so much her Junior, and the latter, tho' very tall & very passionate, was too fond of her Husband to think of such a thing.

Yet in spite of every endeavour on the part of Miss Johnson to discover any attachment to her in him, the cold & indifferent heart of Charles Adams still, to all appearance, preserved its native freedom; polite to all but partial to none, he still remained the lovely, the lively, but insensible Charles Adams.

One evening, Alice finding herself somewhat heated by wine (no very uncommon case) determined to seek a relief for her disordered Head & Love-sick Heart in the Conversation of the intelligent Lady Williams.

She found her Ladyship at home, as was in general the Case, for she was not fond of going out, & like the great Sir Charles Grandison scorned to deny herself when at Home, as she looked on that fashionable method of shutting out disagreable Visitors, as little less than downright Bigamy.

In spite of the wine she had been drinking, poor Alice was uncommonly out of spirits; she could think of nothing but Charles Adams, she could talk of nothing but him, & in short spoke so openly that Lady Williams soon discovered the unreturned affection she bore him, which excited her Pity & Compassion so strongly that she addressed her in the following Manner.

"I perceive but too plainly, my dear Miss Johnson, that your Heart has not been able to withstand the fascinating Charms of this young Man & I pity you sincerely. Is it a first Love?"

"It is."

"I am still more greived to hear that; I am myself a sad example of the Miseries in general attendant on a first Love & I am determined for the future to avoid the like Misfortune. I wish it may not be too late for you to do the same; if it is not, endeavour, my dear Girl, to secure yourself from so great a Danger. A second attachment is seldom attended with any serious consequences; against that therefore I have nothing to say. Preserve yourself from a first Love & you need not fear a second."

"You mentioned, Madam, something of your having yourself been a sufferer by the misfortune you are so good as to wish me to avoid. Will you favour me with your Life & Adventures?"

"Willingly, my Love."

Chapter 3

"MY Father was a gentleman of considerable Fortune in Berkshire; myself & a few more his only Children. I was but six years old when I had the misfortune of losing my Mother, & being at that time young & Tender, my father, instead of sending me to School, procured an able handed Governess to superintend my Education at Home. My Brothers were placed at Schools suitable to their Ages & my Sisters, being all younger than myself, remained still under the Care of their Nurse.

Miss Dickins was an excellent Governess. She instructed me in the Paths of Virtue; under her tuition I daily became more amiable, & might perhaps by this time have nearly attained perfection, had not my worthy Preceptoress been torn from my arms, e'er I had attained my seventeenth year. I never shall forget her last words. ``My dear Kitty'' she said, ``Good night t'ye.'' I never saw her afterwards'', continued Lady Williams, wiping her eyes, "She eloped with the Butler the same night."

"I was invited the following year by a distant relation of my Father's to spend the Winter with her in town. Mrs. Watkins was a Lady of Fashion, Family, & fortune; she was in general esteemed a pretty Woman, but I never thought her very handsome, for my part. She had too high a forehead, Her eyes were too small, & she had too much colour."

"How can that be?" interrupted Miss Johnson, reddening with anger; "Do you think that any one can have too much colour?"

"Indeed I do, & I'll tell you why I do, my dear Alice; when a person has too great a degree of red in their Complexion, it gives their face, in my opinion, too red a look."

"But can a face, my Lady, have too red a look?"

"Certainly, my dear Miss Johnson, & I'll tell you why. When a face has too red a look it does not appear to so much advantage as it would were it paler."

"Pray Ma'am, proceed in your story."

"Well, as I said before, I was invited by this Lady to spend some weeks with her in town. Many Gentlemen thought her Handsome, but in my opinion, Her forehead was too high, her eyes too small, & she had too much colour."

"In that, Madam, as I said before, your Ladyship must have been mistaken. Mrs. Watkins could not have too much colour, since no one can have too much."

"Excuse me, my Love, if I do not agree with you in that particular. Let me explain myself clearly; my idea of the case is this. When a Woman has too great a proportion of red in her Cheeks, she must have too much colour."

"But Madam, I deny that it is possible for any one to have too great a proportion of red in their Cheeks."

"What, my Love, not if they have too much colour?"

Miss Johnson was now out of all patience, the more so, perhaps, as Lady Williams still remained so inflexibly cool. It must be remembered, however, that her Ladyship had in one respect by far the advantage of Alice; I mean in not being drunk, for heated with wine & raised by Passion, she could have little command of her Temper.

The Dispute at length grew so hot on the part of Alice that, "From Words she almost came to Blows", When Mr. Johnson luckily entered, & with some difficulty forced her away from Lady Williams, Mrs. Watkins, & her red cheeks.

Chapter 4

MY Readers may perhaps imagine that after such a fracas, no intimacy could longer subsist between the Johnsons and Lady Williams, but in that they are mistaken; for her Ladyship was too sensible to be angry at a conduct which she could not help perceiving to be the natural consequence of inebriety, & Alice had too sincere a respect for Lady Williams, & too great a relish for her Claret, not to make every concession in her power.

A few days after their reconciliation, Lady Williams called on Miss Johnson to propose a walk in a Citron Grove which led from her Ladyship's pigstye to Charles Adams's Horsepond. Alice was too sensible of Lady Williams's kindness in proposing such a walk, & too much pleased with the prospect of seeing at the end of it a Horsepond of Charles's, not to accept it with visible delight. They had not proceeded far before she was roused from the reflection of the happiness she was going to enjoy, by Lady Williams's thus addressing her.

"I have as yet forborn, my dear Alice, to continue the narrative of my Life, from an unwillingness of recalling to your Memory a scene which (since it reflects on you rather disgrace than credit) had better be forgot than remembered."

Alice had already begun to colour up, & was beginning to speak, when her Ladyship, perceiving her displeasure, continued thus.

"I am afraid, my dear Girl, that I have offended you by what I have just said; I assure you I do not mean to distress you by a retrospection of what cannot now be helped; considering all things, I do not think you so much to blame as many People do; for when a person is in Liquor, there is no answering for what they may do."

"Madam, this is not to be borne; I insist --"

"My dear Girl, don't vex yourself about the matter; I assure you I have entirely forgiven every thing respecting it; indeed I was not angry at the time, because as I saw all along, you were nearly dead drunk. I knew you could not help saying the strange things you did. But I see I distress you; so I will change the subject & desire it may never again be mentioned; remember it is all forgot -- I will now pursue my story; but I must insist upon not giving you any description of Mrs. Watkins; it would only be reviving old stories & as you never saw her, it can be nothing to you, if her forehead was too high, her eyes were too small, or if she had too much colour."

"Again! Lady Williams: this is too much" --

So provoked was poor Alice at this renewal of the old story, that I know not what might have been the consequence of it, had not their attention been engaged by another object. A lovely young Woman lying apparently in great pain beneath a Citron-tree, was an object too interesting not to attract their notice. Forgetting their own dispute, they both with simpathizing tenderness advanced towards her & accosted her in these terms.

"You seem, fair Nymph, to be labouring under some misfortune which we shall be happy to releive, if you will inform us what it is. Will you favour us with your Life & adventures?"

"Willingly, Ladies, if you will be so kind as to be seated." They took their places & she thus began.

Chapter 5

"I AM a native of North Wales & my Father is one of the most capital Taylors in it. Having a numerous family, he was easily prevailed on by a sister of my Mother's, who is a widow in good circumstances & keeps an alehouse in the next Village to ours, to let her take me & breed me up at her own expence. Accordingly, I have lived with her for the last 8 years of my Life, during which time she provided me with some of the first rate Masters, who taught me all the accomplishments requisite for one of my sex and rank. Under their instructions I learned Dancing, Music, Drawing & various Languages, by which means I became more accomplished than any other Taylor's Daughter in Wales. Never was there a happier creature than I was, till within the last half year -- but I should have told you before that the principal Estate in our Neighbourhood belongs to Charles Adams, the owner of the brick House, you see yonder."

"Charles Adams!" exclaimed the astonished Alice; "are you acquainted with Charles Adams?"

"To my sorrow, madam, I am. He came about half a year ago to receive the rents of the Estate I have just mentioned. At that time I first saw him; as you seem, ma'am, acquainted with him, I need not describe to you how charming he is. I could not resist his attractions --"

"Ah! who can," said Alice with a deep sigh.

"My aunt, being in terms of the greatest intimacy with his cook, determined, at my request, to try whether she could discover, by means of her freind, if there were any chance of his returning my affection. For this purpose she went one evening to drink tea with Mrs. Susan, who in the course of Conversation mentioned the goodness of her Place & the Goodness of her Master; upon which my Aunt began pumping her with so much dexterity that in a short time Susan owned, that she did not think her Master would ever marry, ``for'' (said she) ``he has often & often declared to me that his wife, whoever she might be, must possess Youth, Beauty, Birth, Wit, Merit, & Money. I have many a time'' (she continued) ``endeavoured to reason him out of his resolution & to convince him of the improbability of his ever meeting with such a Lady; but my arguments have had no effect, & he continues as firm in his determination as ever.'' You may imagine, Ladies, my distress on hearing this; for I was fearfull that tho' possessed of Youth, Beauty, Wit & Merit, & tho' the probable Heiress of my Aunt's House & business, he might think me deficient in Rank, & in being so, unworthy of his hand."

"However I was determined to make a bold push & therefore wrote him a very kind letter, offering him with great tenderness my hand & heart. To this I received an angry & peremptory refusal, but thinking it might be rather the effect of his modesty than any thing else, I pressed him again on the subject. But he never answered any more of my Letters & very soon afterwards left the Country. As soon as I heard of his departure, I wrote to him here, informing him that I should shortly do myself the honour of waiting on him at Pammydiddle, to which I received no answer; therefore, choosing to take Silence for Consent, I left Wales, unknown to my Aunt, & arrived here after a tedious Journey this Morning. On enquiring for his House, I was directed thro' this Wood, to the one you there see. With a heart elated by the expected happiness of beholding him, I entered it, & had proceeded thus far in my progress thro' it, when I found myself suddenly seized by the leg & on examining the cause of it, found that I was caught in one of the steel traps so common in gentlemen's grounds."

"Ah! cried Lady Williams, how fortunate we are to meet with you; since we might otherwise perhaps have shared the like misfortune --"

"It is indeed happy for you, Ladies, that I should have been a short time before you. I screamed, as you may easily imagine, till the woods resounded again & till one of the inhuman Wretch's servants came to my assistance & released me from my dreadfull prison, but not before one of my legs was entirely broken."

Chapter 6

AT this melancholy recital, the fair eyes of Lady Williams were suffused in tears & Alice could not help exclaiming,

"Oh! cruel Charles, to wound the hearts & legs of all the fair."

Lady Williams now interposed, & observed that the young Lady's leg ought to be set without farther delay. After examining the fracture, therefore, she immediately began & performed the operation with great skill, which was the more wonderfull on account of her having never performed such a one before. Lucy then arose from the ground, & finding that she could walk with the greatest ease, accompanied them to Lady Williams's House at her Ladyship's particular request.

The perfect form, the beautifull face, & elegant manners of Lucy so won on the affections of Alice, that when they parted, which was not till after Supper, she assured her that except her Father, Brother, Uncles, Aunts, Cousins & other relations, Lady Williams, Charles Adams, & a few dozen more of particular freinds, she loved her better than almost any other person in the world.

Such a flattering assurance of her regard would justly have given much pleasure to the object of it, had she not plainly perceived that the amiable Alice had partaken too freely of Lady Williams's claret.

Her Ladyship (whose discernment was great) read in the intelligent countenance of Lucy her thoughts on the subject, & as soon as Miss Johnson had taken her leave, thus addressed her.

"When you are more intimately acquainted with my Alice, you will not be surprised, Lucy, to see the dear Creature drink a little too much; for such things happen every day. She has many rare & charming qualities, but Sobriety is not one of them. The whole Family are indeed a sad drunken set. I am sorry to say too that I never knew three such thorough Gamesters as they are, more particularly Alice. But she is a charming girl. I fancy not one of the sweetest tempers in the world; to be sure I have seen her in such passions! However, she is a sweet young Woman. I am sure you'll like her. I scarcely know any one so amiable. -- Oh! that you could but have seen her the other Evening! How she raved! & on such a trifle too! She is indeed a most pleasing Girl! I shall always love her!"

"She appears, by your ladyship's account, to have many good qualities", replied Lucy. "Oh! a thousand," answered Lady Williams; "tho' I am very partial to her, and perhaps am blinded, by my affection, to her real defects."

Chapter 7

THE next morning brought the three Miss Simpsons to wait on Lady Williams, who received them with the utmost politeness & introduced to their acquaintance Lucy, with whom the eldest was so much pleased that at parting she declared her sole ambition was to have her accompany them the next morning to Bath, whither they were going for some weeks.

"Lucy," said Lady Williams, "is quite at her own disposal & if she chooses to accept so kind an invitation, I hope she will not hesitate from any motives of delicacy on my account. I know not indeed how I shall ever be able to part with her. She never was at Bath & I should think that it would be a most agreable Jaunt to her. Speak, my Love," continued she, turning to Lucy, "what say you to accompanying these Ladies? I shall be miserable without you -- t'will be a most pleasant tour to you -- I hope you'll go; if you do I am sure t'will be the Death of me -- pray be persuaded" --

Lucy begged leave to decline the honour of accompanying them, with many expressions of gratitude for the extream politeness of Miss Simpson in inviting her. Miss Simpson appeared much disappointed by her refusal. Lady Williams insisted on her going -- declared that she would never forgive her if she did not, and that she should never survive it if she did, & in short, used such persuasive arguments that it was at length resolved she was to go. The Miss Simpsons called for her at ten o'clock the next morning & Lady Williams had soon the satisfaction of receiving from her young freind the pleasing intelligence of their safe arrival in Bath.

It may now be proper to return to the Hero of this Novel, the brother of Alice, of whom I beleive I have scarcely ever had occasion to speak; which may perhaps be partly oweing to his unfortunate propensity to Liquor, which so compleatly deprived him of the use of those faculties Nature had endowed him with, that he never did anything worth mentioning. His Death happened a short time after Lucy's departure & was the natural Consequence of this pernicious practice. By his decease, his sister became the sole inheritress of a very large fortune, which as it gave her fresh Hopes of rendering herself acceptable as a wife to Charles Adams, could not fail of being most pleasing to her -- & as the effect was Joyfull, the Cause could scarcely be lamented.

Finding the violence of her attachment to him daily augment, she at length disclosed it to her Father & desired him to propose a union between them to Charles. Her father consented & set out one morning to open the affair to the young Man. Mr. Johnson being a man of few words, his part was soon performed & the answer he received was as follows --

"Sir, I may perhaps be expected to appear pleased at & gratefull for the offer you have made me: but let me tell you that I consider it as an affront. I look upon myself to be, Sir, a perfect Beauty -- where would you see a finer figure or a more charming face. Then, sir, I imagine my Manners & Address to be of the most polished kind; there is a certain elegance, a peculiar sweetness in them that I never saw equalled & cannot describe. -- Partiality aside, I am certainly more accomplished in every Language, every Science, every Art and every thing than any other person in Europe. My temper is even, my virtues innumerable, my self unparalelled. Since such, Sir, is my character, what do you mean by wishing me to marry your Daughter? Let me give you a short sketch of yourself & of her. I look upon you, Sir, to be a very good sort of Man in the main; a drunken old Dog to be sure, but that's nothing to me. Your daughter sir, is neither sufficiently beautifull, sufficiently amiable, sufficiently witty, nor sufficiently rich for me. -- I expect nothing more in my wife than my wife will find in me -- Perfection. These, sir, are my sentiments & I honour myself for having such. One freind I have, & glory in having but one. -- She is at present preparing my Dinner, but if you choose to see her, she shall come & she will inform you that these have ever been my sentiments."

Mr. Johnson was satisfied: & expressing himself to be much obliged to Mr. Adams for the characters he had favoured him with of himself & his Daughter, took his leave.

The unfortunate Alice, on receiving from her father the sad account of the ill success his visit had been attended with, could scarcely support the disappointment -- She flew to her Bottle & it was soon forgot.

Chapter 8

WHILE these affairs were transacting at Pammydiddle, Lucy was conquering every Heart at Bath. A fortnight's residence there had nearly effaced from her remembrance the captivating form of Charles -- The recollection of what her Heart had formerly suffered by his charms & her Leg by his trap, enabled her to forget him with tolerable Ease, which was what she determined to do; & for that purpose dedicated five minutes in every day to the employment of driving him from her remembrance.

Her second Letter to Lady Williams contained the pleasing intelligence of her having accomplished her undertaking to her entire satisfaction; she mentioned in it also an offer of marriage she had received from the Duke of ----, an elderly Man of noble fortune whose ill health was the chief inducement of his Journey to Bath.

"I am distressed" (she continued) "to know whether I mean to accept him or not. There are a thousand advantages to be derived from a marriage with the Duke, for besides those more inferior ones of Rank & Fortune, it will procure me a home, which of all other things is what I most desire. Your

Ladyship's kind wish of my always remaining with you is noble & generous, but I cannot think of becoming so great a burden on one I so much love & esteem. That one should receive obligations only from those we despise, is a sentiment instilled into my mind by my worthy aunt, in my early years, & cannot in my opinion be too strictly adhered to. The excellent woman of whom I now speak is, I hear, too much incensed by my imprudent departure from Wales, to receive me again. -- I most earnestly wish to leave the Ladies I am now with. Miss Simpson is indeed (setting aside ambition) very amiable, but her 2d. Sister, the envious & malvolent Sukey, is too disagreable to live with. I have reason to think that the admiration I have met with in the circles of the Great at this Place, has raised her Hatred & Envy; for often has she threatened, & sometimes endeavoured to cut my throat. -- Your Ladyship will therefore allow that I am not wrong in wishing to leave Bath, & in wishing to have a home to receive me, when I do. I shall expect with impatience your advice concerning the Duke & am your most obliged

&c. Lucy."

Lady Williams sent her her opinion on the subject in the following Manner.

"Why do you hesitate, my dearest Lucy, a moment with respect to the Duke? I have enquired into his Character & find him to be an unprincipaled, illiterate Man. Never shall my Lucy be united to such a one! He has a princely fortune, which is every day encreasing. How nobly will you spend it!, what credit will you give him in the eyes of all!, How much will he be respected on his Wife's account! But why, my dearest Lucy, why will you not at once decide this affair by returning to me & never leaving me again? Altho' I admire your noble sentiments with respect to obligations, yet, let me beg that they may not prevent your making me happy. It will, to be sure, be a great expence to me, to have you always with me -- I shall not be able to support it -- but what is that in comparison with the happiness I shall enjoy in your society? -- 'twill ruin me I know -- you will not therefore surely, withstand these arguments, or refuse to return to yours most affectionately &c. &c.

C. WILLIAMS"

Chapter 9

WHAT might have been the effect of her Ladyship's advice, had it ever been received by Lucy, is uncertain, as it reached Bath a few Hours after she had breathed her last. She fell a sacrifice to the Envy & Malice of Sukey, who jealous of her superior charms, took her by poison from an admiring World at the age of seventeen.

Thus fell the amiable & lovely Lucy, whose Life had been marked by no crime, and stained by no blemish but her imprudent departure from her Aunt's, & whose death was sincerely lamented by every one who knew her. Among the most afflicted of her freinds were Lady Williams, Miss Johnson & the Duke; the 2 first of whom had a most sincere regard for her, more particularly Alice, who had spent a whole evening in her company & had never thought of her since. His Grace's affliction may likewise be easily accounted for, since he lost one for whom he had experienced, during the last ten days, a tender affection & sincere regard. He mourned her loss with unshaken constancy for the next fortnight, at the end of which time, he gratified the ambition of Caroline Simpson by raising her to the rank of a Dutchess. Thus was she at length rendered compleatly happy in the gratification of her favourite passion. Her sister, the perfidious Sukey, was likewise shortly after exalted in a manner she truly deserved, & by her actions appeared to have always desired. Her barbarous Murder was discovered, & in spite of every interceding freind she was speedily raised to the Gallows. -- The beautifull but affected Cecilia was too sensible of her own superior charms, not to imagine that if Caroline could engage a Duke, she might without censure aspire to the affections of some Prince -- & knowing that those of her native Country were cheifly engaged, she left England & I have since heard is at present the favourite Sultana of the great Mogul. --

In the mean time, the inhabitants of Pammydiddle were in a state of the greatest astonishment & Wonder, a report being circulated of the intended marriage of Charles Adams. The Lady's name was still a secret. Mr. & Mrs. Jones imagined it to be Miss Johnson; but she knew better; all *her* fears were centered in his Cook, when to the astonishment of every one, he was publicly united to Lady Williams –

Edgar & Emma

Chapter I

'I cannot imagine,' said Sir Godfrey to his Lady, 'why we continue in such deplorable Lodgings as these, in a paltry Market-town, while we have 3 good Houses of our own situated in some of the finest parts of England, & perfectly ready to receive us!'

'I'm sure, Sir Godfrey,' replied Lady Marlow, 'it has been much against my inclination that we have staid here so long; or why we should ever have come at all indeed, has been to me a wonder, as none of our Houses have been in the least want of repair.'

'Nay, my dear,' answered Sir Godfrey, 'you are the last person who ought to be displeased with what was always meant as a compliment to you; for you cannot but be sensible of the very great inconvenience your Daughters & I have been put to, during the 2 years we have remained crowded in these Lodgings in order to give you pleasure.'

'My dear,' replied Lady Marlow, 'How can you stand & tell such lies, when you very well know that it was merely to oblige the Girls & you, that I left a most commodious House situated in a most delightfull Country & surrounded by a most agreable Neighbourhood, to live 2 years cramped up in Lodgings three pair of Stairs high, in a smokey & unwholesome town, which has given me a continual fever & almost thrown me into a Consumption.'

As, after a few more speeches on both sides, they could not determine which was the most to blame, they prudently laid aside the debate, & having packed up their Cloathes & paid their rent, they set out the next morning with their 2 Daughters for their seat in Sussex.

Sir Godfrey & Lady Marlow were indeed very sensible people & tho' (as in this instance) like many other sensible People, they sometimes did a foolish thing, yet in general their actions were guided by Prudence & regulated by discretion.

After a Journey of two Days & a half they arrived at Marlhurst in good health & high spirits; so overjoyed were they all to inhabit again a place, they had left with mutual regret for two years, that they ordered the bells to be rung & distributed ninepence among the Ringers.

Chapter II

The news of their arrival being quickly spread throughout the Country, brought them in a few Days visits of congratulation from every family in it.

Amongst the rest came the inhabitants of Willmot Lodge a beautifull Villa not far from Marlhurst. Mr Willmot was the representative of a very ancient Family & possessed besides his paternal Estate, a considerable share in a Lead mine & a ticket in the Lottery. His Lady was an agreable Woman. Their Children were too numerous to be particularly described; it is sufficient to say that in general they were virtuously inclined & not given to any wicked ways. Their family being too large to accompany them in every visit, they took nine with them alternately. When their Coach stopped at Sir Godfrey's door, the Miss Marlow's Hearts throbbed in the eager expectation of once more beholding a family so dear to them. Emma the youngest (who was more particularly interested in their arrival, being attached to their eldest Son) continued at her Dressing-room window in anxious Hopes of seeing young Edgar descend from the Carriage.

Mr & Mrs Willmot with their three eldest Daughters first appeared–Emma began to tremble. Robert, Richard, Ralph, & Rodolphus followed–Emma turned pale. Their two youngest Girls were lifted from the Coach–Emma sunk breathless on a Sopha. A footman came to announce to her the arrival of Company; her heart was too full to contain its afflictions. A confidante was necessary–In Thomas she hoped to experience a faithfull one–for one she must have & Thomas was the only one at Hand. To him she unbosomed herself without restraint & after owning her passion for young Willmot, requested his advice in what manner she should conduct herself in the melancholy Disappointment under which she laboured.

Thomas, who would gladly have been excused from listening to her complaint, begged leave to decline giving any advice concerning it, which much against her will, she was obliged to comply with.

Having dispatched him therefore with many injunctions of secrecy, she descended with a heavy heart into the Parlour, where she found the good Party seated in a social Manner round a blazing fire.

Chapter III

Emma had continued in the Parlour some time before she could summon up sufficient courage to ask Mrs Willmot after the rest of her family; & when she did, it was in so low, so faltering a voice that no one knew she spoke. Dejected by the ill success of her first attempt she made no other, till on Mrs Willmot's desiring one of the little Girls to ring the bell for their Carriage, she stepped across the room & seizing the string said in a resolute manner.

'Mrs Willmot, you do not stir from this House till you let me know how all the rest of` your family do, particularly your eldest son.'

They were all greatly surprised by such an unexpected address & the more so, on account of the manner in which it was spoken; but Emma, who would not be again disappointed, requesting an answer, Mrs Willmot made the following eloquent oration.

'Our children are all extremely well but at present most of them from home. Amy is with my sister Clayton. Sam at Eton. David with his Uncle John. Jem & Will at Winchester. Kitty at Queen's Square. Ned with his Grandmother. Hetty & Patty in a Convent at Brussells. Edgar at college, Peter at Nurse, & all the rest (except the nine here) at home.'

It was with difficulty that Emma could refrain from tears on hearing of the absence of Edgar; she remained however tolerably composed till the Willmots were gone when having no check to the overflowings of her greif, she gave free vent to them, & retiring to her own room, continued in tears the remainder of her Life.

Henry and Eliza

Is humbly dedicated to Miss Cooper by her obedient Humble Servant
THE AUTHOR

As Sir George and Lady Harcourt were superintending the Labours of their Haymakers, rewarding the industry of some by smiles of approbation, & punishing the idleness of others by a cudgel, they perceived lying closely concealed beneath the thick foliage of a Haycock, a beautifull little Girl not more than 3 months old.

Touched with the enchanting Graces of her face & delighted with the infantine tho' sprightly answers she returned to their many questions, they resolved to take her home &, having no Children of their own, to educate her with care & cost.

Being good People themselves, their first & principal care was to incite in her a Love of Virtue & a Hatred of Vice, in which they so well succeeded (Eliza having a natural turn that way herself) that when she grew up, she was the delight of all who knew her.

Beloved by Lady Harcourt, adored by Sir George & admired by all the World, she lived in a continued course of uninterrupted Happiness, till she had attained her eighteenth year, when happening one day to be detected in stealing a banknote of 50£, she was turned out of doors by her inhuman Benefactors. Such a transition, to one who did not possess so noble & exalted a mind as Eliza, would have been Death, but she, happy in the conscious knowledge of her own Excellence, amused herself as she sat beneath a tree with making & singing the following Lines.

SONG

Though misfortunes my footsteps may ever attend
I hope I shall never have need of a Freind
as an innocent Heart I will ever preserve
and will never from Virtue's dear boundaries swerve.

Having amused herself some hours, with this song & her own pleasing reflections, she arose & took the road to M., a small market town, of which place her most intimate freind kept the Red Lion.

To this freind she immediately went, to whom having recounted her late misfortune, she communicated her wish of getting into some family in the capacity of Humble Companion.

Mrs. Wilson, who was the most amiable creature on earth, was no sooner acquainted with her Desire, than she sat down in the Bar & wrote the following Letter to the Dutchess of F., the woman whom of all others she most Esteemed.

"To the Dutchess of F.

Receive into your Family, at my request, a young woman of unexceptionable Character, who is so good as to choose your Society in preference to going to Service. Hasten, & take her from the arms of your

SARAH WILSON."

The Dutchess, whose freindship for Mrs. Wilson would have carried her any lengths, was overjoyed at such an opportunity of obliging her, & accordingly sate out immediately on the receipt of her letter for the Red Lion, which she reached the same Evening. The Dutchess of F. was about 45 & a half; Her passions were strong, her freindships firm, & her Enmities unconquerable. She was a widow & had only one Daughter, who was on the point of marriage with a young Man of considerable fortune.

The Dutchess no sooner beheld our Heroine than throwing her arms around her neck, she declared herself so much pleased with her, that she was resolved they never more should part. Eliza was delighted with such a protestation of freindship, & after taking a most affecting leave of her dear Mrs. Wilson, accompanied her grace the next morning to her seat in Surry.

With every expression of regard did the Dutchess introduce her to Lady Harriet, who was so much pleased with her appearance that she besought her, to consider her as her Sister, which Eliza with the greatest Condescension promised to do.

Mr Cecil, the Lover of Lady Harriet, being often with the family was often with Eliza. A mutual Love took place & Cecil having declared his first, prevailed on Eliza to consent to a private union, which was easy to be effected, as the dutchess's chaplain being very much in love with Eliza himself, would, they were certain, do anything to oblige her.

The Dutchess & Lady Harriet being engaged one evening to an assembly, they took the opportunity of their absence & were united by the enamoured Chaplain.

When the Ladies returned, their amazement was great at finding instead of Eliza the following Note.

"MADAM
We are married & gone.

HENRY & ELIZA CECIL"

Her Grace, as soon as she had read the letter, which sufficiently explained the whole affair, flew into the most violent passion & after having spent an agreable half hour, in calling them by all the shocking Names her rage could suggest to her, sent out after them 300 armed Men, with orders not to return without their Bodies, dead or alive; intending that if they should be brought to her in the latter condition to have them put to Death in some torturelike manner, after a few years Confinement.

In the mean time, Cecil & Eliza continued their flight to the Continent, which they judged to be more secure than their native Land, from the dreadfull effects of the Dutchess's vengeance which they had so much reason to apprehend.

In France they remained 3 years, during which time they became the parents of two Boys, & at the end of it Eliza became a widow without any thing to support either her or her Children. They had lived since their Marriage at the rate of 18,000£ a year, of which Mr Cecil's estate being rather less than the twentieth part, they had been able to save but a trifle, having lived to the utmost extent of their Income.

Eliza, being perfectly conscious of the derangement in their affairs, immediately on her Husband's death set sail for England, in a man of War of 55 Guns, which they had built in their more prosperous Days. But no sooner had she stepped on Shore at Dover, with a Child in each hand, than she was seized by the officers of the Dutchess, & conducted by them to a snug little Newgate of their Lady's, which she had erected for the reception of her own private Prisoners.

No sooner had Eliza entered her Dungeon than the first thought which occurred to her, was how to get out of it again.

She went to the Door; but it was locked. She looked at the Window; but it was barred with iron; disappointed in both her expectations, she dispaired of effecting her Escape, when she fortunately perceived in a Corner of her Cell, a small saw & Ladder of ropes. With the saw she instantly went to work & in a few weeks had displaced every Bar but one to which she fastened the Ladder.

A difficulty then occurred which for some time, she knew not how to obviate. Her Children were too small to get down the Ladder by themselves, nor would it be possible for her to take them in her arms when she did. At last she determined to fling down all her Cloathes, of which she had a large Quantity, & then having given them strict Charge not to hurt themselves, threw her Children after them. She herself with ease discended by the Ladder, at the bottom of which she had the pleasure of finding her little boys in perfect Health & fast asleep.

Her wardrobe she now saw a fatal necessity of selling, both for the preservation of her Children & herself. With tears in her eyes, she parted with these last reliques of her former Glory, & with the money she got for them, bought others more usefull, some playthings for Her Boys, and a gold Watch for herself.

But scarcely was she provided with the above-mentioned necessaries, than she began to find herself rather hungry, & had reason to think, by their biting off two of her fingers, that her Children were much in the same situation.

To remedy these unavoidable misfortunes, she determined to return to her old freinds, Sir George & Lady Harcourt, whose generosity she had so often experienced & hoped to experience as often again.

She had about 40 miles to travel before she could reach their hospitable Mansion, of which having walked 30 without stopping, she found herself at the Entrance of a Town, where often in happier times, she had accompanied Sir George & Lady Harcourt to regale themselves with a cold collation at one of the Inns.

The reflections that her adventures since the last time she had partaken of these happy Junketings afforded her, occupied her mind, for some time, as she sat on the steps at the door of a Gentleman's house. As soon as these reflections were ended, she arose & determined to take her station at the very inn she remembered with so much delight, from the Company of which, as they went in & out, she hoped to receive some Charitable Gratuity.

She had but just taken her post at the Inn yard before a Carriage drove out of it, & on turning the Corner at which she was stationed, stopped to give the Postilion an opportunity of admiring the beauty of the prospect. Eliza then advanced to the carriage & was going to request their Charity, when on fixing her Eyes on the Lady, within it, she exclaimed,

"Lady Harcourt!"

To which the lady replied,

"Eliza!"

"Yes Madam, it is the wretched Eliza herself."

Sir George, who was also in the Carriage, but too much amazed to speek, was proceeding to demand an explanation from Eliza of the Situation she was then in, when Lady Harcourt in transports of Joy, exclaimed.

"Sir George, Sir George, she is not only Eliza our adopted Daughter, but our real Child."

"Our real Child! What, Lady Harcourt, do you mean? You know you never even was with child. Explain yourself, I beseech you."

"You must remember, Sir George, that when you sailed for America, you left me breeding."

"I do, I do, go on, dear Polly."

"Four months after you were gone, I was delivered of this Girl, but dreading your just resentment at her not proving the Boy you wished, I took her to a Haycock & laid her down. A few weeks afterwards, you returned, & fortunately for me, made no enquiries on the subject. Satisfied within myself of the wellfare of my Child, I soon forgot I had one, insomuch that when we shortly after found her in the very Haycock I had placed her, I had no more idea of her being my own, than you had, & nothing, I will venture to say, would have recalled the circumstance to my remembrance, but my thus accidentally hearing her voice, which now strikes me as being the very counterpart of my own Child's."

"The rational & convincing Account you have given of the whole affair," said Sir George, "leaves no doubt of her being our Daughter & as such I freely forgive the robbery she was guilty of."

A mutual Reconciliation then took place, & Eliza, ascending the Carriage with her two Children, returned to that home from which she had been absent nearly four years.

No sooner was she reinstated in her accustomed power at Harcourt Hall, than she raised an Army, with which she entirely demolished the Dutchess's Newgate, snug as it was, and by that act, gained the Blessings of thousands, & the Applause of her own Heart.

The Adventures of Mr. Harley

A short, but interesting Tale, is with all imaginable Respect inscribed to Mr. Francis William Austen, Midshipman on board his Majesty's Ship the Perseverance by his Obedient Servant

THE AUTHOR.

MR. HARLEY was one of many Children. Destined by his father for the Church & by his Mother for the Sea, desirous of pleasing both, he prevailed on Sir John to obtain for him a Chaplaincy on board a Man of War. He accordingly cut his Hair and sailed.

In half a year he returned & set-off in the Stage Coach for Hogsworth Green, the seat of Emma. His fellow travellers were, A man without a Hat, Another with two, An old maid, & a young Wife.

This last appeared about 17, with fine dark Eyes & an elegant Shape; in short, Mr. Harley soon found out that she was his Emma & recollected he had married her a few weeks before he left England.

Sir William Mountague

SIR WILLIAM MOUNTAGUE
an unfinished performance
is humbly dedicated to Charles John
Austen Esqre., by his most obedient humble
Servant

THE AUTHOR

SIR WILLIAM MOUNTAGUE was the son of Sir Henry Mountague,

who was the son of Sir John Mountague, a descendant of Sir Christopher Mountague, who was the nephew of Sir Edward Mountague, whose ancestor was Sir James Mountague, a near relation of Sir Robert Mountague, who inherited the Title & Estate from Sir Frederic Mountague.

Sir William was about 17 when his Father died, & left him a handsome fortune, an ancient House, & a Park well stocked with Deer. Sir William had not been long in the possession of his Estate before he fell in Love with the 3 Miss Cliftons of Kilhoobery Park. These young Ladies were all equally young, equally handsome, equally rich & equally amiable -- Sir William was equally in Love with them all, & knowing not which to prefer, he left the Country & took Lodgings in a small Village near Dover.

In this retreat, to which he had retired in the hope of finding a shelter from the Pangs of Love, he became enamoured of a young Widow of Quality, who came for change of air to the same Village, after the death of a Husband, whom she had always tenderly loved & now sincerely lamented.

Lady Percival was young, accomplished & lovely. Sir William adored her & she consented to become his Wife. Vehemently pressed by Sir William to name the Day in which he might conduct her to the Altar, she at length fixed on the following Monday, which was the first of September. Sir William was a Shot & could not support the idea of losing such a Day, even for such a Cause. He begged her to delay the Wedding a short time. Lady Percival was enraged & returned to London the next Morning.

Sir William was sorry to lose her, but as he knew that he should have been much more grieved by the Loss of the 1st of September, his Sorrow was not without a mixture of Happiness, & his Affliction was considerably lessened by his Joy.

After staying at the Village a few weeks longer, he left it & went to a friend's House in Surry. Mr. Brudenell was a sensible Man, & had a beautiful Niece with whom Sir William soon fell in love. But Miss Arundel was cruel; she preferred a Mr. Stanhope: Sir William shot Mr. Stanhope; the lady had then no reason to refuse him; she accepted him, & they were to be married on the 27th of October. But on the 25th Sir William received a visit from Emma Stanhope, the sister of the unfortunate Victim of his rage. She begged some recompence, some atonement for the cruel Murder of her Brother. Sir William bade her name her price. She fixed on 14 shillings. Sir William offered her himself & Fortune. They went to London the next day & were there privately married. For a fortnight Sir William was completely happy, but chancing one day to see a charming young Woman entering a Chariot in Brook Street, he became again most violently in love. On enquiring the name of this fair Unknown, he found that she was the Sister of his old freind Lady Percival, at which he was much rejoiced, as he hoped to have, by his acquaintance with her Ladyship, free access to Miss Wentworth........

Memoirs of Mr. Clifford

An Unfinished Tale
To Charles John Austen Esqre

Sir,

Your generous patronage of the unfinished tale, I have already taken the Liberty of dedicating to you, encourages me to dedicate to you a second, as unfinished as the first.

I am Sir with every expression
of regard for you and yr noble
Family, your most obedt
&c. &c. . . .

The Author

Mr Clifford lived at Bath; and having never seen London, set off one Monday morning determined to feast his eyes with a sight of that great Metropolis. He travelled in his Coach and Four, for he was a very rich young Man and kept a great many Carriages of which I do not recollect half. I can only remember that he had a Coach, a Chariot, a Chaise, a Landeau, a Landeaulet, a Phaeton, a Gig, a Whisky, an Italian Chair, a Buggy, a Curricle & a wheelbarrow. He had likewise an amazing fine stud of Horses. To my knowledge he had six Greys, 4 Bays, eight Blacks and a poney.

In his Coach & 4 Bays Mr Clifford sate forward about 5 o'clock on Monday Morning the 1st of May for London. He always travelled remarkably expeditiously and contrived therefore to get to Devizes from Bath, which is no less than nineteen miles, the first Day. To be sure he did not Set in till eleven at night and pretty tight work, it was as you may imagine.

However when he was once got to Devizes he was determined to comfort himself with a good hot Supper and therefore ordered a whole Egg to be boiled for him and his Servants. The next morning he pursued his Journey and in the course of 3 days hard labour reached Overton, where he was seized with a dangerous fever the Consequence of too violent Exercise.

Five months did our Hero remain in this celebrated City under the care of its no less celebrated Physician, who at length completely cured him of his troublesome Disease.

As Mr Clifford still continued very weak, his first Day's Journey carried him only to Dean Gate where he remained a few Days and found himself much benefited by the change of Air.

In easy Stages he proceeded to Basingstoke. One day Carrying him to Clarkengreen, the next to Worting, the 3d to the bottom of Basingstoke Hill, and the fourth, to Mr Robins's. ...

The Beautifull Cassandra

A Novel in Twelve Chapters
Dedicated by permission to Miss Austen.
Dedication:

MADAM

You are a Phoenix. Your taste is refined, your Sentiments are noble, & your Virtues innumerable. Your Person is lovely, your Figure, elegant, & your Form, majestic. Your Manners are polished, your Conversation is rational & your appearance singular. If, therefore, the following Tale will afford one moment's amusement to you, every wish will be gratified of

Your most obedient
humble servant
THE AUTHOR

Chapter I

CASSANDRA was the Daughter & the only Daughter of a celebrated Millener in Bond Street. Her father was of noble Birth, being the near relation of the Duchess of ----'s Butler.

Chapter II

WHEN Cassandra had attained her 16th year, she was lovely & amiable, & chancing to fall in love with an elegant Bonnet her Mother had just completed, bespoke by the Countess of ----, she placed it on her gentle Head & walked from her Mother's shop to make her Fortune.

Chapter III

THE first person she met, was the Viscount of ----, a young Man, no less celebrated for his Accomplishments & Virtues, than for his Elegance & Beauty. She curtseyed & walked on.

Chapter IV

SHE then proceeded to a Pastry-cook's, where she devoured six ices, refused to pay for them, knocked down the Pastry Cook & walked away.

Chapter V

SHE next ascended a Hackney Coach & ordered it to Hampstead, where she was no sooner arrived than she ordered the Coachman to turn round & drive her back again.

Chapter VI

BEING returned to the same spot of the same Street she had set out from, the Coachman demanded his Pay.

Chapter VII

SHE searched her pockets over again & again; but every search was unsuccessful. No money could she find. The man grew peremptory. She placed her bonnet on his head & ran away.

Chapter VIII

THRO' many a street she then proceeded & met in none the least Adventure, till on turning a Corner of Bloomsbury Square, she met Maria.

Chapter IX

CASSANDRA started & Maria seemed surprised; they trembled, blushed, turned pale & passed each other in a mutual silence.

Chapter X

CASSANDRA was next accosted by her friend the Widow, who squeezing out her little Head thro' her less window, asked her how she did? Cassandra curtseyed & went on.

Chapter XI

A QUARTER of a mile brought her to her paternal roof in Bond Street, from which she had now been absent nearly 7 hours.

Chapter XII

SHE entered it & was pressed to her Mother's bosom by that worthy Woman. Cassandra smiled & whispered to herself "This is a day well spent."

Amelia Webster

an interesting & well written Tale
is dedicated by Permission
to
Mrs Austen
by
Her humble Servant

THE AUTHOR

Letter the first

TO MISS WEBSTER

MY DEAR AMELIA
You will rejoice to hear of the return of my amiable Brother from abroad. He arrived on thursday, & never did I see a finer form, save that of your sincere freind

MATILDA HERVEY

Letter the 2d.

TO H. BEVERLEY ESQre.

DEAR BEVERLEY
I arrived here last thursday & met with a hearty reception from my Father, Mother, & Sisters. The latter are both fine Girls -- particularly Maud, who I think would suit you as a Wife well enough. What say you to this? She will

have two thousand Pounds & as much more as you can get. If you don't marry her you will mortally offend

GEORGE HERVEY

Letter the 3d.

TO MISS HERVEY

DEAR MAUD

Beleive me, I'm happy to hear of your Brother's arrival. I have a thousand things to tell you, but my paper will only permit me to add that I am yr. affect. Freind

AMELIA WEBSTER

Letter the 4th.

TO MISS S. HERVEY

DEAR SALLY

I have found a very convenient old hollow oak to put our Letters in; for you know we have long maintained a private Correspondence. It is about a mile from my House & seven from yours. You may perhaps imagine that I might have made choice of a tree which would have divided the Distance more equally -- I was sensible of this at the time, but as I considered that the walk would be of benefit to you in your weak & uncertain state of Health, I preferred it to one nearer your House, & am yr. faithfull

BENJAMIN BAR

Letter the 5th.

TO MISS HERVEY

DEAR MAUD

I write now to inform you that I did not stop at your house in my way to Bath last Monday. -- I have many things to inform you of besides; but my Paper reminds me of concluding; & beleive me yrs. ever &c.

AMELIA WEBSTER

Letter the 6th.

TO MISS WEBSTER

Saturday

MADAM

An humble Admirer now addresses you -- I saw you, lovely Fair one, as you passed on Monday last, before our House in your way to Bath. I saw you thro' a telescope, & was so struck by your Charms that from that time to this I have not tasted human food.

GEORGE HERVEY

Letter the 7th.

TO JACK

As I was this morning at Breakfast the Newspaper was brought me, & in the list of Marriages I read the following.

"George Hervey Esqre. to Miss Amelia Webster"

"Henry Beverley Esqre. to Miss Hervey"

&

"Benjamin Bar Esqre. to Miss Sarah Hervey".

yours, TOM

The Visit

A COMEDY IN 2 ACTS
Dedication
To the Revd. James Austen

SIR,

The following Drama, which I humbly recommend to your Protection & Patronage, tho' inferior to those celebrated Comedies called "The School for Jealousy" & "The Travelled Man", will I hope afford some amusement to so respectable a Curate as yourself; which was the end in veiw when it was first composed by your Humble Servant the Author.

Dramatis Personae

Men:
    Sir Arthur Hampton
    Lord Fitzgerald
    Stanly
    Willoughby, Sir Arthur's nephew

Women:

    Lady Hampton
    Miss Fitzgerald
    Sophy Hampton
    Cloe Willoughby

The scenes are laid in Lord Fitzgerald's House.

Act The First

Scene the first, a Parlour --
enter LORD FITZGERALD & STANLY

STANLY.

Cousin, your servant.

FITZGERALD.

Stanly, good morning to you. I hope you slept well last night.

STANLY.

Remarkably well, I thank you.

FITZGERALD.

I am afraid you found your Bed too short. It was bought in my Grandmother's time, who was herself a very short woman & made a point of suiting all her Beds to her own length, as she never wished to have any company in the House, on account of an unfortunate impediment in her speech, which she was sensible of being very disagreable to her inmates.

STANLY.

Make no more excuses, dear Fitzgerald.

FITZGERALD.

I will not distress you by too much civility -- I only beg you will consider yourself as much at home as in your Father's house. Remember, "The more free, the more Wellcome."

[exit FITZGERALD

STANLY.

Amiable Youth!
"Your virtues, could he imitate
How happy would be Stanly's fate!"

[exit STANLY

Scene the 2d.
STANLY & MISS FITZGERALD, discovered.

STANLY.

What Company is it you expect to dine with you to Day, Cousin?

MISS F.

Sir Arthur & Lady Hampton; their Daughter, Nephew & Neice.

STANLY.

Miss Hampton & her Cousin are both Handsome, are they not?

MISS F.

Miss Willoughby is extreamly so. Miss Hampton is a fine Girl, but not equal to her.

STANLY.

Is not your Brother attached to the Latter?

MISS F.

He admires her, I know, but I beleive nothing more. Indeed I have heard him say that she was the most beautifull, pleasing, & amiable Girl in the world, & that of all others he should prefer her for his Wife. But it never went any farther, I'm certain.

STANLY.

And yet my Cousin never says a thing he does not mean.

MISS F.

Never. From his Cradle he has always been a strict adherent to Truth

[Exeunt Severally

End of the First Act.

Act The Second

Scene the first. The Drawing Room.

Chairs set round in a row. LORD FITZGERALD, MISS FITZGERALD & STANLY seated.

Enter a Servant.

SERVANT.

Sir Arthur & Lady Hampton. Miss Hampton, Mr. & Miss Willoughby.

[Exit SERVANT

Enter the Company.

MISS F.

I hope I have the pleasure of seeing your Ladyship well. Sir Arthur, your servant. Yrs., Mr. Willoughby. Dear Sophy, Dear Cloe, --

[They pay their Compliments alternately.

Miss F.

Pray be seated.

[They sit

Bless me! there ought to be 8 Chairs & there are but 6. However, if your Ladyship will but take Sir Arthur in your Lap, & Sophy my Brother in hers, I beleive we shall do pretty well.

LADY H.

Oh! with pleasure....

SOPHY.

I beg his Lordship would be seated.

MISS F.

I am really shocked at crouding you in such a manner, but my

Grandmother (who bought all the furniture of this room) as she had never a very large Party, did not think it necessary to buy more Chairs than were sufficient for her own family and two of her particular freinds.

SOPHY.
I beg you will make no apologies. Your Brother is very light.

STANLY, aside)
What a cherub is Cloe!

CLOE, aside)
What a seraph is Stanly!

Enter a Servant.

SERVANT.
Dinner is on table.

[*They all rise.*

MISS F.
Lady Hampton, Miss Hampton, Miss Willoughby.

STANLY *hands* CLOE; LORD FITZGERALD, SOPHY; WILLOUGHBY, MISS FITZGERALD; and SIR ARTHUR, LADY HAMPTON

[*Exeunt.*

Scene the 2d.
The Dining Parlour.

MISS FITZGERALD at top. LORD FITZGERALD at bottom. Company ranged on each side. Servants waiting.

CLOE.
I shall trouble Mr. Stanly for a Little of the fried Cow heel & Onion.

STANLY.
Oh Madam, there is a secret pleasure in helping so amiable a Lady. --

LADY H.
I assure you, my Lord, Sir Arthur never touches wine; but Sophy will toss off a bumper I am sure, to oblige your Lordship.

LORD F.
Elder wine or Mead, Miss Hampton?

SOPHY.
If it is equal to you, Sir, I should prefer some warm ale with a toast and nutmeg.

LORD F.
Two glasses of warmed ale with a toast and nutmeg.

MISS F.
I am afraid, Mr. Willoughby, you take no care of yourself. I fear you don't meet with any thing to your liking.

WILLOUGHBY.

Oh! Madam, I can want for nothing while there are red herrings on table.

LORD F.

Sir Arthur, taste that Tripe. I think you will not find it amiss.

LADY H.

Sir Arthur never eats Tripe; tis too savoury for him, you know, my Lord.

MISS F.

Take away the Liver & Crow, & bring in the suet pudding.

(a short Pause.)

MISS F.

Sir Arthur, shan't I send you a bit of pudding?

LADY H.

Sir Arthur never eats suet pudding, Ma'am. It is too high a Dish for him.

MISS F.

Will no one allow me the honour of helping them? Then John, take away the Pudding, & bring the Wine.

[SERVANTS *take away the things and bring in the Bottles & Glasses.*

LORD F.

I wish we had any Desert to offer you. But my Grandmother in her Lifetime, destroyed the Hothouse in order to build a receptacle for the Turkies with its materials; & we have never been able to raise another tolerable one.

LADY H.

I beg you will make no apologies, my Lord.

WILLOUGHBY.

Come Girls, let us circulate the Bottle.

SOPHY.

A very good notion, Cousin; & I will second it with all my Heart. Stanly, you don't drink.

STANLY.

Madam, I am drinking draughts of Love from Cloe's eyes.

SOPHY.

That's poor nourishment truly. Come, drink to her better acquaintance.

[MISS FITZGERALD goes to a Closet & brings out a bottle

MISS F.

This, Ladies & Gentlemen, is some of my dear Grandmother's own manufacture. She excelled in Gooseberry Wine. Pray taste it, Lady Hampton

LADY H.

How refreshing it is!

MISS F.

I should think, with your Ladyship's permission, that Sir Arthur might taste a little of it.

LADY H.

Not for Worlds. Sir Arthur never drinks any thing so high.

LORD F.

And now my amiable Sophia, condescend to marry me.

[*He takes her hand & leads her to the front*

STANLY.

Oh! Cloe, could I but hope you would make me blessed --

CLOE.

I will.

[*They advance.*

MISS F.

Since you, Willoughby, are the only one left, I cannot refuse your earnest solicitations -- There is my Hand.

LADY H.

And may you all be Happy!

The Mystery

An Unfinished Comedy

To the Revd George Austen

Sir,

I humbly solicit your Patronage to the following Comedy, which tho' an unfinished one is, I flatter myself, as complete a Mystery as any of its kind.

I am Sir your most Humble Servant.

The Author

Dramatis Personae

Men:
Colonel Elliott
Sir Edward Spangle
Old Humbug
Yong Humbug, and

Corydon

Women:
Fanny Elliott
Mrs. Humbug, and
Daphne

Act the First

Scene the First
A Garden.

Enter CORYDON.

Cory
But Hush! I am interrupted.

Exit CORYDON.
Enter OLD HUMBUG and his SON, talking.

Old Hum
It is for that reason I wish you to follow my advice. Are you convinced of
it's propriety?
Young Hum
I am, Sir, and will certainly manner what you have pointed out to me.
Old Hum
Then let us return to the House.
Exeunt.

Scene the Second
A Parlour in Humbug's House.

MRS. HUMBUG and FANNY, discovered at work.

Mrs. Hum
You understand me, my Love?
Fanny
Perfectly ma'am. Pray continue your narration.
Mrs. Hum
Alas! It is nearly concluded, for I have nothing more to say on the Subject.

Enter DAPHNE.

Daphne
My dear Mrs. Humbug, how d'ye do? Oh! Fanny, t'is all over.
Fanny
It is indeed!
Mrs. Hum
I'm very sorry to hear it.
Fanny
Then t'was to no purpose that I...
Daphne
None upon Earth.
Mrs. Hum
And what is to become of...
Daphne
Oh! That's all settled.

Whispers to MRS. HUMBUG

Fanny
And how is it determined?
Daphne
I'll tell you.

Whispers to FANNY.

Mrs. Hum
And is he to...
Daphne
I'll tell you all I know of the matter.

Whispers MRS. HUMBUG and FANNY.

Fanny
Well! Now I know everything about it, I'll go away.
Mrs. Hum and Daphne
And so will I.

Exeunt.

Scene the Third
The Curtain rises and discovers Sir Edward Spangle reclined in an elegant
Attitude on a Sofa, fast asleep.

Enter COLONEL ELLIOTT.

Colonel
My Daughter is not here I see.... . There lies Sir Edward.... . Shall I tell him the secret?... No, he'll certainly blab it.... . But he is asleep and won't hear me.... . So I'll e'en venture.

Goes up to SIR EDWARD, whispers to him, and exits.

The Three Sisters

To Edward Austen Esquire
The following unfinished Novel
is respectfully inscribed
by
his obedient humble servant
THE AUTHOR

Letter 1st

MISS STANHOPE TO MRS. ----

MY DEAR FANNY

I am the happiest creature in the World, for I have received an offer of marriage from Mr. Watts. It is the first I have ever had, and I hardly know how to value it enough. How I will triumph over the Duttons! I do not intend to accept it, at least I believe not, but as I am not quite certain, I gave him an equivocal answer and left him. And now my dear Fanny, I want your Advice whether I should accept his offer or not; but that you may be able to judge of his merits and the situation of affairs, I will give you an account of them. He is quite an old Man, about two and thirty, very plain, so plain that I cannot bear to look at him. He is extremely disagreeable and I hate him more than anybody else in the world. He has a large fortune and will make great Settlements on me; but then he is very healthy. In short, I do not know what to do. If I refuse him, he as good as told me that he should offer himself to Sophia, and if she refused him, to Georgiana, and I could not bear to have either of them married before me. If I accept him I know I shall be miserable all the rest of my Life, for he is very ill tempered and peevish, extremely jealous, and so stingy that there is no living in the house with him. He told me he should mention the affair to Mama, but I insisted upon it that he did not, for very likely she would make me marry him whether I would or no; however probably he has before now, for he never does anything he is desired to do. I believe I shall have him. It will be such a triumph to be married before Sophy, Georgiana, and the Duttons; And he promised to have a new Carriage on the occasion, but we almost quarreled about the color, for I insisted upon its being blue spotted with silver, and he declared it should be a plain Chocolate; and to provoke me more, said it should be just as low as his old one. I won't have him, I declare. He said he should come again tomorrow and take my final answer, so I believe I must get him while I can. I know the Duttons will envy me and I shall be able to chaperone Sophy and Georgiana to all the Winter Balls. But then, what will be the use of that when very likely he won't let me go myself, for I know he hates dancing, and what he hates himself he has no idea of any other person's liking; and besides he talks a great deal of Women's always staying at home and such stuff. I believe I shan't have him; I would refuse him at once if I were certain that neither of my Sisters would accept him, and that if they did not, he would not offer to the Duttons. I cannot run such a risk, so, if he will promise to have the Carriage ordered as I like, I will have him; if not he may ride in it by himself for me. I hope you like my determination; I can think of nothing better;

And am your ever Affectionate

MARY STANHOPE

FROM THE SAME TO THE SAME

DEAR FANNY

I had but just sealed my last letter to you, when my Mother came up and told me she wanted to speak to me on a very particular subject.

"Ah! I know what you mean; (said I) That old fool Mr. Watts has told you all about it, tho' I bid him not. However you shan't force me to have him if I don't like it."

"I am not going to force you, Child, but only want to know what your resolution is with regard to his Proposals, and to insist upon your making up your mind one way or t'other, that if you don't accept him, Sophy may."

"Indeed (replied I hastily) Sophy need not trouble herself, for I shall certainly marry him myself."

"If that is your resolution (said my Mother) why should you be afraid of my forcing your inclinations?"

"Why, because I have not settled whether I shall have him or not."

"You are the strangest Girl in the World, Mary. What you say one moment, you unsay the next. Do tell me once for all, whether you intend to marry Mr. Watts or not."

"Law! Mama, how can I tell you what I don't know myself?"

"Then I desire you will know, and quickly too, for Mr. Watts says he won't be kept in suspense."

"That depends upon me."

"No it does not, for if you do not give him your final answer tomorrow when he drinks Tea with us, he intends to pay his Addresses to Sophy."

"Then I shall tell all the World that he behaved very ill to me."

"What good will that do? Mr. Watts has been too long abused by all the World to mind it now."

"I wish I had a Father or a Brother, because then they should fight him."

"They would be cunning if they did, for Mr. Watts would run away first; and therefore you must and shall resolve either to accept or refuse him before tomorrow evening."

"But why, if I don't have him, must he offer to my Sisters?"

"Why! Because he wishes to be allied to the Family, and because they are as pretty as you are."

"But will Sophy marry him, Mama, if he offers to her?"

"Most likely; Why should not she? If, however, she does not choose it, then Georgiana must, for I am determined not to let such an opportunity escape of settling one of my Daughters so advantageously. So make the most of your time, I leave you to settle the Matter with yourself." And then she went away. The only thing I can think of, my dear Fanny, is to ask Sophy and Georgiana whether they would have him were he to make proposals to them, and if they say they would not, I am resolved to refuse him too, for I hate him more than you can imagine. As for the Duttons, if he marries one of them, I shall still have the triumph of having refused him first. So, adieu my dear Friend --

Yours ever, M. S.

MISS GEORGIANA STANHOPE TO MISS X X X

MY DEAR ANNE

Wednesday

Sophy and I have just been practising a little deceit on our eldest Sister, to which we are not perfectly reconciled, and yet the circumstances were such that if anything will excuse it, they must. Our neighbour Mr. Watts has made proposals to Mary: Proposals which she knew not how to receive, for tho' she has a particular Dislike to him (in which she is not singular), yet she would willingly marry him sooner than risk his offering to Sophy or me, which, in case of a refusal from herself, he told her he should do -- for you must know the poor Girl considers our marrying before her as one of the greatest misfortunes that can possibly befall her, and, to prevent it, would willingly ensure herself everlasting Misery by a Marriage with Mr. Watts. An hour ago she came to us to sound our inclinations respecting the affair, which were to determine hers. A little before she came, my Mother had given us an account of it, telling us that she certainly would not let him go farther than our own family for a Wife. "And therefore (said she) if Mary won't have him, Sophy must; and if Sophy won't, Georgiana shall." Poor Georgiana! -- We neither of us attempted to alter my Mother's resolution, which I am sorry to say is generally more strictly kept, than rationally formed. As soon as she was gone, however, I broke silence to assure Sophy that if Mary should refuse Mr. Watts, I should not expect her to sacrifice her happiness by becoming his Wife from a motive of Generosity to me, which I was afraid her Good nature and sisterly affection might induce her to do.

"Let us flatter ourselves (replied She) that Mary will not refuse him. Yet how can I hope that my Sister may accept a man who cannot make her happy."

"He cannot it is true but his Fortune, his Name, his House, his Carriage will, and I have no doubt but that Mary will marry him; indeed, why should she not? He is not more than two and thirty, a very proper age for a Man to marry at; He is rather plain to be sure, but then what is Beauty in a Man? -- if he has but a genteel figure and a sensible looking face it is quite sufficient."

"This is all very true, Georgiana, but Mr. Watts's figure is unfortunately extremely vulgar and his Countenance is very heavy."

"And then as to his temper; it has been reckoned bad, but may not the World be deceived in their Judgement of it? There is an open Frankness in his Disposition which becomes a Man. They say he is stingy; We'll call that Prudence. They say he is suspicious. That proceeds from a warmth of Heart always excusable in Youth, and in short, I see no reason why he should not make a very good Husband, or why Mary should not be very happy with him."

Sophy laughed; I continued,

"However whether Mary accepts him or not, I am resolved. My determination is made. I never would marry Mr. Watts, were Beggary the only alternative. So deficient in every respect! Hideous in his person, and without one good Quality to make amends for it. His fortune, to be sure, is good. Yet not so very large! Three thousand a year. What is three thousand a year? It is but six times as much as my Mother's income. It will not tempt me."

"Yet it will be a noble fortune for Mary" said Sophy, laughing again.

"For Mary! Yes indeed, it will give me pleasure to see her in such affluence."

Thus I ran on, to the great Entertainment of my Sister, till Mary came into the room, to appearance in great agitation. She sat down. We made room for her at the fire. She seemed at a loss how to begin, and at last said in some confusion,

"Pray Sophy have you any mind to be married?"

"To be married! None in the least. But why do you ask me? Are you acquainted with anyone who means to make me proposals?"

"I -- no, how should I? But mayn't I ask a common question?"

"Not a very common one Mary, surely," (said I). She paused, and after some moments silence went on --

"How should you like to marry Mr. Watts, Sophy?"

I winked at Sophy, and replied for her. "Who is there but must rejoice to marry a man of three thousand a year?"

"Very true (she replied), That's very true. So you would have him if he would offer, Georgiana, and would you Sophy?"

Sophy did not like the idea of telling a lie and deceiving her Sister; she prevented the first and saved half her conscience by equivocation.

"I should certainly act just as Georgiana would do."

"Well then," said Mary, with triumph in her Eyes, "I have had an offer from Mr. Watts."

We were of course very much surprised; "Oh! do not accept him," said I, "and then perhaps he may have me."

In short, my scheme took, and Mary is resolved to do that to prevent our supposed happiness, which she would not have done to ensure it in reality. Yet after all, my Heart cannot acquit me and Sophy is even more scrupulous. Quiet our Minds, my dear Anne, by writing and telling us you approve our conduct. Consider it well over. Mary will have real pleasure in being a married Woman, and able to chaperone us, which she certainly shall do, for I think myself bound to contribute as much as possible to her happiness in a State I have made her choose. They will probably have a new Carriage, which will be paradise to her, and if we can prevail on Mr. W. to set up his Phaeton, she will be too happy. These things, however, would be no consolation to Sophy or me for domestic Misery. Remember all this, and do not condemn us.

Friday

Last night, Mr. Watts by appointment drank tea with us. As soon as his Carriage stopped at the Door, Mary went to the Window.

"Would you believe it, Sophy (said she) the old Fool wants to have his new Chaise just the colour of the old one, and hung as low too. But it shan't -- I will carry my point. And if he won't let it be as high as the Duttons', and blue spotted with silver, I won't have him. Yes I will too. Here he comes. I know he'll be rude; I know he'll be ill-tempered and won't say one civil thing to me! nor behave at all like a Lover." She then sat down and Mr. Watts entered.

"Ladies, your most obedient." We paid our Compliments and he seated himself.

"Fine weather, Ladies." Then turning to Mary, "Well, Miss Stanhope, I hope you have at last settled the Matter in your own mind; and will be so good as to let me know whether you will condescend to marry me or not."

"I think, Sir (said Mary) You might have asked in a gentler way than that. I do not know whether I shall have you if you behave so odd."

"Mary!" (said my Mother). "Well, Mama, if he will be so cross..."

"Hush, hush, Mary, you shall not be rude to Mr. Watts."

"Pray Madam, do not lay any restraint on Miss Stanhope by obliging her to be civil. If she does not choose to accept my hand, I can offer it elsewhere, for as I am by no means guided by a particular preference to you above your Sisters, it is equally the same to me which I marry of the three." Was there ever such a Wretch! Sophy reddened with anger and I felt so spiteful!

"Well then (said Mary in a peevish Accent) I will have you if I must."

"I should have thought, Miss Stanhope, that when such Settlements are offered as I have offered to you, there can be no great violence done to the inclinations in accepting of them." Mary mumbled out something, which I who sat close to her could just distinguish to be "What's the use of a great Jointure, if Men live forever?" And then audibly "Remember the pin-money; two hundred a year."

"A hundred and seventy-five, Madam."

"Two hundred indeed, Sir" said my Mother.

"And Remember, I am to have a new Carriage hung as high as the Duttons', and blue spotted with silver; and I shall expect a new saddle horse, a suit of fine lace, and an infinite number of the most valuable Jewels. Diamonds such as never were seen, and Pearls, Rubies, Emeralds, and Beads out of number. You must set up your Phaeton, which must be cream-coloured with a wreath of silver flowers round it; You must buy 4 of the finest Bays in the Kingdom and you must drive me in it every day. This is not all; You must entirely new furnish your House after my Taste, You must hire two more Footmen to attend me, two Women to wait on me, must always let me do just as I please and make a very good husband."

Here she stopped, I believe rather out of breath.

"This is all very reasonable, Mr. Watts, for my Daughter to expect."

"And it is very reasonable, Mrs. Stanhope, that your daughter should be disappointed." He was going on, but Mary interrupted him: "You must build me an elegant Greenhouse and stock it with plants. You must let me spend every Winter in Bath, every Spring in Town, Every Summer in taking some Tour, and every Autumn at a Watering Place, and if we are at home the rest of the year (Sophy and I laughed) You must do nothing but give Balls and Masquerades. You must build a room on purpose and a Theatre to act Plays in. The first Play we have shall be Which is the Man, and I will do Lady Bell Bloomer."

"And pray, Miss Stanhope (said Mr. Watts), What am I to expect from you in return for all this."

"Expect? Why, you may expect to have me pleased."

"It would be odd if I did not. Your expectations, Madam, are too high for me, and I must apply to Miss Sophy, who perhaps may not have raised her's so much."

"You are mistaken, Sir, in supposing so, (said Sophy) for tho' they may not be exactly in the same Line, yet my expectations are to the full as high as my Sister's; for I expect my Husband to be good-tempered and Cheerful; to consult my Happiness in all his Actions, and to love me with Constancy and Sincerity."

Mr. Watts stared. "These are very odd Ideas, truly, young Lady. You had better discard them before you marry, or you will be obliged to do it afterwards."

My Mother, in the meantime, was lecturing Mary, who was sensible that she had gone too far, and when Mr. Watts was just turning towards me in order, I believe, to address me, she spoke to him in a voice half humble, half sulky.

"You are mistaken, Mr. Watts, if you think I was in earnest when I said I expected so much. However I must have a new Chaise."

"Yes, Sir, you must allow that Mary has a right to expect that."

"Mrs. Stanhope, I mean and have always meant to have a new one on my Marriage. But it shall be the color of my present one."

"I think, Mr. Watts, you should pay my Girl the compliment of consulting her Taste on such Matters."

Mr. Watts would not agree to this, and for some time insisted upon its being a Chocolate color, while Mary was as eager for having it blue with silver Spots. At length, however, Sophy proposed that to please Mr. W. it should be a dark brown, and to please Mary it should be hung rather high and have a silver Border. This was at length agreed to, tho' reluctantly on both sides, as each had intended to carry their point entire. We then proceeded to other Matters, and it was settled that they should be married as soon as the Writings could be completed. Mary was very eager for a Special License and Mr. Watts talked of Banns. A common License was at last agreed on. Mary is to have all the Family Jewels, which are very inconsiderable, I believe, and Mr. W. promised to buy her a Saddle horse; but in return, she is not to expect to go to Town or any other public place for these three Years. She is to have neither Greenhouse, Theatre, or Phaeton; to be contented with one Maid without an additional Footman. It engrossed the whole Evening to settle these affairs; Mr. W. supped with us and did not go till twelve. As soon as he was gone, Mary exclaimed "Thank Heaven! he's off at last; how I do hate him!" It was in vain that Mama represented to her the impropriety she was guilty of, in disliking him who was to be her Husband, for she persisted in declaring her aversion to him and hoping she might never see him again. What a Wedding will this be! Adeiu, my dear Anne. Your faithfully Sincere

GEORGIANA STANHOPE

FROM THE SAME TO THE SAME

DEAR ANNE

Saturday

Mary, eager to have everyone know of her approaching Wedding, and more particularly desirous of triumphing, as she called it, over the Duttons, desired us to walk with her this Morning to Stoneham. As we had nothing else to do, we readily agreed, and had as pleasant a walk as we could have with Mary, whose conversation entirely consisted in abusing the Man she is so soon to marry, and in longing for a blue Chaise spotted with Silver. When we reached the Duttons, we found the two Girls in the dressing-room with a very handsome Young Man, who was of course introduced to us. He is the son of Sir Henry Brudenell of Leicestershire -- Mr. Brudenell is the handsomest Man I ever saw in my Life; we are all three very much pleased with him. Mary, who from the moment of our reaching the Dressing-room had been swelling with the knowledge of her own importance, and with the Desire of making it known, could not remain long silent on the Subject after we were seated, and soon addressing herself to Kitty, said,

"Don't you think it will be necessary to have all the Jewels new set?"

"Necessary for what?"

"For What! Why, for my appearance."

"I beg your pardon, but I really do not understand you. What Jewels do you speak of, and where is your appearance to be made?"

"At the next Ball, to be sure, after I am married."

You may imagine their Surprise. They were at first incredulous, but on our joining in the Story, they at last believed it. "And who is it to?" was of course the first Question. Mary pretended Bashfulness, and answered in Confusion, her Eyes cast down, "to Mr. Watts". This also required Confirmation from us, for that anyone who had the Beauty and fortune (tho' small yet a provision) of Mary would willingly marry Mr. Watts, could by them scarcely be credited. The subject being now fairly introduced, and she found herself the object of every one's attention in company, she lost all her confusion and became perfectly unreserved and communicative.

"I wonder you should never have heard of it before, for in general things of this Nature are very well known in the Neighbourhood."

"I assure you", said Jemima, "I never had the least suspicion of such an affair. Has it been in agitation long?"

"Oh! Yes, ever since Wednesday."

They all smiled, particularly Mr. Brudenell.

"You must know Mr. Watts is very much in love with me, so that it is quite a match of affection on his side."

"Not on his only, I suppose", said Kitty.

"Oh! when there is so much Love on one side, there is no occasion for it on the other. However, I do not much dislike him, tho' he is very plain to be sure."

Mr. Brudenell stared, the Miss Duttons laughed and Sophy and I were heartily ashamed of our Sister. She went on.

"We are to have a new Postchaise, and very likely may set up our Phaeton."

This we knew to be false, but the poor Girl was pleased at the idea of persuading the company that such a thing was to be, and I would not deprive her of so harmless an Enjoyment. She continued,

"Mr. Watts is to present me with the family Jewels, which I fancy are very considerable." I could not help whispering Sophy "I fancy not". "These Jewels are what I suppose must be new set before they can be worn. I shall not wear them till the first Ball I go to after my Marriage. If Mrs. Dutton should not go to it, I hope you will let me chaperone you; I shall certainly take Sophy and Georgiana."

"You are very good (said Kitty) and since you are inclined to undertake the Care of young Ladies, I should advise you to prevail on Mrs. Edgecumbe to let you chaprone her six Daughters, which with your two Sisters and ourselves will make your Entrée very respectable."

Kitty made us all smile except Mary, who did not understand her Meaning and coolly said that she should not like to chaperone so many. Sophy and I now endeavored to change the conversation, but succeeded only for a few Minutes, for Mary took care to bring back their attention to her and her approaching Wedding. I was sorry for my Sister's sake to see that Mr. Brudenell seemed to take pleasure in listening to her account of it, and even encouraged her by his Questions and Remarks, for it was evident that his only Aim was to laugh at her. I am afraid he found her very ridiculous. He kept his Countenance extremely well, yet it was easy to see that it was with difficulty he kept it. At length, however, he seemed fatigued and Disgusted with her ridiculous Conversation, as he turned from her to us, and spoke but little to her for about half an hour before we left Stoneham. As soon as we were out of the House, we all joined in praising the Person and Manners of Mr. Brudenell.

We found Mr. Watts at home.

"So, Miss Stanhope (said he) you see I am come a courting in a true Lover like Manner."

"Well you need not have told me that. I knew why you came very well."

Sophy and I then left the room, imagining of course that we must be in the way, if a Scene of Courtship were to begin. We were surprised at being followed almost immediately by Mary.

"And is your Courting so soon over?" said Sophy.

"Courting! (replied Mary) we have been quarrelling. Watts is such a Fool! I hope I shall never see him again."

"I am afraid you will, (said I) as he dines here today. But what has been your dispute?"

"Why, only because I told him that I had seen a Man much handsomer than he was this Morning, he flew into a great Passion and called me a Vixen, so I only stayed to tell him I thought him a Blackguard and came away."

"Short and sweet; (said Sophy) but pray, Mary, how will this be made up?"

"He ought to ask my pardon; but if he did, I would not forgive him."

"His Submission, then, would not be very useful."

When we were dressed we returned to the Parlour where Mama and Mr. Watts were in close Conversation. It seems that he had been complaining to her of her Daughter's behavior, and she had persuaded him to think no more of it. He therefore met Mary with all his accustomed Civility, and except one touch at the Phaeton and another at the Greenhouse, the Evening went off with great Harmony and Cordiality. Watts is going to Town to hasten the preparations for the Wedding.

I am your affectionate Friend, G.S.

Detached Pieces

Dedication

To Miss Jane Anna Elizabeth Austen

My Dear Niece,

Though you are at this period not many degrees removed from Infancy, Yet trusting that you will in time be older, and that through the care of your excellent Parents, You will one day or another be able to read written hand, I dedicate to You the following Miscellaneous Morsels, convinced that if you seriously attend to them, You will derive from them very important Instructions, with regard to your Conduct in Life. If such my hopes should hereafter be realized, never shall I regret the Days and Nights that have been spent in composing these Treatises for your Benefit. I am, my dear Niece Your very Affectionate Aunt.

The Author

June 2d. 1793

A Fragment written to inculcate the practice of Virtue
(Erased from the original manuscript.)

We all know that many are unfortunate in their progress through the world, but we do not know all that are so. To seek them out to study their wants, & to leave them unsupplied is the duty, and ought to be the Business of Man. But few have time, fewer still have inclination, and no one has either the one or the other for such employments. Who amidst those that perspire away their Evenings in crowded assemblies can have leisure to bestow a thought on such as sweat under the fatigue of their daily Labor.

A beautiful description

of the different effects of sensibility on different minds

I am but just returned from Melissa's Bedside, & in my Life, tho' it has been a pretty long one, & I have during the course of it been at many Bedsides, I never saw so affecting an object as she exhibits. She lies wrapped in a book muslin bedgown, a chambray gauze shift, and a French net nightcap. Sir William is constantly at her bedside. The only repose he takes is on the Sopha in the Drawing room, where for five minutes every fortnight he remains in an imperfect Slumber, starting up every Moment & exclaiming "Oh! Melissa, Ah! Melissa," then sinking down again, raises his left arm and scratches his head. Poor Mrs. Burnaby is beyond measure afflicted. She sighs every now & then, that is about once a week; while the melancholy Charles says every Moment "Melissa how are you?" The lovely Sisters are much to be pitied. Julia is ever lamenting the situation of her friend, while lying behind her pillow & supporting her head. Maria, more mild in her grief, talks of going to Town next week, & Anna is always recurring to the pleasures we once enjoyed when Melissa was well. I am usually at the fire cooking some little delicacy for the unhappy invalid. Perhaps hashing up the remains of an old Duck, toasting some cheese or making a Curry, which are the favorite dishes of our poor friend. In these situations we were this morning surprised by receiving a visit from Dr. Dowkins; "I am come to see Melissa," said he. "How is She?" "Very weak indeed," said the fainting Melissa. "Very weak," replied the punning Doctor, "aye indeed it is more than a very week since you have taken to your bed. How is your appetite?" "Bad, very bad," said Julia. "That is very bad," replied he; "Are her spirits good, Madam?" "So poorly, Sir, that we are obliged to strengthen her with cordials every Minute." "Well then she receives Spirits from your being with her. Does she sleep?" "Scarcely ever." "And Ever Scarcely, I suppose, when she does. Poor thing! Does she think of dying?" "She has not strength to think at all." "Nay, then she cannot think to have Strength."

The Generous Curate

A moral Tale, setting forth the Advantages of being Generous and a Curate.

In a part little known of the County of Warwick, a very worthy Clergyman lately resided. The income of his living which amounted to about two hundred pound, and the interest of his Wife's fortune which was nothing at all, was entirely sufficient for the Wants and Wishes of a Family who neither wanted or wished for anything beyond what their income afforded them. Mr Williams had been in possession of his living above twenty Years, when this history commences, and his Marriage which had taken place soon after his presentation to it, had made him the father of six very fine Children. The eldest had been placed at the Royal Academy for Seamen at Portsmouth when about thirteen years old, and from thence had been discharged on board of one of the Vessels of a small fleet destined for Newfoundland, where his promising and amiable disposition had procured him many friends among the Natives, and from whence he regularly sent home a large Newfoundland Dog every Month to his family. The second, who was also a Son, had been adopted by a neighboring Clergyman with the intention of educating him at his own expense, which would have been a very desirable Circumstance had the Gentleman's fortune been equal to his generosity, but as he had nothing to support himself and a very large family but a Curacy of fifty pound a year, Young Williams knew nothing more at the age of 18 than what a two penny Dame's School in the village could teach him. His Character however was perfectly amiable though his genius might be cramped, and he was addicted to novice, or ever guilty of any fault beyond what his age and situation rendered perfectly excusable. He had indeed; sometimes been detected in flinging Stones at a Duck or putting brickbats into his Benefactor's bed; but these innocent efforts of wit were considered by that good Man rather as the effects of a lively imagination, than of anything bad in his Nature, and if any punishment were decreed for the offence it was in general no greater than that the Culprit should pick up the Stones or take the brickbats away.

Ode to Pity

To Miss Austen

The following Ode to Pity is dedicated, from a thorough knowledge of her pitiful Nature, by her obedt humle Servt.

The Author

    Ever musing I delight to tread
    The Paths of honour and the Myrtle Grove
    Whilst the pale Moon her beams doth shed
    On disappointed Love.
    While Philomel on airy hawthorn Bush
    Sings sweet and Melancholy, And the thrush
    Converses with the Dove.

    Gently brawling down the turnpike road,
    Sweetly noisy falls the Silent Stream—
    The Moon emerges from behind a Cloud
    And darts upon the Myrtle Grove her beam.
    Ah! then what Lovely Scenes appear,
    The hut, the Cot, the Grot, and Chapel queer,
    And eke the Abbey too a mouldering heap,
    Cnceal'd by aged pines her head doth rear
    And quite invisible doth take a peep.

    June 3d 1793

Juvenilia — Volume the Second

Love And Freindship

> TO MADAME LA COMTESSE DE FEUILLIDE THIS NOVEL
> IS INSCRIBED BY HER
> OBLIGED HUMBLE SERVANT
> THE AUTHOR.

"Deceived in Freindship and Betrayed in Love."

Letter The First

From *ISABEL to LAURA*

How often, in answer to my repeated intreaties that you would give my Daughter a regular detail of the Misfortunes and Adventures of your Life, have you said "No, my freind never will I comply with your request till I may be no longer in Danger of again experiencing such dreadful ones."

Surely that time is now at hand. You are this day 55. If a woman may ever be said to be in safety from the determined Perseverance of disagreeable Lovers and the cruel Persecutions of obstinate Fathers, surely it must be at such a time of Life.

Isabel

Letter 2nd

LAURA to ISABEL

Altho' I cannot agree with you in supposing that I shall never again be exposed to Misfortunes as unmerited as those I have already experienced, yet to avoid the imputation of Obstinacy or ill-nature, I will gratify the curiosity of your daughter; and may the fortitude with which I have suffered the many afflictions of my past Life, prove to her a useful lesson for the support of those which may befall her in her own.

Laura

Letter 3rd

LAURA to MARIANNE

As the Daughter of my most intimate freind I think you entitled to that knowledge of my unhappy story, which your Mother has so often solicited me to give you.

My Father was a native of Ireland and an inhabitant of Wales; my Mother was the natural Daughter of a Scotch Peer by an italian Opera-girl—I was born in Spain and received my Education at a Convent in France.

When I had reached my eighteenth Year I was recalled by my Parents to my paternal roof in Wales. Our mansion was situated in one of the most romantic parts of the Vale of Uske. Tho' my Charms are now considerably softened and somewhat impaired by the Misfortunes I have undergone, I was once beautiful. But lovely as I was the Graces of my Person were the least of my Perfections. Of every accomplishment accustomary to my sex, I was Mistress. When in the Convent, my progress had always exceeded my instructions, my Acquirements had been wonderfull for my age, and I had shortly surpassed my Masters.

In my Mind, every Virtue that could adorn it was centered; it was the Rendez-vous of every good Quality and of every noble sentiment.

A sensibility too tremblingly alive to every affliction of my Freinds, my Acquaintance and particularly to every affliction of my own, was my only fault, if a fault it could be called. Alas! how altered now! Tho' indeed my own Misfortunes do not make less impression on me than they ever did, yet now I never feel for those of an other. My accomplishments too, begin to fade—I can neither sing so well nor Dance so gracefully as I once did—and I have entirely forgot the MINUET DELA COUR.

Adeiu.

Laura.

Letter 4th

Laura to MARIANNE

Our neighbourhood was small, for it consisted only of your Mother. She may probably have already told you that being left by her Parents in indigent Circumstances she had retired into Wales on eoconomical motives. There it was our freindship first commenced. Isobel was then one and twenty. Tho' pleasing both in her Person and Manners (between ourselves) she never possessed the hundredth part of my Beauty or Accomplishments. Isabel had seen the World. She had passed 2 Years at one of the first Boarding-schools in London; had spent a fortnight in Bath and had supped one night in Southampton.

"Beware my Laura (she would often say) Beware of the insipid Vanities and idle Dissipations of the Metropolis of England; Beware of the unmeaning Luxuries of Bath and of the stinking fish of Southampton."

"Alas! (exclaimed I) how am I to avoid those evils I shall never be exposed to? What probability is there of my ever tasting the Dissipations of London, the Luxuries of Bath, or the stinking Fish of Southampton? I who am doomed to waste my Days of Youth and Beauty in an humble Cottage in the Vale of Uske."

Ah! little did I then think I was ordained so soon to quit that humble Cottage for the Deceitfull Pleasures of the World.

Adeiu

Laura.

Letter 5th

LAURA to MARIANNE

One Evening in December as my Father, my Mother and myself, were arranged in social converse round our Fireside, we were on a sudden greatly astonished, by hearing a violent knocking on the outward door of our rustic Cot.

My Father started—"What noise is that," (said he.) "It sounds like a loud rapping at the door"—(replied my Mother.) "it does indeed." (cried I.) "I am of your opinion; (said my Father) it certainly does appear to proceed from some uncommon violence exerted against our unoffending door." "Yes (exclaimed I) I cannot help thinking it must be somebody who knocks for admittance."

"That is another point (replied he;) We must not pretend to determine on what motive the person may knock—tho' that someone DOES rap at the door, I am partly convinced."

Here, a 2d tremendous rap interrupted my Father in his speech, and somewhat alarmed my Mother and me.

"Had we better not go and see who it is? (said she) the servants are out." "I think we had." (replied I.) "Certainly, (added my Father) by all means." "Shall we go now?" (said my Mother,) "The sooner the better." (answered he.) "Oh! let no time be lost" (cried I.)

A third more violent Rap than ever again assaulted our ears. "I am certain there is somebody knocking at the Door." (said my Mother.) "I think there must," (replied my Father) "I fancy the servants are returned; (said I) I think I hear Mary going to the Door." "I'm glad of it (cried my Father) for I long to know who it is."

I was right in my conjecture; for Mary instantly entering the Room, informed us that a young Gentleman and his Servant were at the door, who had lossed their way, were very cold and begged leave to warm themselves by our fire.

"Won't you admit them?" (said I.) "You have no objection, my Dear?" (said my Father.) "None in the World." (replied my Mother.)

Mary, without waiting for any further commands immediately left the room and quickly returned introducing the most beauteous and amiable Youth, I had ever beheld. The servant she kept to herself.

My natural sensibility had already been greatly affected by the sufferings of the unfortunate stranger and no sooner did I first behold him, than I felt that on him the happiness or Misery of my future Life must depend.

Adeiu

Laura.

Letter 6th

LAURA to MARIANNE

The noble Youth informed us that his name was Lindsay—for particular reasons however I shall conceal it under that of Talbot. He told us that he was the son of an English Baronet, that his Mother had been for many years no more and that he had a Sister of the middle size. "My Father (he continued) is a mean and mercenary wretch—it is only to such particular freinds as this Dear Party that I would thus betray his failings. Your Virtues my amiable Polydore (addressing himself to my father) yours Dear Claudia and yours my Charming Laura call on me to repose in you, my confidence." We bowed. "My Father seduced by the false glare of Fortune and the Deluding Pomp of Title, insisted on my giving my hand to Lady Dorothea. No never exclaimed I. Lady Dorothea is lovely and Engaging; I prefer no woman to her; but know Sir, that I scorn to marry her in compliance with your Wishes. No! Never shall it be said that I obliged my Father."

We all admired the noble Manliness of his reply. He continued.

"Sir Edward was surprised; he had perhaps little expected to meet with so spirited an opposition to his will. "Where, Edward in the name of wonder (said he) did you pick up this unmeaning gibberish? You have been studying Novels I suspect." I scorned to answer: it would have been beneath my dignity. I mounted my Horse and followed by my faithful William set forth for my Aunts."

"My Father's house is situated in Bedfordshire, my Aunt's in Middlesex, and tho' I flatter myself with being a tolerable proficient in Geography, I know not how it happened, but I found myself entering this beautifull Vale which I find is in South Wales, when I had expected to have reached my Aunts."

"After having wandered some time on the Banks of the Uske without knowing which way to go, I began to lament my cruel Destiny in the bitterest and most pathetic Manner. It was now perfectly dark, not a single star was there to direct my steps, and I know not what might have befallen me had I not at length discerned thro' the solemn Gloom that surrounded me a distant light, which as I approached it, I discovered to be the chearfull Blaze of your fire. Impelled by the combination of Misfortunes under which I laboured, namely Fear, Cold and Hunger I hesitated not to ask admittance which at length I have gained; and now my Adorable Laura (continued he taking my Hand) when may I hope to receive that reward of all the painfull sufferings I have undergone during the course of my attachment to you, to which I have ever aspired. Oh! when will you reward me with Yourself?"

"This instant, Dear and Amiable Edward." (replied I.). We were immediately united by my Father, who tho' he had never taken orders had been bred to the Church.

Adeiu

Laura

Letter 7th

LAURA to MARIANNE

We remained but a few days after our Marriage, in the Vale of Uske. After taking an affecting Farewell of my Father, my Mother and my Isabel, I accompanied Edward to his Aunt's in Middlesex. Philippa received us both with every expression of affectionate Love. My arrival was indeed a most agreable surprise to her as she had not only been totally ignorant of my Marriage with her Nephew, but had never even had the slightest idea of there being such a person in the World.

Augusta, the sister of Edward was on a visit to her when we arrived. I found her exactly what her Brother had described her to be—of the middle size. She received me with equal surprise though not with equal Cordiality, as Philippa. There was a disagreable coldness and Forbidding Reserve in her reception of me which was equally distressing and Unexpected. None of that interesting Sensibility or amiable simpathy in her manners and Address to me when we first met which should have distinguished our introduction to each other. Her Language was neither warm, nor affectionate, her expressions of regard were neither animated nor cordial; her arms were not opened to receive me to her Heart, tho' my own were extended to press her to mine.

A short Conversation between Augusta and her Brother, which I accidentally overheard encreased my dislike to her, and convinced me that her Heart was no more formed for the soft ties of Love than for the endearing intercourse of Freindship.

"But do you think that my Father will ever be reconciled to this imprudent connection?" (said Augusta.)

"Augusta (replied the noble Youth) I thought you had a better opinion of me, than to imagine I would so abjectly degrade myself as to consider my Father's Concurrence in any of my affairs, either of Consequence or concern to me. Tell me Augusta with sincerity; did you ever know me consult his inclinations or follow his Advice in the least trifling Particular since the age of fifteen?"

"Edward (replied she) you are surely too diffident in your own praise. Since you were fifteen only! My Dear Brother since you were five years old, I entirely acquit you of ever having willingly contributed to the satisfaction of your Father. But still I am not without apprehensions of your being shortly obliged to degrade yourself in your own eyes by seeking a support for your wife in the Generosity of Sir Edward."

"Never, never Augusta will I so demean myself. (said Edward). Support! What support will Laura want which she can receive from him?"

"Only those very insignificant ones of Victuals and Drink." (answered she.)

"Victuals and Drink! (replied my Husband in a most nobly contemptuous Manner) and dost thou then imagine that there is no other support for an exalted mind (such as is my Laura's) than the mean and indelicate employment of Eating and Drinking?"

"None that I know of, so efficacious." (returned Augusta).

"And did you then never feel the pleasing Pangs of Love, Augusta? (replied my Edward). Does it appear impossible to your vile and corrupted Palate, to exist on Love? Can you not conceive the Luxury of living in every distress that Poverty can inflict, with the object of your tenderest affection?"

"You are too ridiculous (said Augusta) to argue with; perhaps however you may in time be convinced that..."

Here I was prevented from hearing the remainder of her speech, by the appearance of a very Handsome young Woman, who was ushured into the Room at the Door of which I had been listening. On hearing her announced by the Name of "Lady Dorothea," I instantly quitted my Post and followed her into the Parlour, for I well remembered that she was the Lady, proposed as a Wife for my Edward by the Cruel and Unrelenting Baronet.

Altho' Lady Dorothea's visit was nominally to Philippa and Augusta, yet I have some reason to imagine that (acquainted with the Marriage and arrival of Edward) to see me was a principal motive to it.

I soon perceived that tho' Lovely and Elegant in her Person and tho' Easy and Polite in her Address, she was of that inferior order of Beings with regard to Delicate Feeling, tender Sentiments, and refined Sensibility, of which

Augusta was one.

She staid but half an hour and neither in the Course of her Visit, confided to me any of her secret thoughts, nor requested me to confide in her, any of Mine. You will easily imagine therefore my Dear Marianne that I could not feel any ardent affection or very sincere Attachment for Lady Dorothea.

Adeiu

Laura.

Letter 8th

LAURA to MARIANNE, in continuation

Lady Dorothea had not left us long before another visitor as unexpected a one as her Ladyship, was announced. It was Sir Edward, who informed by Augusta of her Brother's marriage, came doubtless to reproach him for having dared to unite himself to me without his Knowledge. But Edward foreseeing his design, approached him with heroic fortitude as soon as he entered the Room, and addressed him in the following Manner.

"Sir Edward, I know the motive of your Journey here—You come with the base Design of reproaching me for having entered into an indissoluble engagement with my Laura without your Consent. But Sir, I glory in the Act—. It is my greatest boast that I have incurred the displeasure of my Father!"

So saying, he took my hand and whilst Sir Edward, Philippa, and Augusta were doubtless reflecting with admiration on his undaunted Bravery, led me from the Parlour to his Father's Carriage which yet remained at the Door and in which we were instantly conveyed from the pursuit of Sir Edward.

The Postilions had at first received orders only to take the London road; as soon as we had sufficiently reflected However, we ordered them to Drive to M——. the seat of Edward's most particular freind, which was but a few miles distant.

At M——. we arrived in a few hours; and on sending in our names were immediately admitted to Sophia, the Wife of Edward's freind. After having been deprived during the course of 3 weeks of a real freind (for such I term your Mother) imagine my transports at beholding one, most truly worthy of the Name. Sophia was rather above the middle size; most elegantly formed. A soft languor spread over her lovely features, but increased their Beauty—. It was the Charectarestic of her Mind—. She was all sensibility and Feeling. We flew into each others arms and after having exchanged vows of mutual Freindship for the rest of our Lives, instantly unfolded to each other the most inward secrets of our Hearts—. We were interrupted in the delightfull Employment by the entrance of Augustus, (Edward's freind) who was just returned from a solitary ramble.

Never did I see such an affecting Scene as was the meeting of Edward and Augustus.

"My Life! my Soul!" (exclaimed the former) "My adorable angel!" (replied the latter) as they flew into each other's arms. It was too pathetic for the feelings of Sophia and myself—We fainted alternately on a sofa.

Adeiu

Laura.

Letter 9th

From the same to the same

Towards the close of the day we received the following Letter from Philippa.

"Sir Edward is greatly incensed by your abrupt departure; he has taken back Augusta to Bedfordshire. Much as I wish to enjoy again your charming society, I cannot determine to snatch you from that, of such dear and deserving Freinds—When your Visit to them is terminated, I trust you will return to the arms of your" "Philippa."

We returned a suitable answer to this affectionate Note and after thanking her for her kind invitation assured her that we would certainly avail ourselves of it, whenever we might have no other place to go to. Tho' certainly nothing could to any reasonable Being, have appeared more satisfactory, than so gratefull a reply to her invitation, yet I know not how it was, but she was certainly capricious enough to be displeased with our behaviour and in a few weeks after, either to revenge our Conduct, or releive her own solitude, married a young and illiterate Fortune-hunter. This imprudent step (tho' we were sensible that it would probably deprive us of that fortune which Philippa had ever taught us to expect) could not on our own accounts, excite from our exalted minds a single sigh; yet fearfull lest it might prove a source of endless misery to the deluded Bride, our trembling Sensibility was greatly affected when we were first informed of the Event. The affectionate Entreaties of Augustus and Sophia that we would for ever consider their House as our Home, easily prevailed on us to determine never more to leave them, In the society of my Edward and this Amiable Pair, I passed the happiest moments of my Life; Our time was most delightfully spent, in mutual Protestations of Freindship, and in vows of unalterable Love, in which we were secure from being interrupted, by intruding and disagreable Visitors, as Augustus and Sophia had on their first Entrance in the Neighbourhood, taken due care to inform the surrounding Families, that as their happiness centered wholly in themselves, they wished for no other society. But alas! my Dear Marianne such Happiness as I then enjoyed was too perfect to be lasting. A most severe and unexpected Blow at once destroyed every sensation of Pleasure.

Convinced as you must be from what I have already told you concerning Augustus and Sophia, that there never were a happier Couple, I need not I imagine, inform you that their union had been contrary to the inclinations of their Cruel and Mercenery Parents; who had vainly endeavoured with obstinate Perseverance to force them into a Marriage with those whom they had ever abhorred; but with a Heroic Fortitude worthy to be related and admired, they had both, constantly refused to submit to such despotic Power.

After having so nobly disentangled themselves from the shackles of Parental Authority, by a Clandestine Marriage, they were determined never to forfeit the good opinion they had gained in the World, in so doing, by accepting any proposals of reconciliation that might be offered them by their Fathers—to this farther tryal of their noble independance however they never were exposed.

They had been married but a few months when our visit to them commenced during which time they had been amply supported by a considerable sum of money which Augustus had gracefully purloined from his unworthy father's Escritoire, a few days before his union with Sophia.

By our arrival their Expenses were considerably encreased tho' their means for supplying them were then nearly exhausted. But they, Exalted Creatures! scorned to reflect a moment on their pecuniary Distresses and would have blushed at the idea of paying their Debts.—Alas! what was their Reward for such disinterested Behaviour! The beautifull Augustus was arrested and we were all undone. Such perfidious Treachery in the merciless perpetrators of the Deed will shock your gentle nature Dearest Marianne as much as it then affected the Delicate sensibility of Edward, Sophia, your Laura, and of Augustus himself. To compleat such unparalelled Barbarity we were informed that an Execution in the House would shortly take place. Ah! what could we do but what we did! We sighed and fainted on the sofa.

Adeiu

Laura.

Letter 10th

LAURA in continuation

When we were somewhat recovered from the overpowering Effusions of our grief, Edward desired that we would consider what was the most prudent step to be taken in our unhappy situation while he repaired to his imprisoned freind to lament over his misfortunes. We promised that we would, and he set forwards on his journey to Town. During his absence we faithfully complied with his Desire and after the most mature Deliberation, at length agreed that the best thing we could do was to leave the House; of which we every moment expected the officers of Justice to take possession. We waited therefore with the greatest impatience, for the return of Edward in order to impart to him the result of our Deliberations. But no Edward appeared. In vain did we count the tedious moments of his absence—in vain did we weep—in vain even did we sigh—no Edward returned—. This was too cruel, too unexpected a Blow to our Gentle Sensibility—we could not support it— we could only faint. At length collecting all the Resolution I was Mistress of, I arose and after packing up some necessary apparel for Sophia and myself, I dragged her to a Carriage I had ordered and we instantly set out for London. As the Habitation of Augustus was within twelve miles of Town, it was not long e'er we arrived there, and no sooner had we entered Holboun than letting down one of the Front Glasses I enquired of every decent-looking Person that we passed "If they had seen my Edward?"

But as we drove too rapidly to allow them to answer my repeated Enquiries, I gained little, or indeed, no information concerning him. "Where am I to drive?" said the Postilion. "To Newgate Gentle Youth (replied I), to see Augustus." "Oh! no, no, (exclaimed Sophia) I cannot go to Newgate; I shall not be able to support the sight of my Augustus in so cruel a confinement—my feelings are sufficiently shocked by the RECITAL, of his Distress, but to behold it will overpower my Sensibility." As I perfectly agreed with her in the Justice of her Sentiments the Postilion was instantly directed to return into the Country. You may perhaps have been somewhat surprised my Dearest Marianne, that in the Distress I then endured, destitute of any support, and unprovided with any Habitation, I should never once have remembered my Father and Mother or my paternal Cottage in the Vale of Uske. To account for this seeming forgetfullness I must inform you of a trifling circumstance concerning them which I have as yet never mentioned. The death of my Parents a few weeks after my Departure, is the circumstance I allude to. By their decease I became the lawfull Inheritress of their House and Fortune. But alas! the House had never been their own and their Fortune had only been an Annuity on their own Lives. Such is the Depravity of the World! To your Mother I should have returned with Pleasure, should have been happy to have introduced to her, my charming Sophia and should with Chearfullness have passed the remainder of my Life in their dear Society in the Vale of Uske, had not one obstacle to the execution of so agreable a scheme, intervened; which was the Marriage and Removal of your Mother to a distant part of Ireland.

Adeiu

Laura.

Letter 11th

LAURA in continuation

"I have a Relation in Scotland (said Sophia to me as we left London) who I am certain would not hesitate in receiving me." "Shall I order the Boy to drive there?" said I—but instantly recollecting myself, exclaimed, "Alas I fear it will be too long a Journey for the Horses." Unwilling however to act only from my own inadequate Knowledge of the Strength and Abilities of Horses, I consulted the Postilion, who was entirely of my Opinion concerning the Affair. We therefore determined to change Horses at the next Town and to travel Post the remainder of the Journey—. When we arrived at the last Inn we were to stop at, which was but a few miles from the House of Sophia's Relation, unwilling to intrude our Society on him unexpected and unthought of, we wrote a very elegant and well penned Note to him containing an account of our Destitute and melancholy Situation, and of our intention to spend some months with him in Scotland. As soon as we had dispatched this Letter, we immediately prepared to follow it in person and were stepping into the Carriage for that Purpose when our attention was attracted by the Entrance of a coroneted Coach and 4 into the Inn-yard. A Gentleman considerably advanced in years descended from it. At his first Appearance my Sensibility was wonderfully affected and e'er I had gazed at him a 2d time, an instinctive sympathy whispered to my Heart, that he was my Grandfather. Convinced that I could not be mistaken in my conjecture I instantly sprang from the Carriage I had just entered, and following the Venerable Stranger into the Room he had been shewn to, I threw myself on my knees before him and besought him to acknowledge me as his Grand Child. He started, and having attentively examined my features, raised me from the Ground and throwing his Grand-fatherly arms around my Neck, exclaimed, "Acknowledge thee! Yes dear resemblance of my Laurina and Laurina's Daughter, sweet image of my Claudia and my Claudia's Mother, I do acknowledge thee as the Daughter of the one and the Grandaughter of the other." While he was thus tenderly embracing me, Sophia astonished at my precipitate Departure, entered the Room in search of me. No sooner had she caught the eye of the venerable Peer, than he exclaimed with every mark of Astonishment—"Another Grandaughter! Yes, yes, I see you are the Daughter of my Laurina's eldest Girl; your resemblance to the beauteous Matilda sufficiently proclaims it. "Oh!" replied Sophia, "when I first beheld you the instinct of Nature whispered me that we were in some degree related—But whether Grandfathers, or Grandmothers, I could not pretend to determine." He folded her in his arms, and whilst they were tenderly embracing, the Door of the Apartment opened and a most beautifull young Man appeared. On perceiving him Lord St. Clair started and retreating back a few paces, with uplifted Hands, said, "Another Grand-child! What an unexpected Happiness is this! to discover in the space of 3 minutes, as many of my Descendants! This I am certain is Philander the son of my Laurina's 3d girl the amiable Bertha; there wants now but the presence of Gustavus to compleat the Union of my Laurina's Grand-Children."

"And here he is; (said a Gracefull Youth who that instant entered the room) here is the Gustavus you desire to see. I am the son of Agatha your Laurina's 4th and youngest Daughter," "I see you are indeed; replied Lord St. Clair—But tell me (continued he looking fearfully towards the Door) tell me, have I any other Grand-children in the House." "None my Lord." "Then I will provide for you all without farther delay—Here are 4 Banknotes of 50L each—Take them and remember I have done the Duty of a Grandfather." He instantly left the Room and immediately afterwards the House.

Adeiu,

Laura.

Letter 12th

LAURA in continuation

You may imagine how greatly we were surprised by the sudden departure of Lord St Clair. "Ignoble Grand-sire!" exclaimed Sophia. "Unworthy Grandfather!" said I, and instantly fainted in each other's arms. How long we remained in this situation I know not; but when we recovered we found ourselves alone, without either Gustavus, Philander, or the Banknotes. As we were deploring our unhappy fate, the Door of the Apartment opened and "Macdonald" was announced. He was Sophia's cousin. The haste with which he came to our releif so soon after the receipt of our Note, spoke so greatly in his favour that I hesitated not to pronounce him at first sight, a tender and simpathetic Freind. Alas! he little deserved the name—for though he told us that he was much concerned at our Misfortunes, yet by his own account it appeared that the perusal of them, had neither drawn from him a single sigh, nor induced him to bestow one curse on our vindictive stars—. He told Sophia that his Daughter depended on her returning with him to Macdonald-Hall, and that as his Cousin's freind he should be happy to see me there also. To Macdonald-Hall, therefore we went, and were received with great kindness by Janetta the Daughter of Macdonald, and the Mistress of the Mansion. Janetta was then only fifteen; naturally well disposed, endowed with a susceptible Heart, and a simpathetic Disposition, she might, had these amiable qualities been properly encouraged, have been an ornament to human Nature; but unfortunately her Father possessed not a soul sufficiently exalted to admire so promising a Disposition, and had endeavoured by every means on his power to prevent it encreasing with her Years. He had actually so far extinguished the natural noble Sensibility of her Heart, as to prevail on her to accept an offer from a young Man of his Recommendation. They were to be married in a few months, and Graham, was in the House when we arrived. WE soon saw through his character. He was just such a Man as one might have expected to be the choice of Macdonald. They said he was Sensible, well-informed, and Agreable; we did not pretend to Judge of such trifles, but as we were convinced he had no soul, that he had never read the sorrows of Werter, and that his Hair bore not the least resemblance to auburn, we were certain that Janetta could feel no affection for him, or at least that she ought to feel none. The very circumstance of his being her father's choice too, was so much in his disfavour, that had he been deserving her, in every other respect yet THAT of itself ought to have been a sufficient reason in the Eyes of Janetta for rejecting him. These considerations we were determined to represent to her in their proper light and doubted not of meeting with the desired success from one naturally so well disposed; whose errors in the affair had only arisen from a want of proper confidence in her own opinion, and a suitable contempt of her father's. We found her indeed all that our warmest wishes could have hoped for; we had no difficulty to convince her that it was impossible she could love Graham, or that it was her Duty to disobey her Father; the only thing at which she rather seemed to hesitate was our assertion that she must be attached to some other Person. For some time, she persevered in declaring that she knew no other young man for whom she had the the smallest Affection; but upon explaining the impossibility of such a thing she said that she beleived she DID LIKE Captain M'Kenrie better than any one she knew besides. This confession satisfied us and after having enumerated the good Qualities of M'Kenrie and assured her that she was violently in love with him, we desired to know whether he had ever in any wise declared his affection to her.

"So far from having ever declared it, I have no reason to imagine that he has ever felt any for me." said Janetta. "That he certainly adores you (replied Sophia) there can be no doubt—. The Attachment must be reciprocal. Did he never gaze on you with admiration—tenderly press your hand—drop an involantary tear—and leave the room abruptly?" "Never (replied she) that I remember—he has always left the room indeed when his visit has been ended, but has never gone away particularly abruptly or without making a bow." Indeed my Love (said I) you must be mistaken—for it is absolutely impossible that he should ever have left you but with Confusion, Despair, and Precipitation. Consider but for a moment Janetta, and you must be convinced how absurd it is to suppose that he could ever make a Bow, or behave like any other Person." Having settled this Point to our satisfaction, the next we took into consideration was, to determine in what manner we should inform M'Kenrie of the favourable Opinion Janetta entertained of him.... We at length agreed to acquaint him with it by an anonymous Letter which Sophia drew up in the following manner.

"Oh! happy Lover of the beautifull Janetta, oh! amiable Possessor of HER Heart whose hand is destined to another, why do you thus delay a confession of your attachment to the amiable Object of it? Oh! consider that a few weeks will at once put an end to every flattering Hope that you may now entertain, by uniting the unfortunate Victim of her father's Cruelty to the execrable and detested Graham."

"Alas! why do you thus so cruelly connive at the projected Misery of her and of yourself by delaying to communicate that scheme which had doubtless long possessed your imagination? A secret Union will at once secure the felicity of both."

The amiable M'Kenrie, whose modesty as he afterwards assured us had been the only reason of his having so long concealed the violence of his affection for Janetta, on receiving this Billet flew on the wings of Love to Macdonald-Hall, and so powerfully pleaded his Attachment to her who inspired it, that after a few more private interveiws, Sophia and I experienced the satisfaction of seeing them depart for Gretna-Green, which they chose for the celebration of their Nuptials, in preference to any other place although it was at a considerable distance from Macdonald-Hall.

Adeiu

Laura.

Letter 13th

LAURA in continuation

They had been gone nearly a couple of Hours, before either Macdonald or Graham had entertained any suspicion of the affair. And they might not even then have suspected it, but for the following little Accident. Sophia happening one day to open a private Drawer in Macdonald's Library with one of her own keys, discovered that it was the Place where he kept his Papers of consequence and amongst them some bank notes of considerable amount. This discovery she imparted to me; and having agreed together that it would be a proper treatment of so vile a Wretch as Macdonald to deprive him of money, perhaps dishonestly gained, it was determined that the next time we should either of us happen to go that way, we would take one or more of the Bank notes from the drawer. This well meant Plan we had often successfully put in Execution; but alas! on the very day of Janetta's Escape, as Sophia was majestically removing the 5th Bank-note from the Drawer to her own purse, she was suddenly most impertinently interrupted in her employment by the entrance of Macdonald himself, in a most abrupt and precipitate Manner. Sophia (who though naturally all winning sweetness could when occasions demanded it call forth the Dignity of her sex) instantly put on a most forbidding look, and darting an angry frown on the undaunted culprit, demanded in a haughty tone of voice "Wherefore her retirement was thus insolently broken in on?" The unblushing Macdonald, without even endeavouring to exculpate himself from the crime he was charged with, meanly endeavoured to reproach Sophia with ignobly defrauding him of his money... The dignity of Sophia was wounded; "Wretch (exclaimed she, hastily replacing the Bank-note in the Drawer) how darest thou to accuse me of an Act, of which the bare idea makes me blush?" The base wretch was still unconvinced and continued to upbraid the justly-offended Sophia in such opprobious Language, that at length he so greatly provoked the gentle sweetness of her Nature, as to induce her to revenge herself on him by informing him of Janetta's Elopement, and of the active Part we had both taken in the affair. At this period of their Quarrel I entered the Library and was as you may imagine equally offended as Sophia at the ill-grounded accusations of the malevolent and contemptible Macdonald. "Base Miscreant! (cried I) how canst thou thus undauntedly endeavour to sully the spotless reputation of such bright Excellence? Why dost thou not suspect MY innocence as soon?" "Be satisfied Madam (replied he) I DO suspect it, and therefore must desire that you will both leave this House in less than half an hour."

"We shall go willingly; (answered Sophia) our hearts have long detested thee, and nothing but our freindship for thy Daughter could have induced us to remain so long beneath thy roof."

"Your Freindship for my Daughter has indeed been most powerfully exerted by throwing her into the arms of an unprincipled Fortune-hunter." (replied he)

"Yes, (exclaimed I) amidst every misfortune, it will afford us some consolation to reflect that by this one act of Freindship to Janetta, we have amply discharged every obligation that we have received from her father."

"It must indeed be a most gratefull reflection, to your exalted minds." (said he.)

As soon as we had packed up our wardrobe and valuables, we left Macdonald Hall, and after having walked about a mile and a half we sate down by the side of a clear limpid stream to refresh our exhausted limbs. The place was suited to meditation. A grove of full-grown Elms sheltered us from the East—. A Bed of full-grown Nettles from the West—. Before us ran the murmuring brook and behind us ran the turn-pike road. We were in a mood for contemplation and in a Disposition to enjoy so beautifull a spot. A mutual silence which had for some time reigned between us, was at length broke by my exclaiming—"What a lovely scene! Alas why are not Edward and Augustus here to enjoy its Beauties with us?"

"Ah! my beloved Laura (cried Sophia) for pity's sake forbear recalling to my remembrance the unhappy situation of my imprisoned Husband. Alas, what would I not give to learn the fate of my Augustus! to know if he is still in Newgate, or if he is yet hung. But never shall I be able so far to conquer my tender sensibility as to enquire after him. Oh! do not I beseech you ever let me again hear you repeat his beloved name—. It affects me too deeply—. I cannot bear to hear him mentioned it wounds my feelings."

"Excuse me my Sophia for having thus unwillingly offended you—"

replied I—and then changing the conversation, desired her to admire the noble Grandeur of the Elms which sheltered us from the Eastern Zephyr. "Alas! my Laura (returned she) avoid so melancholy a subject, I intreat you. Do not again wound my Sensibility by observations on those elms. They remind me of Augustus. He was like them, tall, magestic—he possessed that noble grandeur which you admire in them."

I was silent, fearfull lest I might any more unwillingly distress her by fixing on any other subject of conversation which might again remind her of Augustus.

"Why do you not speak my Laura? (said she after a short pause) "I cannot support this silence you must not leave me to my own reflections; they ever recur to Augustus."

"What a beautifull sky! (said I) How charmingly is the azure varied by those delicate streaks of white!"

"Oh! my Laura (replied she hastily withdrawing her Eyes from a momentary glance at the sky) do not thus distress me by calling my Attention to an object which so cruelly reminds me of my Augustus's blue sattin waistcoat striped in white! In pity to your unhappy freind avoid a subject so distressing." What could I do? The feelings of Sophia were at that time so exquisite, and the tenderness she felt for Augustus so poignant that I had not power to start any other topic, justly fearing that it might in some unforseen manner again awaken all her sensibility by directing her thoughts to her Husband. Yet to be silent would be cruel; she had intreated me to talk.

From this Dilemma I was most fortunately releived by an accident truly apropos; it was the lucky overturning of a Gentleman's Phaeton, on the road which ran murmuring behind us. It was a most fortunate accident as it diverted the attention of Sophia from the melancholy reflections which she had been before indulging. We instantly quitted our seats and ran to the rescue of those who but a few moments before had been in so elevated a situation as a fashionably high Phaeton, but who were now laid low and sprawling in the Dust. "What an ample subject for reflection on the uncertain Enjoyments of this World, would not that Phaeton and the Life of Cardinal Wolsey afford a thinking Mind!" said I to Sophia as we were hastening to the field of Action.

She had not time to answer me, for every thought was now engaged by the horrid spectacle before us. Two Gentlemen most elegantly attired but weltering in their blood was what first struck our Eyes—we approached— they were Edward and Augustus—. Yes dearest Marianne they were our Husbands. Sophia shreiked and fainted on the ground—I screamed and instantly ran mad—. We remained thus mutually deprived of our senses, some minutes, and on regaining them were deprived of them again. For an Hour and a Quarter did we continue in this unfortunate situation—Sophia fainting every moment and I running mad as often. At length a groan from the hapless Edward (who alone retained any share of life) restored us to ourselves. Had we indeed before imagined that either of them lived, we should have been more sparing of our Greif—but as we had supposed when we first beheld them that they were no more, we knew that nothing could remain to be done but what we were about. No sooner did we therefore hear my Edward's groan than postponing our lamentations for the present, we hastily ran to the Dear Youth and kneeling on each side of him implored him not to die—. "Laura (said He fixing his now languid Eyes on me) I fear I have been overturned."

I was overjoyed to find him yet sensible.

"Oh! tell me Edward (said I) tell me I beseech you before you die, what has befallen you since that unhappy Day in which Augustus was arrested and we were separated—"

"I will" (said he) and instantly fetching a deep sigh, Expired—. Sophia immediately sank again into a swoon—. MY greif was more audible. My Voice faltered, My Eyes assumed a vacant stare, my face became as pale as Death, and my senses were considerably impaired—.

"Talk not to me of Phaetons (said I, raving in a frantic, incoherent manner)—Give me a violin—. I'll play to him and sooth him in his melancholy Hours—Beware ye gentle Nymphs of Cupid's Thunderbolts, avoid the piercing shafts of Jupiter—Look at that grove of Firs—I see a Leg of Mutton—They told me Edward was not Dead; but they deceived me— they took him for a cucumber—" Thus I continued wildly exclaiming on my Edward's Death—. For two Hours did I rave thus madly and should not then have left off, as I was not in the least fatigued, had not Sophia who was just recovered from her swoon, intreated me to consider that Night was now approaching and that the Damps began to fall. "And whither shall we go (said I) to shelter us from either?" "To that white Cottage." (replied she pointing to a neat Building which rose up amidst the grove of Elms and which I had not before observed—) I agreed and we instantly walked to it—we knocked at the door—it was opened by an old woman; on being requested to afford us a Night's Lodging, she informed us that her House was but small, that she had only two Bedrooms, but that However we should be wellcome to one of them. We were satisfied and followed the good woman into the House where we were greatly cheered by the sight of a comfortable fire—. She was a widow and had only one Daughter, who was then just seventeen—One of the best of ages; but alas! she was very plain and her name was Bridget..... Nothing therfore could be expected from her—she could not be supposed to possess either exalted Ideas, Delicate Feelings or refined Sensibilities—. She was nothing more than a mere good-tempered, civil and obliging young woman; as such we could scarcely dislike here—she was only an Object of Contempt—

Adeiu

Laura.

Letter 14th

LAURA in continuation

Arm yourself my amiable young Freind with all the philosophy you are Mistress of; summon up all the fortitude you possess, for alas! in the perusal of the following Pages your sensibility will be most severely tried. Ah! what were the misfortunes I had before experienced and which I have already related to you, to the one I am now going to inform you of. The Death of my Father and my Mother and my Husband though almost more than my gentle Nature could support, were trifles in comparison to the misfortune I am now proceeding to relate. The morning after our arrival at the Cottage, Sophia complained of a violent pain in her delicate limbs, accompanied with a disagreable Head-ake She attributed it to a cold caught by her continued faintings in the open air as the Dew was falling the Evening before. This I feared was but too probably the case; since how could it be otherwise accounted for that I should have escaped the same indisposition, but by supposing that the bodily Exertions I had undergone in my repeated fits of frenzy had so effectually circulated and warmed my Blood as to make me proof against the chilling Damps of Night, whereas, Sophia lying totally inactive on the ground must have been exposed to all their severity. I was most seriously alarmed by her illness which trifling as it may appear to you, a certain instinctive sensibility whispered me, would in the End be fatal to her.

Alas! my fears were but too fully justified; she grew gradually worse—and I daily became more alarmed for her. At length she was obliged to confine herself solely to the Bed allotted us by our worthy Landlady—. Her disorder turned to a galloping Consumption and in a few days carried her off. Amidst all my Lamentations for her (and violent you may suppose they were) I yet received some consolation in the reflection of my having paid every attention to her, that could be offered, in her illness. I had wept over her every Day— had bathed her sweet face with my tears and had pressed her fair Hands continually in mine—. "My beloved Laura (said she to me a few Hours before she died) take warning from my unhappy End and avoid the imprudent conduct which had occasioned it... Beware of fainting-fits... Though at the time they may be refreshing and agreable yet beleive me they will in the end, if too often repeated and at improper seasons, prove destructive to your Constitution... My fate will teach you this.. I die a Martyr to my greif for the loss of Augustus.. One fatal swoon has cost me my Life.. Beware of swoons Dear Laura.... A frenzy fit is not one quarter so pernicious; it is an exercise to the Body and if not too violent, is I dare say conducive to Health in its consequences—Run mad as often as you chuse; but do not faint—"

These were the last words she ever addressed to me.. It was her dieing Advice to her afflicted Laura, who has ever most faithfully adhered to it.

After having attended my lamented freind to her Early Grave, I immediately (tho' late at night) left the detested Village in which she died, and near which had expired my Husband and Augustus. I had not walked many yards from it before I was overtaken by a stage-coach, in which I instantly took a place, determined to proceed in it to Edinburgh, where I hoped to find some kind some pitying Freind who would receive and comfort me in my afflictions.

It was so dark when I entered the Coach that I could not distinguish the Number of my Fellow-travellers; I could only perceive that they were many. Regardless however of anything concerning them, I gave myself up to my own sad Reflections. A general silence prevailed—A silence, which was by nothing interrupted but by the loud and repeated snores of one of the Party.

"What an illiterate villain must that man be! (thought I to myself) What a total want of delicate refinement must he have, who can thus shock our senses by such a brutal noise! He must I am certain be capable of every bad action! There is no crime too black for such a Character!" Thus reasoned I within myself, and doubtless such were the reflections of my fellow travellers.

At length, returning Day enabled me to behold the unprincipled Scoundrel who had so violently disturbed my feelings. It was Sir Edward the father of my Deceased Husband. By his side sate Augusta, and on the same seat with me were your Mother and Lady Dorothea. Imagine my surprise at finding myself thus seated amongst my old Acquaintance. Great as was my astonishment, it was yet increased, when on looking out of Windows, I beheld the Husband of Philippa, with Philippa by his side, on the Coachbox and when on looking behind I beheld, Philander and Gustavus in the Basket. "Oh! Heavens, (exclaimed I) is it possible that I should so unexpectedly be surrounded by my nearest Relations and Connections?" These words roused the rest of the Party, and every eye was directed to the corner in which I sat. "Oh! my Isabel (continued I throwing myself across Lady Dorothea into her arms) receive once more to your Bosom the unfortunate Laura. Alas! when we last parted in the Vale of Usk, I was happy in being united to the best of Edwards; I had then a Father and a Mother, and had never known misfortunes—But now deprived of every freind but you—"

"What! (interrupted Augusta) is my Brother dead then? Tell us I intreat you what is become of him?" "Yes, cold and insensible Nymph, (replied I) that luckless swain your Brother, is no more, and you may now glory in being the Heiress of Sir Edward's fortune."

Although I had always despised her from the Day I had overheard her conversation with my Edward, yet in civility I complied with hers and Sir Edward's intreaties that I would inform them of the whole melancholy affair. They were greatly shocked—even the obdurate Heart of Sir Edward and the insensible one of Augusta, were touched with sorrow, by the unhappy tale. At the request of your Mother I related to them every other misfortune which had befallen me since we parted. Of the imprisonment of Augustus and the absence of Edward—of our arrival in Scotland—of our unexpected Meeting with our Grand-father and our cousins—of our visit to Macdonald-Hall—of the singular service we there performed towards Janetta—of her Fathers ingratitude for it.. of his inhuman Behaviour, unaccountable suspicions, and barbarous treatment of us, in obliging us to leave the House.. of our lamentations on the loss of Edward and Augustus and finally of the melancholy Death of my beloved Companion.

Pity and surprise were strongly depictured in your Mother's countenance, during the whole of my narration, but I am sorry to say, that to the eternal reproach of her sensibility, the latter infinitely predominated. Nay, faultless as my conduct had certainly been during the whole course of my late misfortunes and adventures, she pretended to find fault with my behaviour in many of the situations in which I had been placed. As I was sensible myself, that I had always behaved in a manner which reflected Honour on my Feelings and Refinement, I paid little attention to what she said, and desired her to satisfy my Curiosity by informing me how she came there, instead of wounding my spotless reputation with unjustifiable Reproaches. As soon as she had complied with my wishes in this particular and had given me an accurate detail of every thing that had befallen her since our separation (the particulars of which if you are not already acquainted with, your Mother will give you) I applied to Augusta for the same information respecting herself, Sir Edward and Lady Dorothea.

She told me that having a considerable taste for the Beauties of Nature, her curiosity to behold the delightful scenes it exhibited in that part of the World had been so much raised by Gilpin's Tour to the Highlands, that she had prevailed on her Father to undertake a Tour to Scotland and had persuaded Lady Dorothea to accompany them. That they had arrived at Edinburgh a few Days before and from thence had made daily Excursions into the Country around in the Stage Coach they were then in, from one of which Excursions they were at that time returning. My next enquiries were concerning Philippa and her Husband, the latter of whom I learned having spent all her fortune, had recourse for subsistence to the talent in which, he had always most excelled, namely, Driving, and that having sold every thing which belonged to them except their Coach, had converted it into a Stage and in order to be removed from any of his former Acquaintance, had driven it to Edinburgh from whence he went to Sterling every other Day. That Philippa still retaining her affection for her ungratefull Husband, had followed him to Scotland and generally accompanied him in his little Excursions to Sterling. "It has only been to throw a little money into their Pockets (continued Augusta) that my Father has always travelled in their Coach to veiw the beauties of the Country since our arrival in Scotland—for it would certainly have been much more agreable to us, to visit the Highlands in a Postchaise than merely to travel from Edinburgh to Sterling and from Sterling to Edinburgh every other Day in a crowded and uncomfortable Stage." I perfectly agreed with her in her sentiments on the affair, and secretly blamed Sir Edward for thus sacrificing his Daughter's Pleasure for the sake of a ridiculous old woman whose folly in marrying so young a man ought to be punished. His Behaviour however was entirely of a peice with his general Character; for what could be expected from a man who possessed not the smallest atom of Sensibility, who scarcely knew the meaning of simpathy, and who actually snored—

Adeiu

Laura.

Letter 15th

LAURA in continuation.

When we arrived at the town where we were to Breakfast, I was determined to speak with Philander and Gustavus, and to that purpose as soon as I left the Carriage, I went to the Basket and tenderly enquired after their Health, expressing my fears of the uneasiness of their situation. At first they seemed rather confused at my appearance dreading no doubt that I might call them to account for the money which our Grandfather had left me and which they had unjustly deprived me of, but finding that I mentioned nothing of the Matter, they desired me to step into the Basket as we might there converse with greater ease. Accordingly I entered and whilst the rest of the party were devouring green tea and buttered toast, we feasted ourselves in a more refined and sentimental Manner by a confidential Conversation. I informed them of every thing which had befallen me during the course of my life, and at my request they related to me every incident of theirs.

"We are the sons as you already know, of the two youngest Daughters which Lord St Clair had by Laurina an italian opera girl. Our mothers could neither of them exactly ascertain who were our Father, though it is generally beleived that Philander, is the son of one Philip Jones a Bricklayer and that my Father was one Gregory Staves a Staymaker of Edinburgh. This is however of little consequence for as our Mothers were certainly never married to either of them it reflects no Dishonour on our Blood, which is of a most ancient and unpolluted kind. Bertha (the Mother of Philander) and Agatha (my own Mother) always lived together. They were neither of them very rich; their united fortunes had originally amounted to nine thousand Pounds, but as they had always lived on the principal of it, when we were fifteen it was diminished to nine Hundred. This nine Hundred they always kept in a Drawer in one of the Tables which stood in our common sitting Parlour, for the convenience of having it always at Hand. Whether it was from this circumstance, of its being easily taken, or from a wish of being independant, or from an excess of sensibility (for which we were always remarkable) I cannot now determine, but certain it is that when we had reached our 15th year, we took the nine Hundred Pounds and ran away. Having obtained this prize we were determined to manage it with eoconomy and not to spend it either with folly or Extravagance. To this purpose we therefore divided it into nine parcels, one of which we devoted to Victuals, the 2d to Drink, the 3d to Housekeeping, the 4th to Carriages, the 5th to Horses, the 6th to Servants, the 7th to Amusements, the 8th to Cloathes and the 9th to Silver Buckles. Having thus arranged our Expences for two months (for we expected to make the nine Hundred Pounds last as long) we hastened to London and had the good luck to spend it in 7 weeks and a Day which was 6 Days sooner than we had intended. As soon as we had thus happily disencumbered ourselves from the weight of so much money, we began to think of returning to our Mothers, but accidentally hearing that they were both starved to Death, we gave over the design and determined to engage ourselves to some strolling Company of Players, as we had always a turn for the Stage. Accordingly we offered our services to one and were accepted; our Company was indeed rather small, as it consisted only of the Manager his wife and ourselves, but there were fewer to pay and the only inconvenience attending it was the Scarcity of Plays which for want of People to fill the Characters, we could perform. We did not mind trifles however——. One of our most admired Performances was MACBETH, in which we were truly great. The Manager always played BANQUO himself, his Wife my LADY MACBETH. I did the THREE WITCHES and Philander acted ALL THE REST. To say the truth this tragedy was not only the Best, but the only Play that we ever performed; and after having acted it all over England, and Wales, we came to Scotland to exhibit it over the remainder of Great Britain. We happened to be quartered in that very Town, where you came and met your Grandfather——. We were in the Inn-yard when his Carriage entered and perceiving by the arms to whom it belonged, and knowing that Lord St Clair was our Grandfather, we agreed to endeavour to get something from him by discovering the Relationship——. You know how well it succeeded——. Having obtained the two Hundred Pounds, we instantly left the Town, leaving our Manager and his Wife to act MACBETH by themselves, and took the road to Sterling, where we spent our little fortune with great ECLAT. We are now returning to Edinburgh in order to get some preferment in the Acting way; and such my Dear Cousin is our History."

I thanked the amiable Youth for his entertaining narration, and after expressing my wishes for their Welfare and Happiness, left them in their little Habitation and returned to my other Freinds who impatiently expected me.

My adventures are now drawing to a close my dearest Marianne; at least for the present.

When we arrived at Edinburgh Sir Edward told me that as the Widow of his son, he desired I would accept from his Hands of four Hundred a year. I graciously promised that I would, but could not help observing that the unsimpathetic Baronet offered it more on account of my being the Widow of Edward than in being the refined and amiable Laura.

I took up my Residence in a Romantic Village in the Highlands of Scotland where I have ever since continued, and where I can uninterrupted by unmeaning Visits, indulge in a melancholy solitude, my unceasing Lamentations for the Death of my Father, my Mother, my Husband and my Freind.

Augusta has been for several years united to Graham the Man of all others most suited to her; she became acquainted with him during her stay in Scotland.

Sir Edward in hopes of gaining an Heir to his Title and Estate, at the same time married Lady Dorothea—. His wishes have been answered.

Philander and Gustavus, after having raised their reputation by their Performances in the Theatrical Line at Edinburgh, removed to Covent Garden, where they still exhibit under the assumed names of LUVIS and QUICK.

Philippa has long paid the Debt of Nature, Her Husband however still continues to drive the Stage-Coach from Edinburgh to Sterling:—

Adeiu my Dearest Marianne.

Laura.

June 13th 1790.

Lesley Castle

AN UNFINISHED NOVEL IN LETTERS

To HENRY THOMAS AUSTEN Esqre.

Sir

I am now availing myself of the Liberty you have frequently honoured me with of dedicating one of my Novels to you. That it is unfinished, I greive; yet fear that from me, it will always remain so; that as far as it is carried, it should be so trifling and so unworthy of you, is another concern to your obliged humble Servant

The Author

Messrs Demand and Co—please to pay Jane Austen Spinster the sum of one hundred guineas on account of your Humble Servant.

H. T. Austen

Letter The First

is from Miss MARGARET LESLEY to Miss CHARLOTTE

LUTTERELL. Lesley Castle Janry 3rd—1792.

My Brother has just left us. "Matilda (said he at parting) you and Margaret will I am certain take all the care of my dear little one, that she might have received from an indulgent, and affectionate and amiable Mother." Tears rolled down his cheeks as he spoke these words—the remembrance of her, who had so wantonly disgraced the Maternal character and so openly violated the conjugal Duties, prevented his adding anything farther; he embraced his sweet Child and after saluting Matilda and Me hastily broke from us and seating himself in his Chaise, pursued the road to Aberdeen. Never was there a better young Man! Ah! how little did he deserve the misfortunes he has experienced in the Marriage state. So good a Husband to so bad a Wife! for you know my dear Charlotte that the Worthless Louisa left him, her Child and reputation a few weeks ago in company with Danvers and dishonour. Never was there a sweeter face, a finer form, or a less amiable Heart than Louisa owned! Her child already possesses the personal Charms of her unhappy Mother! May she inherit from her Father all his mental ones! Lesley is at present but five and twenty, and has already given himself up to melancholy and Despair; what a difference between him and his Father! Sir George is 57 and still remains the Beau, the flighty stripling, the gay Lad, and sprightly Youngster, that his Son was really about five years back, and that HE has affected to appear ever since my remembrance. While our father is fluttering about the streets of London, gay, dissipated, and Thoughtless at the age of 57, Matilda and I continue secluded from Mankind in our old and Mouldering Castle, which is situated two miles from Perth on a bold projecting Rock, and commands an extensive veiw of the Town and its delightful Environs. But tho' retired from almost all the World, (for we visit no one but the M'Leods, The M'Kenzies, the M'Phersons, the M'Cartneys, the M'Donalds, The M'kinnons, the M'lellans, the M'kays, the Macbeths and the Macduffs) we are neither dull nor unhappy; on the contrary there never were two more lively, more agreable or more witty girls, than we are; not an hour in the Day hangs heavy on our Hands. We read, we work, we walk, and when fatigued with these Employments releive our spirits, either by a lively song, a graceful Dance, or by some smart bon-mot, and witty repartee. We are handsome my dear Charlotte, very handsome and the greatest of our Perfections is, that we are entirely insensible of them ourselves. But why do I thus dwell on myself! Let me rather repeat the praise of our dear little Neice the innocent Louisa, who is at present sweetly smiling in a gentle Nap, as she reposes on the sofa. The dear Creature is just turned of two years old; as handsome as tho' 2 and 20, as sensible as tho' 2 and 30, and as prudent as tho'

2 and 40. To convince you of this, I must inform you that she has a very fine complexion and very pretty features, that she already knows the two first letters in the Alphabet, and that she never tears her frocks—. If I have not now convinced you of her Beauty, Sense and Prudence, I have nothing more to urge in support of my assertion, and you will therefore have no way of deciding the Affair but by coming to Lesley-Castle, and by a personal acquaintance with Louisa, determine for yourself. Ah! my dear Freind, how happy should I be to see you within these venerable Walls! It is now four years since my removal from School has separated me from you; that two such tender Hearts, so closely linked together by the ties of simpathy and Freindship, should be so widely removed from each other, is vastly moving. I live in Perthshire, You in Sussex. We might meet in London, were my Father disposed to carry me there, and were your Mother to be there at the same time. We might meet at Bath, at Tunbridge, or anywhere else indeed, could we but be at the same place together. We have only to hope that such a period may arrive. My Father does not return to us till Autumn; my Brother will leave Scotland in a few Days; he is impatient to travel. Mistaken Youth! He vainly flatters himself that change of Air will heal the Wounds of a broken Heart! You will join with me I am certain my dear Charlotte, in prayers for the recovery of the unhappy Lesley's peace of Mind, which must ever be essential to that of your sincere freind M. Lesley.

Letter The Second

From Miss C. LUTTERELL to Miss M. LESLEY in answer.

Glenford Febry 12

I have a thousand excuses to beg for having so long delayed thanking you my dear Peggy for your agreable Letter, which beleive me I should not have deferred doing, had not every moment of my time during the last five weeks been so fully employed in the necessary arrangements for my sisters wedding, as to allow me no time to devote either to you or myself. And now what provokes me more than anything else is that the Match is broke off, and all my Labour thrown away. Imagine how great the Dissapointment must be to me, when you consider that after having laboured both by Night and by Day, in order to get the Wedding dinner ready by the time appointed, after having roasted Beef, Broiled Mutton, and Stewed Soup enough to last the new-married Couple through the Honey-moon, I had the mortification of finding that I had been Roasting, Broiling and Stewing both the Meat and Myself to no purpose. Indeed my dear Freind, I never remember suffering any vexation equal to what I experienced on last Monday when my sister came running to me in the store-room with her face as White as a Whipt syllabub, and told me that Hervey had been thrown from his Horse, had fractured his Scull and was pronounced by his surgeon to be in the most emminent Danger. "Good God! (said I) you dont say so? Why what in the name of Heaven will become of all the Victuals! We shall never be able to eat it while it is good. However, we'll call in the Surgeon to help us. I shall be able to manage the Sir-loin myself, my Mother will eat the soup, and You and the Doctor must finish the rest." Here I was interrupted, by seeing my poor Sister fall down to appearance Lifeless upon one of the Chests, where we keep our Table linen. I immediately called my Mother and the Maids, and at last we brought her to herself again; as soon as ever she was sensible, she expressed a determination of going instantly to Henry, and was so wildly bent on this Scheme, that we had the greatest Difficulty in the World to prevent her putting it in execution; at last however more by Force than Entreaty we prevailed on her to go into her room; we laid her upon the Bed, and she continued for some Hours in the most dreadful Convulsions. My Mother and I continued in the room with her, and when any intervals of tolerable Composure in Eloisa would allow us, we joined in heartfelt lamentations on the dreadful Waste in our provisions which this Event must occasion, and in concerting some plan for getting rid of them. We agreed that the best thing we could do was to begin eating them immediately, and accordingly we ordered up the cold Ham and Fowls, and instantly began our Devouring Plan on them with great Alacrity. We would have persuaded Eloisa to have taken a Wing of a Chicken, but she would not be persuaded. She was however much quieter than she had been; the convulsions she had before suffered having given way to an almost perfect Insensibility. We endeavoured to rouse her by every means in our power, but to no purpose. I talked to her of Henry. "Dear Eloisa (said I) there's no occasion for your crying so much about such a trifle. (for I was willing to make light of it in order to comfort her) I beg you would not mind it—You see it does not vex me in the least; though perhaps I may suffer most from it after all; for I shall not only be obliged to eat up all the Victuals I have dressed already, but must if Henry should recover (which however is not very likely) dress as much for you again; or should he die (as I suppose he will) I shall still have to prepare a Dinner for you whenever you marry any one else. So you see that tho' perhaps for the present it may afflict you to think of Henry's sufferings, Yet I dare say he'll die soon, and then his pain will be over and you will be easy, whereas my Trouble will last much longer for work as hard as I may, I am certain that the pantry cannot be cleared in less than a fortnight." Thus I did all in my power to console her, but without any effect, and at last as I saw that she did not seem to listen to me, I said no more, but leaving her with my Mother I took down the remains of The Ham and Chicken, and sent William to ask how Henry did. He was not expected to live many Hours; he died the same day. We took all possible care to break the melancholy Event to Eloisa in the tenderest manner; yet in spite of every precaution, her sufferings on hearing it were too violent for her reason, and she continued for many hours in a high Delirium. She is still extremely ill, and her Physicians are greatly afraid of her going into a Decline. We are therefore preparing for Bristol, where we mean to be in the course of the next week. And now my dear Margaret let me talk a little of your affairs; and in the first place I must inform you that it is confidently reported, your Father is going to be married; I am very unwilling to beleive so unpleasing a report, and at the same time cannot wholly discredit it. I have written to my freind Susan Fitzgerald, for information concerning it, which as she is at present in Town, she will be very able to give me. I know not who is the Lady. I think your Brother is extremely right in the resolution he has taken of travelling, as it will perhaps contribute to obliterate from his remembrance, those disagreable Events, which have lately so much afflicted him—I am happy to find that tho' secluded from all the World, neither you nor Matilda are dull or unhappy—that you may never know what it is to, be either is the wish of your sincerely affectionate

C.L.

P. S. I have this instant received an answer from my freind Susan, which I enclose to you, and on which you will make your own reflections.

The enclosed LETTER

My dear CHARLOTTE You could not have applied for information concerning the report of Sir George Lesleys Marriage, to any one better able to give it you than I am. Sir George is certainly married; I was myself present at the Ceremony, which you will not be surprised at when I subscribe myself your Affectionate

Susan Lesley

Letter The Third

From Miss MARGARET LESLEY to Miss C. LUTTERELL Lesley

Castle February the 16th

I have made my own reflections on the letter you enclosed to me, my Dear Charlotte and I will now tell you what those reflections were. I reflected that if by this second Marriage Sir George should have a second family, our fortunes must be considerably diminushed—that if his Wife should be of an extravagant turn, she would encourage him to persevere in that gay and Dissipated way of Life to which little encouragement would be necessary, and which has I fear already proved but too detrimental to his health and fortune—that she would now become Mistress of those Jewels which once adorned our Mother, and which Sir George had always promised us—that if they did not come into Perthshire I should not be able to gratify my curiosity of beholding my Mother-in-law and that if they did, Matilda would no longer sit at the head of her Father's table—. These my dear Charlotte were the melancholy reflections which crowded into my imagination after perusing Susan's letter to you, and which instantly occurred to Matilda when she had perused it likewise. The same ideas, the same fears, immediately occupied her Mind, and I know not which reflection distressed her most, whether the probable Diminution of our Fortunes, or her own Consequence. We both wish very much to know whether Lady Lesley is handsome and what is your opinion of her; as you honour her with the appellation of your freind, we flatter ourselves that she must be amiable. My Brother is already in Paris. He intends to quit it in a few Days, and to begin his route to Italy. He writes in a most chearfull manner, says that the air of France has greatly recovered both his Health and Spirits; that he has now entirely ceased to think of Louisa with any degree either of Pity or Affection, that he even feels himself obliged to her for her Elopement, as he thinks it very good fun to be single again. By this, you may perceive that he has entirely regained that chearful Gaiety, and sprightly Wit, for which he was once so remarkable. When he first became acquainted with Louisa which was little more than three years ago, he was one of the most lively, the most agreable young Men of the age—. I beleive you never yet heard the particulars of his first acquaintance with her. It commenced at our cousin Colonel Drummond's; at whose house in Cumberland he spent the Christmas, in which he attained the age of two and twenty. Louisa Burton was the Daughter of a distant Relation of Mrs. Drummond, who dieing a few Months before in extreme poverty, left his only Child then about eighteen to the protection of any of his Relations who would protect her. Mrs. Drummond was the only one who found herself so disposed—Louisa was therefore removed from a miserable Cottage in Yorkshire to an elegant Mansion in Cumberland, and from every pecuniary Distress that Poverty could inflict, to every elegant Enjoyment that Money could purchase—. Louisa was naturally ill-tempered and Cunning; but she had been taught to disguise her real Disposition, under the appearance of insinuating Sweetness, by a father who but too well knew, that to be married, would be the only chance she would have of not being starved, and who flattered himself that with such an extroidinary share of personal beauty, joined to a gentleness of Manners, and an engaging address, she might stand a good chance of pleasing some young Man who might afford to marry a girl without a Shilling. Louisa perfectly entered into her father's schemes and was determined to forward them with all her care and attention. By dint of Perseverance and Application, she had at length so thoroughly disguised her natural disposition under the mask of Innocence, and Softness, as to impose upon every one who had not by a long and constant intimacy with her discovered her real Character. Such was Louisa when the hapless Lesley first beheld her at Drummond-house. His heart which (to use your favourite comparison) was as delicate as sweet and as tender as a Whipt-syllabub, could not resist her attractions. In a very few Days, he was falling in love, shortly after actually fell, and before he had known her a Month, he had married her. My Father was at first highly displeased at so hasty and imprudent a connection; but when he found that they did not mind it, he soon became perfectly reconciled to the match. The Estate near Aberdeen which my brother possesses by the bounty of his great Uncle independant of Sir George, was entirely sufficient to support him and my Sister in Elegance and Ease. For the first twelvemonth, no one could be happier than Lesley, and no one more amiable to appearance than Louisa, and so plausibly did she act and so cautiously behave that tho' Matilda and I often spent several weeks together with them, yet we neither of us had any suspicion of her real Disposition. After the birth of Louisa however, which one would have thought would have strengthened her regard for Lesley, the mask she had so long supported was by degrees thrown aside, and as probably she then thought herself secure in the affection of her Husband (which did indeed appear if possible augmented by the birth of his Child) she seemed to take no pains to prevent that affection from ever diminishing. Our visits therefore to Dunbeath, were now less frequent and by far less agreable than they used to be. Our absence was however never either mentioned or lamented by Louisa who in the society of young Danvers with whom she became acquainted at Aberdeen (he was at one of the Universities there,) felt infinitely happier than in that of Matilda and your freind, tho' there certainly never were pleasanter girls than we are. You know the sad end of all Lesleys connubial happiness; I will not repeat it——. Adeiu my dear Charlotte; although I have not yet mentioned anything of the matter, I hope you will do me the justice to beleive that I THINK and FEEL, a great deal for your Sisters affliction. I do not doubt but that the healthy air of the Bristol downs will intirely remove it, by erasing from her Mind the remembrance of Henry. I am my dear Charlotte yrs ever

M. L.

Letter The Fourth

From Miss C. LUTTERELL to Miss M. LESLEY Bristol

February 27th

My Dear Peggy I have but just received your letter, which being directed to Sussex while I was at Bristol was obliged to be forwarded to me here, and from some unaccountable Delay, has but this instant reached me——. I return you many thanks for the account it contains of Lesley's acquaintance, Love and Marriage with Louisa, which has not the less entertained me for having often been repeated to me before.

I have the satisfaction of informing you that we have every reason to imagine our pantry is by this time nearly cleared, as we left Particular orders with the servants to eat as hard as they possibly could, and to call in a couple of Chairwomen to assist them. We brought a cold Pigeon pye, a cold turkey, a cold tongue, and half a dozen Jellies with us, which we were lucky enough with the help of our Landlady, her husband, and their three children, to get rid of, in less than two days after our arrival. Poor Eloisa is still so very indifferent both in Health and Spirits, that I very much fear, the air of the Bristol downs, healthy as it is, has not been able to drive poor Henry from her remembrance.

You ask me whether your new Mother in law is handsome and amiable—I will now give you an exact description of her bodily and mental charms. She is short, and extremely well made; is naturally pale, but rouges a good deal; has fine eyes, and fine teeth, as she will take care to let you know as soon as she sees you, and is altogether very pretty. She is remarkably good-tempered when she has her own way, and very lively when she is not out of humour. She is naturally extravagant and not very affected; she never reads anything but the letters she receives from me, and never writes anything but her answers to them. She plays, sings and Dances, but has no taste for either, and excells in none, tho' she says she is passionately fond of all. Perhaps you may flatter me so far as to be surprised that one of whom I speak with so little affection should be my particular freind; but to tell you the truth, our freindship arose rather from Caprice on her side than Esteem on mine. We spent two or three days together with a Lady in Berkshire with whom we both happened to be connected—. During our visit, the Weather being remarkably bad, and our party particularly stupid, she was so good as to conceive a violent partiality for me, which very soon settled in a downright Freindship and ended in an established correspondence. She is probably by this time as tired of me, as I am of her; but as she is too Polite and I am too civil to say so, our letters are still as frequent and affectionate as ever, and our Attachment as firm and sincere as when it first commenced. As she had a great taste for the pleasures of London, and of Brighthelmstone, she will I dare say find some difficulty in prevailing on herself even to satisfy the curiosity I dare say she feels of beholding you, at the expence of quitting those favourite haunts of Dissipation, for the melancholy tho' venerable gloom of the castle you inhabit. Perhaps however if she finds her health impaired by too much amusement, she may acquire fortitude sufficient to undertake a Journey to Scotland in the hope of its Proving at least beneficial to her health, if not conducive to her happiness. Your fears I am sorry to say, concerning your father's extravagance, your own fortunes, your Mothers Jewels and your Sister's consequence, I should suppose are but too well founded. My freind herself has four thousand pounds, and will probably spend nearly as much every year in Dress and Public places, if she can get it—

she will certainly not endeavour to reclaim Sir George from the manner of living to which he has been so long accustomed, and there is therefore some reason to fear that you will be very well off, if you get any fortune at all. The Jewels I should imagine too will undoubtedly be hers, and there is too much reason to think that she will preside at her Husbands table in preference to his Daughter. But as so melancholy a subject must necessarily extremely distress you, I will no longer dwell on it—.

Eloisa's indisposition has brought us to Bristol at so unfashionable a season of the year, that we have actually seen but one genteel family since we came. Mr and Mrs Marlowe are very agreable people; the ill health of their little boy occasioned their arrival here; you may imagine that being the only family with whom we can converse, we are of course on a footing of intimacy with them; we see them indeed almost every day, and dined with them yesterday. We spent a very pleasant Day, and had a very good Dinner, tho' to be sure the Veal was terribly underdone, and the Curry had no seasoning. I could not help wishing all dinner-time that I had been at the dressing it—. A brother of Mrs Marlowe, Mr Cleveland is with them at present; he is a good-looking young Man, and seems to have a good deal to say for himself. I tell Eloisa that she should set her cap at him, but she does not at all seem to relish the proposal. I should like to see the girl married and Cleveland has a very good estate. Perhaps you may wonder that I do not consider myself as well as my Sister in my matrimonial Projects; but to tell you the truth I never wish to act a more principal part at a Wedding than the superintending and directing the Dinner, and therefore while I can get any of my acquaintance to marry for me, I shall never think of doing it myself, as I very much suspect that I should not have so much time for dressing my own Wedding-dinner, as for dressing that of my freinds. Yours sincerely

C. L.

Letter The Fifth

Miss MARGARET LESLEY to Miss CHARLOTTE LUTTERELL

Lesley-Castle March 18th

On the same day that I received your last kind letter, Matilda received one from Sir George which was dated from Edinburgh, and informed us that he should do himself the pleasure of introducing Lady Lesley to us on the following evening. This as you may suppose considerably surprised us, particularly as your account of her Ladyship had given us reason to imagine there was little chance of her visiting Scotland at a time that London must be so gay. As it was our business however to be delighted at such a mark of condescension as a visit from Sir George and Lady Lesley, we prepared to return them an answer expressive of the happiness we enjoyed in expectation of such a Blessing, when luckily recollecting that as they were to reach the Castle the next Evening, it would be impossible for my father to receive it before he left Edinburgh, we contented ourselves with leaving them to suppose that we were as happy as we ought to be. At nine in the Evening on the following day, they came, accompanied by one of Lady Lesleys brothers. Her Ladyship perfectly answers the description you sent me of her, except that I do not think her so pretty as you seem to consider her. She has not a bad face, but there is something so extremely unmajestic in her little diminutive figure, as to render her in comparison with the elegant height of Matilda and Myself, an insignificant Dwarf. Her curiosity to see us (which must have been great to bring her more than four hundred miles) being now perfectly gratified, she already begins to mention their return to town, and has desired us to accompany her. We cannot refuse her request since it is seconded by the commands of our Father, and thirded by the entreaties of Mr. Fitzgerald who is certainly one of the most pleasing young Men, I ever beheld. It is not yet determined when we are to go, but when ever we do we shall certainly take our little Louisa with us. Adeiu my dear Charlotte; Matilda unites in best wishes to you, and Eloisa, with yours ever

M. L.

Letter The Sixth

LADY LESLEY to Miss CHARLOTTE LUTTERELL Lesley-Castle

March 20th

We arrived here my sweet Freind about a fortnight ago, and I already heartily repent that I ever left our charming House in Portman-square for such a dismal old weather-beaten Castle as this. You can form no idea sufficiently hideous, of its dungeon-like form. It is actually perched upon a Rock to appearance so totally inaccessible, that I expected to have been pulled up by a rope; and sincerely repented having gratified my curiosity to behold my Daughters at the expence of being obliged to enter their prison in so dangerous and ridiculous a manner. But as soon as I once found myself safely arrived in the inside of this tremendous building, I comforted myself with the hope of having my spirits revived, by the sight of two beautifull girls, such as the Miss Lesleys had been represented to me, at Edinburgh. But here again, I met with nothing but Disappointment and Surprise. Matilda and Margaret Lesley are two great, tall, out of the way, over-grown, girls, just of a proper size to inhabit a Castle almost as large in comparison as themselves. I wish my dear Charlotte that you could but behold these Scotch giants; I am sure they would frighten you out of your wits. They will do very well as foils to myself, so I have invited them to accompany me to London where I hope to be in the course of a fortnight. Besides these two fair Damsels, I found a little humoured Brat here who I beleive is some relation to them, they told me who she was, and gave me a long rigmerole story of her father and a Miss SOMEBODY which I have entirely forgot. I hate scandal and detest Children. I have been plagued ever since I came here with tiresome visits from a parcel of Scotch wretches, with terrible hard-names; they were so civil, gave me so many invitations, and talked of coming again so soon, that I could not help affronting them. I suppose I shall not see them any more, and yet as a family party we are so stupid, that I do not know what to do with myself. These girls have no Music, but Scotch airs, no Drawings but Scotch Mountains, and no Books but Scotch Poems—and I hate everything Scotch. In general I can spend half the Day at my toilett with a great deal of pleasure, but why should I dress here, since there is not a creature in the House whom I have any wish to please. I have just had a conversation with my Brother in which he has greatly offended me, and which as I have nothing more entertaining to send you I will gave you the particulars of. You must know that I have for these 4 or 5 Days past strongly suspected William of entertaining a partiality to my eldest Daughter. I own indeed that had I been inclined to fall in love with any woman, I should not have made choice of Matilda Lesley for the object of my passion; for there is nothing I hate so much as a tall Woman: but however there is no accounting for some men's taste and as William is himself nearly six feet high, it is not wonderful that he should be partial to that height. Now as I have a very great affection for my Brother and should be extremely sorry to see him unhappy, which I suppose he means to be if he cannot marry Matilda, as moreover I know that his circumstances will not allow him to marry any one without a fortune, and that Matilda's is entirely dependant on her Father, who will neither have his own inclination nor my permission to give her anything at present, I thought it would be doing a good-natured action by my Brother to let him know as much, in order that he might choose for himself, whether to conquer his passion, or Love and Despair. Accordingly finding myself this Morning alone with him in one of the horrid old rooms of this Castle, I opened the cause to him in the following Manner.

"Well my dear William what do you think of these girls? for my part, I do not find them so plain as I expected: but perhaps you may think me partial to the Daughters of my Husband and perhaps you are right—They are indeed so very like Sir George that it is natural to think"—

"My Dear Susan (cried he in a tone of the greatest amazement) You do not really think they bear the least resemblance to their Father! He is so very plain!—but I beg your pardon—I had entirely forgotten to whom I was speaking—"

"Oh! pray dont mind me; (replied I) every one knows Sir George is horribly ugly, and I assure you I always thought him a fright."

"You surprise me extremely (answered William) by what you say both with respect to Sir George and his Daughters. You cannot think your Husband so deficient in personal Charms as you speak of, nor can you surely see any resemblance between him and the Miss Lesleys who are in my opinion perfectly unlike him and perfectly Handsome."

"If that is your opinion with regard to the girls it certainly is no proof of their Fathers beauty, for if they are perfectly unlike him and very handsome at the same time, it is natural to suppose that he is very plain."

"By no means, (said he) for what may be pretty in a Woman, may be very unpleasing in a Man."

"But you yourself (replied I) but a few minutes ago allowed him to be very plain."

"Men are no Judges of Beauty in their own Sex." (said he).

"Neither Men nor Women can think Sir George tolerable."

"Well, well, (said he) we will not dispute about HIS Beauty, but your opinion of his DAUGHTERS is surely very singular, for if I understood you right, you said you did not find them so plain as you expected to do!"

"Why, do YOU find them plainer then?" (said I).

"I can scarcely beleive you to be serious (returned he) when you speak of their persons in so extroidinary a Manner. Do not you think the Miss Lesleys are two very handsome young Women?"

"Lord! No! (cried I) I think them terribly plain!"

"Plain! (replied He) My dear Susan, you cannot really think so! Why what single Feature in the face of either of them, can you possibly find fault with?"

"Oh! trust me for that; (replied I). Come I will begin with the eldest—with Matilda. Shall I, William?" (I looked as cunning as I could when I said it, in order to shame him).

"They are so much alike (said he) that I should suppose the faults of one, would be the faults of both."

"Well, then, in the first place; they are both so horribly tall!"

"They are TALLER than you are indeed." (said he with a saucy smile.)

"Nay, (said I), I know nothing of that."

"Well, but (he continued) tho' they may be above the common size, their figures are perfectly elegant; and as to their faces, their Eyes are beautifull."

"I never can think such tremendous, knock-me-down figures in the least degree elegant, and as for their eyes, they are so tall that I never could strain my neck enough to look at them."

"Nay, (replied he) I know not whether you may not be in the right in not attempting it, for perhaps they might dazzle you with their Lustre."

"Oh! Certainly. (said I, with the greatest complacency, for I assure you my dearest Charlotte I was not in the least offended tho' by what followed, one would suppose that William was conscious of having given me just cause to be so, for coming up to me and taking my hand, he said) "You must not look so grave Susan; you will make me fear I have offended you!"

"Offended me! Dear Brother, how came such a thought in your head! (returned I) No really! I assure you that I am not in the least surprised at your being so warm an advocate for the Beauty of these girls."—

"Well, but (interrupted William) remember that we have not yet concluded our dispute concerning them. What fault do you find with their complexion?"

"They are so horridly pale."

"They have always a little colour, and after any exercise it is considerably heightened."

"Yes, but if there should ever happen to be any rain in this part of the world, they will never be able raise more than their common stock—except indeed they amuse themselves with running up and Down these horrid old galleries and Antichambers."

"Well, (replied my Brother in a tone of vexation, and glancing an impertinent look at me) if they HAVE but little colour, at least, it is all their own."

This was too much my dear Charlotte, for I am certain that he had the impudence by that look, of pretending to suspect the reality of mine. But you I am sure will vindicate my character whenever you may hear it so cruelly aspersed, for you can witness how often I have protested against wearing Rouge, and how much I always told you I disliked it. And I assure you that my opinions are still the same.—. Well, not bearing to be so suspected by my Brother, I left the room immediately, and have been ever since in my own Dressing-room writing to you. What a long letter have I made of it! But you must not expect to receive such from me when I get to Town; for it is only at Lesley castle, that one has time to write even to a Charlotte Lutterell.—. I was so much vexed by William's glance, that I could not summon Patience enough, to stay and give him that advice respecting his attachment to Matilda which had first induced me from pure Love to him to begin the conversation; and I am now so thoroughly convinced by it, of his violent passion for her, that I am certain he would never hear reason on the subject, and I shall there fore give myself no more trouble either about him or his favourite. Adeiu my dear girl—Yrs affectionately

Susan L.

Letter The Seventh

From Miss C. LUTTERELL to Miss M. LESLEY Bristol the

27th of March

I have received Letters from you and your Mother-in-law within this week which have greatly entertained me, as I find by them that you are both downright jealous of each others Beauty. It is very odd that two pretty

Women tho' actually Mother and Daughter cannot be in the same House without falling out about their faces. Do be convinced that you are both perfectly handsome and say no more of the Matter. I suppose this letter must be directed to Portman Square where probably (great as is your affection for Lesley Castle) you will not be sorry to find yourself. In spite of all that people may say about Green fields and the Country I was always of opinion that London and its amusements must be very agreable for a while, and should be very happy could my Mother's income allow her to jockey us into its Public-places, during Winter. I always longed particularly to go to Vaux-hall, to see whether the cold Beef there is cut so thin as it is reported, for I have a sly suspicion that few people understand the art of cutting a slice of cold Beef so well as I do: nay it would be hard if I did not know something of the Matter, for it was a part of my Education that I took by far the most pains with. Mama always found me HER best scholar, tho' when Papa was alive Eloisa was HIS. Never to be sure were there two more different Dispositions in the World. We both loved Reading. SHE preferred Histories, and I Receipts. She loved drawing, Pictures, and I drawing Pullets. No one could sing a better song than she, and no one make a better Pye than I.—And so it has always continued since we have been no longer children. The only difference is that all disputes on the superior excellence of our Employments THEN so frequent are now no more. We have for many years entered into an agreement always to admire each other's works; I never fail listening to HER Music, and she is as constant in eating my pies. Such at least was the case till Henry Hervey made his appearance in Sussex. Before the arrival of his Aunt in our neighbourhood where she established herself you know about a twelvemonth ago, his visits to her had been at stated times, and of equal and settled Duration; but on her removal to the Hall which is within a walk from our House, they became both more frequent and longer. This as you may suppose could not be pleasing to Mrs Diana who is a professed enemy to everything which is not directed by Decorum and Formality, or which bears the least resemblance to Ease and Good-breeding. Nay so great was her aversion to her Nephews behaviour that I have often heard her give such hints of it before his face that had not Henry at such times been engaged in conversation with Eloisa, they must have caught his Attention and have very much distressed him. The alteration in my Sisters behaviour which I have before hinted at, now took place. The Agreement we had entered into of admiring each others productions she no longer seemed to regard, and tho' I constantly applauded even every Country-dance, she played, yet not even a pidgeon-pye of my making could obtain from her a single word of approbation. This was certainly enough to put any one in a Passion; however, I was as cool as a cream-cheese and having formed my plan and concerted a scheme of Revenge, I was determined to let her have her own way and not even to make her a single reproach. My scheme was to treat her as she treated me, and tho' she might even draw my own Picture or play Malbrook (which is the only tune I ever really liked) not to say so much as "Thank you Eloisa;" tho' I had for many years constantly hollowed whenever she played, BRAVO, BRAVISSIMO, ENCORE, DA CAPO, ALLEGRETTO, CON EXPRESSIONE, and POCO PRESTO with many other such outlandish words, all of them as Eloisa told me expressive of my Admiration; and so indeed I suppose they are, as I see some of them in every Page of every Music book, being the sentiments I imagine of the composer.

I executed my Plan with great Punctuality. I can not say success, for alas! my silence while she played seemed not in the least to displease her; on the contrary she actually said to me one day "Well Charlotte, I am very glad to find that you have at last left off that ridiculous custom of applauding my Execution on the Harpsichord till you made my head ake, and yourself hoarse. I feel very much obliged to you for keeping your admiration to yourself." I never shall forget the very witty answer I made to this speech. "Eloisa (said I) I beg you would be quite at your Ease with respect to all such fears in future, for be assured that I shall always keep my admiration to myself and my own pursuits and never extend it to yours." This was the only very severe thing I ever said in my Life; not but that I have often felt myself extremely satirical but it was the only time I ever made my feelings public.

I suppose there never were two Young people who had a greater affection for each other than Henry and Eloisa; no, the Love of your Brother for Miss Burton could not be so strong tho' it might be more violent. You may imagine therefore how provoked my Sister must have been to have him play her such a trick. Poor girl! she still laments his Death with undiminished constancy, notwithstanding he has been dead more than six weeks; but some People mind such things more than others. The ill state of Health into which his loss has thrown her makes her so weak, and so unable to support the least exertion, that she has been in tears all this Morning merely from having taken leave of Mrs. Marlowe who with her Husband, Brother and Child are to leave Bristol this morning. I am sorry to have them go because they are the only family with whom we have here any acquaintance, but I never thought of crying; to be sure Eloisa and Mrs Marlowe have always been more together than with me, and have therefore contracted a kind of affection for each other, which does not make Tears so inexcusable in them as they would be in me. The Marlowes are going to Town; Cliveland accompanies them; as neither Eloisa nor I could catch him I hope you or Matilda may have better Luck. I know not when we shall leave Bristol, Eloisa's spirits are so low that she is very averse to moving, and yet is certainly by no means mended by her residence here. A week or two will I hope determine our Measures—in the mean time believe me and etc—and etc—

Charlotte Lutterell.

Letter The Eighth

Miss LUTTERELL to Mrs MARLOWE Bristol April 4th

I feel myself greatly obliged to you my dear Emma for such a mark of your affection as I flatter myself was conveyed in the proposal you made me of our Corresponding; I assure you that it will be a great releif to me to write to you and as long as my Health and Spirits will allow me, you will find me a very constant correspondent; I will not say an entertaining one, for you know my situation suffciently not to be ignorant that in me Mirth would be improper and I know my own Heart too well not to be sensible that it would be unnatural. You must not expect news for we see no one with whom we are in the least acquainted, or in whose proceedings we have any Interest. You must not expect scandal for by the same rule we are equally debarred either from hearing or inventing it.—You must expect from me nothing but the melancholy effusions of a broken Heart which is ever reverting to the Happiness it once enjoyed and which ill supports its present wretchedness. The Possibility of being able to write, to speak, to you of my lost Henry will be a luxury to me, and your goodness will not I know refuse to read what it will so much releive my Heart to write. I once thought that to have what is in general called a Freind (I mean one of my own sex to whom I might speak with less reserve than to any other person) independant of my sister would never be an object of my wishes, but how much was I mistaken! Charlotte is too much engrossed by two confidential correspondents of that sort, to supply the place of one to me, and I hope you will not think me girlishly romantic, when I say that to have some kind and compassionate Freind who might listen to my sorrows without endeavouring to console me was what I had for some time wished for, when our acquaintance with you, the intimacy which followed it and the particular affectionate attention you paid me almost from the first, caused me to entertain the flattering Idea of those attentions being improved on a closer acquaintance into a Freindship which, if you were what my wishes formed you would be the greatest Happiness I could be capable of enjoying. To find that such Hopes are realised is a satisfaction indeed, a satisfaction which is now almost the only one I can ever experience.—I feel myself so languid that I am sure were you with me you would oblige me to leave off writing, and I cannot give you a greater proof of my affection for you than by acting, as I know you would wish me to do, whether Absent or Present. I am my dear Emmas sincere friend

E. L.

Letter The Ninth

Mrs MARLOWE to Miss LUTTERELL Grosvenor Street, April

10th

Need I say my dear Eloisa how wellcome your letter was to me I cannot give a greater proof of the pleasure I received from it, or of the Desire I feel that our Correspondence may be regular and frequent than by setting you so good an example as I now do in answering it before the end of the week—. But do not imagine that I claim any merit in being so punctual; on the contrary I assure you, that it is a far greater Gratification to me to write to you, than to spend the Evening either at a Concert or a Ball. Mr Marlowe is so desirous of my appearing at some of the Public places every evening that I do not like to refuse him, but at the same time so much wish to remain at Home, that independant of the Pleasure I experience in devoting any portion of my Time to my Dear Eloisa, yet the Liberty I claim from having a letter to write of spending an Evening at home with my little Boy, you know me well enough to be sensible, will of itself be a sufficient Inducement (if one is necessary) to my maintaining with Pleasure a Correspondence with you. As to the subject of your letters to me, whether grave or merry, if they concern you they must be equally interesting to me; not but that I think the melancholy Indulgence of your own sorrows by repeating them and dwelling on them to me, will only encourage and increase them, and that it will be more prudent in you to avoid so sad a subject; but yet knowing as I do what a soothing and melancholy Pleasure it must afford you, I cannot prevail on myself to deny you so great an Indulgence, and will only insist on your not expecting me to encourage you in it, by my own letters; on the contrary I intend to fill them with such lively Wit and enlivening Humour as shall even provoke a smile in the sweet but sorrowfull countenance of my Eloisa.

In the first place you are to learn that I have met your sisters three freinds Lady Lesley and her Daughters, twice in Public since I have been here. I know you will be impatient to hear my opinion of the Beauty of three Ladies of whom you have heard so much. Now, as you are too ill and too unhappy to be vain, I think I may venture to inform you that I like none of their faces so well as I do your own. Yet they are all handsome—Lady Lesley indeed I have seen before; her Daughters I beleive would in general be said to have a finer face than her Ladyship, and yet what with the charms of a Blooming complexion, a little Affectation and a great deal of small-talk, (in each of which she is superior to the young Ladies) she will I dare say gain herself as many admirers as the more regular features of Matilda, and Margaret. I am sure you will agree with me in saying that they can none of them be of a proper size for real Beauty, when you know that two of them are taller and the other shorter than ourselves. In spite of this Defect (or rather by reason of it) there is something very noble and majestic in the figures of the Miss Lesleys, and something agreably lively in the appearance of their pretty little Mother-in-law. But tho' one may be majestic and the other lively, yet the faces of neither possess that Bewitching sweetness of my Eloisas, which her present languor is so far from diminushing. What would my Husband and Brother say of us, if they knew all the fine things I have been saying to you in this letter. It is very hard that a pretty woman is never to be told she is so by any one of her own sex without that person's being suspected to be either her determined Enemy, or her professed Toad-eater. How much more amiable are women in that particular! One man may say forty civil things to another without our supposing that he is ever paid for it, and provided he does his Duty by our sex, we care not how Polite he is to his own.

Mrs Lutterell will be so good as to accept my compliments, Charlotte, my Love, and Eloisa the best wishes for the recovery of her Health and Spirits that can be offered by her affectionate Freind E. Marlowe.

I am afraid this letter will be but a poor specimen of my Powers in the witty way; and your opinion of them will not be greatly increased when I assure you that I have been as entertaining as I possibly could.

Letter The Tenth

From Miss MARGARET LESLEY to Miss CHARLOTTE LUTTERELL

Portman Square April 13th

MY DEAR CHARLOTTE We left Lesley-Castle on the 28th of last Month, and arrived safely in London after a Journey of seven Days; I had the pleasure of finding your Letter here waiting my Arrival, for which you have my grateful Thanks. Ah! my dear Freind I every day more regret the serene and tranquil Pleasures of the Castle we have left, in exchange for the uncertain and unequal Amusements of this vaunted City. Not that I will pretend to assert that these uncertain and unequal Amusements are in the least Degree unpleasing to me; on the contrary I enjoy them extremely and should enjoy them even more, were I not certain that every appearance I make in Public but rivetts the Chains of those unhappy Beings whose Passion it is impossible not to pity, tho' it is out of my power to return. In short my Dear Charlotte it is my sensibility for the sufferings of so many amiable young Men, my Dislike of the extreme admiration I meet with, and my aversion to being so celebrated both in Public, in Private, in Papers, and in Printshops, that are the reasons why I cannot more fully enjoy, the Amusements so various and pleasing of London. How often have I wished that I possessed as little Personal Beauty as you do; that my figure were as inelegant; my face as unlovely; and my appearance as unpleasing as yours! But ah! what little chance is there of so desirable an Event; I have had the small-pox, and must therefore submit to my unhappy fate.

I am now going to intrust you my dear Charlotte with a secret which has long disturbed the tranquility of my days, and which is of a kind to require the most inviolable Secrecy from you. Last Monday se'night Matilda and I accompanied Lady Lesley to a Rout at the Honourable Mrs Kickabout's; we were escorted by Mr Fitzgerald who is a very amiable young Man in the main, tho' perhaps a little singular in his Taste—He is in love with Matilda—. We had scarcely paid our Compliments to the Lady of the House and curtseyed to half a score different people when my Attention was attracted by the appearance of a Young Man the most lovely of his Sex, who at that moment entered the Room with another Gentleman and Lady. From the first moment I beheld him, I was certain that on him depended the future Happiness of my Life. Imagine my surprise when he was introduced to me by the name of Cleveland—I instantly recognised him as the Brother of Mrs Marlowe, and the acquaintance of my Charlotte at Bristol. Mr and Mrs M. were the gentleman and Lady who accompanied him. (You do not think Mrs Marlowe handsome?) The elegant address of Mr Cleveland, his polished Manners and Delightful Bow, at once confirmed my attachment. He did not speak; but I can imagine everything he would have said, had he opened his Mouth. I can picture to myself the cultivated Understanding, the Noble sentiments, and elegant Language which would have shone so conspicuous in the conversation of Mr Cleveland. The approach of Sir James Gower (one of my too numerous admirers) prevented the Discovery of any such Powers, by putting an end to a Conversation we had never commenced, and by attracting my attention to himself. But oh! how inferior are the accomplishments of Sir James to those of his so greatly envied Rival! Sir James is one of the most frequent of our Visitors, and is almost always of our Parties. We have since often met Mr and Mrs Marlowe but no Cleveland—he is always engaged some where else. Mrs Marlowe fatigues me to Death every time I see her by her tiresome Conversations about you and Eloisa. She is so stupid! I live in the hope of seeing her irrisistable Brother to night, as we are going to Lady Flambeaus, who is I know intimate with the Marlowes. Our party will be Lady Lesley, Matilda, Fitzgerald, Sir James Gower, and myself. We see little of Sir George, who is almost always at the gaming-table. Ah! my poor Fortune where art thou by this time? We see more of Lady L. who always makes her appearance (highly rouged) at Dinner-time. Alas! what Delightful Jewels will she be decked in this evening at Lady Flambeau's! Yet I wonder how she can herself delight in wearing them; surely she must be sensible of the ridiculous impropriety of loading her little diminutive figure with such superfluous ornaments; is it possible that she can not know how greatly superior an elegant simplicity is to the most studied apparel? Would she but Present them to Matilda and me, how greatly should we be obliged to her, How becoming would Diamonds be on our fine majestic figures! And how surprising it is that such an Idea should never have occurred to HER. I am sure if I have reflected in this manner once, I have fifty times. Whenever I see Lady Lesley dressed in them such reflections immediately come across me. My own Mother's Jewels too! But I will say no more on so melancholy a subject—let me entertain you with something more pleasing—Matilda had a letter this morning from Lesley, by which we have the pleasure of finding that he is at Naples has turned Roman-Catholic, obtained one of the Pope's Bulls for annulling his 1st Marriage and has since actually married a Neapolitan Lady of great Rank and Fortune. He tells us moreover that much the same sort of affair has befallen his first wife the worthless Louisa who is likewise at Naples had turned Roman-catholic, and is soon to be married to a Neapolitan Nobleman of great and Distinguished merit. He says, that they are at present very good Freinds, have quite forgiven all past errors and intend in future to be very good Neighbours. He invites Matilda and me to pay him a visit to Italy and to bring him his little Louisa whom both her Mother, Step-mother, and himself are equally desirous of beholding. As to our accepting his invitation, it is at Present very uncertain; Lady Lesley advises us to go without loss of time; Fitzgerald offers to escort us there, but Matilda has some doubts of the Propriety of such a scheme—she owns it would be very agreable. I am certain she likes the Fellow. My Father desires us not to be in a hurry, as perhaps if we wait a few months both he and Lady Lesley will do themselves the pleasure of attending us. Lady Lesley says no, that nothing will ever tempt her to forego the Amusements of Brighthelmstone for a Journey to Italy merely to see our Brother. "No (says the disagreable Woman) I have once in my life been fool enough to travel I dont know how many hundred Miles to see two of the Family, and I found it did not answer, so Deuce take me, if ever I am so foolish again."So says her Ladyship, but Sir George still Perseveres in saying that perhaps in a month or two, they may accompany us. Adeiu my Dear Charlotte Yrs faithful

Margaret Lesley.

The History of England

FROM THE REIGN OF HENRY THE 4TH TO THE DEATH OF CHARLES THE 1ST
BY A PARTIAL, PREJUDICED, AND IGNORANT HISTORIAN.

To Miss Austen, eldest daughter of the Rev. George Austen, this work is inscribed with all due respect by THE AUTHOR.

N.B. There will be very few Dates in this History.

Henry The 4th

Henry the 4th ascended the throne of England much to his own satisfaction in the year 1399, after having prevailed on his cousin and predecessor Richard the 2nd, to resign it to him, and to retire for the rest of his life to Pomfret Castle, where he happened to be murdered. It is to be supposed that Henry was married, since he had certainly four sons, but it is not in my power to inform the Reader who was his wife. Be this as it may, he did not live for ever, but falling ill, his son the Prince of Wales came and took away the crown; whereupon the King made a long speech, for which I must refer the Reader to Shakespear's Plays, and the Prince made a still longer. Things being thus settled between them the King died, and was succeeded by his son Henry who had previously beat Sir William Gascoigne.

Henry The 5th

This Prince after he succeeded to the throne grew quite reformed and amiable, forsaking all his dissipated companions, and never thrashing Sir William again. During his reign, Lord Cobham was burnt alive, but I forget what for. His Majesty then turned his thoughts to France, where he went and fought the famous Battle of Agincourt. He afterwards married the King's daughter Catherine, a very agreable woman by Shakespear's account. In spite of all this however he died, and was succeeded by his son Henry.

Henry The 6th

I cannot say much for this Monarch's sense. Nor would I if I could, for he was a Lancastrian. I suppose you know all about the Wars between him and the Duke of York who was of the right side; if you do not, you had better read some other History, for I shall not be very diffuse in this, meaning by it only to vent my spleen AGAINST, and shew my Hatred TO all those people whose parties or principles do not suit with mine, and not to give information. This King married Margaret of Anjou, a Woman whose distresses and misfortunes were so great as almost to make me who hate her, pity her. It was in this reign that Joan of Arc lived and made such a ROW among the English. They should not have burnt her—but they did. There were several Battles between the Yorkists and Lancastrians, in which the former (as they ought) usually conquered. At length they were entirely overcome; The King was murdered—The Queen was sent home—and Edward the 4th ascended the Throne.

Edward The 4th

This Monarch was famous only for his Beauty and his Courage, of which the Picture we have here given of him, and his undaunted Behaviour in marrying one Woman while he was engaged to another, are sufficient proofs.

His Wife was Elizabeth Woodville, a Widow who, poor Woman! was afterwards confined in a Convent by that Monster of Iniquity and Avarice Henry the 7th. One of Edward's Mistresses was Jane Shore, who has had a play written about her, but it is a tragedy and therefore not worth reading. Having performed all these noble actions, his Majesty died, and was succeeded by his son.

Edward The 5th

This unfortunate Prince lived so little a while that nobody had him to draw his picture. He was murdered by his Uncle's Contrivance, whose name was Richard the 3rd.

Richard The 3rd

The Character of this Prince has been in general very severely treated by Historians, but as he was a YORK, I am rather inclined to suppose him a very respectable Man. It has indeed been confidently asserted that he killed his two Nephews and his Wife, but it has also been declared that he did not kill his two Nephews, which I am inclined to beleive true; and if this is the case, it may also be affirmed that he did not kill his Wife, for if Perkin Warbeck was really the Duke of York, why might not Lambert Simnel be the Widow of Richard. Whether innocent or guilty, he did not reign long in peace, for Henry Tudor E. of Richmond as great a villain as ever lived, made a great fuss about getting the Crown and having killed the King at the battle of Bosworth, he succeeded to it.

Henry The 7th

This Monarch soon after his accession married the Princess Elizabeth of York, by which alliance he plainly proved that he thought his own right inferior to hers, tho' he pretended to the contrary. By this Marriage he had two sons and two daughters, the elder of which Daughters was married to the King of Scotland and had the happiness of being grandmother to one of the first Characters in the World. But of HER, I shall have occasion to speak more at large in future. The youngest, Mary, married first the King of France and secondly the D. of Suffolk, by whom she had one daughter, afterwards the Mother of Lady Jane Grey, who tho' inferior to her lovely Cousin the Queen of Scots, was yet an amiable young woman and famous for reading Greek while other people were hunting. It was in the reign of Henry the 7th that Perkin Warbeck and Lambert Simnel before mentioned made their appearance, the former of whom was set in the stocks, took shelter in

Beaulieu Abbey, and was beheaded with the Earl of Warwick, and the latter was taken into the Kings kitchen. His Majesty died and was succeeded by his son Henry whose only merit was his not being quite so bad as his daughter Elizabeth.

Henry The 8th

It would be an affront to my Readers were I to suppose that they were not as well acquainted with the particulars of this King's reign as I am myself. It will therefore be saving THEM the task of reading again what they have read before, and MYSELF the trouble of writing what I do not perfectly recollect, by giving only a slight sketch of the principal Events which marked his reign. Among these may be ranked Cardinal Wolsey's telling the father Abbott of Leicester Abbey that "he was come to lay his bones among them," the reformation in Religion and the King's riding through the streets of London with Anna Bullen. It is however but Justice, and my Duty to declare that this amiable Woman was entirely innocent of the Crimes with which she was accused, and of which her Beauty, her Elegance, and her Sprightliness were sufficient proofs, not to mention her solemn Protestations of Innocence, the weakness of the Charges against her, and the King's Character; all of which add some confirmation, tho' perhaps but slight ones when in comparison with those before alledged in her favour. Tho' I do not profess giving many dates, yet as I think it proper to give some and shall of course make choice of those which it is most necessary for the Reader to know, I think it right to inform him that her letter to the King was dated on the 6th of May. The Crimes and Cruelties of this Prince, were too numerous to be mentioned, (as this history I trust has fully shown;) and nothing can be said in his vindication, but that his abolishing Religious Houses and leaving them to the ruinous depredations of time has been of infinite use to the landscape of England in general, which probably was a principal motive for his doing it, since otherwise why should a Man who was of no Religion himself be at so much trouble to abolish one which had for ages been established in the Kingdom. His Majesty's 5th Wife was the Duke of Norfolk's Neice who, tho' universally acquitted of the crimes for which she was beheaded, has been by many people supposed to have led an abandoned life before her Marriage— of this however I have many doubts, since she was a relation of that noble Duke of Norfolk who was so warm in the Queen of Scotland's cause, and who at last fell a victim to it. The Kings last wife contrived to survive him, but with difficulty effected it. He was succeeded by his only son Edward.

Edward The 6th

As this prince was only nine years old at the time of his Father's death, he was considered by many people as too young to govern, and the late King happening to be of the same opinion, his mother's Brother the Duke of Somerset was chosen Protector of the realm during his minority. This Man was on the whole of a very amiable Character, and is somewhat of a favourite with me, tho' I would by no means pretend to affirm that he was equal to those first of Men Robert Earl of Essex, Delamere, or Gilpin. He was beheaded, of which he might with reason have been proud, had he known that such was the death of Mary Queen of Scotland; but as it was impossible that he should be conscious of what had never happened, it does not appear that he felt particularly delighted with the manner of it. After his decease the Duke of Northumberland had the care of the King and the Kingdom, and performed his trust of both so well that the King died and the Kingdom was left to his daughter in law the Lady Jane Grey, who has been already mentioned as reading Greek. Whether she really understood that language or whether such a study proceeded only from an excess of vanity for which I beleive she was always rather remarkable, is uncertain. Whatever might be the cause, she preserved the same appearance of knowledge, and contempt of what was generally esteemed pleasure, during the whole of her life, for she declared herself displeased with being appointed Queen, and while conducting to the scaffold, she wrote a sentence in Latin and another in Greek on seeing the dead Body of her Husband accidentally passing that way.

Mary

This woman had the good luck of being advanced to the throne of England, in spite of the superior pretensions, Merit, and Beauty of her Cousins Mary Queen of Scotland and Jane Grey. Nor can I pity the Kingdom for the misfortunes they experienced during her Reign, since they fully deserved them, for having allowed her to succeed her Brother—which was a double peice of folly, since they might have foreseen that as she died without children, she would be succeeded by that disgrace to humanity, that pest of society, Elizabeth. Many were the people who fell martyrs to the protestant Religion during her reign; I suppose not fewer than a dozen. She married Philip King of Spain who in her sister's reign was famous for building Armadas. She died without issue, and then the dreadful moment came in which the destroyer of all comfort, the deceitful Betrayer of trust reposed in her, and the Murderess of her Cousin succeeded to the Throne.——

Elizabeth

It was the peculiar misfortune of this Woman to have bad Ministers— Since wicked as she herself was, she could not have committed such extensive mischeif, had not these vile and abandoned Men connived at, and encouraged her in her Crimes. I know that it has by many people been asserted and beleived that Lord Burleigh, Sir Francis Walsingham, and the rest of those who filled the cheif offices of State were deserving, experienced, and able Ministers. But oh! how blinded such writers and such Readers must be to true Merit, to Merit despised, neglected and defamed, if they can persist in such opinions when they reflect that these men, these boasted men were such scandals to their Country and their sex as to allow and assist their Queen in confining for the space of nineteen years, a WOMAN who if the claims of Relationship and Merit were of no avail, yet as a Queen and as one who condescended to place confidence in her, had every reason to expect assistance and protection; and at length in allowing Elizabeth to bring this amiable Woman to an untimely, unmerited, and scandalous Death. Can any one if he reflects but for a moment on this blot, this everlasting blot upon their understanding and their Character, allow any praise to Lord Burleigh or Sir Francis Walsingham? Oh! what must this bewitching Princess whose only freind was then the Duke of Norfolk, and whose only ones now Mr Whitaker, Mrs Lefroy, Mrs Knight and myself, who was abandoned by her son, confined by her Cousin, abused, reproached and vilified by all, what must not her most noble mind have suffered when informed that Elizabeth had given orders for her Death! Yet she bore it with a most unshaken fortitude, firm in her mind; constant in her Religion; and prepared herself to meet the cruel fate to which she was doomed, with a magnanimity that would alone proceed from conscious Innocence. And yet could you Reader have beleived it possible that some hardened and zealous Protestants have even abused her for that steadfastness in the Catholic Religion which reflected on her so much credit? But this is a striking proof of THEIR narrow souls and prejudiced Judgements who accuse her. She was executed in the Great Hall at Fortheringay Castle (sacred Place!) on Wednesday the 8th of February 1586— to the everlasting Reproach of Elizabeth, her Ministers, and of England in general. It may not be unnecessary before I entirely conclude my account of this ill-fated Queen, to observe that she had been accused of several crimes during the time of her reigning in Scotland, of which I now most seriously do assure my Reader that she was entirely innocent; having never been guilty of anything more than Imprudencies into which she was betrayed by the openness of her Heart, her Youth, and her Education. Having I trust by this assurance entirely done away every Suspicion and every doubt which might have arisen in the Reader's mind, from what other Historians have written of her, I shall proceed to mention the remaining Events that marked Elizabeth's reign. It was about this time that Sir Francis Drake the first English Navigator who sailed round the World, lived, to be the ornament of his Country and his profession. Yet great as he was, and justly celebrated as a sailor, I cannot help foreseeing that he will be equalled in this or the next Century by one who tho' now but young, already promises to answer all the ardent and sanguine expectations of his Relations and Freinds, amongst whom I may class the amiable Lady to whom this work is dedicated, and my no less amiable self.

Though of a different profession, and shining in a different sphere of Life, yet equally conspicuous in the Character of an Earl, as Drake was in that of a Sailor, was Robert Devereux Lord Essex. This unfortunate young Man was not unlike in character to that equally unfortunate one FREDERIC DELAMERE. The simile may be carried still farther, and Elizabeth the torment of Essex may be compared to the Emmeline of Delamere. It would be endless to recount the misfortunes of this noble and gallant Earl. It is sufficient to say that he was beheaded on the 25th of Feb, after having been Lord Lieutenant of Ireland, after having clapped his hand on his sword, and after performing many other services to his Country. Elizabeth did not long survive his loss, and died so miserable that were it not an injury to the memory of Mary I should pity her.

James The 1st

Though this King had some faults, among which and as the most principal, was his allowing his Mother's death, yet considered on the whole I cannot help liking him. He married Anne of Denmark, and had several Children; fortunately for him his eldest son Prince Henry died before his father or he might have experienced the evils which befell his unfortunate Brother.

As I am myself partial to the roman catholic religion, it is with infinite regret that I am obliged to blame the Behaviour of any Member of it: yet Truth being I think very excusable in an Historian, I am necessitated to say that in this reign the roman Catholics of England did not behave like Gentlemen to the protestants. Their Behaviour indeed to the Royal Family and both Houses of Parliament might justly be considered by them as very uncivil, and even Sir Henry Percy tho' certainly the best bred man of the party, had none of that general politeness which is so universally pleasing, as his attentions were entirely confined to Lord Mounteagle.

Sir Walter Raleigh flourished in this and the preceeding reign, and is by many people held in great veneration and respect—But as he was an enemy of the noble Essex, I have nothing to say in praise of him, and must refer all those who may wish to be acquainted with the particulars of his life, to Mr Sheridan's play of the Critic, where they will find many interesting anecdotes as well of him as of his friend Sir Christopher Hatton.—His Majesty was of that amiable disposition which inclines to Freindship, and in such points was possessed of a keener penetration in discovering Merit than many other people. I once heard an excellent Sharade on a Carpet, of which the subject I am now on reminds me, and as I think it may afford my Readers some amusement to FIND IT OUT, I shall here take the liberty of presenting it to them.

SHARADE My first is what my second was to King James the 1st, and you tread on my whole.

The principal favourites of his Majesty were Car, who was afterwards created Earl of Somerset and whose name perhaps may have some share in the above mentioned Sharade, and George Villiers afterwards Duke of Buckingham. On his Majesty's death he was succeeded by his son Charles.

Charles The 1st

This amiable Monarch seems born to have suffered misfortunes equal to those of his lovely Grandmother; misfortunes which he could not deserve since he was her descendant. Never certainly were there before so many detestable Characters at one time in England as in this Period of its History; never were amiable men so scarce. The number of them throughout the whole Kingdom amounting only to FIVE, besides the inhabitants of Oxford who were always loyal to their King and faithful to his interests. The names of this noble five who never forgot the duty of the subject, or swerved from their attachment to his Majesty, were as follows—The King himself, ever stedfast in his own support—Archbishop Laud, Earl of Strafford, Viscount Faulkland and Duke of Ormond, who were scarcely less strenuous or zealous in the cause. While the VILLIANS of the time would make too long a list to be written or read; I shall therefore content myself with mentioning the leaders of the Gang. Cromwell, Fairfax, Hampden, and Pym may be considered as the original Causers of all the disturbances, Distresses, and Civil Wars in which England for many years was embroiled. In this reign as well as in that of Elizabeth, I am obliged in spite of my attachment to the Scotch, to consider them as equally guilty with the generality of the English, since they dared to think differently from their Sovereign, to forget the Adoration which as STUARTS it was their Duty to pay them, to rebel against, dethrone and imprison the unfortunate Mary; to oppose, to deceive, and to sell the no less unfortunate Charles. The Events of this Monarch's reign are too numerous for my pen, and indeed the recital of any Events (except what I make myself) is uninteresting to me; my principal reason for undertaking the History of England being to Prove the innocence of the Queen of Scotland, which I flatter myself with having effectually done, and to abuse Elizabeth, tho' I am rather fearful of having fallen short in the latter part of my scheme.—As therefore it is not my intention to give any particular account of the distresses into which this King was involved through the misconduct and Cruelty of his Parliament, I shall satisfy myself with vindicating him from the Reproach of Arbitrary and tyrannical Government with which he has often been charged. This, I feel, is not difficult to be done, for with one argument I am certain of satisfying every sensible and well disposed person whose opinions have been properly guided by a good Education—and this Argument is that he was a STUART.

Saturday Nov: 26th 1791.

A Collection of Letters

To Miss COOPER

COUSIN Conscious of the Charming Character which in every Country, and every Clime in Christendom is Cried, Concerning you, with Caution and Care I Commend to your Charitable Criticism this Clever Collection of Curious Comments, which have been Carefully Culled, Collected and Classed by your Comical Cousin

The Author.

Letter The First

From a MOTHER to her FREIND.

My Children begin now to claim all my attention in different Manner from that in which they have been used to receive it, as they are now arrived at that age when it is necessary for them in some measure to become conversant with the World, My Augusta is 17 and her sister scarcely a twelvemonth younger. I flatter myself that their education has been such as will not disgrace their appearance in the World, and that THEY will not disgrace their Education I have every reason to beleive. Indeed they are sweet Girls—. Sensible yet unaffected—Accomplished yet Easy—. Lively yet Gentle—. As their progress in every thing they have learnt has been always the same, I am willing to forget the difference of age, and to introduce them together into Public. This very Evening is fixed on as their first ENTREE into Life, as we are to drink tea with Mrs Cope and her Daughter. I am glad that we are to meet no one, for my Girls sake, as it would be awkward for them to enter too wide a Circle on the very first day. But we shall proceed by degrees.— Tomorrow Mr Stanly's family will drink tea with us, and perhaps the Miss Phillips's will meet them. On Tuesday we shall pay Morning Visits—On

Wednesday we are to dine at Westbrook. On Thursday we have Company at home. On Friday we are to be at a Private Concert at Sir John Wynna's—and on Saturday we expect Miss Dawson to call in the Morning—which will complete my Daughters Introduction into Life. How they will bear so much dissipation I cannot imagine; of their spirits I have no fear, I only dread their health.

This mighty affair is now happily over, and my Girls are OUT. As the moment approached for our departure, you can have no idea how the sweet Creatures trembled with fear and expectation. Before the Carriage drove to the door, I called them into my dressing-room, and as soon as they were seated thus addressed them. "My dear Girls the moment is now arrived when I am to reap the rewards of all my Anxieties and Labours towards you during your Education. You are this Evening to enter a World in which you will meet with many wonderfull Things; Yet let me warn you against suffering yourselves to be meanly swayed by the Follies and Vices of others, for beleive me my beloved Children that if you do—I shall be very sorry for it." They both assured me that they would ever remember my advice with Gratitude, and follow it with attention; That they were prepared to find a World full of things to amaze and to shock them: but that they trusted their behaviour would never give me reason to repent the Watchful Care with which I had presided over their infancy and formed their Minds—" "With such expectations and such intentions (cried I) I can have nothing to fear from you—and can chearfully conduct you to Mrs Cope's without a fear of your being seduced by her Example, or contaminated by her Follies. Come, then my Children (added I) the Carriage is driving to the door, and I will not a moment delay the happiness you are so impatient to enjoy." When we arrived at Warleigh, poor Augusta could scarcely breathe, while Margaret was all Life and Rapture. "The long-expected Moment is now arrived (said she) and we shall soon be in the World."—In a few Moments we were in Mrs Cope's parlour, where with her daughter she sate ready to receive us. I observed with delight the impression my Children made on them—. They were indeed two sweet, elegant-looking Girls, and tho' somewhat abashed from the peculiarity of their situation, yet there was an ease in their Manners and address which could not fail of pleasing—. Imagine my dear Madam how delighted I must have been in beholding as I did, how attentively they observed every object they saw, how disgusted with some Things, how enchanted with others, how astonished at all! On the whole however they returned in raptures with the World, its Inhabitants, and Manners. Yrs Ever—

A. F.

Letter The Second

From a YOUNG LADY crossed in Love to her freind

Why should this last disappointment hang so heavily on my spirits? Why should I feel it more, why should it wound me deeper than those I have experienced before? Can it be that I have a greater affection for Willoughby than I had for his amiable predecessors? Or is it that our feelings become more acute from being often wounded? I must suppose my dear Belle that this is the Case, since I am not conscious of being more sincerely attached to Willoughby than I was to Neville, Fitzowen, or either of the Crawfords, for all of whom I once felt the most lasting affection that ever warmed a Woman's heart. Tell me then dear Belle why I still sigh when I think of the faithless Edward, or why I weep when I behold his Bride, for too surely this is the case—. My Freinds are all alarmed for me; They fear my declining health; they lament my want of spirits; they dread the effects of both. In hopes of releiving my melancholy, by directing my thoughts to other objects, they have invited several of their freinds to spend the Christmas with us. Lady Bridget Darkwood and her sister-in-law, Miss Jane are expected on Friday; and Colonel Seaton's family will be with us next week. This is all most kindly meant by my Uncle and Cousins; but what can the presence of a dozen indefferent people do to me, but weary and distress me—. I will not finish my Letter till some of our Visitors are arrived.

Friday Evening Lady Bridget came this morning, and with her, her sweet sister Miss Jane—. Although I have been acquainted with this charming Woman above fifteen Years, yet I never before observed how lovely she is. She is now about 35, and in spite of sickness, sorrow and Time is more blooming than I ever saw a Girl of 17. I was delighted with her, the moment she entered the house, and she appeared equally pleased with me, attaching herself to me during the remainder of the day. There is something so sweet, so mild in her Countenance, that she seems more than Mortal. Her Conversation is as bewitching as her appearance; I could not help telling her how much she engaged my admiration—. "Oh! Miss Jane (said I)—and stopped from an inability at the moment of expressing myself as I could wish—Oh! Miss Jane—(I repeated)—I could not think of words to suit my feelings—She seemed waiting for my speech—. I was confused—distressed—my thoughts were bewildered—and I could only add—"How do you do?" She saw and felt for my Embarrassment and with admirable presence of mind releived me from it by saying—"My dear Sophia be not uneasy at having exposed yourself—I will turn the Conversation without appearing to notice it. "Oh! how I loved her for her kindness!" Do you ride as much as you used to do?" said she—. "I am advised to ride by my Physician. We have delightful Rides round us, I have a Charming horse, am uncommonly fond of the Amusement, replied I quite recovered from my Confusion, and in short I ride a great deal." "You are in the right my Love," said she. Then repeating the following line which was an extempore and equally adapted to recommend both Riding and Candour—

"Ride where you may, Be Candid where you can," she added," I rode once, but it is many years ago—She spoke this in so low and tremulous a Voice, that I was silent—. Struck with her Manner of speaking I could make no reply. "I have not ridden, continued she fixing her Eyes on my face, since I was married." I was never so surprised—"Married, Ma'am!" I repeated. "You may well wear that look of astonishment, said she, since what I have said must appear improbable to you—Yet nothing is more true than that I once was married."

"Then why are you called Miss Jane?"

"I married, my Sophia without the consent or knowledge of my father the late Admiral Annesley. It was therefore necessary to keep the secret from him and from every one, till some fortunate opportunity might offer of revealing it—. Such an opportunity alas! was but too soon given in the death of my dear Capt. Dashwood—Pardon these tears, continued Miss Jane wiping her Eyes, I owe them to my Husband's memory. He fell my Sophia, while fighting for his Country in America after a most happy Union of seven years—. My Children, two sweet Boys and a Girl, who had constantly resided with my Father and me, passing with him and with every one as the Children of a Brother (tho' I had ever been an only Child) had as yet been the comforts of my Life. But no sooner had I lossed my Henry, than these sweet Creatures fell sick and died—. Conceive dear Sophia what my feelings must have been when as an Aunt I attended my Children to their early Grave—. My Father did not survive them many weeks—He died, poor Good old man, happily ignorant to his last hour of my Marriage.'

"But did not you own it, and assume his name at your husband's death?"

"No; I could not bring myself to do it; more especially when in my Children I lost all inducement for doing it. Lady Bridget, and yourself are the only persons who are in the knowledge of my having ever been either Wife or Mother. As I could not Prevail on myself to take the name of Dashwood (a name which after my Henry's death I could never hear without emotion) and as I was conscious of having no right to that of Annesley, I dropt all thoughts of either, and have made it a point of bearing only my Christian one since my Father's death." She paused—"Oh! my dear Miss Jane (said I) how infinitely am I obliged to you for so entertaining a story! You cannot think how it has diverted me! But have you quite done?"

"I have only to add my dear Sophia, that my Henry's elder Brother dieing about the same time, Lady Bridget became a Widow like myself, and as we had always loved each other in idea from the high Character in which we had ever been spoken of, though we had never met, we determined to live together. We wrote to one another on the same subject by the same post, so exactly did our feeling and our actions coincide! We both eagerly embraced the proposals we gave and received of becoming one family, and have from that time lived together in the greatest affection."

"And is this all? said I, I hope you have not done."

"Indeed I have; and did you ever hear a story more pathetic?"

"I never did—and it is for that reason it pleases me so much, for when one is unhappy nothing is so delightful to one's sensations as to hear of equal misery."

"Ah! but my Sophia why are YOU unhappy?"

"Have you not heard Madam of Willoughby's Marriage?"

"But my love why lament HIS perfidy, when you bore so well that of many young Men before?"

"Ah! Madam, I was used to it then, but when Willoughby broke his Engagements I had not been dissapointed for half a year."

"Poor Girl!" said Miss Jane.

Letter The Third

From a YOUNG LADY in distressed Circumstances to her

Friend

A few days ago I was at a private Ball given by Mr Ashburnham. As my Mother never goes out she entrusted me to the care of Lady Greville who did me the honour of calling for me in her way and of allowing me to sit forwards, which is a favour about which I am very indifferent especially as I know it is considered as confering a great obligation on me "So Miss Maria (said her Ladyship as she saw me advancing to the door of the Carriage) you seem very smart to night—MY poor Girls will appear quite to disadvantage by YOU—I only hope your Mother may not have distressed herself to set YOU off. Have you got a new Gown on?"

"Yes Ma'am." replied I with as much indifference as I could assume.

"Aye, and a fine one too I think—(feeling it, as by her permission I seated myself by her) I dare say it is all very smart—But I must own, for you know I always speak my mind, that I think it was quite a needless piece of expence— Why could not you have worn your old striped one? It is not my way to find fault with People because they are poor, for I always think that they are more to be despised and pitied than blamed for it, especially if they cannot help it, but at the same time I must say that in my opinion your old striped Gown would have been quite fine enough for its Wearer—for to tell you the truth (I always speak my mind) I am very much afraid that one half of the people in the room will not know whether you have a Gown on or not—But I suppose you intend to make your fortune to night—. Well, the sooner the better; and I wish you success."

"Indeed Ma'am I have no such intention—"

"Who ever heard a young Lady own that she was a Fortune-hunter?" Miss Greville laughed but I am sure Ellen felt for me.

"Was your Mother gone to bed before you left her?" said her Ladyship.

"Dear Ma'am, said Ellen it is but nine o'clock."

"True Ellen, but Candles cost money, and Mrs Williams is too wise to be extravagant."

"She was just sitting down to supper Ma'am."

"And what had she got for supper?" "I did not observe." "Bread and Cheese I suppose." "I should never wish for a better supper." said Ellen. "You have never any reason replied her Mother, as a better is always provided for you." Miss Greville laughed excessively, as she constantly does at her Mother's wit.

Such is the humiliating Situation in which I am forced to appear while riding in her Ladyship's Coach—I dare not be impertinent, as my Mother is always admonishing me to be humble and patient if I wish to make my way in the world. She insists on my accepting every invitation of Lady Greville, or you may be certain that I would never enter either her House, or her Coach with the disagreable certainty I always have of being abused for my Poverty while I am in them.—When we arrived at Ashburnham, it was nearly ten o'clock, which was an hour and a half later than we were desired to be there; but Lady Greville is too fashionable (or fancies herself to be so) to be punctual. The Dancing however was not begun as they waited for Miss Greville. I had not been long in the room before I was engaged to dance by Mr Bernard, but just as we were going to stand up, he recollected that his Servant had got his white Gloves, and immediately ran out to fetch them. In the mean time the Dancing began and Lady Greville in passing to another room went exactly before me—She saw me and instantly stopping, said to me though there were several people close to us,

"Hey day, Miss Maria! What cannot you get a partner? Poor Young Lady! I am afraid your new Gown was put on for nothing. But do not despair; perhaps you may get a hop before the Evening is over." So saying, she passed on without hearing my repeated assurance of being engaged, and leaving me very much provoked at being so exposed before every one—Mr Bernard however soon returned and by coming to me the moment he entered the room, and leading me to the Dancers my Character I hope was cleared from the imputation Lady Greville had thrown on it, in the eyes of all the old Ladies who had heard her speech. I soon forgot all my vexations in the pleasure of dancing and of having the most agreable partner in the room. As he is moreover heir to a very large Estate I could see that Lady Greville did not look very well pleased when she found who had been his Choice—She was determined to mortify me, and accordingly when we were sitting down between the dances, she came to me with more than her usual insulting importance attended by Miss Mason and said loud enough to be heard by half the people in the room, "Pray Miss Maria in what way of business was your Grandfather? for Miss Mason and I cannot agree whether he was a Grocer or a Bookbinder." I saw that she wanted to mortify me, and was resolved if I

possibly could to Prevent her seeing that her scheme succeeded. "Neither
Madam; he was a Wine Merchant." "Aye, I knew he was in some such low
way—He broke did not he?" "I beleive not Ma'am." "Did not he abscond?"
"I never heard that he did." "At least he died insolvent?" "I was never told so
before." "Why, was not your FATHER as poor as a Rat" "I fancy not." "Was
not he in the Kings Bench once?" "I never saw him there." She gave me
SUCH a look, and turned away in a great passion; while I was half delighted
with myself for my impertinence, and half afraid of being thought too saucy.
As Lady Greville was extremely angry with me, she took no further notice of
me all the Evening, and indeed had I been in favour I should have been
equally neglected, as she was got into a Party of great folks and she never
speaks to me when she can to anyone else. Miss Greville was with her
Mother's party at supper, but Ellen preferred staying with the Bernards and
me. We had a very pleasant Dance and as Lady G—slept all the way home, I
had a very comfortable ride.

The next day while we were at dinner Lady Greville's Coach stopped at
the door, for that is the time of day she generally contrives it should. She sent
in a message by the servant to say that "she should not get out but that Miss
Maria must come to the Coach-door, as she wanted to speak to her, and that
she must make haste and come immediately—" "What an impertinent
Message Mama!" said I—"Go Maria—" replied she—Accordingly I went and
was obliged to stand there at her Ladyships pleasure though the Wind was
extremely high and very cold.

"Why I think Miss Maria you are not quite so smart as you were last
night—But I did not come to examine your dress, but to tell you that you
may dine with us the day after tomorrow—Not tomorrow, remember, do not
come tomorrow, for we expect Lord and Lady Clermont and Sir Thomas
Stanley's family—There will be no occasion for your being very fine for I
shant send the Carriage—If it rains you may take an umbrella—" I could
hardly help laughing at hearing her give me leave to keep myself dry—"And
pray remember to be in time, for I shant wait—I hate my Victuals over-
done—But you need not come before the time—How does your Mother do?
She is at dinner is not she?" "Yes Ma'am we were in the middle of dinner
when your Ladyship came." "I am afraid you find it very cold Maria." said
Ellen. "Yes, it is an horrible East wind—said her Mother—I assure you I can
hardly bear the window down—But you are used to be blown about by the
wind Miss Maria and that is what has made your Complexion so rudely and
coarse. You young Ladies who cannot often ride in a Carriage never mind
what weather you trudge in, or how the wind shews your legs. I would not
have my Girls stand out of doors as you do in such a day as this. But some
sort of people have no feelings either of cold or Delicacy—Well, remember
that we shall expect you on Thursday at 5 o'clock—You must tell your Maid
to come for you at night—There will be no Moon—and you will have an
horrid walk home—My compts to Your Mother—I am afraid your dinner

will be cold—Drive on—" And away she went, leaving me in a great passion with her as she always does.

Maria Williams.

Letter The Fourth

From a YOUNG LADY rather impertinent to her freind

We dined yesterday with Mr Evelyn where we were introduced to a very agreable looking Girl his Cousin. I was extremely pleased with her appearance, for added to the charms of an engaging face, her manner and voice had something peculiarly interesting in them. So much so, that they inspired me with a great curiosity to know the history of her Life, who were her Parents, where she came from, and what had befallen her, for it was then only known that she was a relation of Mr Evelyn, and that her name was Grenville. In the evening a favourable opportunity offered to me of attempting at least to know what I wished to know, for every one played at Cards but Mrs Evelyn, My Mother, Dr Drayton, Miss Grenville and myself, and as the two former were engaged in a whispering Conversation, and the Doctor fell asleep, we were of necessity obliged to entertain each other. This was what I wished and being determined not to remain in ignorance for want of asking, I began the Conversation in the following Manner.

"Have you been long in Essex Ma'am?"

"I arrived on Tuesday."

"You came from Derbyshire?"

"No, Ma'am! appearing surprised at my question, from Suffolk." You will think this a good dash of mine my dear Mary, but you know that I am not wanting for Impudence when I have any end in veiw. "Are you pleased with the Country Miss Grenville? Do you find it equal to the one you have left?"

"Much superior Ma'am in point of Beauty." She sighed. I longed to know for why.

"But the face of any Country however beautiful said I, can be but a poor consolation for the loss of one's dearest Freinds." She shook her head, as if she felt the truth of what I said. My Curiosity was so much raised, that I was resolved at any rate to satisfy it.

"You regret having left Suffolk then Miss Grenville?" "Indeed I do." "You were born there I suppose?" "Yes Ma'am I was and passed many happy years there—"

"That is a great comfort—said I—I hope Ma'am that you never spent any unhappy one's there."

"Perfect Felicity is not the property of Mortals, and no one has a right to expect uninterrupted Happiness.—Some Misfortunes I have certainly met with."

"WHAT Misfortunes dear Ma'am? replied I, burning with impatience to know every thing. "NONE Ma'am I hope that have been the effect of any wilfull fault in me." "I dare say not Ma'am, and have no doubt but that any sufferings you may have experienced could arise only from the cruelties of Relations or the Errors of Freinds." She sighed—"You seem unhappy my dear Miss Grenville—Is it in my power to soften your Misfortunes?" "YOUR power Ma'am replied she extremely surprised; it is in NO ONES power to make me happy." She pronounced these words in so mournfull and solemn an accent, that for some time I had not courage to reply. I was actually silenced. I recovered myself however in a few moments and looking at her with all the affection I could, "My dear Miss Grenville said I, you appear extremely young—and may probably stand in need of some one's advice whose regard for you, joined to superior Age, perhaps superior Judgement might authorise her to give it. I am that person, and I now challenge you to accept the offer I make you of my Confidence and Freindship, in return to which I shall only ask for yours—"

"You are extremely obliging Ma'am—said she—and I am highly flattered by your attention to me—But I am in no difficulty, no doubt, no uncertainty of situation in which any advice can be wanted. Whenever I am however continued she brightening into a complaisant smile, I shall know where to apply."

I bowed, but felt a good deal mortified by such a repulse; still however I had not given up my point. I found that by the appearance of sentiment and Freindship nothing was to be gained and determined therefore to renew my attacks by Questions and suppositions. "Do you intend staying long in this part of England Miss Grenville?"

"Yes Ma'am, some time I beleive."

"But how will Mr and Mrs Grenville bear your absence?"

"They are neither of them alive Ma'am." This was an answer I did not expect—I was quite silenced, and never felt so awkward in my Life——.

Letter The Fifth

From a YOUNG LADY very much in love to her Freind

My Uncle gets more stingy, my Aunt more particular, and I more in love every day. What shall we all be at this rate by the end of the year! I had this morning the happiness of receiving the following Letter from my dear Musgrove.

Sackville St: Janry 7th It is a month to day since I first beheld my lovely Henrietta, and the sacred anniversary must and shall be kept in a manner becoming the day—by writing to her. Never shall I forget the moment when her Beauties first broke on my sight—No time as you well know can erase it from my Memory. It was at Lady Scudamores. Happy Lady Scudamore to live within a mile of the divine Henrietta! When the lovely Creature first entered the room, oh! what were my sensations? The sight of you was like the sight of a wonderful fine Thing. I started—I gazed at her with admiration—She appeared every moment more Charming, and the unfortunate Musgrove became a captive to your Charms before I had time to look about me. Yes Madam, I had the happiness of adoring you, an happiness for which I cannot be too grateful. "What said he to himself is Musgrove allowed to die for Henrietta? Enviable Mortal! and may he pine for her who is the object of universal admiration, who is adored by a Colonel, and toasted by a Baronet! Adorable Henrietta how beautiful you are! I declare you are quite divine! You are more than Mortal. You are an Angel. You are Venus herself. In short Madam you are the prettiest Girl I ever saw in my Life—and her Beauty is encreased in her Musgroves Eyes, by permitting him to love her and allowing me to hope. And ah! Angelic Miss Henrietta Heaven is my witness how ardently I do hope for the death of your villanous Uncle and his abandoned Wife, since my fair one will not consent to be mine till their decease has placed her in affluence above what my fortune can procure—. Though it is an improvable Estate—. Cruel Henrietta to persist in such a resolution! I am at Present with my sister where I mean to continue till my own house which tho' an excellent one is at Present somewhat out of repair, is ready to receive me. Amiable princess of my Heart farewell—Of that Heart which trembles while it signs itself Your most ardent Admirer and devoted humble servt. T. Musgrove.

There is a pattern for a Love-letter Matilda! Did you ever read such a master-piece of Writing? Such sense, such sentiment, such purity of Thought, such flow of Language and such unfeigned Love in one sheet? No, never I can answer for it, since a Musgrove is not to be met with by every Girl. Oh! how I long to be with him! I intend to send him the following in answer to his Letter tomorrow.

My dearest Musgrove—. Words cannot express how happy your Letter made me; I thought I should have cried for joy, for I love you better than any body in the World. I think you the most amiable, and the handsomest Man in England, and so to be sure you are. I never read so sweet a Letter in my Life. Do write me another just like it, and tell me you are in love with me in every other line. I quite die to see you. How shall we manage to see one another? for we are so much in love that we cannot live asunder. Oh! my dear Musgrove you cannot think how impatiently I wait for the death of my Uncle and Aunt—If they will not Die soon, I beleive I shall run mad, for I get more in love with you every day of my Life.

How happy your Sister is to enjoy the pleasure of your Company in her house, and how happy every body in London must be because you are there. I hope you will be so kind as to write to me again soon, for I never read such sweet Letters as yours. I am my dearest Musgrove most truly and faithfully yours for ever and ever Henrietta Halton.

I hope he will like my answer; it is as good a one as I can write though nothing to his; Indeed I had always heard what a dab he was at a Love-letter. I saw him you know for the first time at Lady Scudamores—And when I saw her Ladyship afterwards she asked me how I liked her Cousin Musgrove?

"Why upon my word said I, I think he is a very handsome young Man."

"I am glad you think so replied she, for he is distractedly in love with you."

"Law! Lady Scudamore said I, how can you talk so ridiculously?"

"Nay, t'is very true answered she, I assure you, for he was in love with you from the first moment he beheld you."

"I wish it may be true said I, for that is the only kind of love I would give a farthing for—There is some sense in being in love at first sight."

"Well, I give you Joy of your conquest, replied Lady Scudamore, and I beleive it to have been a very complete one; I am sure it is not a contemptible one, for my Cousin is a charming young fellow, has seen a great deal of the World, and writes the best Love-letters I ever read."

This made me very happy, and I was excessively pleased with my conquest. However, I thought it was proper to give myself a few Airs—so I said to her—

"This is all very pretty Lady Scudamore, but you know that we young Ladies who are Heiresses must not throw ourselves away upon Men who have no fortune at all."

"My dear Miss Halton said she, I am as much convinced of that as you can be, and I do assure you that I should be the last person to encourage your marrying anyone who had not some pretensions to expect a fortune with you. Mr Musgrove is so far from being poor that he has an estate of several hundreds an year which is capable of great Improvement, and an excellent House, though at Present it is not quite in repair."

"If that is the case replied I, I have nothing more to say against him, and if as you say he is an informed young Man and can write a good Love-letter, I am sure I have no reason to find fault with him for admiring me, tho' perhaps I may not marry him for all that Lady Scudamore."

"You are certainly under no obligation to marry him answered her Ladyship, except that which love himself will dictate to you, for if I am not greatly mistaken you are at this very moment unknown to yourself, cherishing a most tender affection for him."

"Law, Lady Scudamore replied I blushing how can you think of such a thing?"

"Because every look, every word betrays it, answered she; Come my dear Henrietta, consider me as a freind, and be sincere with me—Do not you prefer Mr Musgrove to any man of your acquaintance?"

"Pray do not ask me such questions Lady Scudamore, said I turning away my head, for it is not fit for me to answer them."

"Nay my Love replied she, now you confirm my suspicions. But why Henrietta should you be ashamed to own a well-placed Love, or why refuse to confide in me?"

"I am not ashamed to own it; said I taking Courage. I do not refuse to confide in you or blush to say that I do love your cousin Mr Musgrove, that I am sincerely attached to him, for it is no disgrace to love a handsome Man. If he were plain indeed I might have had reason to be ashamed of a passion which must have been mean since the object would have been unworthy. But with such a figure and face, and such beautiful hair as your Cousin has, why should I blush to own that such superior merit has made an impression on me."

"My sweet Girl (said Lady Scudamore embracing me with great affection) what a delicate way of thinking you have in these matters, and what a quick discernment for one of your years! Oh! how I honour you for such Noble Sentiments!"

"Do you Ma'am said I; You are vastly obliging. But pray Lady Scudamore did your Cousin himself tell you of his affection for me I shall like him the better if he did, for what is a Lover without a Confidante?"

"Oh! my Love replied she, you were born for each other. Every word you say more deeply convinces me that your Minds are actuated by the invisible power of simpathy, for your opinions and sentiments so exactly coincide. Nay, the colour of your Hair is not very different. Yes my dear Girl, the poor despairing Musgrove did reveal to me the story of his Love—. Nor was I surprised at it—I know not how it was, but I had a kind of presentiment that he would be in love with you."

"Well, but how did he break it to you?"

"It was not till after supper. We were sitting round the fire together talking on indifferent subjects, though to say the truth the Conversation was cheifly on my side for he was thoughtful and silent, when on a sudden he interrupted me in the midst of something I was saying, by exclaiming in a most Theatrical tone—

Yes I'm in love I feel it now And Henrietta Halton has undone me

"Oh! What a sweet way replied I, of declaring his Passion! To make such a couple of charming lines about me! What a pity it is that they are not in rhime!"

"I am very glad you like it answered she; To be sure there was a great deal of Taste in it. And are you in love with her, Cousin? said I. I am very sorry for it, for unexceptionable as you are in every respect, with a pretty Estate capable of Great improvements, and an excellent House tho' somewhat out of repair, yet who can hope to aspire with success to the adorable Henrietta who has had an offer from a Colonel and been toasted by a Baronet"— "THAT I have—" cried I. Lady Scudamore continued. "Ah dear Cousin replied he, I am so well convinced of the little Chance I can have of winning her who is adored by thousands, that I need no assurances of yours to make me more thoroughly so. Yet surely neither you or the fair Henrietta herself will deny me the exquisite Gratification of dieing for her, of falling a victim to her Charms. And when I am dead"—continued her—

"Oh Lady Scudamore, said I wiping my eyes, that such a sweet Creature should talk of dieing!"

"It is an affecting Circumstance indeed, replied Lady Scudamore." "When I am dead said he, let me be carried and lain at her feet, and perhaps she may not disdain to drop a pitying tear on my poor remains."

"Dear Lady Scudamore interrupted I, say no more on this affecting subject. I cannot bear it."

"Oh! how I admire the sweet sensibility of your Soul, and as I would not for Worlds wound it too deeply, I will be silent."

"Pray go on." said I. She did so.

"And then added he, Ah! Cousin imagine what my transports will be when I feel the dear precious drops trickle on my face! Who would not die to haste such extacy! And when I am interred, may the divine Henrietta bless some happier Youth with her affection, May he be as tenderly attached to her as the hapless Musgrove and while HE crumbles to dust, May they live an example of Felicity in the Conjugal state!"

Did you ever hear any thing so pathetic? What a charming wish, to be lain at my feet when he was dead! Oh! what an exalted mind he must have to be capable of such a wish! Lady Scudamore went on.

"Ah! my dear Cousin replied I to him, such noble behaviour as this, must melt the heart of any woman however obdurate it may naturally be; and could the divine Henrietta but hear your generous wishes for her happiness, all gentle as is her mind, I have not a doubt but that she would pity your affection and endeavour to return it." "Oh! Cousin answered he, do not endeavour to raise my hopes by such flattering assurances. No, I cannot hope to please this angel of a Woman, and the only thing which remains for me to do, is to die." "True Love is ever desponding replied I, but I my dear Tom will give you even greater hopes of conquering this fair one's heart, than I have yet given you, by assuring you that I watched her with the strictest attention during the whole day, and could plainly discover that she cherishes in her bosom though unknown to herself, a most tender affection for you."

"Dear Lady Scudamore cried I, This is more than I ever knew!"

"Did not I say that it was unknown to yourself? I did not, continued I to him, encourage you by saying this at first, that surprise might render the pleasure still Greater." "No Cousin replied he in a languid voice, nothing will convince me that I can have touched the heart of Henrietta Halton, and if you are deceived yourself, do not attempt deceiving me." "In short my Love it was the work of some hours for me to Persuade the poor despairing Youth that you had really a preference for him; but when at last he could no longer deny the force of my arguments, or discredit what I told him, his transports, his Raptures, his Extacies are beyond my power to describe."

"Oh! the dear Creature, cried I, how passionately he loves me! But dear Lady Scudamore did you tell him that I was totally dependant on my Uncle and Aunt?"

"Yes, I told him every thing."

"And what did he say."

"He exclaimed with virulence against Uncles and Aunts; Accused the laws of England for allowing them to Possess their Estates when wanted by their Nephews or Neices, and wished HE were in the House of Commons, that he might reform the Legislature, and rectify all its abuses."

"Oh! the sweet Man! What a spirit he has!" said I.

"He could not flatter himself he added, that the adorable Henrietta would condescend for his sake to resign those Luxuries and that splendor to which she had been used, and accept only in exchange the Comforts and Elegancies which his limited Income could afford her, even supposing that his house were in Readiness to receive her. I told him that it could not be expected that she would; it would be doing her an injustice to suppose her capable of giving up the power she now possesses and so nobly uses of doing such extensive Good to the poorer part of her fellow Creatures, merely for the gratification of you and herself."

"To be sure said I, I AM very Charitable every now and then. And what did Mr Musgrove say to this?"

"He replied that he was under a melancholy necessity of owning the truth of what I said, and that therefore if he should be the happy Creature destined to be the Husband of the Beautiful Henrietta he must bring himself to wait, however impatiently, for the fortunate day, when she might be freed from the power of worthless Relations and able to bestow herself on him."

What a noble Creature he is! Oh! Matilda what a fortunate one I am, who am to be his Wife! My Aunt is calling me to come and make the pies, so adeiu my dear freind, and beleive me yours etc—

H. Halton.

The Female Philosopher

To Miss FANNY CATHERINE AUSTEN

MY Dear Neice As I am prevented by the great distance between Rowling and Steventon from superintending your Education myself, the care of which will probably on that account devolve on your Father and Mother, I think it is my particular Duty to Prevent your feeling as much as possible the want of my personal instructions, by addressing to you on paper my Opinions and Admonitions on the conduct of Young Women, which you will find

expressed in the following pages.—I am my dear Neice
Your affectionate Aunt

The Author.

A Letter

My Dear Louisa Your friend Mr Millar called upon us yesterday in his way to Bath, whither he is going for his health; two of his daughters were with him, but the eldest and the three Boys are with their Mother in Sussex. Though you have often told me that Miss Millar was remarkably handsome, you never mentioned anything of her Sisters' beauty; yet they are certainly extremely pretty. I'll give you their description.—Julia is eighteen; with a countenance in which Modesty, Sense and Dignity are happily blended, she has a form which at once presents you with Grace, Elegance and Symmetry. Charlotte who is just sixteen is shorter than her Sister, and though her figure cannot boast the easy dignity of Julia's, yet it has a pleasing plumpness which is in a different way as estimable. She is fair and her face is expressive sometimes of softness the most bewitching, and at others of Vivacity the most striking. She appears to have infinite Wit and a good humour unalterable; her conversation during the half hour they set with us, was replete with humourous sallies, Bonmots and repartees; while the sensible, the amiable Julia uttered sentiments of Morality worthy of a heart like her own. Mr Millar appeared to answer the character I had always received of him. My Father met him with that look of Love, that social Shake, and cordial kiss which marked his gladness at beholding an old and valued freind from whom thro' various circumstances he had been separated nearly twenty years. Mr Millar observed (and very justly too) that many events had befallen each during that interval of time, which gave occasion to the lovely Julia for making most sensible reflections on the many changes in their situation which so long a period had occasioned, on the advantages of some, and the disadvantages of others. From this subject she made a short digression to the instability of human pleasures and the uncertainty of their duration, which led her to observe that all earthly Joys must be imperfect. She was proceeding to illustrate this doctrine by examples from the Lives of great Men when the Carriage came to the Door and the amiable Moralist with her Father and Sister was obliged to depart; but not without a promise of spending five or six months with us on their return. We of course mentioned you, and I assure you that ample Justice was done to your Merits by all. "Louisa Clarke (said I) is in general a very pleasant Girl, yet sometimes her good humour is clouded by Peevishness, Envy and Spite. She neither wants Understanding or is without some pretensions to Beauty, but these are so very trifling, that the value she sets on her personal charms, and the adoration she expects them to be offered are at once a striking example of her vanity, her pride, and her folly." So said I, and to my opinion everyone added weight by the concurrence of their own. Your affectionate Arabella Smythe.

The First Act of A Comedy

Characters
Popgun Maria Charles Pistolletta Postilion Hostess Chorus of ploughboys Cook and and Strephon Chloe

Scene
An Inn

ENTER Hostess, Charles, Maria, and Cook.

Hostess: (to Maria) If the gentry in the Lion should want beds, shew them number 9.
Maria: Yes Mistress.—EXIT Maria
Hostess (to Cook): If their Honours in the Moon ask for the bill of fare, give it them.
Cook: I wull, I wull.

EXIT Cook.

Hostess (to Charles): If their Ladyships in the Sun ring their Bell— answerit.
Charles: Yes Madam.

EXEUNT Severally.

SCENE CHANGES TO THE MOON, and discovers Popgun and Pistoletta.

Pistoletta: Pray papa how far is it to London?
Popgun: My Girl, my Darling, my favourite of all my Children, who art the picture of thy poor Mother who died two months ago, with whom I am going to Town to marry to Strephon, and to whom I mean to bequeath my whole Estate, it wants seven Miles.

SCENE CHANGES TO THE SUN—

ENTER Chloe and a chorus of ploughboys.

Chloe: Where am I? At Hounslow.—Where go I? To London—. What to do? To be married—. Unto whom? Unto Strephon. Who is he? A Youth. Then I will sing a song.

SONG

I go to Town
And when I come down,
I shall be married to Streephon
And that to me will be fun.
Chorus: Be fun, be fun, be fun, And that to me will be fun.

ENTER Cook

Cook: Here is the bill of fare.
Chloe (reads): 2 Ducks, a leg of beef, a stinking partridge, and a tart.—I will have the leg of beef and the partridge.

EXIT Cook.
And now I will sing another song.

SONG

I am going to have my dinner,
After which I shan't be thinner,
I wish I had here Strephon
For he would carve the partridge if it should be a tough one.
Chorus: Tough one, tough one, tough one For he would carve the partridge if it Should be a tough one.

EXIT Chloe and Chorus.—

SCENE CHANGES TO THE INSIDE OF THE LION.

Enter Strephon and Postilion.

Streph: You drove me from Staines to this place, from whence I mean to go to Town to marry Chloe. How much is your due?
Post: Eighteen pence.
Streph: Alas, my freind, I have but a bad guinea with which I mean to support myself in Town. But I will pawn to you an undirected Letter that I received from Chloe.
Post: Sir, I accept your offer.

A Letter From a Young Lady

whose feelings being too strong for her Judgement led her into the commission of Errors which her Heart disapproved.

Many have been the cares and vicissitudes of my past life, my beloved Ellinor, and the only consolation I feel for their bitterness is that on a close examination of my conduct, I am convinced that I have strictly deserved them. I murdered my father at a very early period of my Life, I have since murdered my Mother, and I am now going to murder my Sister. I have changed my religion so often that at present I have not an idea of any left. I have been a perjured witness in every public tryal for these last twelve years; and I have forged my own Will. In short there is scarcely a crime that I have not committed—But I am now going to reform. Colonel Martin of the Horse guards has paid his Addresses to me, and we are to be married in a few days. As there is something singular in our Courtship, I will give you an account of it. Colonel Martin is the second son of the late Sir John Martin who died immensely rich, but bequeathing only one hundred thousand pound apeice to his three younger Children, left the bulk of his fortune, about eight Million to the present Sir Thomas. Upon his small pittance the Colonel lived tolerably contented for nearly four months when he took it into his head to determine on getting the whole of his eldest Brother's Estate. A new will was forged and the Colonel produced it in Court—but nobody would swear to it's being the right will except himself, and he had sworn so much that Nobody beleived him. At that moment I happened to be passing by the door of the Court, and was beckoned in by the Judge who told the Colonel that I was a Lady ready to witness anything for the cause of Justice, and advised him to apply to me. In short the Affair was soon adjusted. The Colonel and I swore to its' being the right will, and Sir Thomas has been obliged to resign all his illgotten wealth. The Colonel in gratitude waited on me the next day with an offer of his hand—. I am now going to murder my Sister.

Yours Ever,

Anna Parker.

A Tour Through Wales

in a LETTER from a YOUNG LADY—

My Dear Clara I have been so long on the ramble that I have not till now had it in my power to thank you for your Letter—. We left our dear home on last Monday month; and proceeded on our tour through Wales, which is a principality contiguous to England and gives the title to the Prince of Wales. We travelled on horseback by preference. My Mother rode upon our little poney and Fanny and I walked by her side or rather ran, for my Mother is so fond of riding fast that she galloped all the way. You may be sure that we were in a fine perspiration when we came to our place of resting. Fanny has taken a great many Drawings of the Country, which are very beautiful, tho' perhaps not such exact resemblances as might be wished, from their being taken as she ran along. It would astonish you to see all the Shoes we wore out in our Tour. We determined to take a good Stock with us and therefore each took a pair of our own besides those we set off in. However we were obliged to have them both capped and heelpeiced at Carmarthen, and at last when they were quite gone, Mama was so kind as to lend us a pair of blue Sattin Slippers, of which we each took one and hopped home from Hereford delightfully—

I am your ever affectionate

Elizabeth Johnson.

A Tale

A Gentleman whose family name I shall conceal, bought a small Cottage in Pembrokeshire about two years ago. This daring Action was suggested to him by his elder Brother who promised to furnish two rooms and a Closet for him, provided he would take a small house near the borders of an extensive Forest, and about three Miles from the Sea. Wilhelminus gladly accepted the offer and continued for some time searching after such a retreat when he was one morning agreably releived from his suspence by reading this advertisement in a Newspaper.

TO BE LETT: A Neat Cottage on the borders of an extensive forest and about three Miles from the Sea. It is ready furnished except two rooms and a Closet.

The delighted Wilhelminus posted away immediately to his brother, and shewed him the advertisement. Robertus congratulated him and sent him in his Carriage to take possession of the Cottage. After travelling for three days and six nights without stopping, they arrived at the Forest and following a track which led by it's side down a steep Hill over which ten Rivulets meandered, they reached the Cottage in half an hour. Wilhelminus alighted, and after knocking for some time without receiving any answer or hearing any one stir within, he opened the door which was fastened only by a wooden latch and entered a small room, which he immediately perceived to be one of the two that were unfurnished—From thence he proceeded into a Closet equally bare. A pair of stairs that went out of it led him into a room above, no less destitute, and these apartments he found composed the whole of the House. He was by no means displeased with this discovery, as he had the comfort of reflecting that he should not be obliged to lay out anything on furniture himself—. He returned immediately to his Brother, who took him the next day to every Shop in Town, and bought what ever was requisite to furnish the two rooms and the Closet, In a few days everything was completed, and Wilhelminus returned to take possession of his Cottage. Robertus accompanied him, with his Lady the amiable Cecilia and her two lovely Sisters Arabella and Marina to whom Wilhelminus was tenderly attached, and a large number of Attendants.—An ordinary Genius might probably have been embarrassed, in endeavouring to accomodate so large a party, but Wilhelminus with admirable presence of mind gave orders for the immediate erection of two noble Tents in an open spot in the Forest adjoining to the house. Their Construction was both simple and elegant—A couple of old blankets, each supported by four sticks, gave a striking proof of that taste for architecture and that happy ease in overcoming difficulties which were some of Wilhelminus's most striking Virtues.

Juvenilia — Volume the Third

Evelyn

To Miss Mary Lloyd

The following Novel is by permission Dedicated, by her Obedt. humble Servt.

The Author

In a retired part of the County of Sussex there is a village (for what I know to the Contrary) called Evelyn, perhaps one of the most beautiful Spots in the south of England. A Gentleman passing through it on horseback about twenty years ago, was so entirely of my opinion in this respect, that he put up at the little Alehouse in it and enquired with great earnestness whether there were any house to be let in the parish. The Landlady, who as well as everyone else in Evelyn was remarkably amiable, shook her head at this question, but seemed unwilling to give him any answer. He could not bear this uncertainty—yet knew not to obtain the information he desired. To repeat a question which had already appeared to make the good woman uneasy was impossible. He turned from her in visible agitation. "What a situation am I in!" said he to himself as he walked to the window and threw up the sash. He found himself revived by the Air, which he felt to a much greater degree when he had opened the window than he had done before. Yet it was but for a moment. The agonizing pain of Doubt and Suspense again weighed down his Spirits. The good woman who had watched in eager silence every turn of his Countenance with that benevolence, which characterizes the inhabitants of Evelyn, entreated him to tell her the cause of his uneasiness. "Is there anything, Sir, in my power to do that may relieve your Greifs? Tell me in what manner I can sooth them, and believe me that the friendly balm of Comfort and Assistance shall not be wanting; for indeed, Sir, I have a sympathetic Soul."

"Amiable Woman" (said Mr. Gower, affected almost to tears by this generous offer) "This Greatness of mind in one to whom I am almost a Stranger, serves but to make me the more warmly wish for a house in this sweet village. What would I not give to be your neighbor, to be blessed with your Acquaintance, and with the farther knowledge of your virtues! Oh! With what pleasure would I form myself by such an example! Tell me then, best of Women, is there no possibility?—I cannot speak—you know my Meaning—."

"Alas! Sir," replied Mrs. Willis, "there is none. Every house in this village, from the sweetness of the Situation, and the purity of the Air, in which neither Misery, Ill health, or vice are ever wafted, is inhabited. And yet," (after a short pause) "there is a Family, who tho' warmly attached to the spot, yet from a peculiar Generosity of Disposition would perhaps be willing to oblige you with their house." He eagerly caught at this idea, and having gained a direction to the place, he set off immediately on his walk to it. As he approached the House, he was delighted with its situation. It was in the exact centre of a small circular paddock, which was enclosed by a regular paling, and bordered with a plantation of Lombardy poplars, and Spruce firs alternatively placed in three rows. A gravel walk ran through this beautiful Shrubbery, and as the remainder of the paddock was unencumbered with any other Timber, the surface of it perfectly even and smooth, and grazed by four white Cows which were disposed at equal distances from each other, the whole appearance of the place as Mr. Gower entered the Paddock was uncommonly striking. A beautifully-rounded, gravel road without any turn or interruption led immediately to the house. Mr. Gower rang; the Door was soon opened. "Are Mr. and Mrs. Webb at home?" "My Good Sir, they are," replied the Servant; And leading the way, conducted Mr. Gower upstairs into a very elegant Dressing room, where a Lady rising from her seat, welcomed him with all the Generosity which Mrs. Willis had attributed to the Family.

"Welcome best of Men. Welcome to this House, and to everything it contains. William, tell your Master of the happiness I enjoy—invite him to partake of it. Bring up some Chocolate immediately; Spread a Cloth in the dining Parlor, and carry in the venison pasty. In the meantime let the Gentleman have some sandwiches, and bring in a Basket of Fruit. Send up some Ices and a bason of Soup, and do not forget some Jellies and Cakes." Then turning to Mr. Gower, and taking out her purse, "Accept this, my good Sir. Believe me you are welcome to everything that is in my power to bestow. I wish my purse were weightier, but Mr. Webb must make up my deficiencies. I know he has cash in the house to the amount of an hundred pounds, which he shall bring you immediately." Mr. Gower felt overpowered by her generosity as he put the purse in his pocket, and from the excess of his Gratitude, could scarcely express himself intelligibly when he accepted her offer of the hundred pounds. Mr. Webb soon entered the room, and repeated every protestation of Friendship and Cordiality which his Lady had already made. The Chocolate, the Sandwiches, the Jellies, the Cakes, the Ice, and the Soup soon made their appearance, and Mr. Gower having tasted something of all, and pocketed the rest, was conducted into the dining parlor, where he eat a most excellent Dinner and partook of the most exquisite Wines, while Mr. and Mrs. Webb stood by him still pressing him to eat and drink a little more. "And now my good Sir," said Mr. Webb, when Mr. Gower's repast was concluded, "what else can we do to contribute to your happiness and express the Affection we bear you. Tell us what you wish more to receive, and depend upon our gratitude for the communication of your wishes." "Give me then your house and Grounds; I ask for nothing else." "It is yours," exclaimed both at once; "from this moment it is yours." The Agreement concluded on and the present accepted by Mr. Gower, Mr. Webb rang to have the Carriage ordered, telling William at the same time to call the Young Ladies.

"Best of Men," said Mrs. Webb, "we will not long intrude upon your Time."

"Make no Apologies, dear Madam," replied Mr. Gower, "You are welcome to stay this half hour if you like it."

They both burst forth into raptures of Admiration at his politeness, which they agreed served only to make their Conduct appear more inexcusable in trespassing on his time.

The Young Ladies soon entered the room. The eldest of them was about seventeen, the other, several years younger. Mr. Gower had no sooner fixed his Eyes on Miss Webb than he felt that something more was necessary to his happiness than the house he had just received. Mrs. Webb introduced him to her daughter. "Our dear friend Mr. Gower, my Love—He has been so good as to accept of this house, small as it is, and to promise to keep it forever." "Give me leave to assure you, Sir," said Miss Webb, "that I am highly sensible of your kindness in this respect, which from the shortness of my Father's and Mother's acquaintance with you, is more than usually flattering."

Mr. Gower bowed, "You are too obliging, Ma'am. I assure you that I like the house extremely, and if they would complete their generosity by giving me their eldest daughter in marriage with a handsome portion, I should have nothing more to wish for." This compliment brought a blush into the cheeks of the lovely Miss Webb, who seemed however to refer herself to her father and Mother. They looked delighted at each other. At length Mrs. Webb, breaking silence, said, "We bend under a weight of obligations to you which we can never repay. Take our girl, take our Maria, and on her must the difficult task fall, of endeavoring to make some return to so much Beneficence." Mr. Webb added, "Her fortune is but ten thousand pounds, which is almost too small a sum to be offered." This objection however being instantly removed by the generosity of Mr. Gower, who declared himself satisfied with the sum mentioned, Mr. and Mrs. Webb, with their youngest daughter took their leave, and on the next day, the nuptials of their eldest with Mr. Gower were celebrated.

This amiable Man now found himself perfectly happy; united to a very lovely and deserving young woman, with an handsome fortune, an elegant house, settled in the village of Evelyn, and by that means enabled to cultivate his acquaintance with Mrs. Willis, could he have a wish ungratified? For some months he found that he could not, till one day as he was walking in the Shrubbery with Maria leaning on his arm, they observed a rose full-blown lying on the gravel; it had fallen from a rose tree which with three others had been planted by Mr. Webb to give a pleasing variety to the walk. These four Rose trees served also to mark the quarters of the Shrubbery, by which means the Traveller might always know how far in his progress round the Paddock he was got. Maria stooped to pick up the beautiful flower, and with all her Family Generosity presented it to her Husband. "My dear Frederic," said she, "pray take this charming rose." "Rose!" exclaimed Mr. Gower. "Oh! Maria, of what does not that remind me! Alas, my poor Sister, how have I neglected you!" The truth was that Mr. Gower was the only son of a very large Family, of which Miss Rose Gower was the thirteenth daughter. This Young Lady whose merits deserved a better fate than she met with, was the darling of her relations. From the clearness of her skin and the Brilliancy of her Eyes, she was fully entitled to all their partial affection. Another circumstance contributed to the general Love they bore her, and that was one of the finest heads of hair in the world. A few Months before her Brother's Marriage, her heart had been engaged by the attentions and charms of a young Man whose high rank and expectations seemed to foretell objections from his Family to a match which would be highly desirable to theirs. Proposals were made on the young Man's part, and proper objections on his Father's. He was desired to return from Carlisle where he was with his beloved Rose, to the family seat in Sussex. He was obliged to comply, and the angry father then finding from his Conversation how determined he was to marry no other woman, sent him for a fortnight to the Isle of Wight under the care of the Family Chaplin, with the hope of overcoming his Constancy by Time and Absence in a foreign Country. They accordingly prepared to bid a long adieu to England. The young Nobleman was not allowed to see his Rosa. They set sail. A storm arose which baffled the arts of the Seamen. The Vessel was wrecked on the coast of Calshot and every Soul on board perished. This sad Event soon reached Carlisle, and the beautiful Rose was affected by it, beyond the power of Expression. It was to soften her affliction by obtaining a picture of her unfortunate Lover that her brother undertook a Journey into Sussex, where he hoped that his petition would not be rejected, by the severe yet afflicted Father. When he reached Evelyn he was not many miles from —— Castle, but the pleasing events which befell him in that place had for a while made him totally forget the object of his Journey and his unhappy Sister. The little incident of the rose however brought everything concerning her to his recollection again, and he bitterly repented his neglect. He returned to the house immediately and agitated by Greif, Apprehension and Shame wrote the following Letter to Rosa.

Evelyn
July 14th

My dearest Sister,

As it is now four months since I left Carlisle, during which period I have not once written to you, You will perhaps unjustly accuse me of Neglect and Forgetfulness. Alas! I blush when I own the truth of your Accusation. Yet if you are still alive, do not think too harshly of me, or suppose that I could for a moment forget the situation of my Rose. Believe me I will forget you no longer, but will hasten as soon as possible to —— Castle if I find by your answer that you are still alive. Maria joins me in every dutiful and affectionate wish, and I am yours sincerely.

F. Gower.

He waited in the most anxious expectation for an answer to his Letter, which arrived as soon as the great distance from Carlisle would admit of. But alas, it came not from Rosa.

Carlisle
July 17th

Dear Brother,

My Mother has taken the liberty of opening your Letter to poor Rose, as she has been dead these six weeks. Your long absence and continued Silence gave us all great uneasiness and hastened her to the Grave. Your Journey to —— Castle therefore may be spared. You do not tell us where you have been since the time of your quitting Carlisle, nor in any way account for your tedious absence, which gives us some surprise. We all unite in Compliments to Maria, and beg to know who she is.

Yr affectionate Sister,

M. Gower.

This Letter, by which Mr. Gower was obliged to attribute to his own conduct, his Sister's death, was so violent a shock to his feelings, that in spite of his living at Evelyn where Illness was scarcely ever heard of, he was attacked by a fit of the gout, which confining him to his own room afforded an opportunity to Maria of shining in that favorite character of Sir Charles Grandison's, a nurse. No woman could ever appear more amiable than Maria did under such circumstances, and at last by her unremitting attentions had the pleasure of seeing him gradually recover the use of his feet. It was a blessing by no means lost on him, for he was no sooner in a condition to leave the house, that he mounted his horse, and rode to —— Castle, wishing to find whether his Lordship softened by his Son's death, might have been brought to consent to the match, had both he and Rosa been alive. His amiable Maria followed him with her Eyes till she could see him no longer, and then sinking into her chair overwhelmed with Greif, found that in his absence she could enjoy no comfort.

Mr. Gower arrived late in the evening at the castle, which was situated on a woody Eminence commanding a beautiful prospect of the Sea. Mr. Gower did not dislike the situation, tho' it was certainly greatly inferior to that of his own house. There was an irregularity in the fall of the ground, and a profusion of old Timber which appeared to him ill-suited to the style of the Castle, for it being a building of a very ancient date, he thought it required the Paddock of Evelyn lodge to form a Contrast, and enliven the structure. The gloomy appearance of the old Castle frowning on him as he followed it's winding approach, struck him with terror. Nor did he think himself safe, till he was introduced into the Drawing room where the Family were assembled to tea. Mr. Gower was a perfect stranger to everyone in the Circle but tho' he was always timid in the Dark and easily terrified when alone, he did not want that more necessary and more noble courage which enabled him without a Blush to enter a large party of superior Rank, whom he had never seen before, and to take his Seat amongst them with perfect Indifference. The name of Gower was not unknown to Lord ——. He felt distressed and astonished; Yet rose and received him with all the politeness of a well-bred Man. Lady —— who felt a deeper Sorrow at the loss of her Son, than his Lordship's harder heart was capable of, could hardly keep her Seat when she found that he was the Brother of her lamented Henry's Rosa. "My Lord," said Mr. Gower as soon as he was seated, "You are perhaps surprised at receiving a visit from a Man whom you could not have the least expectation of seeing here. But my Sister, my unfortunate Sister, is the real cause of my thus troubling you: That luckless Girl is now no more—and tho' she can receive no pleasure from the intelligence, yet for the satisfaction of her Family I wish to know whether the Death of this unhappy Pair has made an impression on your heart sufficiently strong to obtain that consent to their Marriage which in happier circumstances you would not be persuaded to give Supposing that they now were both alive." His Lordship seemed lossed in astonishment. Lady —— could not support the mention of her son, and left the room in tears; the rest of the Family remained attentively listening, almost persuaded that Mr. Gower was distracted. "Mr. Gower," replied his Lordship, "this is a very odd question. It appears to me that you are supposing an impossibility. No one can more sincerely regret the death of my Son than I have always done, and it gives me great concern to know that Miss Gower's was hastened by his. Yet to suppose them alive is destroying at once the Motive for a change in my sentiments concerning the affair." "My Lord," replied Mr. Gower in anger, "I see that you are a most inflexible Man, and that not even the death of your Son can make you wish his future Life happy. I will no longer detain your Lordship. I see, I plainly see that you are a very vile Man. And now I have the honor of wishing all your Lordships, and Ladyships a good Night." He immediately left the room, forgetting in the heat of his Anger the lateness of the hour, which at any other time would have made him tremble, and leaving the whole Company unanimous in their opinion of his being Mad. When however he had mounted his horse and the great Gates of the Castle had shut him out, he felt an universal tremor throughout his whole frame. If we consider his Situation indeed, alone, on horseback, as late in the year as August, and in the day, as nine o'clock, with no light to direct him but that of the Moon almost full, and the Stars which alarmed him by their twinkling, who can refrain from pitying him? No house within a quarter of a mile, and a Gloomy Castle blackened by the deep shade of Walnuts and

Pines, behind him. He felt indeed almost distracted with his fears, and shutting his Eyes till he arrived at the Village to prevent his seeing either Gipsies or Ghosts, he rode on a full gallop all the way.

On his return home, he rang the house bell, but no one appeared, a second time he rang, but the door was not opened, a third and a fourth with as little success, when observing the dining parlor window open he leapt in, and perused his way through the house till he reached Maria's Dressing room, where he found all the Servants assembled at tea. Surprised at so very unusual a sight, he fainted, on his recovery he found himself on the Sofa, with his wife's maid kneeling by him, chafing his temples with Hungary water. From her he learned that his beloved Maria had been so much grieved at his departure that she died of a broken heart about 3 hours after his departure.

He then became sufficiently composed to give necessary orders for her funeral which took place the Monday following this being the Saturday. When Mr. Gower had settled the order of the procession he set out himself to Carlisle, to give vent to his sorrow in the bosom of his family. He arrived there in high health and spirits, after a delightful journey of 3 days and a 1/2. What was his surprise on entering the Breakfast parlor to see Rosa, his beloved Rosa, seated on a Sofa; at the sight of him she fainted and would have fallen had not a Gentleman sitting with his back to the door, started up and saved her from sinking to the ground—She very soon came to herself and then introduced this gentleman to her Brother as her Husband a Mr. Davenport.

"But my dearest Rosa," said the astonished Gower, "I thought you were dead and buried." "Why, my dear Frederick," replied Rosa "I wished you to think so, hoping that you would spread the report about the country and it would thus by some means reach —— Castle. By this I hoped somehow or other to touch the hearts of its inhabitants. It was not till the day before yesterday that I heard of the death of my beloved Henry which I learned from Mr. Davenport who concluded by offering me his hand. I accepted it with transport, and was married yesterday." Mr. Gower, embraced his sister and shook hands with Mr. Davenport, he then took a stroll into the town. As he passed by a public house he called for a pot of beer, which was brought him immediately by his old friend Mrs. Willis.

Great was his astonishment at seeing Mrs. Willis in Carlisle. But not forgetful of the respect he owed her, he dropped on one knee, and received the frothy cup from her, more grateful to him than Nectar. He instantly made her an offer of his hand and heart, which she graciously condescended to accept, telling him that she was only on a visit to her cousin, who kept the Anchor and should be ready to return to Evelyn, whenever he chose. The next morning they were married and immediately proceeded to Evelyn. When he reached home, he recollected that he had never written to Mr. and Mrs. Webb to inform them of the death of their daughter, which he rightly supposed they knew nothing of, as they never took in any newspapers. He immediately dispatched the following Letter.

Evelyn
August 19th 180—

Dearest Madam,

How can words express the poignancy of my feelings! Our Maria, our beloved Maria is no more, she breathed her last, on Saturday the 12th of August. I see you now in an agony of grief lamenting not your own, but my loss. Rest satisfied I am happy, possessed of my lovely Sarah what more can I wish for? I remain respectfully Yours.

F. Gower

Westgate Builgs
Augst 22nd

Generous, Best of Men,

How truly we rejoice to hear of your present welfare and happiness! and how truly grateful are we for your unexampled generosity in writing to condole with us on the late unlucky accident which befell our Maria. I have enclosed a draught on our banker for 30 pounds, which Mr. Webb joins with me in entreating you and the amiable Sarah to accept.

Your most grateful,

Anne Augusta Webb

Mr. and Mrs. Gower resided many years at Evelyn enjoying perfect happiness the just reward of their virtues. The only alteration which took place at Evelyn was that Mr. and Mrs. Davenport settled there in Mrs. Willis's former abode and were for many years the proprietors of the White Horse Inn.

Catharine

(Also known as Kitty or The Bower)

To Miss Austen

Madam,

Encouraged by your warm patronage of The beautiful Cassandra, and The History of England, which through your generous support, have obtained a place in every library in the Kingdom, and run through threescore Editions, I take the liberty of begging the same Exertions in favor of the following Novel, which I humbly flatter myself, possesses Merit beyond any already published, or any that will ever in future appear, except such as may proceed from the pen of Your Most Grateful Humble Servt.

The Author
Steventon, August 1792

Catharine had the misfortune, as many heroines have had before her, of losing her parents when she was very young, and of being brought up under the care of a maiden aunt, who while she tenderly loved her, watched over her conduct with so scrutinizing a severity, as to make it very doubtful to many people, and to Catharine amongst the rest, whether she loved her or not. She had frequently been deprived of a real pleasure through this jealousy; been sometimes obliged to relinquish a ball because an officer was to be there, or to dance with a partner of her aunt's introduction in preference to one of her own choice. But her spirits were naturally good, and not easily depressed, and she possessed such a fund of vivacity and good humor as could only be damped by some very serious vexation. Besides these antidotes against every disappointment, and consolations under them, she had another, which afforded her constant relief in all her misfortunes, and that was a fine shady bower, the work of her own infantine labors assisted by those of two young companions who had resided in the same village. To this bower, which terminated a very pleasant and retired walk in her aunt's garden, she always wandered whenever anything disturbed her, and it possessed such a charm over her senses, as constantly to tranquillize her mind and quiet her spirits. Solitude and reflection might perhaps have had the same effect in her bed chamber, yet habit had so strengthened the idea which fancy had first suggested, that such a thought never occurred to Kitty who was firmly persuaded that her bower alone could restore her to herself. Her imagination was warm, and in her friendships, as well as in the whole tenure of her mind, she was enthusiastic. This beloved bower had been the united work of herself and two amiable girls, for whom since her earliest years, she had felt the tenderest regard. They were the daughters of the clergyman of the parish with whose family, while it had continued there, her aunt had been on the most intimate terms, and the little girls tho' separated for the greatest part of the year by the different modes of their education, were constantly together during the holidays of the Miss Wynnes. In those days of happy childhood, now so often regretted by Kitty, this arbor had been formed, and separated perhaps forever from these dear friends, it encouraged more than any other place the tender and melancholy recollections of hours rendered pleasant by them, at once so sorrowful, yet so soothing!

It was now two years since the death of Mr. Wynne, and the consequent dispersion of his family who had been left by it in great distress. They had been reduced to a state of absolute dependence on some relations, who though very opulent and very nearly connected with them, had with difficulty been prevailed on to contribute anything towards their support. Mrs. Wynne was fortunately spared the knowledge and participation of their distress, by her release from a painful illness a few months before the death of her husband. The eldest daughter had been obliged to accept the offer of one of her cousins to equip her for the East Indies, and the infinitely against her inclinations had been necessitated to embrace the only possibility that was offered to her, of a maintenance. Yet it was one, so opposite to all her ideas of propriety, so contrary to her wishes, so repugnant to her feelings, that she would almost have preferred servitude to it, had choice been allowed her. Her personal attractions had gained her a husband as soon as she had arrived at Bengal, and she had now been married nearly a twelve month. Splendidly yet unhappily married. United to a man of double her own age, whose disposition was not amiable, and whose manners were unpleasing, though his character was respectable. Kitty had heard twice from her friend since her marriage, but her letters were always unsatisfactory, and though she did not openly avow her feelings, yet every line proved her to be unhappy. She spoke with pleasure of nothing, but of those amusements which they had shared together and which could return no more, and seemed to have no happiness in view but that of returning to England again. Her sister had been taken by another relation the Dowager Lady Halifax as a companion to her daughters, and had accompanied her family into Scotland about the same time of Cecilia's leaving England. From Mary therefore Kitty had the power of hearing more frequently, but her letters were scarcely more comfortable. There was not indeed that hopelessness of sorrow in her situation as in her sister's; she was not married, and could yet look forward to a change in her circumstances, but situated for the present without any immediate hope of it, in a family where, tho' all were her relations, she had no friend, she wrote usually in depressed spirits, which her separation from her sister and her sister's marriage had greatly contributed to make so. Divided thus from the two she loved best on Earth, while Cecilia and Mary were still more endeared to her by their loss, everything that brought a remembrance of them was doubly cherished, and the shrubs they had planted, and the keepsakes they had given were rendered sacred.

The living of Chetwynde was now in the possession of a Mr. Dudley, whose family unlike the Wynnes were productive only of vexation and trouble to Mrs. Percival and her niece. Mr. Dudley, who was the younger son of a very noble family, of a family more famed for their pride than their opulence, tenacious of his dignity, and jealous of his rights, was forever quarrelling, if not with Mrs. Percival herself, with her steward and tenants concerning tithes, and with the principal neighbors themselves concerning the respect and parade, he exacted. His wife, an ill-educated, untaught woman of ancient family, was proud of that family almost without knowing why, and like him too was haughty and quarrelsome, without considering for what. Their only daughter, who inherited the ignorance, the insolence, and pride of her parents, was from that beauty of which she was unreasonably vain, considered by them as an irresistible creature, and looked up to as the future restorer, by a Splendid Marriage, of the dignity which their reduced situation and Mr. Dudley's being obliged to take orders for a country living had so much lessened. They at once despised the Percivals as people of mean family, and envied them as people of fortune. They were jealous of their being more respected than themselves and while they affected to consider them as of no consequence, were continually seeking to lessen them in the opinion of the neighborhood by scandalous and malicious reports. Such a family as this, was ill-calculated to console Kitty for the loss of the Wynnes, or to fill up by their society, those occasionally irksome hours which in so retired a situation would sometimes occur for want of a companion. Her aunt was most excessively fond of her, and miserable if she saw her for a moment out of spirits; Yet she lived in such constant apprehension of her marrying imprudently if she were allowed the opportunity of choosing, and was so dissatisfied with her behavior when she saw her with young men, for it was, from her natural disposition remarkably open and unreserved, that though she frequently wished for her niece's sake, that the neighborhood were larger, and that she had used herself to mix more with it, yet the recollection of there being young men in almost every family in it, always conquered the wish. The same fears that prevented Mrs. Percival's joining much in the society of her neighbors, led her equally to avoid inviting her relations to spend any time in her house. She had therefore constantly regretted the annual attempt of a distant relation to visit her at Chetwynde, as there was a young man in the family of whom she had heard many traits that alarmed her. This son was however now on his travels, and the repeated solicitations of Kitty, joined to a consciousness of having declined with too little ceremony the frequent overtures of her friends to be admitted, and a real wish to see them herself, easily prevailed on her to press with great earnestness the pleasure of a visit from them during the summer. Mr. and Mrs. Stanley were accordingly to come, and Catharine, in having an object to look forward to, a something to expect that must inevitably relieve the dullness of a constant tête à tête with her aunt, was so delighted, and her spirits so elevated, that for the three or four days immediately preceding their arrival, she could scarcely fix herself to any employment. In this point Mrs. Percival always thought her defective, and frequently complained of a want of steadiness and perseverance in her occupations, which were by no means congenial to the eagerness of Kitty's disposition, and perhaps not often met with in any young person. The tediousness too of her aunt's conversation and the want of agreeable companions greatly increased this desire of change in her employments, for Kitty found herself much sooner tired of reading, working, or drawing, in Mrs. Percival's parlor than in her own arbor, where Mrs. Percival for fear of its being damp never accompanied her.

As her aunt prided herself on the exact propriety and neatness with which everything in her family was conducted, and had no higher satisfaction than that of knowing her house to be always in complete order, as her fortune was good, and her establishment ample, few were the preparations necessary for the reception of her visitors. The day of their arrival so long expected, at length came, and the noise of the coach and as it drove round the sweep, was to Catharine a more interesting sound, than the music of an Italian opera, which to most heroines is the height of enjoyment. Mr. and Mrs. Stanley were people of large fortune and high fashion. He was a Member of the House of Commons, and they were therefore most agreeably necessitated to reside half the year in Town; where Miss Stanley had been attended by the most capital masters from the time of her being six years old to the last spring, which comprehending a period of twelve years had been dedicated to the acquirement of accomplishments which were now to be displayed and in a few years entirely neglected. She was elegant in her appearance, rather handsome, and naturally not deficient in abilities; but those years which ought to have been spent in the attainment of useful knowledge and mental improvement, had been all bestowed in learning drawing, Italian and music, more especially the latter, and she now united to these accomplishments, an understanding unimproved by reading and a mind totally devoid either of taste or judgment. Her temper was by nature good, but unassisted by reflection; she had neither patience under disappointment, nor could sacrifice her own inclinations to promote the happiness of others. All her ideas were towards the elegance of her appearance, the fashion of her dress, and the admiration she wished them to excite. She professed a love of books without reading, was lively without wit, and generally good humored without merit. Such was Camilla Stanley; and Catharine, who was prejudiced by her appearance, and who from her solitary situation was ready to like anyone, tho' her understanding and judgment would not otherwise have been easily satisfied, felt almost convinced when she saw her, that Miss Stanley would be the very companion she wanted, and in some degree make amends for the loss of Cecilia and Mary Wynne. She therefore attached herself to Camilla from the first day of her arrival, and from being the only young people in the house, they were by inclination constant companions. Kitty was herself a great reader, tho' perhaps not a very deep one, and felt therefore highly delighted to find that Miss Stanley was equally fond of it. Eager to know that their sentiments as to books were similar, she very soon began questioning her new acquaintance on the subject; but though she was well read in modern history herself, she chose rather to speak first of books of a lighter kind, of books universally read and admired.

"You have read Mrs. Smith's novels, I suppose!" said she to her companion. "Oh! Yes," replied the other, "and I am quite delighted with them. They are the sweetest things in the world." "And which do you prefer of them?" "Oh! dear, I think there is no comparison between them— Emmeline is so much better than any of the others." "Many people think so, I know; but there does not appear so great a disproportion in their merits to me; do you think it is better written?" "Oh! I do not know anything about that—but it is better in everything. Besides, Ethelinde is so long." "That is a very common objection I believe," said Kitty, "But for my own part, if a book is well written, I always find it too short." "So do I, only I get tired of it before it is finished." "But did not you find the story of Ethelinde very interesting? And the descriptions of Grasmere, are not they beautiful?" "Oh! I missed them all, because I was in such a hurry to know the end of it." Then from an easy transition she added, "We are going to the Lakes this autumn, and I am quite mad with joy; Sir Henry Devereux has promised to go with us, and that will make it so pleasant, you know."

"I dare say it will; but I think it is a pity that Sir Henry's powers of pleasing were not reserved for an occasion where they might be more wanted. However I quite envy you the pleasure of such a scheme."

"Oh! I am quite delighted with the thoughts of it; I can think of nothing else. I assure you I have done nothing for this last month but plan what clothes I should take with me, and I have at last determined to take very few indeed besides my travelling dress, and so I advise you to do, whenever you go; for I intend in case we should fall in with any races, or stop at Matlock or Scarborough, to have some things made for the occasion."

"You intend then to go into Yorkshire?"

"I believe not—indeed I know nothing of the route, for I never trouble myself about such things. I only know that we are to go from Derbyshire to Matlock and Scarborough, but to which of them first, I neither know nor care. I am in hopes of meeting some particular friends of mine at Scarborough. Augusta told me in her last letter that Sir Peter talked of going; but then you know that is so uncertain. I cannot bear Sir Peter, he is such a horrid creature."

"He is, is he?" said Kitty, not knowing what else to say.

"Oh! he is quite shocking." Here the conversation was interrupted, and Kitty was left in a painful uncertainty, as to the particulars of Sir Peter's character; she knew only that he was horrid and shocking, but why, and in what, yet remained to be discovered. She could scarcely resolve what to think of her new acquaintance; she appeared to be shamefully ignorant as to the geography of England, if she had understood her right, and equally devoid of taste and information. Kitty was however unwilling to decide hastily; she was at once desirous of doing Miss Stanley justice, and of having her own wishes in her answered; she determined therefore to suspend all judgment for some time. After supper, the conversation turning on the state of affairs in the political world, Mrs. Percival, who was firmly of opinion that the whole race of mankind were degenerating, said that for her part, everything she believed was going to rack and ruin, all order was destroyed over the face of the World, the House of Commons she heard did not break up sometimes till five in the morning, and depravity never was so general before; concluding with a wish that she might live to see the manners of the people in Queen Elizabeth's reign, restored again. "Well, ma'am," said her niece, "But I hope you do not mean with the times to restore Queen Elizabeth herself."

"Queen Elizabeth," said Mrs. Stanley, who never hazarded a remark on history that was not well founded, "lived to a good old age, and was a very clever woman." "True, ma'am", said Kitty; "But I do not consider either of those circumstances as meritorious in herself, and they are very far from making me wish her return, for if she were to come again with the same abilities and the same good constitution she might do as much mischief and last as long as she did before." Then turning to Camilla who had been sitting very silent for some time, she added, "What do you think of Elizabeth, Miss Stanley? I hope you will not defend her."

"Oh! dear," said Miss Stanley, "I know nothing of politics, and cannot bear to hear them mentioned." Kitty started at this repulse, but made no answer; that Miss Stanley must be ignorant of what she could not distinguish from politics she felt perfectly convinced. She retired to her own room, perplexed in her opinion about her new acquaintance, and fearful of her being very unlike Cecilia and Mary. She arose the next morning to experience a fuller conviction of this, and every future day increased it. She found no variety in her conversation; She received no information from her but in fashions, and no amusement but in her performance on the harpsichord; and after repeated endeavors to find her what she wished, she was obliged to give up the attempt and to consider it as fruitless. There had occasionally appeared a something like humor in Camilla which had inspired her with hopes, that she might at least have a natural genius, tho' not an improved one, but these sparklings of wit happened so seldom, and were so ill-supported that she was at last convinced of their being merely accidental. All her stock of knowledge was exhausted in a very few days, and when Kitty had learnt from her, how large their house in Town was, when the fashionable amusements began, who were the celebrated beauties and who the best milliner, Camilla had nothing further to teach, except the characters of any of her acquaintance as they occurred in conversation, which was done with equal ease and brevity, by saying that the person was either the sweetest creature in the world, and one of whom she was dotingly fond, or horrid, shocking and not fit to be seen.

As Catharine was very desirous of gaining every possible information as to the characters of the Halifax family, and concluded that Miss Stanley must be acquainted with them, as she seemed to be so with every one of any consequence, she took an opportunity as Camilla was one day enumerating all the people of rank that her mother visited, of asking her whether Lady Halifax were among the number.

"Oh! Thank you for reminding me of her; she is the sweetest woman in the world, and one of our most intimate acquaintance, I do not suppose there is a day passes during the six months that we are in Town, but what we see each other in the course of it. And I correspond with all the girls."

"They are then a very pleasant family!" said Kitty. "They ought to be so indeed, to allow of such frequent meetings or all conversation must be at end."

"Oh! dear, not at all," said Miss Stanley, "for sometimes we do not speak to each other for a month together. We meet perhaps only in public, and then you know we are often not able to get near enough; but in that case we always nod and smile."

"Which does just as well. But I was going to ask you whether you have ever seen a Miss Wynne with them?"

"I know who you mean perfectly—she wears a blue hat. I have frequently seen her in Brook Street, when I have been at Lady Halifax's balls. She gives one every month during the winter. But only think how good it is in her to take care of Miss Wynne, for she is a very distant relation, and so poor that, as Miss Halifax told me, her Mother was obliged to find her in clothes. Is not it shameful?"

"That she should be so poor? It is indeed, with such wealthy connections as the family have."

"Oh! no; I mean, was not it shameful in Mr. Wynne to leave his children so distressed, when he had actually the living of Chetwynde and two or three curacies, and only four children to provide for. What would he have done if he had had ten, as many people have?"

"He would have given them all a good education and have left them all equally poor."

"Well I do think there never was so lucky a family. Sir George Fitzgibbon you know sent the eldest girl to India entirely at his own expense, where they say she is most nobly married and the happiest creature in the world. Lady Halifax you see has taken care of the youngest and treats her as if she were her daughter; She does not go out into public with her to be sure; but then she is always present when her Ladyship gives her balls, and nothing can be kinder to her than Lady Halifax is; she would have taken her to Cheltenham last year, if there had been room enough at the lodgings, and therefore I do not think that she can have anything to complain of. Then there are the two sons; one of them the Bishop of M—— has got into the Army as a Lieutenant I suppose; and the other is extremely well off I know, for I have a notion that somebody puts him to school somewhere in Wales. Perhaps you knew them when they lived here?"

"Very well, we met as often as your family and the Halifaxes do in Town, but as we seldom had any difficulty in getting near enough to speak, we seldom parted with merely a nod and a smile. They were indeed a most charming family, and I believe have scarcely their equals in the world; the neighbors we now have at the Parsonage, appear to more disadvantage in coming after them."

"Oh! horrid wretches! I wonder you can endure them."

"Why, what would you have one do?"

"Oh! Lord, if I were in your place, I should abuse them all day long."

"So I do, but it does no good."

"Well, I declare it is quite a pity that they should be suffered to live. I wish my father would propose knocking all their brains out, some day or other when he is in the House. So abominably proud of their family! And I dare say after all, that there is nothing particular in it."

"Why yes, I believe they have reason to value themselves on it, if anybody has; for you know he is Lord Amyatt's brother."

"Oh! I know all that very well, but it is no reason for their being so horrid. I remember I met Miss Dudley last spring with Lady Amyatt at Ranelagh, and she had such a frightful cap on, that I have never been able to bear any of them since. And so you used to think the Wynnes very pleasant?"

"You speak as if their being so were doubtful! Pleasant! Oh! they were everything that could interest and attach. It is not in my power to do justice to their merits, tho' not to feel them, I think must be impossible. They have unfitted me for any society but their own!"

"Well, that is just what I think of the Miss Halifaxes; by the bye, I must write to Caroline tomorrow, and I do not know what to say to her. The Barlows too are just such other sweet girls; but I wish Augusta's hair was not so dark. I cannot bear Sir Peter—horrid wretch! He is always laid up with the gout, which is exceedingly disagreeable to the family."

"And perhaps not very pleasant to himself. But as to the Wynnes; do you really think them very fortunate?"

"Do I? Why, does not everybody? Miss Halifax and Caroline and Maria all say that they are the luckiest creatures in the world. So does Sir George Fitzgibbon and so do everybody."

"That is, everybody who have themselves conferred an obligation on them. But do you call it lucky, for a girl of genius and feeling to be sent in quest of a husband to Bengal, to be married there to a man of whose disposition she has no opportunity of judging till her judgment is of no use to her, who may be a tyrant, or a fool or both for what she knows to the contrary. Do you call that fortunate?"

"I know nothing of all that; I only know that it was extremely good in Sir George to fit her out and pay her passage, and that she would not have found many who would have done the same."

"I wish she had not found one," said Kitty with great eagerness, "she might then have remained in England and been happy."

"Well, I cannot conceive the hardship of going out in a very agreeable manner with two or three sweet girls for companions, having a delightful voyage to Bengal or Barbadoes or wherever it is, and being married soon after one's arrival to a very charming man immensely rich. I see no hardship in all that."

"Your representation of the affair," said Kitty laughing, "certainly gives a very different idea of it from mine. But supposing all this to be true, still, as it was by no means certain that she would be so fortunate either in her voyage, her companions, or her husband; in being obliged to run the risk of their proving very different, she undoubtedly experienced a great hardship. Besides, to a girl of any delicacy, the voyage in itself, since the object of it is so universally known, is a punishment that needs no other to make it very severe."

"I do not see that at all. She is not the first girl who has gone to the East Indies for a husband, and I declare I should think it very good fun if I were as poor."

"I believe you would think very differently then. But at least you will not defend her sister's situation! Dependent even for her clothes on the bounty of others, who of course do not pity her, as by your own account, they consider her as very fortunate."

"You are extremely nice upon my word; Lady Halifax is a delightful woman, and one of the sweetest tempered creatures in the world; I am sure I have every reason to speak well of her, for we are under most amazing obligations to her. She has frequently chaperoned me when my mother has been indisposed and last spring she lent me her own horse three times, which was a prodigious favor, for it is the most beautiful creature that ever was seen, and I am the only person she ever lent it to."

"And then," continued she, "the Miss Halifaxes are quite delightful. Maria is one of the cleverest girls that ever were known—draws in oils, and plays anything by sight. She promised me one of her drawings before I left Town, but I entirely forgot to ask her for it. I would give anything to have one."

"But was not it very odd," said Kitty, "that the Bishop should send Charles Wynne to sea, when he must have had a much better chance of providing for him in the Church, which was the profession that Charles liked best, and the one for which his father had intended him? The Bishop I know had often promised Mr. Wynne a living, and as he never gave him one, I think it was incumbent on him to transfer the promise to his son."

"I believe you think he ought to have resigned his Bishopric to him; you seem determined to be dissatisfied with everything that has been done for them."

"Well," said Kitty, "this is a subject on which we shall never agree, and therefore it will be useless to continue it farther, or to mention it again." She then left the room, and running out of the house was soon in her dear bower where she could indulge in peace all her affectionate anger against the relations of the Wynnes, which was greatly heightened by finding from Camilla that they were in general considered as having acted particularly well by them. She amused herself for some time in abusing, and hating them all, with great spirit, and when this tribute to her regard for the Wynnes, was paid, and the bower began to have its usual influence over her spirits, she contributed towards settling them, by taking out a book, for she had always one about her, and reading. She had been so employed for nearly an hour, when Camilla came running towards her with great eagerness, and apparently great pleasure. "Oh! My dear Catharine," said she, half out of breath, "I have such delightful news for you. But you shall guess what it is. We are all the happiest creatures in the world; would you believe it, the Dudleys have sent us an invitation to a ball at their own house. What charming people they are! I had no idea of there being so much sense in the whole family. I declare I quite dote upon them. And it happens so fortunately too, for I expect a new cap from Town tomorrow which will just do for a ball—gold net. It will be a most angelic thing—everybody will be longing for the pattern." The expectation of a ball was indeed very agreeable intelligence to Kitty, who fond of dancing and seldom able to enjoy it, had reason to feel even greater pleasure in it than her friend; for to her, it was now no novelty. Camilla's delight however was by no means inferior to Kitty's, and she rather expressed the most of the two. The cap came and every other preparation was soon completed; while these were in agitation the days passed gaily away, but when directions were no longer necessary, taste could no longer be displayed, the difficulties no longer overcome, the short period that intervened before the day of the ball hung heavily on their hands, and every hour was too long. The very few times that Kitty had ever enjoyed the amusement of dancing was an excuse for her impatience, and an apology for the idleness it occasioned to a mind naturally very active; but her friend without such a plea was infinitely worse than herself. She could do nothing but wander from the house to the garden, and from the garden to the avenue, wondering when Thursday would come, which she might easily have ascertained, and counting the hours as they passed which served only to lengthen them.

They retired to their rooms in high spirits on Wednesday night, but Kitty awoke the next morning with a violent toothache. It was in vain that she endeavored at first to deceive herself; her feelings were witnesses too acute of its reality; with as little success did she try to sleep it off, for the pain she suffered prevented her closing her eyes. She then summoned her maid and with the assistance of the housekeeper, every remedy that the receipt book or the head of the latter contained, was tried, but ineffectually; for though for a short time relieved by them, the pain still returned. She was now obliged to give up the endeavor, and to reconcile herself not only to the pain of a toothache, but to the loss of a ball; and though she had with so much eagerness looked forward to the day of its arrival, had received such pleasure in the necessary preparations, and promised herself so much delight in it, yet she was not so totally void of philosophy as many girls of her age might have been in her situation. She considered that there were misfortunes of a much greater magnitude than the loss of a ball, experienced every day by some part of mortality, and that the time might come when she would herself look back with wonder and perhaps with envy on her having known no greater vexation. By such reflections as these, she soon reasoned herself into as much resignation and patience as the pain she suffered, would allow of, which after all was the greatest misfortune of the two, and told the sad story when she entered the breakfast room, with tolerable composure. Mrs. Percival more grieved for her toothache than her disappointment, as she feared that it would not be possible to prevent her dancing with a Man if she went, was eager to try everything that had already been applied to alleviate the pain, while at the same time she declared it was impossible for her to leave the house. Miss Stanley who joined to her concern for her friend, felt a mixture of dread lest her mother's proposal that they should all remain at home, might be accepted, was very violent in her sorrow on the occasion, and though her apprehensions on the subject were soon quieted by Kitty's protesting that sooner than allow anyone to stay with her, she would herself go, she continued to lament it with such unceasing vehemence as at last drove Kitty to her own room. Her fears for herself being now entirely dissipated left her more than ever at leisure to pity and persecute her friend who the safe when in her own room, was frequently removing from it to some other in hopes of being more free from pain, and then had no opportunity of escaping her.

"To be sure, there never was anything so shocking," said Camilla; "To come on such a day too! For one would not have minded it you know had it been at any other time. But it always is so. I never was at a ball in my life, but what something happened to prevent somebody from going! I wish there were no such things a teeth in the world; they are nothing but plagues to one, and I dare say that people might easily invent something to eat with instead of them; poor thing! what pain you are in! I declare it is quite shocking to look at you. But you won't have it out, will you! For Heaven's sake don't; for there is nothing I dread so much. I declare I have rather undergo the greatest tortures in the world than have a tooth drawn. Well! how patiently you do bear it! How can you be so quiet! Lord, if I were in your place I should make such a fuss, there would be no bearing me. I should torment you to death."

"So you do, as it is," thought Kitty.

"For my own part, Catharine" said Mrs. Percival "I have not a doubt but that you caught this toothache by sitting so much in that arbour, for it is always damp. I know it has ruined your constitution entirely; and indeed I do not believe it has been of much service to mine; I sat down in it last May to rest myself, and I have never been quite well since. I shall order John to pull it all down I assure you."

"I know you will not do that, ma'am," said Kitty, "as you must be convinced how unhappy it would make me."

"You talk very ridiculously, child; it is all whim and nonsense. Why cannot you fancy this room an arbor!"

"Had this room been built by Cecilia and Mary, I should have valued it equally, ma'am, for it is not merely the name of an arbor, which charms me."

"Why indeed, Mrs. Percival," said Mrs. Stanley, "I must think that Catharine's affection for her bower is the effect of a sensibility that does her credit. I love to see a friendship between young persons and always consider it as a sure mark of an amiable affectionate disposition. I have from Camilla's infancy taught her to think the same, and have taken great pains to introduce her to young people of her own age who were likely to be worthy of her regard. Nothing forms the taste more than sensible and elegant letters. Lady

Halifax thinks just like me. Camilla corresponds with her daughters, and I believe I may venture to say that they are none of them the worse for it."

These ideas were too modern to suit Mrs. Percival who considered a correspondence between girls as productive of no good, and as the frequent origin of imprudence and error by the effect of pernicious advice and bad example. She could not therefore refrain from saying that for her part, she had lived fifty years in the world without having ever had a correspondent, and did not find herself at all the less respectable for it. Mrs. Stanley could say nothing in answer to this, but her daughter who was less governed by propriety, said in her thoughtless way, "But who knows what you might have been, ma'am, if you had had a correspondent; perhaps it would have made you quite a different creature. I declare I would not be without those I have for all the world. It is the greatest delight of my life, and you cannot think how much their letters have formed my taste as Mama says, for I hear from them generally every week."

"You received a letter from Augusta Barlow today, did not you, my love" said her mother. "She writes remarkably well I know."

"Oh! Yes ma'am, the most delightful letter you ever heard of. She sends me a long account of the new Regency walking dress Lady Susan has given her, and it is so beautiful that I am quite dying with envy for it."

"Well, I am prodigiously happy to hear such pleasing news of my young friend; I have a high regard for Augusta, and most sincerely partake in the general joy on the occasion. But does she say nothing else? it seemed to be a long letter. Are they to be at Scarborough?"

"Oh! Lord, she never once mentions it, now I recollect it; and I entirely forgot to ask her when I wrote last. She says nothing indeed except about the Regency." "She must write well" thought Kitty, "to make a long letter upon a bonnet and pelisse." She then left the room tired of listening to a conversation which tho' it might have diverted her had she been well, served only to fatigue and depress her, while in pain. Happy was it for her, when the hour of dressing came, for Camilla satisfied with being surrounded by her mother and half the maids in the house did not want her assistance, and was too agreeably employed to want her society. She remained therefore alone in the parlor, till joined by Mr. Stanley and her aunt, who however after a few enquiries, allowed her to continue undisturbed and began their usual conversation on politics. This was a subject on which they could never agree, for Mr. Stanley who considered himself as perfectly qualified by his seat in the House, to decide on it without hesitation, resolutely maintained that the Kingdom had not for ages been in so flourishing and prosperous a state, and Mrs. Percival with equal warmth, tho' perhaps less argument, as vehemently asserted that the whole nation would speedily be ruined, and everything as she expressed herself be at sixes and sevens. It was not however amusing to Kitty to listen to the dispute, especially as she began then to be more free from pain, and without taking any share in it herself, she found it very entertaining to observe the eagerness with which they both defended their opinions, and could not help thinking that Mr. Stanley would not feel more disappointed if her aunt's expectations were fulfilled, than her Aunt would be mortified by their failure. After waiting a considerable time Mrs. Stanley and her daughter appeared, and Camilla in high spirits, and perfect good humor with her own looks, was more violent than ever in her lamentations over her friend as she practiced her Scotch steps about the room. At length they departed, and Kitty better able to amuse herself than she had been the whole day before, wrote a long account of her misfortunes to Mary Wynne.

When her letter was concluded she had an opportunity of witnessing the truth of that assertion which says that sorrows are lightened by communication, for her toothache was then so much relieved that she began to entertain an idea of following her friends to Mr. Dudley's. They had been gone an hour, and as everything relative to her dress was in complete readiness, she considered that in another hour since there was so little a way to go, she might be there. They were gone in Mr. Stanley's carriage and therefore she might follow in her aunt's. As the plan seemed so very easy to be executed, and promising so much pleasure, it was after a few minutes deliberation finally adopted, and running up stairs, she rang in great haste for her maid. The bustle and hurry which then ensued for nearly an hour was at last happily concluded by her finding herself very well dressed and in high beauty. Anne was then dispatched in the same haste to order the carriage, while her mistress was putting on her gloves, and arranging the folds of her dress. In a few minutes she heard the carriage drive up to the door, and tho' at first surprised at the expedition with which it had been got ready, she concluded after a little reflection that the men had received some hint of her intentions beforehand, and was hastening out of the room, when Anne came running into it in the greatest hurry and agitation, exclaiming "Lord, ma'am! Here's a gentleman in a chaise and four come, and I cannot for the life conceive who it is! I happened to be crossing the hall when the carriage drove up, and I knew nobody would be in the way to let him in but Tom, and he looks so awkward you know, ma'am, now his hair is just done up, that I was not willing the gentleman should see him, and so I went to the door myself. And he is one of the handsomest young men you would wish to see; I was almost ashamed of being seen in my apron, ma'am, but however he is vastly handsome and did not seem to mind it at all. And he asked me whether the family were at home; and so I said everybody was gone out but you, ma'am, for I would not deny you because I was sure you would like to see him. And then he asked me whether Mr. and Mrs. Stanley were not here, and so I said yes, and then—"

"Good Heavens!" said Kitty, "what can all this mean! And who can it possibly be! Did you never see him before! And did not he tell you his name!"

"No, ma'am, he never said anything about it. So then I asked him to walk into the parlor, and he was prodigious agreeable, and—"

"Whoever he is," said her mistress, "he has made a great impression upon you, Nanny. But where did he come from? and what does he want here?"

"Oh! Ma'am, I was going to tell you, that I fancy his business is with you; for he asked me whether you were at leisure to see anybody, and desired I would give his compliments to you, and say he should be very happy to wait on you. However I thought he had better not come up into your dressing room, especially as everything is in such a litter, so I told him if he would be so obliging as to stay in the parlor, I would run up stairs and tell you he was come, and I dared to say that you would wait upon him. Lord, ma'am, I'd lay anything that he is come to ask you to dance with him tonight, and has got his chaise ready to take you to Mr. Dudley's."

Kitty could not help laughing at this idea, and only wished it might be true, as it was very likely that she would be too late for any other partner. "But what, in the name of wonder, can he have to say to me! Perhaps he is come to rob the house. He comes in style at least; and it will be some consolation for our losses to be robbed by a gentleman in a chaise and four. What livery has his servants?"

"Why that is the most wonderful thing about him, ma'am, for he has not a single servant with him, and came with hack horses; but he is as handsome as a Prince for all that, and has quite the look of one. Do, dear ma'am, go down, for I am sure you will be delighted with him."

"Well, I believe I must go; but it is very odd! What can he have to say to me." Then giving one look at herself in the glass, she walked with great impatience, tho' trembling all the while from not knowing what to expect, down stairs, and after pausing a moment at the door to gather courage for opening it, she resolutely entered the room. The stranger, whose appearance did not disgrace the account she had received of it from her maid, rose up on her entrance, and laying aside the newspaper he had been reading, advanced towards her with an air of the most perfect ease and vivacity, and said to her, "It is certainly a very awkward circumstance to be thus obliged to introduce myself, but I trust that the necessity of the case will plead my excuse, and prevent your being prejudiced by it against me. Your name, I need not ask, ma'am—Miss Percival is too well known to me by description to need any information of that."

Kitty, who had been expecting him to tell his own name, instead of hers, and who from having been little in company, and never before in such a situation, felt herself unable to ask it, tho' she had been planning her speech all the way down stairs, was so confused and distressed by this unexpected address that she could only return a slight curtsy to it, and accepted the chair he reached her, without knowing what she did. The gentleman then continued. "You are, I dare say, surprised to see me returned from France so soon, and nothing indeed but business could have brought me to England; a very melancholy affair has now occasioned it, and I was unwilling to leave it without paying my respects to the family in Devonshire whom I have so long wished to be acquainted with." Kitty, who felt much more surprised at his supposing her to be so, than at seeing a person in England, whose having ever left it was perfectly unknown to her, still continued silent from wonder and perplexity, and her visitor still continued to talk.

"You will suppose, madam, that I was not the less desirous of waiting on you, from your having Mr. and Mrs. Stanley with you. I hope they are well? And Mrs. Percival, how does she do?" Then without waiting for an answer he gaily added, "But my dear Miss Percival, you are going out I am sure; and I am detaining you from your appointment. How can I ever expect to be forgiven for such injustice! Yet how can I, so circumstanced, forbear to offend! You seem dressed for a ball! But this is the land of gaiety I know; I have for many years been desirous of visiting it. You have dances I suppose at least every week. But where are the rest of your party gone, and what kind angel in compassion to me, has excluded you from it?"

"Perhaps sir," said Kitty extremely confused by his manner of speaking to her, and highly displeased with the freedom of his conversation towards one who had never seen him before and did not now know his name, "Perhaps sir, you are acquainted with Mr. and Mrs. Stanley; and your business may be with them?"

"You do me too much honor, ma'am," replied he laughing, "in supposing me to be acquainted with Mr. and Mrs. Stanley; I merely know them by sight; very distant relations; only my father and mother. Nothing more I assure you."

"Gracious Heaven!" said Kitty, "Are you Mr. Stanley then? I beg a thousand pardons. Though really upon recollection I do not know for what— for you never told me your name."

"I beg your pardon. I made a very fine speech when you entered the room, all about introducing myself; I assure you it was very great for me."

"The speech had certainly great merit," said Kitty smiling; "I thought so at the time; but since you never mentioned your name in it, as an introductory one it might have been better."

There was such an air of good humor and gaiety in Stanley, that Kitty, tho' perhaps not authorized to address him with so much familiarity on so short an acquaintance, could not forbear indulging the natural unreserved and vivacity of her own disposition, in speaking to him, as he spoke to her. She was intimately acquainted too with his family who were her relations, and she chose to consider herself entitled by the connection to forget how little a while they had known each other. "Mr. and Mrs. Stanley and your sister are extremely well," said she, "and will I dare say be very much surprised to see you. But I am sorry to hear that your return to England has been occasioned by an unpleasant circumstance."

"Oh, don't talk of it," said he, "it is a most confounded shocking affair, and makes me miserable to think of it; But where are my father and mother, and your aunt gone! Oh! Do you know that I met the prettiest little waiting maid in the world, when I came here; she let me into the house; I took her for you at first."

"You did me a great deal of honor, and give me more credit for good nature than I deserve, for I never go to the door when any one comes."

"Nay do not be angry; I mean no offence. But tell me, where are you going to so smart? Your carriage is just coming round."

"I am going to a dance at a neighbor's, where your family and my aunt are already gone."

"Gone, without you! what's the meaning of that? But I suppose you are like myself, rather long in dressing."

"I must have been so indeed, if that were the case for they have been gone nearly these two hours; the reason however was not what you suppose. I was prevented going by a pain—"

"By a pain!" interrupted Stanley, "Oh! Heavens, that is dreadful indeed! No matter where the pain was. But my dear Miss Percival, what do you say to my accompanying you! And suppose you were to dance with me too? I think it would be very pleasant."

"I can have no objection to either I am sure," said Kitty laughing to find how near the truth her maid's conjecture had been; "on the contrary I shall be highly honored by both, and I can answer for your being extremely welcome to the family who give the ball."

"Oh! hang them; who cares for that; they cannot turn me out of the house. But I am afraid I shall cut a sad figure among all your Devonshire beaux in this dusty, travelling apparel, and I have not wherewithal to change it. You can procure me some powder perhaps, and I must get a pair of shoes from one of the men, for I was in such a devil of a hurry to leave Lyons that I had not time to have anything packed up but some linen." Kitty very readily undertook to procure for him everything he wanted, and telling the footman to show him into Mr. Stanley's dressing room, gave Nanny orders to send in some powder and pomatum, which orders Nanny chose to execute in person. As Stanley's preparations in dressing were confined to such very trifling articles, Kitty of course expected him in about ten minutes; but she found that it had not been merely a boast of vanity in saying that he was dilatory in that respect, as he kept her waiting for him above half an hour, so that the clock had struck ten before he entered the room and the rest of the party had gone by eight.

"Well," said he as he came in, "have not I been very quick! I never hurried so much in my life before."

"In that case you certainly have," replied Kitty, "for all merit you know is comparative."

"Oh! I knew you would be delighted with me for making so much haste. But come, the carriage is ready; so, do not keep me waiting." And so saying he took her by the hand, and led her out of the room.

"Why, my dear Cousin," said he when they were seated, "this will be a most agreeable surprise to everybody to see you enter the room with such a smart young fellow as I am. I hope your aunt won't be alarmed."

"To tell you the truth," replied Kitty, "I think the best way to prevent it, will be to send for her, or your mother before we go into the room, especially as you are a perfect stranger, and must of course be introduced to Mr. and Mrs. Dudley."

"Oh! Nonsense," said he; "I did not expect you to stand upon such ceremony; Our acquaintance with each other renders all such prudery, ridiculous; Besides, if we go in together, we shall be the whole talk of the country."

"To me" replied Kitty, "that would certainly be a most powerful inducement; but I scarcely know whether my aunt would consider it as such. Women at her time of life, have odd ideas of propriety you know."

"Which is the very thing that you ought to break them of; and why should you object to entering a room with me where all our relations are, when you have done me the honor to admit me without any chaperone into your carriage? Do not you think your aunt will be as much offended with you for one, as for the other of these mighty crimes?"

"Why really" said Catharine, "I do not know but that she may; however, it is no reason that I should offend against decorum a second time, because I have already done it once."

"On the contrary, that is the very reason which makes it impossible for you to prevent it, since you cannot offend for the first time again."

"You are very ridiculous," said she laughing, "but I am afraid your arguments divert me too much to convince me."

"At least they will convince you that I am very agreeable, which after all, is the happiest conviction for me, and as to the affair of propriety we will let that rest till we arrive at our journey's end. This is a monthly ball I suppose. Nothing but dancing here."

"I thought I had told you that it was given by a Mr. and Mrs. Dudley."

"Oh! Aye so you did; but why should not Mr. Dudley give one every month! By the bye who is that man? Everybody gives balls now I think; I believe I must give one myself soon. Well, but how do you like my father and mother? And poor little Camilla too, has not she plagued you to death with the Halifaxes" Here the carriage fortunately stopped at Mr. Dudley's, and Stanley was too much engaged in handing her out of it, to wait for an answer, or to remember that what he had said required one. They entered the small vestibule which Mr. Dudley had raised to the dignity of a hall, and Kitty immediately desired the footman who was leading the way upstairs, to inform either Mrs. Percival, or Mrs. Stanley of her arrival, and beg them to come to her, but Stanley unused to any contradiction and impatient to be amongst them, would neither allow her to wait, or listen to what she said, and forcibly seizing her arm within his, overpowered her voice with the rapidity of his own, and Kitty half angry, and half laughing was obliged to go with him up stairs, and could even with difficulty prevail on him to relinquish her hand before they entered the room.

Mrs. Percival was at that very moment engaged in conversation with a lady at the upper end of the room, to whom she had been giving a long account of her niece's unlucky disappointment, and the dreadful pain that she had with so much fortitude, endured the whole day. "I left her however," said she, "thank heaven, a little better, and I hope she has been able to amuse herself with a book, poor thing! for she must otherwise be very dull. She is probably in bed by this time, which while she is so poorly, is the best place for her you know, ma'am." The lady was going to give her assent to this opinion, when the noise of voices on the stairs, and the footman's opening the door as if for the entrance of company, attracted the attention of everybody in the room; and as it was in one of those intervals between the dances when everyone seemed glad to sit down, Mrs. Percival had a most unfortunate opportunity of seeing her niece whom she had supposed in bed, or amusing herself as the height of gaiety with a book, enter the room most elegantly dressed, with a smile on her countenance, and a glow of mingled cheerfulness and confusion on her cheeks, attended by a young man uncommonly handsome, and who without any of her confusion, appeared to have all her vivacity. Mrs. Percival, coloring with anger and astonishment, rose from her seat, and Kitty walked eagerly towards her, impatient to account for what she saw appeared wonderful to everybody, and extremely offensive to her, while Camilla on seeing her brother ran instantly towards him, and very soon explained who he was by her words and actions. Mr. Stanley, who so fondly doted on his son, that the pleasure of seeing him again after an absence of three months prevented his feeling for the time any anger against him for returning to England without his knowledge, received him with equal surprise and delight; and soon comprehending the cause of his journey, forbore any further conversation with him, as he was eager to see his mother, and it was necessary that he should be introduced to Mr. Dudley's family. This introduction to anyone but Stanley would have been highly unpleasant, for they considered their dignity injured by his coming uninvited to their house, and received him with more than their usual haughtiness. But Stanley who with a vivacity of temper seldom subdued, and a contempt of censure not to be overcome, possessed an opinion of his own consequence, and a perseverance in his own schemes which were not to be damped by the conduct of others, appeared not to perceive it. The civilities therefore which they coldly offered, he received with a gaiety and ease peculiar to himself, and then attended by his father and sister walked into another room where his mother was playing at cards, to experience another meeting, and undergo a repetition of pleasure, surprise and explanations. While these were passing, Camilla eager to communicate all she felt to someone who would attend to her, returned to Catharine, and seating herself by her, immediately began, "Well, did you ever know anything so delightful as this! But it always is so; I never go to a ball in my life but what something or other happens unexpectedly that is quite charming!"

"A ball" replied Kitty, "seems to be a most eventful thing to you."

"Oh! Lord, it is indeed. But only think of my brother's returning so suddenly. And how shocking a thing it is that has brought him over! I never heard anything so dreadful!"

"What is it pray that has occasioned his leaving France! I am sorry to find that it is a melancholy event."

"Oh! it is beyond anything you can conceive! His favorite hunter who was turned out in the park on his going abroad, somehow or other fell ill. No, I believe it was an accident, but however it was something or other, or else it was something else, and so they sent an express immediately to Lyons where my brother was, for they knew that he valued this mare more than anything else in the world besides; an So my brother set off directly for England, and without packing up another coat; I am quite angry with him about it; it was so shocking you know to come away without a change of clothes."

"Why indeed," said Kitty, "it seems to have been a very shocking affair from beginning to end."

"Oh! it is beyond anything you can conceive! I would rather have had anything happen than that he should have lost that mare."

"Except his coming away without another coat."

"Oh! yes, that has vexed me more than you can imagine. Well, and so Edward got to Brampton just as the poor thing was dead; but as he could not bear to remain there then, he came off directly to Chetwynde on purpose to see us. I hope he may not go abroad again."

"Do you think he will not?"

"Oh! Dear, to be sure he must, but I wish he may not with all my heart. You cannot think how fond I am of him! By the bye are not you in love with him yourself?"

"To be sure I am," replied Kitty laughing, "I am in love with every handsome man I see."

"That is just like me. I am always in love with every handsome man in the world."

"There you outdo me," replied Catharine, "for I am only in love with those I do see." Mrs. Percival who was sitting on the other side of her, and who began now to distinguish the words, Love and handsome man, turned hastily towards them and said, "What are you talking of, Catharine!" To which Catharine immediately answered with the simple artifice of a child, "Nothing, ma'am." She had already received a very severe lecture from her aunt on the imprudence of her behavior during the whole evening; She blamed her for coming to the ball, for coming in the same carriage with Edward Stanley, and still more for entering the room with him. For the last-mentioned offence Catharine knew not what apology to give, and tho' she longed in answer to the second to say that she had not thought it would be civil to make Mr.

Stanley walk, she dared not so to trifle with her aunt, who would have been but the more offended by it. The first accusation however she considered as very unreasonable, as she thought herself perfectly justified in coming. This conversation continued till Edward Stanley entering the room came instantly towards her, and telling her that everyone waited for her to begin the next dance led her to the top of the room, for Kitty, impatient to escape from so unpleasant a companion, without the least hesitation, or one civil scruple at being so distinguished, immediately gave him her hand, and joyfully left her seat. This conduct however was highly resented by several young ladies present, and among the rest by Miss Stanley whose regard for her brother tho' excessive, and whose affection for Kitty tho' prodigious, were not proof against such an injury to her importance and her peace. Edward had however only consulted his own inclinations in desiring Miss Percival to begin the dance, nor had he any reason to know that it was either wished or expected by anyone else in the party. As an heiress she was certainly of consequence, but her birth gave her no other claim to it, for her father had been a merchant. It was this very circumstance which rendered this unfortunate affair so offensive to Camilla, for tho' she would sometimes boast in the pride of her heart, and her eagerness to be admired that she did not know who her grandfather had been, and was as ignorant of everything relative to genealogy as to astronomy, (and she might have added, geography) yet she was really proud of her family and connections, and easily offended if they were treated with neglect. "I should not have minded it," said she to her mother, "if she had been anybody else's daughter; but to see her pretend to be above me, when her father was only a tradesman, is too bad! It is such an affront to our whole family! I declare I think Papa ought to interfere in it, but he never cares about anything but politics. If I were Mr. Pitt or the Lord Chancellor, he would take care I should not be insulted, but he never thinks about me; And it is so provoking that Edward should let her stand there. I wish with all my heart that he had never come to England! I hope she may fall down and break her neck, or sprain her ankle." Mrs. Stanley perfectly agreed with her daughter concerning the affair, and tho' with less violence, expressed almost equal resentment at the indignity. Kitty in the meantime remained insensible of having given any one offence, and therefore unable either to offer an apology, or make a reparation; her whole attention was occupied by the happiness she enjoyed in dancing with the most elegant young man in the room, and everyone else was equally unregarded. The evening indeed to her, passed off delightfully; he was her partner during the greatest part of it, and the united attractions that he possessed of person, address and vivacity, had easily gained that preference from Kitty which they seldom fail of obtaining from every one. She was too happy to care either for her aunt's ill humor which she could not help remarking, or for the alteration in Camilla's behavior which forced itself at last on her observations. Her spirits were elevated above the influence of displeasure in any one, and she was equally indifferent as to the cause of

Camilla's, or the continuance of her aunt's. Though Mr. Stanley could never be really offended by any imprudence or folly in his son that had given him the pleasure of seeing him, he was yet perfectly convinced that Edward ought not to remain in England, and was resolved to hasten his leaving it as soon as possible; but when he talked to Edward about it, he found him much less disposed towards returning to France, than to accompany them in their projected tour, which he assured his father would be infinitely more pleasant to him, and that as to the affair of travelling he considered it of no importance, and what might be pursued at any little odd time, when he had nothing better to do. He advanced these objections in a manner which plainly showed that he had scarcely a doubt of their being complied with, and appeared to consider his father's arguments in opposition to them, as merely given with a view to keep up his authority, and such as he should find little difficulty in combating. He concluded at last by saying, as the chaise in which they returned together from Mr. Dudley's reached Mrs. Percival's, "Well sir, we will settle this point some other time, and fortunately it is of so little consequence, that an immediate discussion of it is unnecessary." He then got out of the chaise and entered the house without waiting for his father's reply.

It was not till their return that Kitty could account for that coldness in Camilla's behavior to her, which had been so pointed as to render it impossible to be entirely unnoticed. When however they were seated in the coach with the two other ladies, Miss Stanley's indignation was no longer to be suppressed from breaking out into words, and found the following vent.

"Well, I must say this, that I never was at a stupider ball in my life! But it always is so; I am always disappointed in them for some reason or other. I wish there were no such things."

"I am sorry, Miss Stanley," said Mrs. Percival drawing herself up, "that you have not been amused; everything was meant for the best I am sure, and it is a poor encouragement for your Mama to take you to another if you are so hard to be satisfied."

"I do not know what you mean, ma'am, about Mama's taking me to another. You know I am come out."

"Oh! dear Mrs. Percival," said Mrs. Stanley, "you must not believe everything that my lively Camilla says, for her spirits are prodigiously high sometimes, and she frequently speaks without thinking. I am sure it is impossible for anyone to have been at a more elegant or agreeable dance, and so she wishes to express herself I am certain."

"To be sure I do," said Camilla very sulkily, "only I must say that it is not very pleasant to have anybody behave so rude to one as to be quite shocking! I am sure I am not at all offended, and should not care if all the world were to stand above me, but still it is extremely abominable, and what I cannot put up with. It is not that I mind it in the least, for I had just as soon stand at the bottom as at the top all night long, if it was not so very disagreeable—. But to have a person come in the middle of the evening and take everybody's place is what I am not used to, and tho' I do not care a pin about it myself, I assure you I shall not easily forgive or forget it."

This speech which perfectly explained the whole affair to Kitty, was shortly followed on her side by a very submissive apology, for she had too much good sense to be proud of her family, and too much good nature to live at variance with any one. The excuses she made, were delivered with so much real concern for the offence, and such unaffected sweetness, that it was almost impossible for Camilla to retain that anger which had occasioned them; She felt indeed most highly gratified to find that no insult had been intended and that Catharine was very far from forgetting the difference in their birth for which she could now only pity her, and her good humor being restored with the same ease in which it had been affected, she spoke with the highest delight of the evening, and declared that she had never before been at so pleasant a ball. The same endeavors that had procured the forgiveness of Miss Stanley ensured to her the cordiality of her mother, and nothing was wanting but Mrs. Percival's good humor to render the happiness of the others complete; but she, offended with Camilla for her affected superiority, still more so with her brother for coming to Chetwynde, and dissatisfied with the whole evening, continued silent and gloomy and was a restraint on the vivacity of her companions. She eagerly seized the very first opportunity which the next morning offered to her of speaking to Mr. Stanley on the subject of his son's return, and after having expressed her opinion of its being a very silly affair that he came at all, concluded with desiring him to inform Mr. Edward Stanley that it was a rule with her never to admit a young man into her house as a visitor for any length of time.

"I do not speak, sir," she continued, "out of any disrespect to you, but I could not answer it to myself to allow of his stay; there is no knowing what might be the consequence of it, if he were to continue here, for girls nowadays will always give a handsome young man the preference before any other, tho' for why, I never could discover, for what after all is youth and beauty! It is but a poor substitute for real worth and merit; Believe me Cousin that, whatever people may say to the contrary, there is certainly nothing like virtue for making us what we ought to be, and as to a young man's being young and handsome and having an agreeable person, it is nothing at all to the purpose for he had much better be respectable. I always did think so, and I always shall, and therefore you will oblige me very much by desiring your son to leave Chetrynde, or I cannot be answerable for what may happen between him and my niece. You will be surprised to hear me say it," she continued, lowering her voice, "But truth will out, and I must own that Kitty is one of the most impudent girls that ever existed. I assure you sir, that I have seen her sit and laugh and whisper with a young man whom she has not seen above half a dozen times. Her behavior indeed is scandalous, and therefore I beg you will send your son away immediately, or everything will be at sixes and sevens."

Mr. Stanley, who from one part of her speech had scarcely known to what length her insinuations of Kitty's impudence were meant to extend, now endeavored to quiet her fears on the occasion, by assuring her, that on every account he meant to allow only of his son's continuing that day with them, and that she might depend on his being more earnest in the affair from a wish of obliging her. He added also that he knew Edward to be very desirous himself of returning to France, as he wisely considered all time lost that did not forward the plans in which he was at present engaged, tho' he was but too well convinced of the contrary himself. His assurance in some degree quieted Mrs. Percival, and left her tolerably relieved of her cares and alarms, and better disposed to behave with civility towards his son during the short remainder of his stay at Chetwynde. Mr. Stanley went immediately to Edward, to whom he repeated the conversation that had passed between Mrs. Percival and himself, and strongly pointed out the necessity of his leaving Chetwynde the next day, since his world was already engaged for it. His son however appeared struck only by the ridiculous apprehensions of Mrs. Percival; and highly delighted at having occasioned them himself, seemed engrossed alone in thinking how he might increase them, without attending to any other part of his father's conversation. Mr. Stanley could get no determinate answer from him, and tho' he still hoped for the best, they parted almost in anger on his side.

His son though by no means disposed to marry, or any otherwise attached to Miss Percival than as a good natured lively girl who seemed pleased with him, took infinite pleasure in alarming the jealous fears of her aunt by his attentions to her, without considering what effect they might have on the lady herself. He would always sit by her when she was in the room, appear dissatisfied if she left it, and was the first to enquire whether she meant soon to return. He was delighted with her drawings, and enchanted with her performance on the harpsichord; Everything that she said, appeared to interest him; his conversation was addressed to her alone, and she seemed to be the sole object of his attention. That such efforts should succeed with one so tremblingly alive to every alarm of the kind as Mrs. Percival, is by no means unnatural, and that they should have equal influence with her niece whose imagination was lively, and whose disposition romantic, who was already extremely pleased with him, and of course desirous that he might be so with her, is as little to be wondered at. Every moment as it added to the conviction of his liking her, made him still more pleasing, and strengthened in her mind a wish of knowing him better. As for Mrs. Percival, she was in tortures the whole day; Nothing that she had ever felt before on a similar occasion was to be compared to the sensations which then distracted her; her fears had never been so strongly, or indeed so reasonably excited.—Her dislike of Stanley, her anger at her niece, her impatience to have them separated conquered every idea of propriety and good breeding, and though he had never mentioned any intention of leaving them the next day, she could not help asking him after dinner, in her eagerness to have him gone, at what time he meant to set out.

"Oh! Ma'am," replied he, "if I am off by twelve at night, you may think yourself lucky; and if I am not, you can only blame yourself for having left so much as the hour of my departure to my own disposal." Mrs. Percival cultured very highly at this speech, and without addressing herself to any one in particular, immediately began a long harangue on the shocking behavior of modern young men, and the wonderful alteration that had taken place in them, since her time, which she illustrated with many Instructive anecdotes of the decorum and modesty which had marked the characters of those whom she had known, when she had been young. This however did not prevent his walking in the garden with her niece, without any other companion for nearly an hour in the course of the evening. They had left the room for that purpose with Camilla at a time when Mrs. Percival had been out of it, nor was it for some time after her return to it, that she could discover where they were. Camilla had taken two or three turns with them in the walk which led to the arbor, but soon growing tired of listening to a conversation in which she was seldom invited to join, and from its turning occasionally on books, very little able to do it, she left them together in the arbor, to wander alone to some other part of the garden, to eat the fruit, and examine Mrs. Percival's greenhouse. Her absence was so far from being regretted; that it was scarcely noticed by them, and they continued conversing together on almost every subject, for Stanley seldom dwelt long on any, and had something to say on all, till they were interrupted by her aunt.

Kitty was by this time perfectly convinced that both in natural abilities, and acquired information, Edward Stanley was infinitely superior to his sister. Her desire of knowing that he was so, had induced her to take every opportunity of turning the conversation on history and they were very soon engaged in an historical dispute, for which no one was more calculated than Stanley who was so far from being really of any party, that he had scarcely a fixed opinion on the subject. He could therefore always take either side, and always argue with temper. In his indifference on all such topics he was very unlike his companion, whose judgment being guided by her feelings which were eager and warm, was easily decided, and though it was not always infallible, she defended it with a spirit and enthusiasm which marked her own reliance on it. They had continued therefore for some time conversing in this manner on the character of Richard the Third, which she was warmly defending when he suddenly seized hold of her hand, and exclaiming with great emotion, "Upon my honor you are entirely mistaken," pressed it passionately to his lips, and ran out of the arbor. Astonished at this behavior, for which she was wholly unable to account, she continued for a few moments motionless on the seat where he had left her, and was then on the point of following him up the narrow walk through which he had passed, when on looking up the one that lay immediately before the arbor, she saw her aunt walking towards her with more than her usual quickness. This explained at once the reason for his leaving her, but his leaving her in such manner was rendered still more inexplicable by it. She felt a considerable degree of confusion at having been seen by her in such a place with Edward, and at having that part of his conduct, for which she could not herself account, witnessed by one to whom all gallantry was odious. She remained therefore confused, distressed and irresolute, and suffered her aunt to approach her, without leaving the arbor.

Mrs. Percival's looks were by no means calculated to animate the spirits of her niece, who in silence awaited her accusation, and in silence meditated her defense. After a few moments suspense, for Mrs. Percival was too much fatigued to speak immediately, she began with great anger and asperity, the following harangue. "Well; this is beyond anything I could have supposed. Profligate as I knew you to be, I was not prepared for such a sight. This is beyond anything you ever did before; beyond any thing I ever heard of in my life! Such impudence, I never witnessed before in such a girl! And this is the reward for all the cares I have taken in your education; for all my troubles and anxieties; and Heaven knows how many they have been! All I wished for, was to breed you up virtuously; I never wanted you to play upon the harpsicord, or draw better than anyone else; but I had hoped to see you respectable and good; to see you able and willing to give an example of modesty and virtue to the young people here abouts. I bought you Blair's Sermons, and Coelebs' In Search of a Wife, I gave you the key to my own library, and borrowed a great many good books of my neighbors for you, all to this purpose. But I might have spared myself the trouble. Oh! Catharine, you are an abandoned creature, and I do not know what will become of you. I am glad however," she continued softening into some degree of mildness, "to see that you have some shame for what you have done, and if you are really sorry for it, and your future life is a life of penitence and reformation perhaps you may be forgiven. But I plainly see that everything is going to sixes and sevens and all order will soon be at an end throughout the Kingdom." "Not however, ma'am, the sooner, I hope, from any conduct of mine," said Catharine in a tone of great humility, "for upon my honor I have done nothing this evening that can contribute to overthrow the establishment of the kingdom."

"You are mistaken, child," replied she "the welfare of every nation depends upon the virtue of its individuals, and anyone who offends in so gross a manner against decorum and propriety is certainly hastening its ruin. You have been giving a bad example to the world, and the world is but too well disposed to receive such."

"Pardon me, madam," said her niece; "but I can have given an example only to you, for you alone have seen the offence. Upon my word however there is no danger to fear from what I have done; Mr. Stanley's behavior has given me as much surprise, as it has done to you, and I can only suppose that it was the effect of his high spirits, authorized in his Opinion by our relationship. But do you consider, madam, that it is growing very late! Indeed you had better return to the house." This speech as she well knew, would be unanswerable with her aunt, who instantly rose, and hurried away under so many apprehensions for her own health, as banished for the time all anxiety about her niece, who walked quietly by her side, revolving within her own mind the occurrence that had given her aunt so much alarm. "I am astonished at my own imprudence," said Mrs. Percival; "How could I be so forgetful as to sit down out of doors at such a time of night! I shall certainly have a return of my rheumatism after it. I begin to feel very chill already. I must have caught a dreadful cold by this time. I am sure of being lain-up all the winter after it." Then reckoning with her fingers, "Let me see; This is July; the cold weather will soon be coming in—August—September—October—November— December—January—February—March—April. Very likely I may not be tolerable again before May. I must and will have that arbor pulled down—it will be the death of me; who knows now, but what I may never recover. Such things have happened. My particular friend Miss Sarah Hutchinson's death was occasioned by nothing more. She stayed out late one evening in April, and got wet through for it rained very hard, and never changed her clothes when she came home. It is unknown how many people have died in consequence of catching cold! I do not believe there is a disorder in the world except the smallpox which does not spring from it." It was in vain that Kitty endeavored to convince her that her fears on the occasion were groundless; that it was not yet late enough to catch cold, and that even if it were, she might hope to escape any other complaint, and to recover in less than ten months. Mrs. Percival only replied that she hoped she knew more of ill health than to be convinced in such a point by a girl who had always been perfectly well, and hurried up stairs leaving Kitty to make her apologies to Mr. and Mrs. Stanley for going to bed. Tho' Mrs. Percival seemed perfectly satisfied with the goodness of the apology herself, yet Kitty felt somewhat embarrassed to find that the only one she could offer to their visitors was that her aunt had perhaps caught cold, for Mrs. Percival charged her to make light of it, for fear of alarming them. Mr. and Mrs. Stanley however who well knew that their cousin was easily terrified on that score, received the account of it with very little surprise, and all proper concern.

Edward and his sister soon came in, and Kitty had no difficulty in gaining an explanation of his conduct from him, for he was too warm on the subject himself, and too eager to learn its success, to refrain from making immediate enquiries about it; and she could not help feeling both surprised and offended at the ease and indifference with which he owned that all his intentions had been to frighten her aunt by pretending an affection for her, a design so very incompatible with that partiality which she had at one time been almost convinced of his feeling for her. It is true that she had not yet seen enough of him to be actually in love with him, yet she felt greatly disappointed that so handsome, so elegant, so lively a young man should be so perfectly free from any such sentiment as to make it his principal sport. There was a novelty in his character which to her was extremely pleasing; his person was uncommonly fine, his spirits and vivacity suited to her own, and his manners at once so animated and insinuating, that she thought it must be impossible for him to be otherwise than amiable, and was ready to give him credit for being perfectly so. He knew the powers of them himself; to them he had often been indebted for his father's forgiveness of faults which had he been awkward and inelegant would have appeared very serious; to them, even more than to his person or his fortune, he owed the regard which almost everyone was disposed to feel for him, and which young women in particular were inclined to entertain.

Their influence was acknowledged on the present occasion by Kitty, whose anger they entirely dispelled, and whose cheerfulness they had power not only to restore, but to raise. The evening passed off as agreeably as the one that had preceded it; they continued talking to each other, during the chief part of it, and such was the power of his address, and the brilliancy of his eyes, that when they parted for the night, tho' Catharine had but a few hours before totally given up the idea, yet she felt almost convinced again that he was really in love with her. She reflected on their past conversation, and tho' it had been on various and indifferent subjects, and she could not exactly recollect any speech on his side expressive of such a partiality, she was still however nearly certain of its being so; But fearful of being vain enough to suppose such a thing without sufficient reason, she resolved to suspend her final determination on it, till the next day, and more especially till their parting which she thought would infallibly explain his regard if any he had. The more she had seen of him, the more inclined was she to like him, and the more desirous that he should like her. She was convinced of his being naturally very clever and very well disposed, and that his thoughtlessness and negligence, which tho' they appeared to her as very becoming in him, she was aware would by many people be considered as defects in his character, merely proceeded from a vivacity always pleasing in young men, and were far from testifying a weak or vacant understanding. Having settled this point within herself, and being perfectly convinced by her own arguments of its truth, she went to bed in high spirits; determined to study his character, and watch his behavior still more the next day.

She got up with the same good resolutions and would probably have put them in execution, had not Anne informed her as soon as she entered the room that Mr. Edward Stanley was already gone. At first she refused to credit the information, but when her maid assured her that he had ordered a carriage the evening before to be there at seven o'clock in the morning and that she herself had actually seen him depart in it a little after eight, she could no longer deny her belief to it. "And this," thought she to herself blushing with anger at her own folly, "this is the affection for me of which I was so certain. Oh! what a silly thing is woman! How vain, how unreasonable! To suppose that a young man would be seriously attached in the course of four and twenty hours, to a girl who has nothing to recommend her but a good pair of eyes! And he is really gone! Gone perhaps without bestowing a thought on me! Oh! why was not I up by eight o'clock! But it is a proper punishment for my laziness and folly, and I am heartily glad of it. I deserve it all, and ten times more for such insufferable vanity. It will at least be of service to me in that respect; it will teach me in future not to think everybody is in love with me. Yet I should like to have seen him before he went, for perhaps it may be many years before we meet again. By his manner of leaving us however, he seems to have been perfectly indifferent about it. How very odd, that he should go without giving us notice of it, or taking leave of any one! But it is just like a young man, governed by the whim of the moment, or actuated merely by the love of doing anything odd! Unaccountable beings indeed! And young women are equally ridiculous! I shall soon begin to think like my aunt that everything is going to sixes and sevens, and that the whole race of mankind are degenerating." She was just dressed, and on the point of leaving her room to make her personal enquires after Mrs. Percival, when Miss Stanley knocked at her door, and on her being admitted began in her usual strain a long harangue upon her father's being so shocking as to make Edward go at all, and upon Edward's being so horrid as to leave them at such an hour in the morning. "You have no idea," said she, "how surprised I was, when he came into my room to bid me good bye."

"Have you seen him then, this morning?" said Kitty.

"Oh yes! And I was so sleepy that I could not open my eyes. And so he said, 'Camilla, goodbye to you for I am going away. I have not time to take leave of anybody else, and I dare not trust myself to see Kitty, for then you know I should never get away.'"

"Nonsense," said Kitty; "he did not say that, or he was in joke if he did."

"Oh! no I assure you he was as much in earnest as he ever was in his life; he was too much out of spirits to joke then. And he desired me when we all met at breakfast to give his compliments to your aunt, and his love to you, for you was a nice girl he said and he only wished it were in his power to be more with you. You were just the girl to suit him, because you were so lively and good-natured, and he wished with all his heart that you might not be married before he came back, for there was nothing he liked better than being here. Oh! You have no idea what fine things he said about you, till at last I fell asleep and he went away. But he certainly is in love with you. I am sure he is. I have thought so a great while I assure you."

"How can you be so ridiculous?" said Kitty smiling with pleasure; "I do not believe him to be so easily affected. But he did desire his love to me then? And wished I might not be married before his return? And said I was a nice girl, did he?"

"Oh! dear, yes, and I assure you it is the greatest praise in his opinion, that he can bestow on anybody; I can hardly ever persuade him to call me one, tho' I beg him sometimes for an hour together."

"And do you really think that he was sorry to go."

"Oh! you can have no idea how wretched it made him. He would not have gone this month, if my father had not insisted on it; Edward told me so himself yesterday. He said that he wished with all his heart he had never promised to go abroad, for that he repented it more and more every day; that it interfered with all his other schemes, and that since Papa had spoken to him about it, he was more unwilling to leave Chetwynde than ever."

"Did he really say all this? And why would your father insist upon his going?" "His leaving England interfered with all his other plans, and his conversation with Mr. Stanley had made him still more averse to it." "What can this mean!" "Why that he is excessively in love with you to be sure; what other plans can he have? And I suppose my father said that if he had not been going abroad, he should have wished him to marry you immediately. But I must go and see your aunt's plants. There is one of them that I quite dote on—and two or three more besides."

"Can Camilla's explanation be true?" said Catharine to herself, when her friend had left the room. "And after all my doubts and uncertainties, can Stanley really be averse to leaving England for my sake only? 'His plans interrupted.' And what indeed can his plans be, but towards marriage. Yet so soon to be in love with me! But it is the effect perhaps only of the warmth of heart which to me is the highest recommendation in any one. A heart disposed to love—and such under the appearance of so much gaiety and inattention, is Stanley's. Oh! how much does it endear him to me! But he is gone—gone perhaps for years—obliged to tear himself from what he most loves, his happiness is sacrificed to the vanity of his father! In what anguish he must have left the house! Unable to see me, or to bid me adieu, while I, senseless wretch, was daring to sleep. This, then explained his leaving us at such a time of day. He could not trust himself to see me. Charming young man! How much must you have suffered! I knew that it was impossible for one so elegant, and so well bred, to leave any family in such a manner, but for a motive like this unanswerable." Satisfied, beyond the power of change, of this, she went in high spirits to her aunt's apartment, without giving a moment's recollection on the vanity of young women, or the unaccountable conduct of young men.

Kitty continued in this state of satisfaction during the remainder of the Stanleys' visit—who took their leave with many pressing invitations to visit them in London, when as Camilla said, she might have an opportunity of becoming acquainted with that sweet girl Augusta Halifax. Or rather (thought Kitty,) of seeing my dear Mary Wynne again. Mrs. Percival in answer to Mrs. Stanley's invitation replied that she looked upon London as the hot house of vice where virtue had long been banished from society and wickedness of every description was daily gaining ground—that Kitty was of herself sufficiently inclined to give way to and indulge in vicious inclinations, and therefore was the last girl in the world to be trusted in London, as she would be totally unable to withstand temptation.

After the departure of the Stanleys, Kitty returned to her usual occupations, but alas! they had lost their power of pleasing. Her bower alone retained its interest in her feelings, and perhaps that was owing to the particular remembrance it brought to her mind of Edward Stanley.

The summer passed away unmarked by any incident worth narrating, or any pleasure to Catharine save one, which arose from the receipt of a letter from her friend Cecilia now Mrs. Lascelles, announcing the speedy return of herself and husband to England.

A correspondence productive indeed of little pleasure to either party had been established between Camilla and Catharine. The latter had now lost the only satisfaction she had ever received from the letters of Miss Stanley, as that young lady having informed her friend of the departure of her brother to Lyons now never mentioned his name—her letters seldom contained any intelligence except a description of some new article of dress, an enumeration of various engagements, a panegyric on Augusta Halifax and perhaps a little abuse of the unfortunate Sir Peter.

The Grove, for so was the mansion of Mrs. Percival at Chetwynde denominated, was situated within five miles from Exeter, but though that lady possessed a carriage and horses of her own, it was seldom that Catharine could prevail on her to visit that town for the purpose of shopping, on account of the many officers perpetually quartered there and who infested the principal streets. A company of strolling players on their way from some neighbouring races having opened a temporary theatre there, Mrs. Percival was prevailed on by her niece to indulge her by attending the performance once during their stay. Mrs. Percival insisted on paying Miss Dudley the compliment of inviting her to join the party, when a new difficulty arose, from the necessity of having some gentleman to attend them.

Printed in Great Britain
by Amazon